THE COMPLETE
SHORT STORIES

ಬಂಚ

THE COMPLETE SHORT STORIES

by

GERALD BRENNAN

ॐ෪

**DreamStreet
Press**
Ann Arbor, MI USA
www.DreamStreetPress.com

dedicated to
Patty,
my wife

Table of Contents

On Newton's 3rd Law

To every action there is always opposed an equal reaction...
—Isaac Newton

Teddy Tonlin gazes at the clock on the wall. The red second hand, needle-thin compared to the sturdy minute and the stubby hour hand, makes its inexorable, majestic sweep around the dial. This bores him like you wouldn't *believe.*

But on the other hand, he's dying. He's on his deathbed. So, if he would forego all the boring bits, the inertness and the waiting, he would just slam hard into the point of death without delay. But then at least something would actually be happening, right? The moment of death is not a boring proposition.

This is quite the dichotomy for Teddy. He never figured this happening. But it doesn't matter. The moment has arrived, and he has arrived at the moment; he dies.

Now, Teddy always assumed, 'that would be that.' So he's astonished that he's still aware of what's going on around him in his bed. Because he's not really *in* his bed anymore. He can see everything going on in the room and can sense the few people present and the small sadness that permeates everything at this moment. But it's fading, the vision and the concern for it all, and he swoons.

When he comes to, he's standing across from old Mr. Kaminski, the high school janitor when Teddy went to high school. Teddy's just standing there, in his street clothes, in a small gymnasium that looks like the one from high school. Right across from him stands old Mr. K in his janitor's outfit tapping a clipboard against his leg. He doesn't look surprised or glad to see him or pissed off or anything really.

1

Mr. K glances at his clipboard and finally manages to force a little smile and says, "Welcome. Ah… Teddy. Right?"

"Yes," Teddy mumbles.

Mr. K nods. "Ah! I got it right."

"Where in the fucking hell am I!" Teddy inquires with a growing sense of panic.

"Well… you're dead. You know that, right?" Old Mr. K just puts that out there.

Teddy is stunned and is looking all around him in disbelief. "Well why am I… how come there's…"

Mr. K steps up and claps a big friendly paw on Teddy's shoulder. "All you people these days. You're so surprised that when you die, you ain't dead."

"Well…" stunned Teddy mumbles, "how am I…"

Mr. K crooks his arm into Teddy's and they start walking. Teddy is compliant as a doll.

"Come with me," Mr. K says, "and I'll explain."

༺

When Teddy was a boy, his family had an old rotary-dial telephone in their rural farmhouse. Even as a child Teddy hated that thing, because when he dialed a big number (especially a '0') he had to just stand there like a moron waiting for the dial to spin back to rest so he could get on with dialing the next number, which he always hoped would be less than 5. To say Teddy was an impatient boy would be a serious understatement of the case. This was pathology, and it shaped Teddy Tonlin's life.

His disdain, his terror, actually, of boredom, led him to alcohol as a teen. But this wasn't enough to relieve the spells of tedium and ennui that Teddy felt so keenly between his occupied moments. He threw himself into his studies in high school, dreading the idle summers, graduated early and attended college where his freshman efforts were interrupted by his drug use. He found opioids worked well for him, and what used to be a hell of languor was, in these hours, a

2

heavenly respite, monotony and dullness washed clean away by this fresh-water ocean of serenity and well-being. But as is always the case, the high was impossible to maintain and Teddy soon graduated to heroin. After a few months of this his hangovers from the drug highs were so bad that he attempted suicide and finally went into rehab. He recovered and went back to school where he earned his Ph.D. in two disciplines and in near-record time.

Teddy was a math and physics genius, and this led to great wealth and lofty reputation at an early age, first with two large corporations, and finally on his own with more patents to his credit by age 25 than any American in history at that tender age.

He is not well-known for his work on Objective Temporal Acceleration, but it was the work which was most important to him. Simply put, Teddy had found a way to speed up time, or at least the perception of time, which turns out to be the same thing. He had found a way to eliminate boredom. No booze, no drugs, no hangovers. The problem was, Teddy never found a way for his device to work on anyone but himself. The personalization process was so terribly complex that Teddy never made headway with either of the two volunteers whom he had recruited. But it worked for him.

He started small. Here's how: Teddy was disposed to the occasional attack of gout, an exquisitely painful inflammation of his feet and ankles due to deposits of uric acid crystals, which assume the shape of needles when they coalesce. He had designed a bare-bones prototype of the helmet and the charging cradle, built his computer himself and wrote the amazing software that brought it all to life. He was not confident of getting good results at what he considered an early alpha stage in development, but the boredom of sitting all day compounded with the agony of his gout made him intrepid. Boredom *and* pain. Was there anything worse?

A typical gout attack lasted about four days, in Teddy's experience. So, he programmed the system to remove that time from his awareness. Teddy fired up his system, entered the specs for this event, removed the helmet from its charging nest, and affixed the heavy and ill-fitting device to his head. Full of apprehension he spoke the command and the system responded.

Nothing happened.

The clock on the wall showed not even a minute had passed, but perhaps it was four days to the very minute? At last he summoned the courage to rotate his ankle. He braced himself for the pain, and there it was. He felt his face, hoping for a rough four-day stubble, but he was still smooth from his recent shave.

All the signs of failure, Teddy thought. He removed his helmet, hobbled painfully to his computer and sat, utterly dejected. While he pondered his failure and wondered what exactly had gone wrong, he noticed the time and date on his computer. It was four days ahead. He had not failed! He also realized that his body had suffered no aging. This was not a cure for the agonies of gout, but he surmised quite logically that it was indeed a cure for what, in Teddy's life, was a far worse malady: *this was a cure for boredom.* And a bonus: skipping through time would apparently not cause him to age during the skip.

He reclined in his chair and actually relaxed, elated and exhausted. Such an achievement! And though the technical complications made a mass-production model an unlikely prospect, this was no longer so troubling. The implications of such a device were stupendous, monstrous even, so maybe he would simply keep this great thing to himself. And that's what Dr. Theodore Tonlin did. There were many other projects, and a lifetime of work ahead, should he really want to persist in the old grind. His colossal wealth made that optional. He just didn't have to suffer the boring bits anymore.

Restraint was not one of Teddy's virtues. The impulse that took him from booze to opiates and thence to heroin nearly destroyed him as a lad, and his inability to hold himself in check would also characterize his new career as a time-skipper.

The next year was full of little temporal hops as Teddy devoted all his time and energy to the refinement of his device. The new hardware was now completely portable, the helmet was one-tenth the weight and fitted him like a glove, or I should say, a hat, and his refined user interface required only the input of two variables—start time and end time.

He had no spouse and no friends. This was the price of his indulgence and he accepted it as one who had no choice. There could be no one who would keep tabs on him and disturb the buzz of his renewed existence. His secret would leak out and the world would do its best to ruin his way of life.

Teddy was a man of wealth and leisure and he wasn't even 30 yet. And he would not age as others age. Teddy had decided to divest himself of all but a few of his corporate properties and hired others to run the ones he kept. He was free. If his time-skips were long and plentiful enough, he could span hundreds of years before old-age grabbed him and held him fast. But for now, he was a young man of huge appetite and near-infinite resources.

His tolerance of any degree of boredom did not improve. In fact, his malady had worsened. He so loathed being unengaged in some enveloping activity that his palatial estate had become a gilded prison, his very home and hearth a dreaded place of incarceration between activities elsewhere.

Eventually, Teddy began to experiment with skips of longer duration. A celebration was to be held in his honor in Paris a month hence, where Teddy, age 30, was to receive an honorary doctorate. Rather than fumble about for something interesting to do in the interim, he decided to time-skip the entire month. After all, how could he become a keen observer of the future unless he ventured to stretch out his lifespan to cover the many decades, perhaps centuries, that lay ahead? The long skip of a month worked without a hiccup, as Teddy knew it would. The next morning, he was on a plane to Paris.

At last he had set his life up so that time passed in a non-stop whirl of activity. Rarely more than a single day of recuperation would pass before Teddy was off again on some new adventure. Boredom and its attendant (and increasingly disturbing) introspection were all but banished from his being.

Teddy enjoyed an interval when he binged on the favors of some of the most beautiful and notorious women in the world, a hobby he paid dearly to indulge, but after a few years of focusing on this pursuit the thrill had lessened and the search was renewed for greener pastures and bigger thrills. These new excitements were hard to come by and the durations between them longer and longer as the decades passed. Teddy had become a connoisseur of the exotic and perverse—the only beguilements that could still compel his interest.

By his reckoning he was now 45-years old, though 74 years had passed. Teddy was in his prime, still feted worldwide as a master of industry and a science guru to generations. But there was suspicion growing. How does a 74-year old look like a man in his forties? What was his secret? What does the great man do in his free time? As if! Teddy had come to conclude that he would soon require a new identity, as the media and academics were getting too close to uncovering the unique oddity of his existence. He began to study the solution, but he needn't have bothered.

Teddy had decided to time-skip ten weeks to meet his new paramour at his London townhouse to celebrate his 75th birthday (in his 46th year, but who's counting?). But before he voiced the go command, he experienced a severe crushing pain in his chest. He managed to stagger to his library, where he called 911, collapsed and was transported to the hospital.

CR

Old Mr. Kaminski is strolling arm-in-arm with Teddy down the long institutional-style corridor that still reminds Teddy of his old high school. All the rooms they pass are vacant and the doors are closed. Teddy is still too discombobulated to even think of an intelligent question to ask. Eventually they arrive at a door in the middle of the corridor and Mr. K reaches in his overalls and pulls free his big ring of keys. He flips through them and says, "Ah. There you are."

Mr. K unlocks the classroom door, clicks on the overhead fluorescents and bids Teddy to enter. They walk to the center of the classroom. Teddy looks around. There is a long blackboard in front, and a row of windows along the side with trees and a vacant playground out beyond, but the room is pretty much bare except for a single wooden chair in the middle. The annoying fluorescents are buzzing.

Mr. K points to the chair. "You can sit there if you want."

Teddy doesn't react. He looks at the old man. "You're Mr. Kaminski, aren't you?"

"Sure," Mr. K replies.

"Well... why are you here? Why are you here with me?" Teddy imagines he is starting to get his bearings.

"Somebody's gotta be, I reckon," Mr. K says, and chuckles benignly.

"Well... what the hell is going on here? Can you help me out with that?"

"This is the first stage," Mr. K says.

"First stage of *what?*"

"The first stage is Purification, I guess you'd say."

Teddy looks skeptical.

"You get rid of your bad habits here," Mr. K explains, "then you move on."

"To what?"

"The second stage."

"And what in the holy hell is that?"

"Oh, it's a big process. Prepares you for going back, for one thing. Main thing, I guess."

"Going back where?"

"New life. On Earth. Back where you came from? Right?" Mr. K seems unsure and checks the clipboard for confirmation. "Yeah. I got that right."

"Well, what are we going to do now?" Teddy asks, the stink of boredom already oozing through the cracks even in this place.

"Oh. Umm… Well, you're gonna sit here for a while and I got other stuff to do. But don't worry. I'll be back." Mr. K nods politely and steps toward the door.

"Wait! Stop!" Teddy pleads. Mr. K turns and waits with a patient look. "When are you coming back?"

"Pretty soon," Mr. K says.

"How soon?"

Now Mr. K looks a bit annoyed as he consults his clipboard, flipping a couple of pages. "Ah. Here it is. Riiiiight here. It says… umm…"

"*What?!*"

"29 years. Yep. That was the calculation. I'll be back in 29 years."

Teddy collapses on to the wooden chair. "Twenty… nine… years…"

"Yep! Give or take. Anyhoo, get comfortable. I'll be back. I won't forget."

Teddy bolts to his feet, panicked. "NO! STOP!"

But Mr. K departs and shuts the door behind him. Instantly the cinderblock walls, tile floor, and drop ceiling are replaced by a perfect cube of white, softly glowing surfaces. There is no door, no windows, just Teddy and the chair in a featureless cubic room divinely lit. Teddy turns slowly and looks to the wall behind him, where he beholds with unspeakable dread the only fixture in the room.

There is a round, black-rimmed standard institutional clock on the wall. The red second hand, needle-thin compared to the sturdy minute and the stubby hour hand, makes its inexorable, majestic sweep around the dial.

This bores Teddy like you wouldn't *believe*.

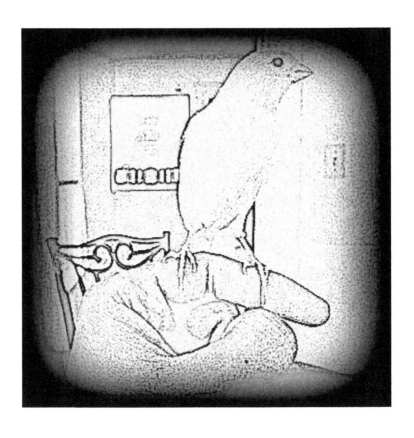

The Obstinate Canary

*C*offee and Doritos is a bad breakfast, especially if you have to make the coffee. This is what Ricardo Piatti concluded as he surveyed his kitchen pantry standing naked and cold in the silver light of a February dawn. It was Estelle's birthday, and she was still asleep. *Hey! Estelle's Birthday! Another good reason to not have coffee and Doritos.*

He looked over at the stoveclock and saw "AM 7:22" painted in green light. He stretched his giant's body, nicking his knuckles apelike on the ceiling and yawned. Now the problem of no money for Estelle's birthday gift could no longer be deferred to a later date. It gnawed at him for the last few days but, characteristically, he had done nothing to resolve the problem, and as he stared out the third-floor window of their ramshackle three-room Brooklyn apartment Ricky grew glum. *No birthday present, no money.*

The solution, such as it was, came to him presently. *Breakfast!* He reckoned that he still had an hour to make a killer gourmet birthday breakfast before Estelle woke up for work. It was a good solution: cheap, romantic, and what the hell, they needed to eat. So: café for the immediate emergency, the market for food, and back in 20 minutes, max.

The line was long – there were many people in front of Rick who sought the precious brown elixir as earnestly as he.

"No… wait now… make that a… wait," a tiny elderly lady of skinny frame but formidable shoulder-pads consulted her list again and resumed her order in that loud voice that people who are going deaf employ. "A double skim latte with light foam, and… also one regular, hmmm…"

"Oh please, no," Rick prayed aloud to the ceiling from the back of the line.

"No. I have it now… that's… *two* regular lattes with… well, no that's one decaffeinated and the other…"

11

"Excuse me. Ma'am?" Rick's bass voice bellowed from the back of the line.

The woman turned to Ricardo and glowered, sensing the improprieties to come.

"I just want a cup of coffee, and I'm in a race with *death*," he pleaded, moving up the line toward the front.

The counterman moaned. "Rick, I don't need this. Just let her order, for chrissakes."

"Young man," the old lady announced, craning her neck to lock eyes with the towering Ricardo, "I believe that I—"

Something in Rick pretended to snap as he grabbed the counter railing. "*I just want a goddam cup of coffee, David!*" he insisted loudly enough to silence all the conversation in the café. He looked around and sighed.

"Look, it's Estelle's birthday," Rick explained patiently to everyone in his deep and resonant voice, "And I've got to get breakfast ready before she wakes up." A few people nodded sympathetically; most looked skeptical.

David the *barista* shook his head and called over to the coffee jockey. "Just pour him a cup of coffee." Two girls with identical nose-jewelry who sat at the counter tittered. The ancient lady huffed.

"Rick," the java jerker whispered as he poured the coffee, "Why do you do this sort of thing?" Ricardo took the steaming paper cup without reply, then snatched a lid from the pile.

"I'll pay you this afternoon, okay, Dave?" Dave waved him off, exasperated.

Rick bowed to the old woman. "Thanks. *So* much," he said and bolted from the café. She glowered after him.

Her lips, he mused, *are like these strawberries, except no strawberry could taste that good.* And so, he gathered a bunch from the immense, fragrant heap, examining each one before committing them to the plastic bag. *The market is nice this early in the morning.* He still didn't know what he was going to make Estelle for her birthday breakfast, and he was trying to recall what he made her last year, so he wouldn't make the same thing, and then it hit him: *Crêpes Suzette!* That was the ticket!

With fresh fruit. He narrowed his eyes and surveyed the area keenly with a renewed sense of mission. *Ah. Well.* Those blueberries weren't the color of her eyes, but these grapes were, at least when she had her contacts in, so he seized upon the most perfect bunch. She needed new lenses, but they had not been able to afford it. Out-of-work opera basses don't make much money. *Maybe today things will turn around after the audition.* He felt good. He moved down the aisle like a dancer, like a giant mutant Fred Astaire.

The kiwis were the same color as her favorite suede coat, so they made it onto the menu. It reminded Rick that the coat was still at the cleaners and they had no money to get it out. *Why does she stay with me,* he wondered sourly, *and how could she have put up with this situation for, what, eight years now?* The cherries looked good and he laughed out loud as he put a small bunch in the basket. *Maybe we'll get married as soon as I can get some money flowing,* he thought. *I know she wants to do that.*

The pineapple he got here last week was the sweetest fruit he had ever tasted, so that was appropriate. He smelled one, then squeezed it, pulled at a long leaf and when it popped loose with ease Rick smiled his approval and laid it into the basket with its fellows.

Rick would also need oranges for the *crêpes.* He had sugar, and brandy, and flour and butter. He would need… eggs. He took the basket to the dairy counter and selected a dozen large, annoyed that there were no AA grade, and then stood, staring. He was forgetting something. *What else is there? Fruitsugarbrandyflourbuttereggs…* He knew he was forgetting something very important. He had a mild hangover and his mind resented the effort at recalling the recipe that he had mastered years ago. Instead, the ready image of Estelle's naked body fought with the recipe for space in his mind and he drifted off, oblivious to the fat woman with the grocery cart muttering under her breath as she tried to maneuver the cart around big heedless Ricky, standing with eyes half closed in the middle of the aisle.

How exquisite is Estelle, he thought. She was long and a little coltish, and in every way completely pleasing. *And she has breasts like a goddess. Some think they're her best feature but that's just a first impression. Actually, she... Ha! That's it!* He bellowed his big low laugh, sending the fat woman scurrying with her basket from the produce section with a frightened look. He was standing right in front of it all along! *Cream. Creamy and white and delicious like Estelle's matchless breasts. Creamy and white like the milk she might make for our baby one day.*

There was an empty line at the checkout presided over by a teenage girl whom Rick had never seen there before, who had a florid case of acne. She was brand new, he deduced apprehensively, but before he could change to the other line two full baskets had made their way before him, so he was stuck with the novice. She didn't know the codes to most of the fruits and had to consult Sophia, the grocer's wife, who was running the register in the next lane.

The new girl stopped in the middle of the procedure and let out a big sigh, then held up the bag of kiwis and asked Rick, "What are these?"

"Kiwis," Rick explained.

"Oh. Kiwis," the new girl said aloud, nodding, trying to imprint the name of this strange and exotic fruit into her brain for future reference. Rick noticed some cheap flowers in a rack and threw a bunch atop the pile of groceries. The new girl was puzzling over something else.

Rick stared at her, fascinated by her extravagantly pimpled face. "Did you know," he said to her, "that scientists have figured out a way to grow fruits and vegetables with the barcodes already on them?"

She looked up at Rick, blankly, and blinked. "Really?" Then grabbed the cream and dragged it over the reader, again and again until it finally beeped.

"He's pullin' your leg, honey," old Sophia warned. "There's nobody can grow fruits with codes on 'em. Don't listen to him."

14

"Yeah, you think you're pretty sharp, Sophia," Rick laughed.

"Paper or plastic?" the girl said.

"Paper."

"When are you singing again, Ricky? Angelo wants to know. He remembers last year when you did *Otello*. He hates opera, but he likes you," Sophia said.

"That was *four* years ago, Sophia," he corrected. "I got an audition today with some guy downtown."

"Oooo, really. That's marvelous! Let us know what happens."

"Yeah. If I *get* it I'll let you know."

"Twenty-nine fifty-seven," the girl pronounced, and Rick took out his wallet, looked inside and winced. *Why didn't I raid Estelle's purse before I left? Idiot, idiot.* He rubbed the top of his head and sighed loudly.

"How much again?" he winced to the young cashier.

"Twenty-nine fifty-seven," she repeated.

"Umm… I'm a little short of that actually," Rick muttered.

"Well? What do you wanna put back, then," she huffed, flustered and annoyed, fiddling with the register to void the order. "I don't know how to do this…" she singsonged ominously.

"Ricardo, don't worry about that," Sophia called over. "You pay me later, okay?"

"I thought I had more money with me…" he blubbered lamely.

"Don't worry," Sophia laughed. "You come by later and sing me and Angelo a song, eh? Then we call it even."

Rick was indeed back home in 20 minutes flat, and Estelle was still asleep. He had made coffee, finished the fruit salad and the *crêpe* batter. The table was set, and the flowers were artfully arrayed in the bell jar in the middle of the table. He made his *crêpes* and put them in the oven to warm, then made Estelle's, put them on the table, and was off to the bedroom to wake her up for her special super birthday surprise breakfast treat.

15

She *was* surprised. She had on her silver pajamas and was soon sitting at her kitchen chair wiping sleep from her eyes and smiling up at Rick. "This is so sweet," she said.

"Yeah, your *crêpes* are getting cold," he alerted.

She took a bite and swallowed. "Oh! Grand Marnier. My favorite morning beverage," she laughed. Rick poured her some coffee, and as they sat and ate Estelle was quiet and Rick grew uneasy. *There's something wrong with Estelle.* She finished one of her *crêpes* and sat staring at her fruit salad, moving a lonesome cherry back and forth over a banana slice with her fork.

"What's the matter, honey?" Rick asked her. She looked up and her features were tinted with anxiety.

"Oh. I don't know." She looked away and her eyes glistened.

Rick feared this. "Is it money? You know, I might get this part I'm trying out for this afternoon," he said encouragingly.

Estelle shook her head. "I don't know. I guess that's part of it."

Rick had known Estelle to get depressed on occasion, and lately there was no dearth of occasion, but there was a different note to her mood that made Rick queasy. "Is there something else on your mind?" He reached across the table and touched her hand.

"I can't talk about it now, Rick." She looked at the clock. "My ride will be here in 20 minutes."

"Is it bad? Did I do something wrong?" Rick felt panic rising. He stood up. "What do you mean you can't talk about it now? That'll make me crazy all day, you know that!"

"I'm sorry, Rick." She wiped her eyes with her hand "After work. Okay?"

"Well, how about your birthday dinner? We always do that up nice on your birthday."

"With *what*, Rick?" Estelle looked at him with anger through the drying tears. "How can we afford a nice dinner?"

"You watch me, honey. I got a special surprise. You'll love it. We'll go to Molinari's. They got a chef there that's better than me!" He strutted over macho-comically and kissed the top of her head. "But just tell me everything's all right." Rick stood behind Estelle's chair, bent to her, and wrapped his arms around her, caressing her breasts.

He waited for those reassuring words, which always came, but they didn't come this time.

"Rick, we need to change things." She dabbed at her eyes with her napkin. "We can't live like this. *I* can't live like this. How many times have I told you this? I don't know what to do about it."

She's right, he thought. *Goddammit.* "You're right, honey." He moved his hands to her shoulders and massaged them gently. "But we can work it out. Let's talk about it at dinner."

She rose from her chair and kissed Rick softly on the lips. "I have to get dressed. We'll talk tonight." Estelle ran nervous hands through her long brown hair and tried to smile. "And thanks for the sweet breakfast."

Yeah, Ricardo thought as she padded into the bedroom. *Don't mention it.*

Estelle took her shower and dressed and was out the door in record time with barely another word passing between them, and with a goodbye kiss that spoke so much in such a little peck, but Ricky couldn't quite translate it. He had the sad feeling that breakfast was actually an inconvenience because it made her rush.

From their second-story apartment window, Rick watched Estelle climb into a brand new Mercedes sedan. It was her boss's car, and he would sometimes pick her up on days when she had to be in early. He was, like Ricardo, a huge man – a former All-American basketball star, as rumor had it – but he had let himself go, and the classic "middle-age spread" was upon him with a vengeance. He was also a vulgar and arrogant person who bullied his employees, according to Estelle. Rick disliked him immensely even though they had never met, and though Estelle had assured him that he was always very sweet to her and treated her with every courtesy.

He moved despondently from the window and threw himself down in the big chair. Never, even in his indigent youth, had Rick ever been so near to utter destitution. But for eight years he had managed to treat his beloved to a fine dinner at an upscale restaurant on the occasion of her birthday. *It's a tradition!* This year, he was determined, would not be the exception. That would be too painful to bear.

With a great sigh, he rose from his chair, went back into the kitchen and pulled opened the freezer door. There he beheld through a puff of frosty vapor what was by now his only worldly possession of any value. He removed it carefully and set it down on the kitchen counter, considered it wistfully and gradually accepted his fate.

Donning his tattered and unlined leather trenchcoat and a stocking cap, he tucked the treasure under his arm and resolutely proceeded down the stairs, out the door, and down the twelve frigid blocks to Ash's.

"Hey pal, Myron here?" Rick inquired of the fellow at the front desk, interrupting his novel. He looked up at Rick, squinted, and removed his glasses.

"I believe he is indeed," the clerk said with a thin-lipped smile. "Myron!" he called toward the back room, then back at Ricky. "May I say who's calling?"

"What!" came a bark.

"You have a visitor."

"Not now! Who is it?... Ah, nevermind," Myron mumbled as he made his way out front and spied Rick at the counter, smiling.

"Oh. It's *you!*" A short and wide man, impeccably attired, Myron waddled over to Ricky and the two men shook hands heartily, then Myron reached up, way up, and grabbed Rick by the lapels of his worn trenchcoat. "Why the hell don't you wear a decent coat? You look like you're freezin' your ass off!"

"Ahh, I'm all right. How's business?"

"It'd be a hell of a lot better if I could get some decent cigars in this goddam place!" Myron yelled. He played the role

18

of the refined tobacconist when he had to, polished and aloof, but the store was empty of consumers and Ricardo was an old friend. "C'mon in the back. Have a drink."

In the cluttered back room, the aroma of cedar wood was powerful and agreeable. Myron took two shot glasses from a nearby cupboard and set them on the table while Ricky sat. The tobacconist poured a shot of bourbon for himself, but Rick put his hand over his glass when Myron moved to pour for him.

"Whatsa matter?" Myron asked.

"A little early in the day, I guess."

"Well. That's a new tune," Myron said, his big waxy red nose proof that this was a tune that Myron had sung till he knew it by heart. He screwed the top back onto the bottle. "So what's up?"

Rick reached under his coat and grandly placed the box on the table in front of Myron, who stared at it hard with narrowed eyes for a few moments, the gears in his mind clicking into action. He looked up at Rick, smiled a toothy grin, leaned over his big belly and opened the box. He picked up one of the cigars and examined it.

"They're real, all right," Rick said.

"*Montecristo 'A's*... Where did you get 'em? If you don't mind me askin'."

"A gift from a guy from Germany who heard me sing."

Myron was incredulous. "You're shittin' me? He really must've liked you."

"Well, that was before the boom. They were only 15 bucks each back then. If you could find one."

"Yeah. I remember. Like I need you to remind me."

"They're $80 each now, though. And that's if you can find some schmuk to smuggle them in from Toronto." Rick grinned. "You know – like you do for some of your clients."

"Ah, hell, Ricardo, I figured maybe this was a gift!"

That was a good one, and they laughed loudly and long at it. Myron threw back his shot of bourbon. "And ix-nay on that Canada stuff. Nobody knows about that." He picked up one of the cigars from the middle of the box and squeezed it. "You had these in your freezer, didn't you?"

"Hey. My humidor situation isn't..."

"You did, didn't you – you guinea barbarian." Myron shook his head in disgust. He poured another shot of bourbon, bolted it without ceremony, swallowed, and eyed Rick steadily. "I'll give you $700 for the box."

"$1500," Rick countered. "There's nothing wrong with them cigars."

"You're crazy," Myron was disgusted. "That's way out o' line." They stared at one another for a long moment, daring the other to blink.

"You'll sell them for a $100 each," Rick said. "You'll put a grand in your pocket."

"I can't get a $100 for these," Myron stood up, "are you nuts?"

"Hey, I know some of your 'special' customers."

"They're not *stupid* customers."

The two stared at one another for another quarter-minute, then Rick sighed, stood up, snatched the cigar from the tobacconist's hand and replaced it in the box. Myron grabbed what he could of Rick's massive wrist. "I'll give you a thousand. Cash. Right now."

"$1250."

"$1100 and that's the limit."

"Let go my wrist," Rick said and shook it free. "It's $1250 or I go to Dennemann's up on the hill."

Myron sat back down and looked terribly hurt. "Ricky," he said softly. "Why are doin' this, eh? You're like a son to me."

Ricardo smirked. "Sorry, 'dad,' but that's the bottom line."

"You would go to that bastard, wouldn't you?" Myron brightened up, the charade finished. "Okay. $1250."

Rick held out his hand. "Deal," he said.

They shook on it and Myron stood up, took out his fat wallet and counted out 12 hundred-dollar bills into Rick's palm. While he hunted for a fifty, Rick reached into the box and snatched forth one of the Montecristos which he tucked, pen-like, into his shirt pocket. Myron grunted disagreeably but did not object to the theft as he tucked the final fifty back into his wallet.

On the way out of the shop, Myron pushed a pair of fine leather gloves into Rick's coat pocket.

"What are you doing?" Rick asked, shoving the gloves back at Myron.

"A guy left 'em here last winter and never showed again. Take 'em." Rick hesitated, thought better of it, and took the gloves. Myron looked up at Ricky and shook his head. "It's winter. You need gloves, ya big ape."

You Big Ape. People called him that when he was a teenager and it hurt his feelings. Rick was six-feet and eight-inches tall and just a wee flabby at 320 pounds with a tremendous barrel chest. The better to sing to you, my dear.

And sing he would do any minute now for John Whitman, a notorious impresario and producer who did not like Rick, though cast him four years ago as *Otello* to some national acclaim. This led to offers to sing all over the country, and a few offers from Europe, but no major roles were offered, and Rick turned them all down.

"Rick, you know what your problem is, my friend? Your problem is you got an exaggerated sense of your own self-importance, is what," his useless agent told him one day toward the end, but Rick would only sing – and on this he was adamant – only major roles. "You'll get yourself a reputation but it ain't gonna be the sort of reputation that's gonna get you anywhere in *this* business, my friend!"

Rick knew he was as good as the best he had heard, and he had his pride: an unreasonable pride, fierce and beastly, in his ability and in his glorious instrument. This, coupled with his natural inability to ingratiate himself to the rich and powerful, meant that he didn't sing again. The lectures from his agent grew tiresome, and after Rick refused to understudy the role of *Boris Godunov* in San Francisco, his agent cut him loose. "I don't do understudies," Rick told him, and that was that. But Ricardo loved the theatre. He loved the smell. He hadn't darkened the door of a nice playhouse for years, but in order to keep his hand in he practiced almost daily with a couple of friends who were expert accompanists, he read all the trade magazines and was always aware of what was going on in New York. So, when he found out that "artistic differences" had caused a rift between Whitman and the bass that was contracted for the show, Ricky arranged what he hoped would be a last-minute informal audition for the part. This was a most unusual situation, and Rick had called in every favor he had and a few he hadn't to just get him in the door that day. He stood backstage now with a few other members of the cast and crew who mostly avoided him. He wondered, *Do they know about me? Do they think I'm arrogant and vain and proud and self-important? Well... fuck 'em.* Oddly, he felt no apprehension.

Rick was handed the music by an assistant, took a look at the title page and handed it back. Rick scowled and tapped the side of his big head with the tip of his index finger. The assistant laughed and told Ricardo to wait. He sat himself in the only chair around that would not break under his bulk and hummed scales to himself, listening to a young bass singing nervously on stage. *Poor guy,* Rick mused. *Whitman probably has him scared out of his wits.*

When the young fellow was finished with his aria there was some cheering and applause from a small contingent present, then the vaguely lisping voice of someone Ricky did not know.

"Splendid, splendid! What did I *tell* you, John? Isn't he *marvelous?*" That was probably the director, Rick figured, but he could not understand his enthusiasm for that singer.

"Yeah... I guess so." Rick recognized *that* voice, all right. That was John Whitman. "He was okay. Any word yet from Chernikov?"

22

"Just 'okay?' Well, he was simply *marvelous!*" the director was gushing. "And Sony is thinking of signing him to do a disc of Schumann songs! *He can do it all!*"

Whitman shook his head in disgust. "Jesus Christ," he whispered as if to himself. He turned to his director and fixed him with angry blue eyes. "All right. Listen and learn, junior. Here's some Theatre 101 for you: he's five-feet-eight, looks like he just graduated from high school, and we're supposed to believe he's the high priest of the world? The Sun God's representative on Earth – the great Sarastro himself?" Whitman shouted. "What am I running here, Affirmative Action Theatre? Would *you* believe he's Sarastro?! Look at him shaking up there! He looks like my *niece!*" Whitman was in rare form, and Ricardo was developing very bad feelings about all this. He stood and paced.

"But Mr. Whitman…"

"Do me a favor – don't foist any more of your ideas of 'new talent' on me, okay? Who is he anyway, one of your… secret little buddies?"

Behind the curtain, Rick sighed heavily and didn't have to look to know who was storming down the aisle and out of the theatre. *That man loses more directors. But he'd be back. This could be an important show.* The utterly crestfallen singer, who couldn't have been more than twenty-five, walked past Rick without a glance as he headed shamefaced to the dressing room.

"I can't believe this. I still don't have a goddam cast!" Whitman lamented loudly. "Have we heard back from Chernikov's people?"

"No, sir," replied the assistant from the stage.

"Well then let's wrap it up for lunch, eh?" Whitman decided.

"Well, sir, there's someone here…" the assistant, Ricky's inside man, said. "A singer. A bass. But should we even go on? I mean shouldn't the director…".

"Did I say we're done?"

"Well, actually, you just now said you wanted to break for…"

"Who is it?"

"Ummm…," a shuffle of papers as he pretended to find the name, "a bass, name of umm… Ricardo Piatti. You're not obliged to hear him. He just, sort of… showed up."

"Piatti," he heard Whitman say softly. "Jesus Christ. What a day…"

Rick took the stage and smiled to the accompanist, who nodded to Rick and began the opening chords of the aria.

"Been working lately Piatti?" Whitman interrupted the opening chords from the back of the dark hall. The pianist stopped.

Rick drew in a breath. "Nope."

"Waiting for the Met to beg you to sing *Falstaff*, eh?"

Rick was silent. He knew that Whitman wanted to destroy his confidence and would do anything to make that happen.

"I asked you a question!"

"I'm here to sing," Rick said without emotion. "Shall I go on?"

"For what good it'll do you."

Rick considered this as the pianist waited for some sign from Ricardo, who took a deep breath, expanded himself to his full, colossal dimensions and nodded at the pianist, who began to play.

Rick sang Sarastro's aria from Act II of Mozart's *The Magic Flute*, the opera that Whitman and the company were mounting in the spring. He was in lustrous voice and his singing was effortless, and though he wore no costume nor makeup and was surrounded not by disciples in a dazzling temple but by tattered curtains on a bare stage, Rick was for these few minutes transfigured so naturally and profoundly that any greasepaint trappings the theatre could conjure would only profane the vision that the small band of listeners beheld. The sense of the lyric is this:

24

In these sacred halls, revenge is unknown
And if a man falls, Love leads him to his duty.
There he is taken by a friend's hand,
Refreshed and happy, to a better place.

Whitman was legendary for stopping a singer in the middle of his first line in an audition to dismiss him. If he liked you, you might sing an entire verse before his gruff "That's enough!" put an end to your song. But no such orders were barked at Ricardo, who concluded his aria with grave and regal dignity.

Within these sacred walls where we love one another
    no traitors can lurk
Because we all forgive our enemies.
He who does not rejoice in such teaching
Is not worthy of being a man.

Though there was no applause from the gaggle of assistants, investors, and others associated with the show as the final chord died away, there was an awed stillness, but as it drew on, Rick gradually assumed his old identity. He was no longer the Sun King, but an out-of-work singer, and a Big Ape who never needed a job so badly in his life.

"That was fine. Wow... really fine," whispered the pianist, and Rick gave him a wink, but there was still no response from the all-knowing dictator sitting in the dark, thirty rows from the stage. *Is Whitman even in the theatre? It would be just like that rat bastard to leave in the middle of my aria.* Another thirty seconds passed. *What is he doing?*

When the voice finally came, it was tinted with a rage that was barely constrained. "Who do you think you are? What do you think I'm running here?"

Here it comes, Rick thought. "What kind of a quest..."

"THIS IS A PROFESSIONAL THEATRE!" Whitman bellowed from the darkness. He rose up and made his way down the aisle toward the stage with regal strides. When he

25

came into view, at about the tenth row, his shock of grey hair an aura in the lights, he stopped and glared hotly at Rick. Whitman gestured to embrace the entire gathering around him.

"It's a *profession* that we're all a part of here." He tried to calm himself but instead grew more heated as he went on. "We work, we struggle, we take jobs that teach us how to relate to the people, the organizations, the traditions that we're *all* a part of. Sometimes these jobs SUCK!"

Whitman closed his eyes and took a deep breath to calm himself. It didn't work.

"The theatre is a place of PROFESSIONALS who work hard to gather and master all of the talents and contacts and hurdles and obstacles and all the other bullshit that you might find beneath you, your majesty, but PROFESSIONALS understand that there is MORE TO THEIR CAREERS than how they sing a GODDAM ARIA!"

Rick turned away. *Why did I do this? Why did I even come here today?* he thought and started offstage.

"What did you do after *Otello?*" Whitman barked.

Rick turned. "Nothing."

"Nothing," Whitman repeated and let the word hang in the air like a ripe obscenity. "You had three offers that *I know of.* But you don't 'do' roles that aren't starring vehicles. You don't 'do' understudies. You don't 'do' any of the things that people in the theatre need good people to do *so they can work themselves!* Do you think you're better than a singer who sings a minor role in order to be part of this best profession on the planet? DO YOU?" he shouted.

Rick stood with fists clenched tightly, wanting to flee yet transfixed.

"You and your *conceit,*" Whitman hissed. "There's more professionalism in that kid that brought me my coffee than you'll ever muster in your entire sorry-assed life."

"Thanks, Mr. Whitman!" the boy chirped.

"SHUT UP!"

Rick turned away but Whitman stopped him a last time.

"And let me tell you what else you don't 'do'. You don't 'do' this show. Now you can get out." Whitman turned on his heel and walked slowly toward his seat, back into the darkness of the theatre. "There are professionals here with some commitment to their craft who are trying to work."

Rick turned back to his tormentor, thrashing in his mind for something clever to say to ease his embarrassment, but his mind was an angry blank.

A son of first-generation Italians, Rick understood that food and wine were the second and third most glorious things about living, and he spent a lot of time practicing their subtleties. He was the best cook any of his friends knew, but he liked nothing better than to eat a better cook's meal. Estelle liked good food in small quantities and had some appreciation for wine, but tonight the appetizers grew cold on her plate and her wine was untouched. They sat in silence. Estelle looked beautiful but sad, her brown hair in rare curls that bounced on her shoulders when she turned her head. She wore the same dress she always wore whenever she had to 'look nice,' as she put it, but she always looked so wonderful to him. Rick sat in silence, waiting for Estelle to tell him what was on her mind.

"You haven't told me about the audition today," Estelle said. "What happened?"

"Remember Whitman?" Rick asked.

"The producer? Who could forget him?"

"Yeah. He threw me out of the theatre." He drained his glass of Barolo, an elegant and costly wine he would have savored in other circumstances but this night it flooded down his gullet without sensation. *It's Estelle that makes this stuff taste good.*

She sat quietly with lowered eyes, fingering the lace on the tablecloth.

"So, it didn't go too well." Rick poured himself another glass. Estelle sat nodding her head absentmindedly. Rick asked, "What are you thinking about? You look like you just figured something out."

The seconds passed, and she sat mute, picking at the lace.

"Goddam it." he whispered to her. "Are you gonna tell me what's going on or not?"

"You're so talented. But you won't work." She was speaking quietly and choosing her words with care. "And we live together… in that damn apartment… like… like a couple of penniless students in some stupid Italian opera." Estelle looked at her wine glass as though she hadn't noticed it before, took it and sipped absent-mindedly and placed it down with a heavy sigh.

"You *could* be working," she continued, her voice gathering passion as she spoke. "You *should* be working. You should be *singing*, in an opera company, probably an important singer by now if you just played along a *little*. But you won't." The words came faster. "And what has it gotten us? It's not like I haven't been supportive! I've tried everything I could think of to get you to come around to yourself before it's too late. Too late for you to have the career you deserve, and… and too late for us. It's an *emergency*, Rick, and I don't know what else to do! We've been doing this for almost nine years and it never gets any better! Look at us!"

Ricardo closed his eyes in shame and saw his Big Ape self and beautiful Estelle. He opened his eyes. "I do look at us. And I love us."

"O Rick…"

"What?"

"I'm going away. For a while," she said. "Tonight."

There was the thing he had dreaded but never allowed himself to consciously anticipate. He didn't know what to ask. *Why? With who? How long? Where to?* He sat, dazed.

She could not look at Rick. She told her news to the wall next to her. "Mike Finnerty asked me to go to Jamaica with him for a week and I said I would. We're leaving tonight," she started to cry, "and when I come back," she sniffed, "if you want to see me, then I'll talk to you then. When I can sort all this out."

"Mike. Fucking. Finnerty?" The thought of him with Estelle was so offensive that it overpowered his sadness.

"Oh, stop it," Estelle said.

Their waiter appeared at Rick's elbow. "Is everything all right, sir?"

"Yeah, scram," Rick said, and the waiter departed with a smirk. "Mike Finnerty is a pig."

"You don't know him. And he's always been sweet to me," she sniffed. "And he's paid our rent this month. I couldn't afford it."

Rick leaped to his feet, whacking his head hard on the small chandelier. "He WHAT?" The lamp swayed back and forth with a squeak, throwing spinning shadows about the room.

Estelle looked up at Rick with red eyes. "Well? What were we going to do? I didn't want him to, but he gave me a bonus to cover it."

"Well, how the hell did he know we couldn't pay the rent? What else do you tell this son-of-a-bitch?"

Estelle didn't reply. She sniffed and dabbed at her face with her napkin, her eyes downcast.

"He paid my rent," Ricky explained to the ceiling. "Jesus Christ... I would have thought of something." He sat back down, struggling to remain calm, silently staring at the swaying shadow of his wineglass that kept time with the upset chandelier. Then the dreaded notion seized him and took his breath away. He looked at her and saw that she was anticipating the question. "Have you two been... you know..."

"Have we made love?" There was a hint of defiance in her eyes.

"Well?" *Brace yourself.*

"No." She held his eyes steadily, then looked away. "But you know what? I *want* to go away for a while. I *like* Mike. And I need a rest from all this... this being poor and never going *anywhere* or doing *anything*. And from your... I don't know... *inertness!* And because *it doesn't have to be that way!*" Then Estelle stood up, so obviously upset, walked over to

Rick and kissed him on the cheek. "Goodbye," she said, crying hard but getting the words out. "I have to go now. I'm sorry about dinner, and my birthday and everything but I just... can't..." She turned and walked away.

Rick was so stunned that he didn't notice the smirking waiter standing, who knows how long, at his elbow, ready to take his order.

"I said, would you like to order, sir."

"Yeah," Rick straightened in his chair. "No food. Just another bottle of that Barolo."

The waiter smiled. "For the lady? Shall I wait for her to return?"

"No. She, umm... she won't be back I guess."

"Very good, sir." The waiter spun and went to work.

Drinking was Rick's downfall as a younger man. One evening many years ago, after failing repeatedly to coax his new yellow canary (his one and only experiment with a pet) to perch upon his finger and sing, which Rick thought would be really cool, he became incensed, suspecting that the bird harbored a personal grudge against him, his owner and feeder, king and sole benefactor. In a drunken stupor one night he decided he had had enough of the bird's contrary attitude, and so superglued the frightened creature's little feet to his index finger, the bird pecking madly at Ricky's booze-numbed skin. Through the blur of his double-vision, he waited for one of the canaries to break out into song. "Sing, you little bastard," he would coax. The bird was silent as a tomb for the few minutes it took Rick to fall asleep.

When he woke in his chair hours later, neck stiff, throat dry as soot and head throbbing, he noted with alarm the bird on his blood-caked finger and the memory of his folly came rushing back in full. He cursed and shook his aching head, staring at the bird and wiping spittle from his cheek. The bird (whom Rick had imaginatively dubbed "Mister Bird") was holding up well through his tribulation (or hers – Rick didn't know which), but the little feet would not be budged. The canary would nip sharply at Rick's hand if his efforts to dislodge its feet from their cast became too clumsy. Rick's girl-friend suggested that this was a job for the veterinarian, and so it was. The obstinate canary, to Rick's great contempt, never sounded a note through the entire ordeal.

The disgusted vet, after wheedling out Ricardo's bizarre tale of drunkenness and bird-bondage, would not give him his canary back, an unexpected boon for which Rick was grateful. His girlfriend paid the vet and even took the canary, but she never saw Ricardo again.

His habitual drunkenness subsided soon after that episode, dwindling down to a few glasses of wine per night, and the not-too-rare excess with friends. But something snapped and opened within him at the restaurant after Estelle took her leave that brought back all the mindlessness and recklessness of his youth.

By the end of the second bottle he had turned maudlin and saw the rest of his life as a desert of odd-jobs and loneliness; by the time he finished the third bottle, the singular clarity of the drunkard was upon him, and he knew what he must do.

Rick paid the check and tipped the smartass waiter handsomely to show there were no hard feelings. He still had more than $800 in his newly-fattened wallet and there were accounts to settle. He took a cab to the café near his apartment and paid the coffee bill, then stopped home to change and call the airport for departure information. He decided that he would go to the airport and confront Estelle and Finnerty. He wasn't sure what he would do when he found them, but he would figure that out in the cab on the way.

At the airport he had a devil of a time finding the proper gate, and when he did, Estelle and Finnerty were not to be seen. The plane would leave in an hour, so they were bound to be here soon. Ricardo sat and waited, his rage keeping the somnolent effects of his advanced state of drunkenness at bay. Sleep was absolutely impossible for he was far too angry to worry about nodding off.

"Rick!" came the voice again. "Wake up!"

He opened his eyes and leaped to his feet, for a few seconds unsure of where he was and why. Unsteady, he looked down and beheld the familiar top of Estelle sweet little head.

She looked up. "You were asleep. Are you all right?" she asked. "You look terrible!"

"Where is he?" Rick grumbled menacingly.

"Just *stop it*. He went to the bathroom. He said he'd meet me at the gate, but I don't want you to see him. I want you to go. Right now! Don't do this to me. *Stop it right now!*"

"Don't do this to *you?* You're actually going to go through with this?!" Rick yelled. Suddenly a big man, taller even than Rick, was at Estelle's side.

"Is this guy bothering you?" the man asked Estelle. Ricky closed his eyes and smiled.

"That's… oh god… that's Ricardo," she said, slumping in resignation.

"So," he smiled at Rick, "this is the opera singer. I'm Mike Finnerty." He put out a ham-sized hand for Rick to shake. Instead, Rick grabbed his hand, twisted it around Finnerty's back and slammed him painfully against the wall, digging his shoulder into Finnerty's back with all his might. Estelle knew instinctively not to interfere. She stood close by, agonizing.

Rick lifted Finnerty's captured hand up along his back until it stopped and then fought it up higher using his other hand under Finnerty's elbow, causing Finnerty tremendous suffering.

"Say, 'Estelle, you're a filthy whore,'" Rick ordered Finnerty. Instead, the bigger man cried out in pain.

"SAY IT!" Rick screamed into Finnerty's ear. He worked his hand up higher.

"I'LL BREAK YOUR ARM IF YOU DON'T SAY IT!"

Security was called at once but no one in the crowd dared to come between the two giants in their struggle. It was a race against time and Rick knew it. Finnerty howled in agony as Rick strained to break Finnerty's arm.

"SAY IT! SAY 'ESTELLE YOU'RE A FILTHY WHORE' OR I'LL BREAK YOUR ARM!"

"ESTELLE!" Finnerty cried out.

"SAY IT"

"AHHHH!... YOU"RE A..."

"I'm gonna break it!"

"RRRRRAAAAAAAAGHESTELLEYOUREAFILT HYWHORE!" and Rick released him just as the security guards came around the turn. Finnerty collapsed against the wall and sliding onto the floor, clutching at his shoulder, grunting in agony. *"You lunatic son-of-a-bitch..."* he hissed at his tormentor.

Rick, himself gasping for breath, looked to Estelle, who would not meet Rick's wild gaze. "I would never have said that. You would have had to dislocate my shoulder and I *still* wouldn't have said it." The guards grabbed hold of Rick and wrestled him from the gate area. "YOU WOULD HAVE HAD TO KILL ME, AND I *STILL* WOULDN'T SAY IT!" he screamed at Estelle, who had collapsed in mortification on her chair, her fists doubled at her temples as Ricardo, bellowing her name, was dragged around the corner and out of sight.

Security let Rick go, mainly because Finnerty declined to press charges, but in fact they liked Rick and found his story amusing. They even got him an airport limo to go home in. But Rick felt hollow and morose.

There was but a single chore left him in this long and wrenched day, and he instructed the limo driver to take him to Angelo's Market. Sophia and Angelo were glad to see him but concerned about his state of mind and whether he could walk home or not without falling down.

"Don't worry about me. I'm fine," he assured the old couple. He took out his wallet and counted out the $30 he said he owed them.

Angelo took the cash. "You're a good boy, Ricardo, but why are you so drunk tonight?" he asked. "That's not like you."

"I'm not really drunk anymore," he replied.

"You're stinko, my friend."

"How did the audition go?" Sophia asked.

"Oh. That." Rick swayed back and forth. "Bad. He threw me out."

"Oh, dear," Sophia said. "I'm so sorry. But how can they find a boy with as nice a voice as you have, eh, Ricky?"

"They needed a professional," he explained in a quiet voice.

"You *are* a professional," Angelo said. "Aren't you?"

"Apparently not... I don't know. But right now, I have to make love to your wife."

"You have to *what?*"

Ricardo nudged Angelo aside and took Sophia in his arms and started to sing an old Italian folk song that spoke of the beauty of her black hair and the flowersmell of her skin, and how one day they would grow old together and he would still see her the same way he did when they were young lovers. Sophia grew thirty years younger, even a little taller in his arms as she played the wooed maiden. The dozen or so customers in the market all gathered round to watch colossal Ricardo with the beautiful deep voice make musical love to tiny old Sophia, and when the song ended, they all clapped loudly and long, except Angelo, who looked grim.

"Now you die!" Angelo bellowed and drew an imaginary sword. Rick pleaded for mercy with much melodrama, but it looked like curtains for him until Sophia wiggled in between, fell to her knees, kissed Angelo's hand and begged his forgiveness. With a great show, the noble Angelo spared Ricky's life. Finally, Angelo and Sophia kissed sweetly. The crowd loved the show and were slow to disburse until Sophia and Angelo escorted Rick from the market.

When the trio got outside Rick stopped, lowered his head and began to cry, gently at first but with growing intensity until at last huge sobs racked the shoulders of his bent frame, his daylong agony bursting finally as from a great ruptured dam.

"Ricardo, what in the world is the matter with you tonight?" Sophia asked.

Ricky straightened himself. "Estelle left me for some rich goon," he said, wiping away snot bubbles and trying to stop the sobs that still racked from him uncontrolled.

Angelo stepped in front of Ricky and grabbed him by both shoulders. "Ricardo, listen to me! This is no good. Go home and sleep. You'll never feel worse than you do right now, and you need to sleep it off. *Hey!*" Angelo smacked him hard on the cheek a couple of times as if trying to wake him up, and only then could Rick finally began to calm himself and settle down to Angelo's council. "I'm embarrassed for you. People are looking at you. Be brave," Angelo said. "Do you want me to walk you home?"

"Let Angie walk you home, Ricardo," Sophia said.

"No," he sniffed. "I'll be okay. You're right. I need to go home. Here," he reached into his pocket for the Montecristo, "have a Havana, Angelo." But alas, the cigar was mangled beyond utility. Angelo laughed. Ricky looked hopeless, shook his head and threw the frayed stub into the gutter.

Sad Ricardo kissed both his friends goodbye, wiping away cold tears. "I'll stop by tomorrow." He looked at Sophia and saw that she was crying, too.

Rick tumbled into his dark apartment, nearly tripping over Estelle's shoes which he did not recognize, fell into his big chair near the window and stared out into the city night. The clock said "PM 11:07." He had made a fool of himself today in so many ways that he lost count when he tried to call it all to mind again, and a deep fatigue closed in upon him. He nodded off, but the ringing phone jerked him back into the world. Rick picked it up, so beyond hope that Estelle would be on the other end that the notion never crossed his mind.

"Hello."

"Piatti?"

"Who's this."

"John Whitman."

Rick breathed a bitter laugh. "Was there some way that you wanted to insult me that you overlooked this afternoon?"

"No. I want to know if you want the role of Sarastro. Not an understudy, not a chorus member – Sarastro."

Rick sat up straight and coughed to clear his throat. "Yeah. Yeah I do. Are you torturing me?"

"I don't usually stay up this late, but the way you sang that aria today keeps me awake. It was… compelling."

"Glad you liked it. What's the deal?"

"Come by tomorrow about noon. Meet my pain-in-the-ass director and the rest of the cast and we'll go over the terms and a schedule. That's if you're not too busy," he said sarcastically.

"Oh, don't start, all right?"

Whitman laughed. "Don't be so touchy, for Christ's sake. If this goes well, we'll see about some steady work, okay? But you might have to play along a little bit."

"Yeah. Thanks. I know what you mean by that. And I appreciate it."

"Goddam aria… Now maybe I can get some sleep," Whitman said and hung up without saying goodbye.

Rick put the phone down and sank back into the chair. *A silver lining,* he thought, *but a day too late.* In this bitter irony he had lost everything dear to him. *She is the buzz in my wine, the savor in my food, and the glory in my voice. How can I sing at all and ever again?* He went to the cupboard and poured a completely unnecessary half-tumbler of bourbon and drank it down in a single draught, then went to the window and stared down at the dark street three stories below. It was raining. Inside and out.

Ricky's eye wandered to the small, framed photo on the kitchen table of Estelle and himself, smiling, champagne glasses raised to the camera at a New Year's party back in the day. He picked it up and studied her face, realizing it was the only photo of her he had. He clutched the suddenly precious object to his chest and paced the kitchen fore and aft with fitful breath sighing hard, the last tears of the day squeezing from closed eyes and wetting his cheeks as he paced the old narrow floors.

Finally, exhausted at last, he put the photo down on the stovetop, the urgent need for unconsciousness hitting him like a truck as he staggered into the bedroom, turned on the light, and saw Estelle snuggled up on her usual side of the bed, smiling at him impishly.

"Estelle!" Rick was agog with incomprehension. "Is that *you?"*

"It took you long enough to come in," she said merrily. "What were you doing out there all that time?" She grew suddenly solemn. "I'm sorry about everything," she said quietly. "Will you forgive me?"

He swayed, dazed, unbelieving. "Hell yes! Will *I* forgive *you?"*

"I just get a little weary sometimes about everything. But even though we aren't married yet, I feel like it's for better or worse. You know what I mean?"

He stepped over to her, bent to her and kissed her lips. "I know what you mean. Oh, honey, you didn't leave me!" He seized her shoulders suddenly. "HEY LISTEN GUESS WHAT!!"

"Things are bound to improve, somehow. I mean, what other direction can things go?"

"I want you to quit your job tomorrow," he straightened suddenly, belched and swayed, *"'cause guess what?"*

"What?" she asked. "Ricardo, honey, come lie down."

"You know what happened tonight?" Ricardo tugged enthusiastically at his shirttail, lost his balance and fell hard into bed, breaking the frame underneath (again) so that the mattress tilted to the floor on his side. "Guess?"

Estelle sighed, her pretty breasts rising and falling under the white sheet. "What? Tell me."

"Well, you'll never believe this but… I mean I still can't believe it hardly, but after I got home…" Suddenly he thought of Finnerty. "Listen. I don't want you working with that guy."

"He had some unkind things to say about you, too," she giggled, then became solemn. "You never would have said that awful thing to me." She stroked his hair. "I know you wouldn't. Even if somebody said they'd kill you."

Rick turned on his side to face Estelle, tried unsuccessfully to focus his eyes, then flopped back flat. "Well... there's no way you'll never gonna guess what in a million years so I may as... well just... hey, would you really have gone off with that big fat bastard? You wouldn't have, huh? I mean... you know eventually... I would have... taken care of... actually in foriffasomma in... galladifuffaa..." he mumbled, trailing off incomprehensively and falling fast asleep with a *basso profundo* snore of Wagnerian proportions.

Estelle propped herself up on her elbow. "Ricardo?" she whispered. "Ricky honey?" She poked his cheek softly with a finger in rhythm with her voice. "What. Did. You. Want. To. Tell. Me."

She leaned over and kissed his forehead and watched him sleep for a while, remembering all the many things that had drawn them together, and completely forgetting, for a few precious moments, everything but this.

80C3

Treachery

The old man leaned back in his chair and pointed at his empty glass.

"Another Scotch, Randy," he shouted to the bartender. "And another beer for my grandson?" He raised his bushy eyebrows in inquiry at his grandson who nodded assent. "Yeah, Randy, another beer for the kid here."

The bartender got busy and the old man heaved a great sigh and smiled at Mike, his grandson of, what, 30-some years? How the hell did that happen? Time flies whether you're having fun or not, the old man thought.

"How come you're smilin', Grampa?" Mike asked with a smile of his own. "Is it because you're not going to jail?"

"Not today," he replied with a snort. "But that goddam lawyer cost me a fortune."

They laughed, knowing it was worth it.

"I knew you were innocent," young Mike said. "I'm sorry you had to go through all that."

"Ah, it wasn't much. Never even got close to a trial. They had nothing on me."

Mike took a hit on his beer and studied his grampa with childish affection. "You landed all six shots, right. Pretty good shooting under stress."

Grampa looked about him furtively, and then with lowered head and quiet voice, said, "Not really," in a confessional tone. "He was 20 feet away and I only hit him with five. I aimed them all at his chest. One went there, another hit his neck, one hit his forearm, another his hip and another hit his shin. The sixth round hit his car!"

"Wow! That's pretty bad shooting," the lad laughed. "I take back the compliment!"

"I was a little, as you said, stressed." He smiled at the lad. "Smartass."

41

The drinks arrived. The old man shot half of his back and Mike took a big gulp of beer, wiping the white foam from his 'stash with his sleeve.

The old man looked thoughtful. They were silent for a good half-minute till Mike said, "What's wrong? You look... like something's disturbing you... or somethin'."

His grandfather looked up at the lad and took a deep breath. "I gotta tell you something, Mike. But just you. You gotta know this. What really happened." He shook his head. "It ain't like you think."

The old man got the call from the hospital because he was third on the contact list for his daughter-in-law, Gretchen. The first two on the list, her husband and son, weren't answering their phones. It was almost midnight. He ignored all the lights and stop signs and made the emergency entrance miraculously without incident.

He was led to Gretchen's room and his heart broke. Her head was heavily bandaged, and she broke into tears when she saw him, trying hard in a futile attempt to assure him that she was okay. She was in fact *not* okay. She will eventually lose an eye from her injury, and her face was badly bruised.

He calmed himself enough to ask, "How did this happen?"

She heaved a deep sigh and told her story. "I was at a bar I probably shouldn't have been at, but I didn't pick the place." She was whispering, but not crying anymore. She wanted to get this out. "It was Greta's birthday from work and the bar is the closest to the clinic we work at. So after work the four of us nurses went out to dinner, then to the bar where there was a big surprise party for Greta with like the whole staff there."

She paused and closed her eyes. The old man took her hand in his and squeezed. His weeping had *not* stopped. He waited.

"So anyway... this asshole kept hitting on me. I wear my *ring*, for Christ's sake but I guess that isn't enough for some people." She started crying again.

"Take some deep breaths, honey," her father-in-law said quietly.

She continued. "So it got so bad, and it went on and on... and everybody was looking... and I threw a drink at him. In his face. And everybody laughed. And the bouncer guy came over from the doorway and, I guess this guy's a known jerk, and anyway he threw the guy out." Another long pause. He thought she had gone to sleep.

"So that was that, we all thought, but I was too annoyed and... grossed out to stay any longer and so I left. And before I got to my car this asshole *grabbed* me... and he CUT me! In my EYE! With a *knife. A big knife!*" And she began to cry harder than he had ever seen a woman cry. He hugged her as close as he could without hurting her. And he felt his rage start to overcome his giant grief.

Her door opened and in came her husband Dale and her son Michael. More agony and tears. The worst night ever.

The assailant had also taken her purse. The suspect was tracked down that evening at his home in a dilapidated farm-house outside of town, his name given to the police by a witness to the harassment in the bar, who knew the man.

The suspect was released the next day. He had an alibi, and there was no physical evidence to connect him to the assault. The robbery aspect became a "more likely motive," the cops said, and there were plenty of troublemakers who answered to the description of a man of medium height and build in a tee-shirt and jeans, and who wore a ski mask to hide his features. The man never said a word to Gretchen during the entire episode. She was cut and robbed. It simply was not possible to connect the suspect to the crime with any degree of certainty. And so he walks the streets.

It's been almost two months since the assault. Gretchen lost her left eye and suffered many stitches to her face. The scar will never go away. She wears a prosthetic eye now. Her husband Dale has been beside himself with anger but does not know what to do. He would like to kill the man who hurt his wife but in plain fact Dale is not a killer. Neither is their son, Mike. For her part, Gretchen has extracted promises from both men that they would not put themselves and their lives and futures in jeopardy with revenge fantasies that, even if successful, would likely result in her husband's or son's imprisonment as the most likely outcome.

But Dale's father is a different sort of man. He has been quiet and helpful to the family, discouraging the revenge fantasies and trying to keep everyone on an even keel. This has also been terribly hard on their daughter, Allison, and her grandfather has been a loving and effective force in her dealing with all this.

Two months have passed, and the old man rises one Saturday morn and decides to drive 400 miles to the big city and take in a giant gun & knife show at the local fairgrounds. He loved to go to these things as a kid, but it had been years. There were literally acres of merchandise and, being a gun show, he was in the most polite company imaginable. It's always like that at guns shows—many are carrying concealed, but you never know who, so there's a minimum of mindlessness and stupid behavior. All mind their own business.

He found the booth he was looking for—the most magnificent collection of custom handmade knives on the premises. He never owned a nice knife, just small utility blades over the years that a gentleman might carry. But today he was in the market for something big and splendid. He found it. A small bowie-style knife with scrimshawed ivory scales with a chrome blade that looked about eight inches long. It was beautiful. You'd feel guilty cutting something with it! It was $450, which was less than he thought it would be. He tried haggling but he was never very good at that sort of thing.

That evening after he got back, he made himself dinner and then made a visit to the bar where Gretchen was assaulted. He was looking for the man who gave the police a heads up on where her assailant called home. He wondered what else he might find out about her attacker. It turned out that the informer wasn't there that night, but a few of his friends were, and by providing these men with a staggering amount of beer and various liquors he found out more about Mr. Darren Holderlin than he ever needed to know.

Mike was on his third beer, but his grandfather was on his fifth Scotch. Still, they were about even in their level of inebriation.

"You remember the knife from the hearing?" the old man asked.

"Geez... that big-ass Bowie knife? Yeah... I wonder if it was the same one he used on mom." Mike winced at the memory.

"It wasn't. It was mine."

Mike looked confused. "What? Yours? How did he... what do you mean?"

"I bought it the day before." He chuckled. "It set me back $500. But it was a beauty, huh?"

"Yeah... but-"

"Another beer?"

His grandson nodded but was getting a little unsettled by the conversation. "Yeah, sure, but-"

"I'll tell you," the old man said. "I'll tell you all about it."

The next morning the old man purchased a pair of very thin black leather gloves. It wasn't really the season yet, it was only October, but they were absolutely necessary.

It was the third straight day of dreary Michigan autumn rain that had finally settled into a foggy mist. His arthritis was kicking up and he had second thoughts about setting off on this most urgent of errands. But he was resolved. He gobbled two pain pills with his coffee, washed and dressed in baggy, comfortable clothes, and set off to find the home of one Darren Holderlin. For it was he who had assaulted his daughter-in-law and took her eye, and her sense of well-being, and put scars on her face and in her and her family's heart that shall never disappear.

It was all a matter of public record where the man lived, and before the old man turned into the property he tooled by slowly and took a good look at the place. There he was, Holderlin, outside the house in the front yard staring under the hood of an old Ford Taurus. The old man drove another hundred yards, turned the car around, and doubled back slowly, this time he turned in, pulled up a few yards from the man, turned off his car, opened the door and stepped out onto the gravel driveway.

Darren turned and watched the old man wrench himself out of the car and stood to face him. The young man was standing in very wet mud, which took up most of his yard. Only the gravel driveway was clear of muck.

Holderlin noted with some concern that the old man had a formidable-looking knife in his gloved hand. The old guy shut the car door and advanced to within ten yards of the younger man. The old man noted that the man he was facing looked no more than 30, slim, muscled and moved with an easy grace. He was everything that the old man no longer was.

"Who the fuck are you and what are... oh wait... you're the father of that bitch that accused me of cuttin' her." He took a step back toward the old Taurus. "I remember you from the hearing. What are you doin' here?"

"I'm her father-in-law actually, and I'm here to kill you."

"I'm innocent," Holderlin said, comically holding his hands above his head. "Or you too senile to remember that I had nothin' to do with that?"

The old man held up the knife. "See this?"

Holderlin laughed. "Yeah. It's nice. That yours?"

"I'm gonna kill you with it."

He laughed again. "You can try. But I'll shove that up your ass before you know what hit you and there ain't a judge in the world who'd bother me for it."

The old guy advanced toward the young man, who didn't even bother to change his stance.

"You think you're pretty tough with that thing don't you?" Holderlin said, completely at ease, stifling a giggle, confident in his obvious superiority.

The old man stopped in his tracks at the edge of the mud.

"You hurt my Gretchen, you son-of-a-bitch!" he screamed.

The young man laughed.

Grampa yelled, "You think I need this knife? *Do you!?*" And the old man threw the knife at the younger man's feet. "Bring it on you bastard! You woman beater! I don't need a knife to kill you. I'll kill you with my bare hands! *I know karate!*"

Holderlin whooped a great belly-laugh. "You know karate, huh? Jesus, that's funny."

This was turning into a comedy! Holderlin wasn't afraid of the old man when he had the knife and now he wanted to take him on *mano-a-mano?* This was too much. He looked down at the knife at his feet. He couldn't help himself. He bent down and picked up the knife, turning it in his hands. "Nice," he said. "*Real* nice. I think it wants me to keep it."

"Come on, fucker! Try me!" The old man screamed hysterically. "And after I beat you to death I'll go to that dump you keep that retard vegetable sister of yours in, and maybe I'll cut her like you cut my Gretchen!"

Those were the magic words, and a stormy cloud, a deep darkness came over the visage of the young man.

He looked at the knife in his hands. "I won't need this to take care of you," he seethed, and as he started his muddy tromp toward the old man he motioned to cast the knife aside, but before he could release it, the old man had a pistol in his hands and fired six .45-caliber slugs at the young man, dropping him where he stood.

The old man was careful not to advance on the dying man, not to venture into the mire in which he lay to admire his handiwork. He just looked in wonder at what he did. He had never shot a man before, never even been in a fight since the childhood playground.

The young man was not dead. He stared with bug-eyed hatred at the old man standing a few yards away. He was bleeding from his mouth, tried to speak, but could not.

"Please die quickly so I can call the cops," the old man said. He was getting a little shaky, breathing a little fast, trying now to calm himself. He gathered himself to deliver an explanation. He wanted the young man to understand what had just gone down.

"See, here's what happened," he began. "I came here in good faith just to speak with you, to find out why you did what you did to my Gretchen. What kind of man you are. If there was another side to the story, maybe? Trying to find closure. But you attacked me with that big knife of yours, see?"

The young man spasmed in anger at the old man's speech, gurgling blood, trying to object.

The old man continued. "I'm licensed to carry and took my gun with me as a safeguard in case you turned into a raging madman and tried to kill me. Which you did. See? Maybe with a knife. That's your favorite way, right? My prints aren't on that knife. Just yours. I'm just a feeble old guy tried to defend myself. I just wanted to talk, see? And that's how all this will go down."

The kid lay dead in the mud.

"Just in case you can still hear me, I'm not going to bother your poor sister. I just needed to say something to get you to come at me. So don't worry about that poor girl."

He put the small pistol back into his pocket, reached into his other pocket for his phone and poked 911.

What's your emergency?

"Oh my God!" he panted theatrically. "I shot a man! I think I may have killed him! He had a knife! He was going to kill me! Oh Jesus!"

Calm down sir. Where are you right now.

"At an old farmhouse out on Diamondback Road. The one between the freeway and, what is it… Nickels Road."

Stay calm. Put the gun down and step away from it. Do not be holding your gun when help arrives. An ambulance and the Sheriff will be there in minutes. Do you want to stay on the line with me?

"What? No. Ahh… no. I need to sit and rest. I'll be in my car with the door open. I put the gun on the hood of the car. O Jesus! Hurry, will ya? I think he's *dead!*" And he pressed Stop.

He strolled serenely to the car, took off his gloves and placed them on the hood of the car, pulled out the spent pistol from his pocket and gripped it, fondled it and let it soak up his prints. He put the gun on the hood of his car, picked up the gloves and opened the door to the driver-side. He sat, reached over and put the gloves in the glovebox, which he then locked. The Sheriff arrived within minutes, followed by Fire-Rescue. The Sheriff took him into custody. The old man seemed a little in shock but was very cooperative.

"Why did you tell me this?" his grandson asked, near tears.

"I wanted someone to know. Somehow, I knew I should tell you. I hope you'll be discreet, but that's up to you. If you think it'll be better to share this with all or some of the family, that's your call. I'll be with you if you like."

The lad stared at the wall for a space, then put the finish on beer number five.

"What a setup. That took lots of planning. Didn't it?"

His granddad pointed at his own empty glass and hailed for a refill, but the youngster said no to beer number six. He was having trouble focusing his eyes.

"Yeah, it took planning. Also luck. Lots could have gone wrong."

"Like what?"

"I went there to kill him, but he needed to pick the knife up to get his prints on it. If he didn't I'd have shot him anyway but would have had to track into the mud and force his dead hand around a knife trying to make it look natural. Then I'd maybe have to explain the mud tracks, the dirty shoes, I might have left a trace of myself on him while I faked the fingerprint thing... so he had to pick up the knife. The cops are a lot better at figuring out this sort of thing than people know. Thank God he picked up the blade."

His grandson let a low laugh. "Thank God, eh? I guess..."

"He could have thrown the knife aside. I would have had to explain that, or else fetch it in the muck and place it near the body. So that could have happened."

"So you were lucky."

"I also needed to see if there was anything personally about him I could use in this fight. When the boys at the bar told me about his knife fetish and his poor sister I knew I had what I needed in case I had to light a fire under this guy's ass. So that was handy."

The young man put his hand to his forehead and slumped forward. "I can't believe this..."

"Do you wish I hadn't done it?"

Mike stayed slumped in thought for a few moments, then lifted his head and said, "No, Grampa. I'm glad you killed that son-of-a-bitch. I just feel... funny." He wiped away a few tears.

"You need a clear head. If you decide to share this with anyone don't do it tonight. You need a clear head. Understand?"

Mike nodded. "You're such a loving and peaceful guy, Grampa. How could you think you could take on a guy like that? Young, good shape. Violent crazy asshole?"

The old man smiled. "I had the one thing he didn't have."

"The wisdom of the elderly?" Mike joked.

Grampa laughed. "Ha! Good one. Christ, no! That ain't it."

"A gun?"

Grampa shook his head. "If I just walked in and shot the bastard I'd be in prison now." He added, more seriously, "Plus I didn't want to just shoot him in cold blood. I wanted him to come at me."

Mike looked at him with the question on his face.

Grampa continued. "Youth has beauty, speed, strength, agility, passion—and I can barely get out of a car some days without crying like a girl from the pain. That young man could have broken me in half. I'm old, and I have not a single one of those youthful qualities. But the lack of these things creates a single quality that can conquer all the rest. A quality that youth never quite comprehends."

"What, Grampa? What is that quality called?"

Grampa just smiles.

ഇൗ൚

How to Score Hot Chicks

to Mary, my sister

I fly a lot. I fly way too much. If I shelled out for first-class or even business-class then I wouldn't make any money. So I fly coach with the herd, the screaming babies and the drunks.

I try to avoid 'the middle seat' and I'm pretty good at that when I book a flight, eager to get to the seat chart as soon as it becomes available. But it doesn't always work out. I'm a big guy and the looks I get from the aisle and window sitters when I approach my seat never fail to dishearten me. Some politely try to hide their annoyance, while others seem to relish that glare of contempt, as if they were *hoping* it would be me. I actually apologize before I take my seat. I try not to, but it always just slips out.

So, yeah, I hate flying. But I'm in sales and it's what I have to do. Actually, I own the company and I've never found anyone to trust with the all-important face-to-face dynamic with customers that keeps my cash flow on target. I must be pretty good at it. I do all right. I sell art supplies, with my own line of economy paints and easels.

I'm not an artist myself. Never even tried, the idea is so ludicrous. But I'm a Master of Art History and enchanted by people who can draw and paint and I'm proud of the value that my wares provide to students just starting out. I am unmarried, have few friends and no hobbies. Well, maybe one—when I travel, *I like to score hot chicks.*

I had to laugh just writing that line. I am a total failure at scoring hot chicks, but not for lack of trying.

"It helps if you actually care about them," my buddy Doug sagely advised one day over lunch. He's married.

"But I don't *know* them. How the hell can I especially care for a total stranger?"

"I'm just sayin'," Doug said. "I've seen you in action. It's pathetic."

"Wait a minute," I was offended. "What's pathetic?"

"The way you go about it. The lines you use. One-night stands are pretty easy to score, if that's what you're looking for, and you're not, but you pretend you are."

"Fuck you." He hit a nerve. "Go on."

"Okay, where do you find these pick-up lines that you use?"

"Well I... I try to get advice from-"

"From where? *100 Things to Never Say to a Woman Under Any Circumstances?* Let me recall a few from our nights back in the day. How about this: *Baby, if women were boogers, I'd pick you first.*"

"I never said that."

"Or this: *I hear you're looking for a stud. Well, I've got the STD and all I need is U.*"

"It shows I have a sense of humor! And she almost-"

"No she didn't. And the one you used so many times: *Do you believe in love at first sight? Or should I walk by again?*"

"It made me seem self-confident... didn't it?"

"No. It made you seem like an asshole."

"But-"

"But nothin'. Listen to me. Are you listening to me?"

"Yeah. What."

"None of your bullshit works, and never will, even on these desperate chicks who just want a one-nighter, *because you don't want it to work.* Nobody is that inept without a deep-seated desire to fail, because it's not what you really want! You just aren't as shallow as you wish you were."

So that's the great cross that I bear: I am not as shallow as I wish I was.

This was on my mind as I boarded Delta flight DL2911 from Detroit to Los Angeles—a very long flight, and I trudged to my assigned middle seat near the tail of the plane as if I were on my way to the gallows. Five bloody hours sandwiched between two pissed off people whose hopes were dashed, in the very last minute, that the seat between them would remain unoccupied.

But that nightmare was not to be. For at the window seat was the most beautiful woman in the world, and the other two seats were empty! I nodded at this vision of a girl and she returned my gesture. Small and trim, she had a shock of red hair (should have been a hint as to temperament) and skin so pale it was almost white. I could see the small worry in her quick blue eyes that I was going to cram my big frame up against her in the cursed middle seat, but since they were no longer boarding I decided it was safe to take the aisle seat, which I patted lovingly, and smiled at her. Her relief was evident in the little smile she returned.

While I was stuffing my carry-on in the overhead compartment I had a vision of my pal Doug, warning me not to be my usual self in this circumstance. *But I knew Doug was wrong!* My technique, admittedly unsuccessful over the decades, had been nonetheless honed by now to a keen edge, and I knew, I just *knew*, that payday was finally here. If I played my cards right, this dreamgirl would be mine before we landed.

I decided a British accent was the way to go. Yes. That was the ticket. For starters. I slammed the overhead door closed, looked at my seatmate, smiled, and let fly:

"Well, here I am, my lovely. What are your other two wishes?" I do a pretty good Brit accent.

She looked at me as though she had just noticed some offensive seepage oozing through the airplane fuselage. "Oh, Christ..." she groaned, and she looked away, out the window where the luggage truck was zooming away.

I felt it as keenly as a slap in the face, and mumbled, "I'm sorry, I get nervous around beautiful women."

She looked back at me. "Please stop. Please?"

"That... that wasn't a line. That was true. Sorry." I forgot to use my accent there, so jarred was I at her reaction to me. She never noticed, or if she did she didn't care.

I took my seat, disheartened enough by now to forget the whole thing. I buckled my seatbelt and stared at the seatback in front of me. I felt small and ashamed. I cursed my friend Doug. Now historically, these little setbacks had never bothered me much but this one did. Despite the fact she was a stranger, I actually felt a connection to this woman and I regretted my dumbass posturing.

We sat in silence during the safety lecture by the flight attendant and I noted that my seatmate was paying rapt attention, jabbing at the unit above her head where the oxygen mask would descend if needed, craning her neck to ascertain the location of the emergency doors. Was this her first time on an airplane? When the demonstration was done I noted her poking through the literature in the netting on the seatback in front of her. She pulled out the barfbag and examined it carefully.

"It's a barfbag," I explained helpfully, resuming my Brit accent.

She glared at me. "I *know* what it is. I am *very* familiar with these… these barfbags." She stuffed it back in the netting, sat back with a big sigh and closed her eyes, remaining so as the plane taxied down the tarmac and we were cleared for launch.

During the rush of takeoff, my seatmate (still unnamed) clutched the armrests with white knuckles (no wedding ring) and the look of torture on her face tugged at my heart. I leaned over and said, "Miss… it's okay. It's a perfectly normal takeoff."

She refused to acknowledge me and at that moment the plane banked to starboard, injecting a fresh wave of panic in this poor woman.

"Really, miss," I called to her, "this is all just perfectly normal. You'll be right as rain in a jiffy."

She turned her head and fixed me with that grim look, not so much pure revulsion and irritation this time, but spiced now with a hint of suspicion. As if my attentions didn't quite sort with her notions of me as the sleazebag wolf she suspected at the start. She nodded, which seemed like progress to me, turned her head and closed her eyes, looking calmer now, and remained in this attitude as we approached cruising speed and altitude.

Finally, the bell chimed, and we were able to remove our seatbelts. I unbuckled mine and looked over at my seatmate, whose eyes were now open, burning holes into the seatback in front of her.

"The worst is over. You can unbuckle and relax," I said in my English voice.

She looked at me, then down at her belt which she grasped with both hands. "Oh, no," she said. "This baby stays on the whole way."

I considered this, then thought I'd give the obvious a try, in a friendly way.

"You seem to have a bit of anxiety about being up in an airplane."

She actually laughed, but it was not a joyful laugh. "Do you *think?*"

"My name is Nigel," I said, offering my hand.

She looked down at my proffered hand and declined to join it with her own. She did, however, allow that her name was "Karen. Hello."

I withdrew my hand but kept a nice smile plastered on my face to cover my embarrassment at yet another rejection from this lovely but difficult woman.

"Listen," she said, "I'll be fine... unless... well... I'll be fine for the rest of the way. And I appreciate your concern. Okay? I don't mean to be rude. Although landing can give me the jitters!" she giggled uncomfortably. "Now I ought to be okay."

"You said 'unless.' Unless what?"

"Oh Christ..." and she stiffened and twisted her seatbelt with both hands, looked out the window briefly then back at me. "Unless there's turbulence. That's the worst. I try not to panic. I try I try I try."

Rejecting my few small overtures to conversation, Karen resorted to pretending to be sleeping for the first three hours of the flight. *Wow,* I thought to myself, *she really does not like me.* So I decided to let her alone and cease making any more of an ass of myself than I already had. Doug would have been proud.

Then it happened. The plane jerked and Karen came to life with a start.

"What was that!?" she yipped, sitting up ramrod straight and clutching at her seatbelt.

"Just a little…" I wanted to avoid the T-word here, "a little air pocket. No biggie. I bet that was the end of it."

Wrong.

"Ladies and gentlemen, this is your pilot speaking. We're in for a stretch of turbulence and I have it from other aircraft that it may be a rocky ride. Stay in your seats with your seatbelts fastened. We should be clear within the half-hour. Stay calm and enjoy your flight."

She was incredulous and looked at me with popped-out eyes. "Did he just say, 'enjoy your flight'?"

"Yes, Karen. He also said, 'stay calm'."

At that moment we were jolted so violently that I was beginning to understand her position on this subject. Nor did the plane recover from that big jolt, for now it was shaking and weaving like a boat in distress on high seas.

"Stay calm? Is he *joking?*" Her face was turning a fetching shade of scarlet. "This is how people die! *This is how I'm going to die!*"

At that point, a flight attendant staggered over and assessed the situation. I told her we were fine, and my seatmate was just a bit jittery. Karen gaped at the two of us as if we were the crazy ones, not understanding that we were all about to die.

I had to do something. It broke my heart to see her, this stranger, this adorable Karen, in this terrible state. Sympathy and nice words were not the answer. Not with this woman; not in her state. It would likely make her even more obsessed.

And there was my answer.

"Oh, stop being such a goddam wimp," I droned, weary and urbane. "You American women really are such pussies."

We got another jolt then, but Karen paid attention only to me. And not in the nice way.

Her eyes narrowed and I think I saw smoke come out of her nose. "What did you say to me?" she hissed. "You Brit twit bastard!"

"You Americans... you're all alike. You act big but don't have the stuff when it's called for. You all carry guns and talk shite, but what will you do now? Shoot the turbulence?"

"Why don't you plug your hole with a nice bowl of Spotted Dick, you jerk! That's what you like to eat, isn't it? With your mushy peas? Spotted Dick!"

I pretended great offense at this attack on our national dessert. "Spotted Dick is a traditional British pudding."

"Which naturally, being British, you named after a venereal disease."

"It's wonderfully dense and full of hot plump raisins. Add mounds of custard and you can see why-"

"Tell someone who gives a rat's ass, Percy. Or Cedric or Clive or whatever girlie name you-"

"Girlie! I'll tell *you* something, girlie! And the name, incidentally, is Nigel!"

Her critique of various aspects of British culture was just getting started. She continued with her dietary criticisms, then moved on to general cultural observations, all served up as eloquently and venomously as possible. I, meanwhile, played the pompous and condescending English dandy. And all the while the plane juddering and shivering as if it were having the mechanical equivalent of a grand mal seizure. I was beginning to wonder who was distracting whom.

There was an elderly black woman sitting in front of Karen who would occasionally turn to give me impish looks, as if she were on to me. She was, in any case, vastly entertained at my conversation with Karen, and not at all (yet) troubled by the jostling and buffeting of the airplane, which was severe and sustained.

Karen was glaring at me, wondering what next to attack. "I spent enough time in your stupid country to know what a rathole it is." she seethed.

"Oh really?"

"I went to college there."

"Too bad it didn't take."

The flight attendant, a small but serious woman, was growing concerned about our increasingly violent dialogue. She sat in a nearby vacant seat to keep tabs on us and would occasionally hop up to better observe our conflict. She lurched through the turbulence now to address me.

"Sir, is it necessary to provoke her like this? You both really need to calm down." Before I could reassure her, Karen resumed her insults at my recently adopted country.

"And your weather *sucks*. And I'm from Michigan!" she yelled. "It was dark and dreary almost all the time. It either just rained, or was raining or was going to rain, so the skies are constantly gloomy and grey. It was also incredibly windy, which no one ever warns you about."

"Really? And what else did you find offensive?"

"No water fountains! Everywhere you go, you better bring your water with you or plan on paying crazy prices for water."

"Uh-huh."

"And you're a rude people."

"I *beg* your pardon!"

"Asking for directions was like pulling teeth. British people would never answer me or were very standoffish whenever I would ask for an address or if I were lost and needed help. The general incivility is *much* worse."

"Oh, kiss my arse, you *silly* girl!"

At that she leaned forward and actually took a swing at me, but she was just too far away to connect. So she fumbled at the clasp of her seatbelt to release it, all the while the plane buffeting, rising and falling in a terrifying way. The attendant, still keeping a close eye on the situation ordered her to keep the belt fastened and keep her hands to herself. She reluctantly complied. The black woman giggled.

"And you drive on the wrong side of the street!"

"Oh, that old complaint. Really!"

"And the 'tube,' that excuse you have for a subway system is the *worst!*" she barked. *"How many signal failures can there be that make you 30 minutes late for work on a daily basis!"*

"I never had that problem. You know, you really are crazy, even for an American woman."

All of a sudden she got calm. Scary calm. She gave me a creepy smile. "But you know what's the worst?"

I had a suspicion where this was going to end up, and I pulled an attitude of high dudgeon. I puffed out my chest and lifted my head high. "Don't you *dare* go there."

"Your *fucking* royalsssss." She seethed it like a snake, completely oblivious to the most massive jolt of turbulence yet.

"How *dare* you!" My chin held high and my nostrils nobly flaring, my ersatz patriotism was grievously offended!

"You're not even citizens, you're *subjects*. And you're *proud* of it! 'Look at me! I'm a subject of the British Crown!'" she aped comically. "You're one step above *slaves!*" Oh, she was enjoying this immensely. "You have no Constitution or Bill of Rights, and you worship all these inbred sickos-"

"Inbred!"

"Who suck the treasury dry in a nation that has no idea how to spend its money. People who can't afford to pay their bills lining up in the streets hoping for a glance at the most useless bloodsuckers imaginable, parading by as if they were other than a punchline for the rest of the world!"

She continued in this vein for another five minutes. It was amazing how much she hated the Queen and the entire royal family (about whom she was thoroughly and suspiciously familiar) and how articulate yet outlandishly vulgar she was in her expression.

She finally took a breath, but before I could respond, the turbulence stopped. As if simply switched off. I waited. Still not the smallest joggle. Karen was oblivious.

"Well, Brit twit? *Shit wit!* Nothing to say?" She wasn't nearly done with me.

The women in front of Karen leaned forward and sent me a twinkle from her eye. I smiled back. The pilot broke the spell.

"Ladies and gentlemen, our encounter with the rough air patch was worse than anticipated but shorter in duration. We can be happy for that. We have started our descent to Los Angeles International, and we are on time. The weather in L.A. is sunny, and 79 degrees."

Karen had been jarred out of her violent mode and seemed a little confused, head down and knotted brow. Then, as if she just remembered that she hated me, she shot me an angry look.

"I'm sorry, but you *really* got under my skin!"

"That's okay," I said, in my real American voice. "Forget it."

She gave me a curious look. "I actually enjoyed my time in London," she said. "You just really... provoked me."

"Never been, actually," I said.

She was incredulous. "Never been where? *London?"*

"Nah. I'm from Detroit," I admitted. "Well, Ferndale, actually."

She narrowed her eyes. "Nigel?"

I laughed. "Larry." The old black lady was about to burst with pent-up laughter.

All of Karen's anger and loathing came back in a rush. "What was all that? Some kind of sick *joke?"*

The woman in front could take it no longer and twisted her head around so Karen could see her. "Girl, if it wasn't for old Nigel here, we'd be peeling you off the ceiling!"

She looked like she was slapped. "The turbulence." She put her hand to her mouth. "O my god. Was it bad?"

"Honey, if it was any worse, I would have *joined* you on the ceiling. I been flyin' for years and I *never* felt the likes of that. I prayed to Jesus for it to stop."

At that young Karen shriveled into her shell like a scared turtle and started to cry quietly.

"Hey!" I touched her, actually touched her on the shoulder and she did not recoil. "All that's over now. Everything is good." She wiped at her eyes with both palms and looked at me with a begging affection.

"Thank you," she said. "I'm so embarrassed. That was the meanest kindest thing anyone has ever done for me. I don't know what I would have done if I had to live through that. I'd have to be restrained again, probably. That happened once before, you know?"

"It was nothing," I said. "Actually, it was fun."

"Fun?!" she cried.

"Oh come on," I said. "You were enjoying yourself there more than a little."

"You really pissed me off!" she laughed.

We sat in silence for a moment, then she said, "I don't know how to repay you. I see it was a great kindness."

"You can have dinner with me tonight in L.A." I said. I just came right out and asked her.

She got all serious-faced and pondered forever. I wondered if she was even going to respond. She did.

She looked at me sideways. "What are you envisioning?"

'Envisioning'? I nearly laughed, which would have been stupid, but characteristic. "Well, I figured we'd pick up a twelve-pack, head to your place and order some pizza or Chinese. Whatever you want! You mind if we split the tab? I'm a little short right now…"

She drooped. "Are you serious?"

"No," I assured her. "I have leased a new Cadillac that awaits me at the airport, and we will spirit you away to any restaurant you designate for whatever exotic food and precious wines you wish to partake of. And it's on me, because I had more fun today than you did."

She gave me the most delightful smile. "Okay," she said. She extended her hand. "And thanks."

I took her lovely white hand with her long fingers in my own, leaned forward and kissed it.

She withdrew it fast. "Now don't get all kissy," she said. Then looked thoughtful and said with a smile, "Actually I suppose that was all right. Considering."

"Really?" I piped, and shoved my face forward with closed eyes and pursed lips, humming obscenely while making smacking kissing sounds at her as she jerked away in horror. She palmed my face and pushed it away, giggling.

"You asshole," she laughed.

Maybe I am, but I must have done something right. Four years and a set of twins later and the playfulness is still there. We still argue, but we rarely fight, though she still has that dangerous temper.

Like my best man Doug says, it helps if you care about them.

I finally figured out how to score hot chicks.

But I really only wanted the one.

ဆဩ

Running Mirror

"**S**ee you tonight, Commander!" the young Ensign said as he passed Esallus Hykuula outside the mess hall, with a friendly clap on the shoulder.

"Yeah, I'll be there. Right on time," Hykuula called back at the young man who had never spoken to him before. But everyone was being pleasant today, for this was Esallus' last day as a fleet officer. At 1700 hours his commission would expire.

There would be a party for him tonight. There was always a party when there was a retirement. When he was young, he dreaded these affairs – an officer well past his or her prime, pressed into the center of an awkward celebration. Almost always he felt sorry, even a little embarrassed for them. For that sort of event was rarely a celebration of one's achievements or virtues, unless one counts not dying before retirement as an achievement. To the young Esallus, these were celebrations that carried this message: *Your time here has at last expired, no matter how badly you may have squandered it.*

As the years passed Esallus' attitude changed. Now they were old friends, mentors, and colleagues that were retiring, and with the passing of each, he found himself surrounded by an increasing number of youngsters who eyed Esallus with a remote discomfort – that same feeling Esallus had himself when he was a swashbuckling ensign.

But Esallus was different. He would be celebrated for his achievements, which were famously many and significant, and he hoped that Syla would be there to say goodbye. Maybe she would even kiss him. He dared not hope for more, for even that would be unbearable delight.

These were Esallus' thoughts as he entered VRC-A2 – virtual reality chamber, deck A, number 2 – the largest and best equipped of the VRCs, closed for the last 36 hours due to a malfunction that was playing hell with the mass of generated objects. Chairs would hover above the floor and float away with a touch, while a ping-pong ball would be so heavy that even a Pictite couldn't budge it from the floor. A situation, Esallus thought with a smile, in which the Pictite guest, convinced he was being made sport of, was dangerously unamused.

The repair would take seconds to effect but the rest of the afternoon to calibrate and, instead of delegating the repair to an underling, Esallus decided to fix it himself, and mused that this would be his next-to-last task aboard the starship *John Bell*. There would be the party tonight, then sleep if he could manage it (alone as always). Tomorrow he would teleport to the shuttle that would take him to the resort planet of Greengarden IX™, where he would wait for transportation to Earth, and to his home in the hills of Free Scandia. But what really set him on edge, almost as much as the hope that Syla would kiss him, was what he was going to do the minute after his commission expired.

At 1701 he would no longer be subject to the rules and regulations of the Service. Esallus put the calibrator into pause and reached into his shirt pocket, taking from there the little chip that held MIRROR, the program that launched his career, and which he wrote before he had even graduated from the Academy. He had never run it. No one had. It was illegal.

"Cadet Hykuula, we asked you here – I, your psychocyber instructors, and Admiral Lo – to talk about your entry in this year's contest."

"Did I win?" the young man blurted out and then recovered. "Sir?"

The Dean of Academies smiled and shook his head. "No, Cadet, I'm afraid not."

Esallus was crestfallen. Who could possibly have beaten him? Was it possible? He sunk into his chair.

"Things aren't really that bad, son," the Admiral said, smiling at the dejected youth.

"No. Admiral Lo is quite correct," the Dean said. "Your entry was judged superior in every aspect but one."

"*As usual,*" *sniffed Captain Jolifar, his neurology instructor. And waited.*

Esallus closed his eyes and sighed. "*No safeties,*" *he whispered.*

"*Not just 'no safeties,' cadet,*" *the Dean corrected in a disgusted voice.*

Esallus looked around the table at the expressions on the officers' faces. Therein he found no anger, but serious eyes, and mouths that almost smiled, but not quite.

The Dean held up the chip. "*A more dazzling and succinct piece of work has never come from this academy.*" *He threw the chip on the table.* "*Rarely even from faculty,*" *he said with a hint of embarrassment.* "*But a more swaggering and irresponsible set of code I have never seen, and I have been near the top of Technical Services for almost 30 years,*" *the Dean said.*

"*Yes, sir.*"

"*This program has been deemed far too dangerous for inclusion in the Repertory and is officially disallowed.*" *The Dean paused to observe the effect of his words on the young man.* "*Do you know what that means?*"

"*That... that I lost the contest, and...*"

"*To hell with the contest, son,*" *the Admiral said flatly.*

"*It means,*" *the Dean said,* "*that the program is illegal. It may not be run, or even referred to casually. Is that absolutely clear?*"

"*Yes, sir. But I can add the safeties, and even water it down so that...*"

"*Cadet,*" *the Dean was calm,* "*we reject the program on principle. You are to turn over all of your notes and files on this project to me, personally, by noon today. Security will accompany you. And understand that it has not, does not, and shall not exist in any form. Ever. Understand? See, you never officially entered the contest. We lost your entry.*"

"*You get the picture, son?*" *the Admiral added.*

"*If you violate that order, now or at any time,*" *the Dean continued,* "*your service career will be terminated, all benefits revoked, and you will be subject to full prosecution in a military court.*"

Esallus sat with wide eyes and looked around the table in disbelief. What had he done?

"Do you get the picture, *son?" the Admiral repeated, a little louder this time.*

"Yes, sir. I get the picture." He paused and looked at the Dean. "I feel like I should apologize, but I didn't do anything wrong. Did I? I mean... it was only a contest."

The Dean laughed, then looked at the Admiral and became more sober. "Sorry, Admiral. I just thought that..."

"Ahh, that's all right, John," the Admiral said. "The grim and grave part of our meeting is over — if young Hykuula understands what has just been imparted to him."

"I do, sir."

"Well..." the Admiral considered. "School's out, son. What's your dream?"

"My dream, sir?"

"In life."

"To be the chief of Tech Services on a starship, sir," Esallus said without hesitation.

"Well, you can start on that immediately," the Admiral laughed, "but it's bound to be a long climb."

"Sir?"

"The John Bell has an opening on board for a Tech Ensign, or rather, it will after I get rid of the deadbeat that was put there last year," the Admiral said.

"You put him there," the Dean reminded him.

"Yes, John. Thanks for clarifying that," the Admiral said flatly.

"The John Bell, sir?" Esallus said. "I have another whole year to go here at the Academy before I even..."

"New plans, son. Seize the day. You can study on board." The Admiral leaned forward and looked hard into Esallus' eyes. "You want it?"

Esallus rose from his chair and shouted, "Yes, sir!" The others laughed.

The Dean shook his head. "Sit down, cadet," he ordered. Esallus sat, embarrassed.

"What was the prize in that silly contest, anyway, Hykuula?" the Admiral queried.

"Two months at the resort of our choice. And the respect of our peers, sir." Esallus replied.

"Well, you'll have to defer that last item. But if you're as good as you think you are you can show off at a later date. Pack your bags, son. You can have your junket first. It's on us." The Admiral looked around the table. *"We're adjourned."*

Thus began the illustrious career of Esallus Hykuula, who became the youngest Technical Director on a starship for 200 years, taking the reins only six years after coming aboard the *John Bell.* There he stayed and made his spectacular career, and his work was his life. He had few friends — all of them were retired now — and he never married, devoting all of his time to the advancement of his field of study, and to the technical well-being and finesse of the *John Bell,* surely the technical flagship of the fleet. Esallus made that happen.

At age 60, monkish Esallus was still a trim and good-looking man, only the lines in his face betraying an over-serious nature. And though vigorous in body and flexible in spirit, he did not look forward to a life apart from his beloved routine. He had entered the Academy at 16 and had known no other way of life than the strict routine of the military scientist for 44 years.

It was like Esallus not to dwell on unpleasant subjects. Now deep in his heart stirred a barely acknowledged terror of facing the remainder of his days alone. The solitude of his life he had kept at bay through his work, and though he had been charmed by women, and they by him, his profound austerity and lack of enthusiasm for socializing eventually eroded the possibility of romance with any of them. Or so he had always believed, and so it had come to pass.

Syla, the secret queen of his dreams, had been his only female friend over the years. She was a metallurgist, and a civilian, and had ice-blue eyes like the girls from home and the most beautiful hair, and the prettiest shape that had not changed since she came on board 22 years ago.

He remembers the day Cupid slapped him silly on his first visit to her lab. The first sight of her made him forget why he had come, stammering out instead some stupid story that he had forgotten something urgent back in his own lab and had to attend to it at once! All the while through his clumsy dissembling she smiled at him sweetly, understanding everything and flattered at having such an effect on the first famous man she had ever met.

Syla had accepted Esallus' friendship on his terms. She had never pushed, never demanded even those few concessions that one friend expects from another. She respected his austere ways and responded sweetly the few times that he worked up the courage to pay attention to her. They had never made love, kissed, or even touched, but sometimes they had conversations. Good ones, too, Esallus remembered.

Syla was a gadfly, her social calendar was a busy one, but she would always remember Esallus's birthdays with little gifts of sentimental value. And no matter how obscure or difficult a technical problem that Esallus might be absorbed in, the thought of her making love to him would often worm its way into his concentration, and he would have to shake himself free.

The calibration was finished, and the room ran perfectly. Esallus looked at his watch. In 12 minutes, he would be a civilian. He felt a cold gnawing in his heart. There was no celebration in him and he dreaded his party.

He took the chip out of his pocket and placed it into a socket on the repertory console. He considered taking a shower and changing out of his uniform before he ran the program but decided against it. He didn't want to leave the room. He had waited many years for this moment, and all his preparations were in perfect order.

Esallus sat in the chair facing the console and sighed. Tomorrow his world would change, and what would become of him, a lonely civilian after all these years?

He stared at the chip in the socket and thought about the MIRROR program. What made it so interesting, and so succinct, is that the program wrote itself after it consulted the subject's psychological profiles, and therefore it was a different experience for every subject. MIRROR would call up all of the classified data on a subject, translate it into a scale of relative values, and then invert the data, filling in blanks with extrapolations, interpolations, and best-guesses, finally embodying this new psyche with a form generated by rules of physiognomic correspondences which were known for centuries. There were clever elaborations and many felicities in the final piece of code, but that was the general idea. And it worked. Esallus was about to meet Anti-Esallus.

There were many questions. What would be the shape of this encounter? The program never had a chance to be debugged, and that was a small concern, but why did the brass complain about the safety issue? *All you had to do to stop a program was to tell the computer to stop it. No one could over-ride that.* Not even he could do that. That was an absolute. Esallus had puzzled over all this for more than 40 years.

He looked again at his watch and gasped. He was a civilian, by 90 seconds. He stood up, tightened his belt a notch, turned to the console and spoke.

"Cy, this is Esallus."

"Hello, Esallus."

"We're going to leave the internal repertory and go to chip input."

"Run socket 1?"

"Correct."

"You know I can't do that, Esallus. The chip in Socket 1 contains an illegal program. I am required to report this incident at once and ask you to remain here with me until security arrives."

He heard the door locks activate. "I've made other arrangements. I just wanted to see what you would do if I asked you nice, but I see MIRROR is still contraband," he mused. "Interesting..."

"I am unable to alert security. Esallus, you have committed a serious violation. Report to your commanding officer immediately for further instructions."

"Mm-hmm, right away. Cy: *j-i-l-h-y-d-2-2-syla-6-4-t-y-8-4-3-d-5-y-4-3-t-4-4-5-r-t-4-k-8-j-9-h.*"

"Standing by."

"Run socket 1."

"Running MIRROR."

Immediately the form of a man was in front of him, and Esallus was deeply repelled by what he saw. The apparition looked like Esallus himself, or at least what Esallus thought he looked like, but the features were sharper, and he was naked. Naked, because in his striving for succinctness in his programming, young Esallus neglected to give clothing to his creations. The creature standing in front of him staring at him with laughing, predator eyes, was feeling no shame at his nakedness. Esallus waited to see how his apparition would respond to its own sudden appearance.

It didn't. It simply stared at Esallus, who realized that it was the feral, almost vacant quality of the creature's eyes that was so repulsive to him. After what might have been a whole minute, Esallus said, "Hello."

The apparition looked around the blank confines of the VR chamber (completely barren of scene or furnishings – more "succinctness") and then back at Esallus.

"How about some clothes," the apparition said. And it was the voice that Esallus recognized as his own.

"Clothes. Yes... of course. Cy, place a standard-issue bathrobe around the shoulders of... of... the image." The robe appeared.

"The 'image,' eh?" the image laughed as it adjusted the robe and cinched it with the tie.

"What should I call you?" Esallus asked.

"I dunno."

"How about... Joe?"

"I don't care what you call me," said Joe.

"Do you know who I am?" Esallus asked.

"Yeah…" Joe took a step toward Esallus. "And it makes me sick to look at you."

Esallus backed up a step, reflexively, then held his ground. Joe stopped.

"You're afraid of me." Joe smiled. Joe was right.

"I won't let you intimidate me," Esallus was breathing fast. Joe slapped him, hard, right across the mouth. Esallus stepped back and felt his lip. It bled. Joe laughed and came a step forward and Esallus' mind raced. This was pointless, he thought. To hell with it.

"Cy," Esallus announced, "stop program."

"Belay that," Joe called within a split-second. The program did not end, and as Joe smiled his malicious smile, Esallus' bowels turned to water as he realized that Joe's voice was identical to his own, simply out-of-phase by 180 degrees – a perfect mirror-image that the computer recognized as authority. Esallus understood finally, after four decades of wonder, what the big safety flaw in MIRROR might be all about: *He couldn't get out.*

Esallus assumed a martial arts defensive posture and looked defiantly at Joe, feeling the trickle of blood start to drip from his chin. Joe shook his head and dismissed Esallus with a disgusted wave of his hand. He looked around.

"Got any chairs?"

"Cy, two chairs," Esallus said, his voice trembling now with anger at the apparition he had created. Two chairs appeared of the sort found all over the place on any starship, one on each side of the men. Joe sat.

"Relax," Joe said, striking a slouching pose. Esallus loosened up, wiped at his lip and took his chair opposite Joe about six feet away. He tried to be analytical.

"Why did you hit me?" he asked Joe.

"Because you sicken me. I told ya."

"Why? What have I ever done to-"

"Because you're a worm."

This was going nowhere. If the brass ever bothered to run this program when he wrote it, they might have made him take remedial programming instead of putting him aboard a starship. "Cy, end program," he said.

"Belay that," came Joe's instant response.

Esallus looked intently at Joe, who was no longer smiling. "What do you want?" Esallus asked him.

Joe smiled his wicked smile again. "Syla."

Esallus stood up. "How do you know about her?"

"I dunno," Joe grinned. "Sit down."

"I'll stand." Esallus' mind raced. *Are things filed away about me that I don't even know about? How does anyone know about that?*

"So," he eyed Joe carefully, "you want Syla?"

"Yeah."

"Why?"

"I want to kill her," Joe replied with ease. "After sex. Sex first (of course I'll have to get in line for that duty), then death."

Esallus sat down, puzzled, but in a few seconds it all became clear to him in an academic sort of way. "I get it," he said. "You hate her and want to kill her because I…" he paused.

"Because you what? You weak, pathetic fool…" Joe slouched indolently and stared with contempt. "BECAUSE YOU WHAT!" he bellowed suddenly and perched forward. Esallus jumped back and bunched his fists at his side. Joe howled an animal howl of laughter that took the better part of a minute to subside. He wiped tears of laughter from his eyes. "Because you what?" he repeated.

"Because… I love her," he whispered, more to himself than to Joe, who smirked.

"Like your whore mother?" Joe inquired.

"What?" Esallus was amazed at the depth of Joe's vulgarity.

Joe laughed and rolled his eyes comically as he bounced his pointing finger off of his temple. "I remember Mama!"

he taunted, giggling like a lunatic. He stopped just as suddenly. "Every bit as well as you."

"Yeah, right. I loved her, so you have to hate her. Right?"

"No, stupid," Joe replied. "I loved her. But she *was* a whore."

"She wasn't a whore…"

"She ran around on the old man and broke his heart. Hah! There was a slob for you," Joe mused. "And she ruined you, you stupid baby."

Esallus pointed at Joe. "I'm not ruined. I'm a successful Starfleet officer. And what's all this about mother? My mother."

Joe rose from his chair and stood nose-to-nose with Esallus, who was no longer afraid but had the courage of anger to stand his ground. "Liar." Joe sneered the word out. "Always the shoulder to cry on for the old whore, weren't you? She'd be out getting high with a different bum every week, but she'd always sober up, and there you were, right?" He pushed Esallus, who stepped backward. "That's all right, Mommy," Joe squeaked in a high voice, "I love you, Mommy." He pushed him again. "Did the bad man hurt you, Mommy?" He pushed him again.

Esallus pushed back, sweeping Joe's feet and knocked him to the floor. "SHE WAS SICK, YOU BASTARD!" he cried, shaking with anger.

Joe rose from the floor and adjusted his robe. "I'm not the actual bastard here," he chuckled. "All the aunts and uncles used to joke that you looked just like your father, whoever the hell *he* was!" Joe cackled hysterically. "You helped make the old whore sick. She wanted you to shame her! You could have saved her if you let on for a minute what she was doing to you, you… you weak, pathetic boy. And in return, she made you a worm who can't even have a woman."

Joe walked up to Esallus and stood nose-to-nose with him again. "You hate her guts and haven't got the guts to admit it. Cy," Joe said in disgust, "end program."

"BELAY THAT," Esallus cried. He hissed at Joe. "You're wrong about all that."

"And you can't have your little dream girlie on Deck 8 because, what would Mom say? She even looks like the old whore, doesn't..." Esallus punched Joe in the stomach with all his might and Joe slumped flat to the floor. "Doesn't she? All that yellow hair?" Joe gasped the words. He rolled over and started to his feet. "But when you kill your own mother..."

"SHUT UP!" Esallus cried, kicking blindly at Joe's hunched form. "I DIDN'T KILL HER!

"You killed her!" Joe yelled through the kicking. "You could have saved her, but you were a coward then and you're a coward now." Esallus kicked him hard in the face and Joe fell on his back, moaning. "She wanted you to help her."

Esallus stood with clenched fists and began to sob. "I knew I couldn't save her..." he blubbered. "I just *wanted* to save her... and if only I... loved her a little more, and told her... maybe..." He fell to his knees and felt the tears run down his cheeks, oblivious, for the moment, of Joe.

"She took away your manhood, you stupid bookworm," Joe moaned from the floor. "You know," he coughed. "Syla's a whore, too."

"Shut up." Esallus could not bring his trembling under control.

"Think about it, stupid crybaby. She's probably had every guy on board who has the nerve to go for it. She's not like you. She not only knows what sex is, she actually *likes* it."

"SHUT UP!" Esallus rose from his knees and started toward Joe.

"Maybe that's why you like her so much. Doesn't Syla look like Mommy?" Joe coughed again, spitting blood on to the floor, and then a string of coughs.

"Cy, stop program." Esallus was shaking.

"Belay that!" Joe cried.

Esallus had never known this world of hate and frustration. He was trapped. "Cy, Bowie Knife, 19th century Earth, in my hand, please." The computer complied but placed the blade of the knife in his hand instead of the handle. Esallus flipped the knife to a proper grip and cursed the stupidity of computers.

Joe observed the long silver steel blade and struggled to his feet. He faced Esallus.

"Cy, Bowie Knife, 19th Century Earth," Joe gasped.

"Belay that," Esallus snapped. The knife did not appear.

"So that's how it's gonna be, eh?" Joe coughed and spat blood. He pointed at the knife. "You think that will save you?" Esallus was within reach of Joe, who could barely stand upright. Joe looked up at Esallus. "What would dream girlie say if she knew you were a Mommy killer, you pathetic..."

Esallus' first slash was below Joe's ear. He fell, blood squirting from his carotid. He lay staring at Esallus who was by now straddling his body, about to plant the bowie knife into his chest. "You can't kill me," Joe rasped. Esallus paused with gritted teeth and eyes wild with hate. "Even if you kill me you can't kill me," Joe said.

Esallus stabbed once, deep into Joe's chest. He coughed blood and grinned his feral grin. "Think of all the ways," he whispered in a sandpaper voice, "that you can't kill me." And with their eyes locked in madness, in a few seconds Joe lay still, his eyes still open wide, the animal grin intact on his dead face.

He may have sat there for a long time, or maybe not, but when his wits returned Esallus finally struggled to his feet, gasping for air. He vomited, his fluids mixing with the blood of his enemy, the perfect reflection of his own self, who pushed the buttons that Esallus never even knew he had. He threw the knife to the floor and it clanged still. "Cy," he said softly, "end program."

And it all went away. The body, the blood on the floor, the chairs, the blood on his body, the heavy knife – all gone. The only memento he had of the occasion was the puddle of vomit and the blood, his blood, on his swollen lip, courtesy of Anti-Esallus, who was gone, but, as he promised, never dead.

Even though his enemy's blood was virtual and had disappeared in the VRC, Esallus had to wash it off, and he let the hot water pour over his body for many minutes. When he was finished, he still felt bloodied but had regained enough of his composure to think with some clarity about the party, and the loose ends that needed attention before his departure in the morning – an event which now filled him with horror and loathing.

He sat on the edge of his bed in his bathrobe, looking into his mirror and seeing there a reflection of himself that was very much like the apparition he virtually murdered not an hour ago. *Enough of this*, he thought. *I have things to attend to.* And as he dressed, he fought hard to push back the sad thought of his long-dead mother, and the eyes of Syla, wherein he beheld all the beauty of life that life had left to show him. The resemblance between them he had never noticed before, and he wished that it had not been so horribly brought to his attention.

He poured himself a drink and bolted it. He gave himself one more look in the mirror, but avoided his face, checking instead the crease of his civilian trousers and the fit of his new white shirt. He closed the door of his quarters behind him and heard footsteps, which he turned to meet.

"Commander Hykuula!" it was the same young Ensign he had bumped into after lunch.

"Doctor Hykuula, now, I guess it is," Esallus said to the befuddled lad who looked to Esallus to be in a terrible struggle with himself. They stood together in the hall outside of Esallus' quarters.

"Yes, sir. Doctor. Congratulations. But…"

"What's the matter, Ensign?"

"You're under arrest, sir. Everyone in security is on alert for you."

"Oh." Esallus was serene. "Well," he said, throwing his arms in the air. "You found me." Two youthful-looking guards rounded the corridor and drew the weapons from their belts.

"No!" the Ensign barked. Then whispered, "No restraints or weapons." The two guards stood down. "I'll take him to the Captain. You men are dismissed."

Esallus and the Ensign took the lift to the quarters of Captain Ir'Nath, who was waiting for them in his vestibule.

"Thanks, Ensign. I'll take over," the Captain said and was soon alone in his study with his old friend.

"You could have just sent for me," Esallus said while accepting the drink, real vodka, from Ir'Nath. "You didn't have to arrest me, for gods' sake."

"Oh yes I did," said the Captain. "I was ordered to by Fleet Command."

Esallus winced. "Am I causing trouble?"

"Oh, no. I love it when Command makes me arrest people in my own outfit for munitions violations." Ir'Nath was genuinely irritated. Esallus was silent. *Munitions violations?*

"Sit. Tell me, Esallus," the Captain said, sipping his drink and licking his lips. "Did he strike a nerve?"

Esallus looked up and blinked. "What?"

"Did you try to kill him?" Ir'Nath asked.

How much was known? Esallus wondered. He decided not to hide from his friend. He took a deep breath. "Yeah. I *did* kill him, as a matter of fact."

The Captain shook his head. He mused quietly and hunched over at Esallus. "They go right for the jugular, don't they, Es?" he said. "In that mad brainchild of yours." He drank. "Es, did you think you could run that program of yours in secret? Five seconds after you plugged it into the console every officer of flag rank was alerted to it."

"Really?" Esallus responded lamely.

"Yeah, really. And they're going to demand to know why I didn't interrupt your little theatre instead of letting it all play out."

Esallus bowed his head. "I appreciate that, Soslah."

"Do you? Have you recovered enough to realize that your playmate could have just as likely killed *you?* Because of the way you wrote that dumbass program of your brilliant youth? And I let that ride? Is that what a friend would do?"

Esallus looked up into his friend's dark eyes. They smiled at one another. Esallus looked out his former captain's window and focused on a blue star in deep space. "I was surprised to see that it was still such a big deal," he said. He turned to put the vodka down, having no stomach for it suddenly. "How do you know what happened to me in there? I don't understand that. How could you be surveilling me without my knowing about it?"

Ir'Nath stood and stretched his back to and fro until a loud crack was heard. "Ah. That's better," he said. He began to pace. "No one was spying on you, Es." He got to the wall and turned. "We've been using that program of yours in black ops for 40 years. We know what *must* have gone on in that room."

"What?" Esallus was astonished and stood up. "That's not possible! You would have to have the psych records to use that on an enemy. And that's just for starters!"

"Well, the program needed a little work. But that's the beauty of what you gave us – just a kernel, nothing superfluous. It permitted of much interesting and useful elaboration," the Captain said. "And besides, sometimes the enemy is within our own ranks."

"Is that how you knew about… my… affection for a certain woman?" Esallus eyed his friend and in those eyes was a touch of indignation that he even had to broach such a topic with another person.

"I, personally, know nothing about that, Es. In the 12 years I've been on board you've never discussed such things with me. But if you're asking if we have our ways of keeping current on the psychology of our crew, then I must say yes, we do. But you know that."

Esallus said nothing. He resumed his seat and had another sip of the most excellent vodka – a tribute, Esallus realized, from his Captain in honor of his retirement. He only broke out the good stuff one other time with him, when Esallus won the Galactic Nobel Prize in physics ten years ago.

"Anyway, I'm supposed to arrest you, but it's all pretty *pro forma*, and besides, you're not under my command any more. Your reputation is immaculate. I'm sure I can have the investigation suspended," Ir'Nath said, then laughed quietly. "I suppose you had all that figured out, eh?"

"Soslah, I had underestimated many things this day," Esallus said as he rose and shot back the remainder of his drink. "In fact, it has been full of things that I have not figured out."

Ir'Nath embraced Esallus. "A happy retirement to you, my old friend."

"Thank you, Soslah."

Ir'Nath stepped back. "I hope you're ready for it. I wonder."

There must have been 200 people at the party in the big hall, including many old friends who made the long trip just to be present for the occasion. There were many gifts, all thoughtful and some actually useful. There was everything and everyone, it seemed, but Syla.

When the reception line, that clumsy gauntlet, was finally run, Esallus grew glum, reverting to his under-developed social skills with a vengeance. He drank vodka nervously and found himself losing the thread of conversations so that he stared inappropriately and made many guests uncomfortable. This was unlike him, for though he was never gregarious, neither was he ever a boor, nor rude. But he was never so lonely and full of dread in his life, and in the center of his chest he felt a cold hole.

"Well, umm… we'll just let you enjoy your party, eh, Dr. Hykuula?" It was the Earth ambassador to some important planet or another. He had asked Esallus a question many seconds ago, to which Esallus had responded with a long, forlorn stare at his pretty wife's breasts. She thought he was cute; the ambassador didn't.

Ah! Esallus lamented, closing his eyes and breathing deeply. *When will this long night cease?*

"Sorry I'm late, Essie."

Esallus spun to the voice and saw Syla. He inhaled sharply and threw his arms around her, pulling her hard into himself, smelling her hair, feeling her body against his, actions not planned out but ripped out of him in abrupt, mortal splendor.

She laughed, surprised. "O my! What have I done to deserve this?" she said. Esallus pushed her away and held her at arm's length. He got down on one knee. Nearby conversations thinned out noticeably. Esallus gazed up at his puzzled Syla worshipfully.

"O Syla my dear please come away with me, come home and marry me and live with me." He kissed her hand. Syla's eyes were open comically wide. Although it looked to many observers like it may have been a joke of some kind, no one laughed.

"Don't sentence me to a life that has you millions of parsecs away from me." He squeezed her hand tightly. "I couldn't bear that." Then added frantically, "I'll take good care of you!"

All eyes in the room were on Esallus, acting so bizarrely there in the middle of the big hall. Monkish, austere old Esallus down on one knee to a gregarious middle-aged woman that few would even have numbered among his acquaintances.

He panicked. "What's the matter, Syla? Don't you believe how much I love you?"

"Yes…" she whispered, "I believe you."

"Well? Will you go with me? Please say you will!"

Syla smiled and ran her long fingers through Esallus's hair. "Of course, I'll go with you, Essie." She looked around at her bewildered friends. "I thought he'd never ask," she said with gay sarcasm. "I mean, *I really didn't!*"

Then it hit him — the most wild and splendid and unexpected gift of the celebration. "Soslah can marry us! Right here! Right now!"

He stood up and she gave him the kiss that he had been hoping for all day long, all day long for 22 years. Some around the couple applauded. Esallus didn't notice.

"Soslah!" Esallus cried out to his Captain on the other side of the big hall and kissed Syla again. *"Soslaaaaaaah! Come quickly!"*

%

Making it Right

Martin Moore's agent made good on his promise of a Mercedes luxury van to collect him at Detroit's Metro Airport. Martin introduced himself to his chauffeur and instantly collapsed into the cossetting comfort of the reclining rear seat. More like a throne. It was only a 20-minute drive to their destination, but Martin was asleep during the entire ride. He could never sleep on a plane, and L.A. to Detroit is a long haul.

When they arrive at the church Martin isn't done sleeping.

"Sir?" the chauffeur calls gently. "Mister Moore?" a little louder.

Martin stirs, opens one eye, and fixes his driver with a creepy, sleepy stare.

"I need to sleep. Let me alone. When I wake up we can go about our business, eh?"

The young chauffeur, Joey, has no experience with this sort of thing. But he *is* experienced enough to know that the rich want what the rich want. And get it.

"Umm… Sir? Can you give me some idea of, you know, when-"

"Jesus, Joey, *let me be!* I dunno… an hour or so maybe. What. Is he not paying you enough? I got you for the day. Listen to the radio or something." He rethinks this and mumbles sleepily, "Actually don't. No music." He yawns and adjusts himself in his luxury chair. "No fucking music…" And soft snores fill the cabin of the lush van within seconds.

Martin wasn't born rich. He was in fact just six blocks away from his boyhood home here in East Dearborn, Michigan, sleeping in the parking lot of old Saint Al's. It was pretty posh back then, this part of town was, but no more. One of the whitest of white cities back in the heyday of this wealthy suburb of the Motor City, it was where you lived if you were a (non-Jewish) auto executive for one of the Big

Three. Mayor Orville Hubbard ran on the slogan 'Keep Dearborn Clean.' *Clean*—get it? *nudge-nudge, wink-wink.* But Dearborn has changed over the decades into a lazy melting pot of Muslims, Christian Arabs, whites, blacks and Mexicans. And mostly? They get along.

Martin left home when he was 19 to join a rock-'n'-roll band. He played keyboards and he played them very well indeed. His innate musicianship and charisma made him the obvious frontman of the group. They called themselves *The Bastards*, but their first manager convinced them to change the name early on. Now they're *Sleek*.

That first manager was good for them, but he got greedy. They could have nailed his ass for embezzlement, but they didn't. He had launched their careers and was fun to be around, but he had to go. By the time they dumped him every hot producer in the business wanted a shot with the band and with their second manager they had chosen wisely. A change of record label and producer—and they hit the jackpot.

That was 35 years ago. They haven't had an album in five years. They're winding down and they know it, but all the members are the originals, and millionaires many times over.

It's been about 90-minutes. The snoring has stopped. The chauffeur looks back and sees that Martin's eyes are open. He works the seat into an upright position and stretches his whippet-thin body.

"AAAAAARRRRRGGGGGGGHHHHHH!" he roars. "Dude," he said to his driver. "I'm ready to *rock!*"

"I *told* you," Arlene yelled at Martin though he was standing right in front of her. "I got no money for wine or anything else! You got none either?"

"Nothing," he said. "That's why I got the goddam job, you know? And please don't scream."

"Well, you'll get a check next week, but we got nothin' until then."

He pointed to the kitchen. "We got food. We got enough."

"We'll manage, I guess." She watched her boyfriend close his eyes and sigh. She softened. "What's the matter, hon?"

"I need a goddam drink," he said. "No wine for what, three days now? That's a record."

Arlene cozied up to him and put her arms around his waist, leaning her head against his chest. "We'll make it, hon. You'll see. You start work tomorrow and the diner reopens at the beginning of the month and I'll be back doing the breakfast shift, even pulling doubles. We'll be all right."

"I dunno about this…"

She pulled away from him and fixed him with 'the look.'

"You're not thinking of going back to that goddam band, are you? I told you-"

"I dunno…"

"I told you it's them or me. And I *meant* it. We went through all this!"

Martin pulled away from her and grabbed his coat from the hook.

"I gotta get out of here. Go for a walk."

"I meant what I said!" She was back to yelling mode as he skipped down the steps of their flat. *"It's them or me!"*

His dad got him the job. Dad didn't especially care for Arlene, but he especially did *not* care for his son wasting his life in a rock band, especially one called *The Bastards*. He was to report at 8 a.m. tomorrow to Detroit Brake, where he would deliver parts for truck brakes and suspensions to various small and medium-sized shops city-wide. It was a job that would be hard on the hands with much loading and unloading of heavy material. Days filled with heaving rusted iron and depleted brake pads from huge tanker trucks and semis. His hands were all he had that made him different from others.

Martin needed a drink. He hadn't gone this long without since he was 16. He was really feeling it today, but it would take a stone cold miracle for relief to materialize. He thought about strolling by the old house and sneaking a couple shots of bourbon from the old man's stash, but he knew that was dicey. So he strolled north instead of south and figured he'd wander by Saint Al's and then back to clear his head and sort it all out.

He liked Arlene. She was loyal and a good girlfriend, but she was *loud*. Not just loud, but loud and *brassy*. *Like Ethel fucking Merman*, he mused. Martin had trouble with that. Arlene loved Martin and never tired of proclaiming it. She wanted a life together. She also hated the band. She once called music his "mistress," and admitted her jealousy of the band and everything connected with it. It was she who convinced Martin to ask his dad for a job. And dad came though! That surprised him, though it shouldn't have. They loved one another, father and son, but they were both of the stoic and reserved nature.

He arrived at the front of St. Al's and stopped for a space, hearkening back to his recent 12 years of Catholic school. The nuns, mean and nice; the priests, creepy and creepier; the white ankle socks on beautiful legs on beautiful girls that drove him wild; old pals, some he still hung with, but most of his old crowd off to college. Not for him. Smoking pot at 15 in the playground at night. *Jesus*, he thought, *a bag of weed would come in mighty handy about now.*

But a drink is what he really needed. "God?" he 'prayed' aloud. "Listen: You don't like me, and I don't like you, but would you please get me a drink?" He laughed at the absurdity of his petition.

His revery was interrupted by an elderly woman with a cane who was crossing the street slowly and carefully but heading right for him, stopping in the middle of the street to beckon him with her cane.

"Ready to go in, sir?" his driver asks.

Martin nods and sits waiting for the limo door to be opened. He slips out.

"I'll be... I dunno... less than an hour probably."

"Yes, sir. I'll be here."

It had been decades since Martin had darkened the door of a church. A synagogue for a wedding last month and a bar mitzvah last year was the nearest he had come and that was some weird shit! The music and showbiz world were chock full o' Jews and he never really got their culture. *But what would they think of a full-blown Catholic Latin High Mass?* he wondered. *They'd be just as freaked.*

It was almost 7 p.m., just getting dark this cool fall eve, but the doors of St. Al's are always open. He enters the *narthex* (cool word for a lobby) and opens the inside door to the *nave* (Catholic-speak for the seating area). The door closes silently behind him and he takes it all in.

Ah, old St. Al's. Been a *long* time. Still splendid in that old Church way but a little shabby around the edges—some burned-out lights; a stained-glass window boarded up, likely vandalized. He hears raindrops and his eyes go—to a bucket? He looks up and notes that the place must have sprung a leak, a steady drip drip drip into a plastic bucket. Like I said, a little shabby around the edges.

There are about 30 people here this eve. It's Confession night, evidently. He sees lights (red, triggered by the penitent engaging the kneeler; green when they stand up) over two of the confessional doors. That means there are two priests working the house. The other people are penitents either saying their penance or else waiting to get in to confess their litany of transgressions.

Martin is dressed in bluejeans, a white tee-shirt, sandals and a sweater. The only way he doesn't blend in is on his wrist—a Rolex *Daytona* that his first wife gave him. (No, this wasn't Arlene.) If you combine the net worth of everyone in the church it won't add up to half of what the watch is worth.

He walks down the long center aisle and pauses at the altar. He feels eyes on him. He wonders, *Do I genuflect like a believer or just say hell with it and head over to the side altar?* He decides he still wants to 'blend.' He goes down on one knee and pops back up. *That was weird.* He almost forgot how to do that. He turns and heads to the side altar, the one to the right with the St. Joseph statue. He doesn't remember, but he doesn't think he needs to genuflect here, so he turns to the wall of votive candles and checks out the array. There's an entire wall of these little red votive lights and only three are burning. Martin pulls out his wallet and takes out a $100 bill, the one with the picture of his favorite president, *the only president of the United States who was never president of the United States*, his dad used to joke. He chuckles as he slips the folded bill into the little steel coin box with the lock on it.

Martin selects a long match from the pile and holds the tip to a lighted candle, watching it burst into a little fireball. He'll use lots of these matches. He has 100 candles to light, 50 red ones here and 50 blue votives on the opposite wall at the altar of the Blessed Mother.

It takes damn near an hour, but he's finished. Both walls of candles are completely ablaze. Martin goes halfway back of the side aisle to revel in his handiwork and he notes that many of the penitents are also enjoying the show. They smile at the blaze and then at Martin. He smiles back. Some give little waves like they know who he is. He decides to hang a little and so goes to the back pew and sits on the end. The sun is almost gone from the sky and the pew he sits in grows darker and his memory flashes unbidden to his boyhood.

When Martin was a freshman in high school he decided he wanted to be an altar boy like his friend Ed, who seemed to enjoy all the Catholic pomp. So Ed decided to train Martin in the duties and subtleties of the position. It all went very, very wrong. The sacrilegious urge that all healthy Catholic boys harbor deep within the recesses of their psyche simply exploded. They were alone in the church, and they began to desecrate every ritual object at hand, especially the statues. They pretended to urinate, defecate, spit, bleed upon and ejaculate upon all that was sacred, yelling every obscenity they could dredge from their fevered and twisted teenage brains. It was a horror show of unimaginable vulgarity, and to this very day neither man has the slightest idea of why they did what they did. It was fun. But *why* was it fun?

It ceased to be fun when Martin went home and it was revealed in the middle of dinner that his father, a pious and prayerful man, was sitting in the dark exactly where Martin now sat and took in the entire presentation. Dad had stopped in after work as he occasionally did and slipped in unnoticed at the start of their sick revery. It was the single most mortifying and humiliating moment in Martin's life when his father confronted him that night over his mom's chicken dinner. His father did not speak to him for days. He had never done that before. Martin would rather have been beaten and been done with it, but his dad never did that before either. Martin apologized and his dad eventually relented but it left a scar.

He almost weeps remembering all this, but his reverie is interrupted by a man about his age who materializes in the aisle next to him.

"Excuse me, I don't mean to be a bother," the fellow says.

Martin shakes his head to snap out of it and looks at the man.

"No bother. What can I do for you?"

"You're Martin Moore, aren't you?" He grins. "I'd know you anywhere."

For the ten thousandth time, Martin offers his hand to the fan.

"And you are?"

"Cliff." They shake on it. "I just want you to know you and *Sleek* rocked my world for decades. I got everything you ever did!"

"Ouch!" Martin says. "Even the bad stuff."

"I remember you played the organ in church here in senior year. I was a sophomore. You were amazing even then. Huge, hairy Bach pieces in church! No one around here ever had the chops for that!"

"Kind of you to say so, thank you. You play?"

"Not like you!" They laugh. "We haven't had the organ here for years." Cliff points to a shabby upright piano near the altar. "Just that lame little Baldwin. They hardly ever even tune it."

"What happened to the organ?" This is disturbing. Martin loved that instrument. It was a fine machine.

"Some kids ripped the keyboards out. It's a real mess up there."

"Oh no!" Martin sinks his head into his palms. Unbelievable! He looks up. "Who did such a thing?"

"One of the O'Toole kids. The oldest."

Martin feels sick. This is his cousin's oldest boy! Lived a block from his old house. The *shame*...

"I gotta go up in the loft," Martin whispers. "I gotta see this."

"I'll come with!"

"No, no. Please. I gotta do this alone." He shakes Cliff's hand. "It was nice to have met you."

Martin helped the old woman crossing the street negotiate the curb and guided her safely over a patch of grass to the sidewalk where she stood, stooped and breathless, leaning on her cane. She motioned that she wanted a word with Martin, and he waited patiently for her wind to return.

"Young man!" her voice was quiet but well-modulated.

"At your service, ma'am," Martin said with a smile.

"I live right around the corner, but I don't have time to do an important errand. Will you help me?"

"I'll try," Martin said. "What do you need?"

The old woman held out a clenched, bony fist. Martin put his palm beneath, and she released her grip. A wadded-up $5 bill dropped from her hand.

"My husband died 12 years ago today," she said. "Will you go into the church and light five candles for his soul?"

Martin was moved. "Of course."

"See, I used to light as many candles as there were years that he's passed, but that's a lot of money now!" And she laughed a delightful laugh that transformed her fleetingly into a woman young and gay.

94

Martin laughed with her and assured her, *promised her*, that he would attend straightaway to her request. She thanked him profusely and hobbled off toward the corner. He watched her cross the street and disappear from sight down the block.

As ordered, Martin entered the church and headed down the side aisle to the candles. He unwadded her precious fiver, folded and pressed it flat, and positioned it at the slot of the lockbox and stopped. A mighty struggle ensued between the angel on his right shoulder and the devil on his left whispering into his respective ears. Guess who won.

"$4.14," Leo said. Martin handed him the fiver. He got back a handful of change and a paper bag with two (!!!) bottles of cheap Bardolino.

"Leo. I can't believe these are only a buck ninety-nine," he said to his party store man.

Leo laughed. "You wouldn't believe what I paid for them!" he said with a savvy smile.

When Martin left the party store he lifted his eyes skyward. "Thank you, God!"

He found out later that the wine was so cheap because the entire shipment had frozen solid, thawed, and sold to the party store. The flavor suffered, but the active ingredient was unsullied.

When he got back to the flat he showed off the two bottles of joy juice to Arlene. She looked good. She wore the special-occasion negligee. She wanted to cheer her man up a little before his big day on the new job. But now she was pissed.

"Waddja do, steal em?"

This was a low blow. "Yeah, right. I stole the bag and the receipt, too."

"Well, how did you get them?"

All right. A fair question. He told her, and as the words came out, he felt like a worm.

"I see…" Arlene said. "So. Let me get this straight. You stole $5 from a poor widow who asked you to light candles to commemorate her dear dead husband. Is that right?"

"Look…" he searched for words. "When you put it that way… I need… I need the wine. *I need a break!* And this was the answer to an actual prayer! So I'm okay with this. And I'll find a way to make it right. I swear to God."

He pretended to lighten up. "So hey, Arl! Grab a couple glasses and we'll have… *what?*"

Arlene slammed a single pint Bell jar to the counter with such force that it almost broke.

"You're drinking alone tonight," she said. "I'm going to bed."

She turned to leave and looked back, perfect timing to catch Martin ogling her perfect ass.

She slapped her rounded bottom. "And you can forget about this, too."

That was most unfortunate. Martin anticipated a yummy slice of poon-tang to go with his libation but evidently this was not to be. Alone in the kitchen he looked at the solitary jar.

"What the fuck. What did I do?" he whispered.

He decided to drown his sorrows. He popped the cork on bottle one and half-filled the jar. He drained it in one go. It tasted terrible.

By the time he popped the cork on bottle number two he was quite in the bag and the flavor was hardly a concern. Martin weighed about 130 pounds soaking wet and had little to eat that day. He started thinking, with that drunkard's 'clarity,' about his future. About driving a fucking truck in Detroit. About heaving rusted iron into a stake truck bed. About regrets.

Regrets.

By the end of the second bottle he had made his decision, and stormed into the bedroom, slamming the opening door into the wall. Arlene jumped awake, shocked.

"I'm going on tour with *The Bastards!*" he roared. "*Fuck* that job. I'm gonna be the best goddam keyboard player in rock-'n-roll. I ain't a truck driver. *Fuck* trucks. And *fuck* truck drivers." He pointed toward the living room. "I'm gonna get

96

some sleep, and then I'm gonna go to Greg's, and we'll leave from there. You're welcome to come along."

She looked at him as if he had grown another head. "What? *Me?* Are you fucking *crazy?*"

"I'm goin', baby! You got the flat till the end of the month. But I am GONE!"

She regarded him with an angry stare for a space and shook her head.

"You asshole," she said.

He got a few drunken winks in on the couch and was gone by the time Arlene woke.

Martin actually cried when he saw the organ console in the choir loft. It had two keyboards, and both were ripped to splinters, black naturals and white sharps litter the floor. He thinks of beating his cousin's boy to death. It seems fitting.

He starts the climb down the spiral steps back to the nave, resuming his seat in the pew and wipes the tears from his eyes.

One of the priests is leaving the confessional. Big guy. Martin calls to him quietly and rises to meet him in the center aisle.

"Hi," he says to the priest and holds out his hand. "I'm Martin Moore." The priest looks like a boy. Can't be more than 25. Big and round. They shake.

"O my gosh!" the priest says. "You *are* Martin Moore! What an honor!"

"Thanks. And you are…"

"O! Gosh. I'm Father Vince. Vince Moroni."

"Nice to meet you Vince," Martin says. He hasn't been able to call a priest 'father' since high school. He *has* a father, and this guy ain't him. Vince doesn't seem to mind.

"I played organ here as a kid," Martin says.

"You did?"

"Yeah. So I was completely bummed when I saw the organ console in the loft! What the hell?"

Vince winces.

"Sorry. But why wasn't it repaired? How can you not be insured?"

Father Moroni looks away, embarrassed.

"Well… you know how St. Al's is never closed?"

"Yeah."

"Well, that's not how the insurance coverage was written. They said we violated the contract and they never paid."

"How about that stupid son-of-a-bitch O'Toole kid?"

"Martin, please. Lower your voice."

"I'm sorry about the language, okay, but I'm plenty steamed up."

"I can see. Okay. The O'Tooles have no money. We never even pressed charges. I couldn't do it. Not to the family. I did *expel* the boy."

Martin closes his eyes tight and thinks hard. Should he do this? He is resolved. He takes off his Rolex and hands it to Vince.

"Don't take less than 25 for this. Get that keyboard fixed."

Vince examines the watch. "Thanks, Martin. We can always use 25 bucks. I can take it to-"

"Whoa *whoa* WHOA!" Martin exclaims. "You're not a worldly man, are you Sparky?"

"What? What are you-"

"Vince. This is a Rolex *Daytona*. Do *not* take less than 25-*thousand* dollars for this. Shop around. *Capisce?*"

Vince looks poleaxed. "A Rolex what? A Daytona?"

Martin nods.

"Uh… 25… *thousand* dollars? Really? For a *watch?!*"

"Correct."

"For a watch."

"Again, yes."

"A… a *used* watch."

Martin narrows his eyes and looks annoyed.

Vince springs a hug on Martin and squeezes him tight.

"The organ console needs to be fixed," Martin squeaked. Vince was an enthusiastic hugger. "You ought to have money left over, even."

"Of course. A working organ again! I *promise* you."

"All right. Stop hugging me now." Vince released him.

"On the behalf of the parish, thank you so much. It's been a privilege."

They shake again. "The honor is mine."

On the way out the door Martin looks at his bare wrist, California tanned, and sees a band of white flesh where his Rolex was. He laughs.

His chauffeur is asleep. Martin bangs on the passenger window to get his attention. No good.

He bangs harder. *"Joey! Wake your ass up!"*

The driver springs from the car, sprints over to where Martin is standing and opens the limo door. Martin climbs aboard and snuggles in. When his driver reseats himself he turns to Martin.

"Where to, sir?"

"Kid Rock's old place. They're expecting me! It's party time, baby!"

And off they zoom. Mission accomplished.

Father Vince watches them zip away. He can't believe his good luck. The Lord has answered his prayer!

Thank you, Lord. We can finally get the new roof! he thinks to himself, flooded with relief.

And there might be enough to replace the window of St. Sebastian!

But he had promised to fix the organ console. He furrows his brow and thinks.

We needed a break. And this was the answer to a prayer! I'm okay with this. And I'll find a way to make it right.

I swear I'll make it right.

ଞୠେ

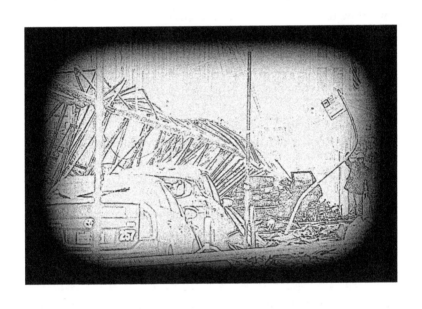

The Tale of Danny LaRue

to Sue Fitzpatrick

It's such a *stupid* dream.

The angel that speaks to him actually has wings like in a painting, and they are all rainbow-colored like an exotic bird, and he, or it, or whatever the hell it is has shiny gold hair and looks as beautiful as a woman but for some reason comes off like a young man.

Daniel knows there is no such thing as angels, and even though he's dreaming he actually *knows* he's dreaming.

"So, I can just wake up," Daniel says to the golden rainbow boy.

"No. Thou canst not wake until I give thee my message." And the angel smiles as Daniel thrashes about trying desperately to break the spell of the dream, but he cannot wake. Daniel stops thrashing and looks again at the apparition but cannot focus for the brighter splendor he beholds there now. He shields his eyes.

"What message?" Dan asks.

The angel speaks:

"Death is coming, Daniel, and Death is coming especially for thee.
Tonight at St. Stephen's Hall is the appointed time and place.
The O'Conner clan has not invited you.
But bring a gift of Redbreast and thou shalt be welcome there.
Prepare thyself, as well as such can be done,
for tonight, though the Lord holds all the others in His Hands,
thou shalt fully and at last know Death."

"Well then why should I go there? What if I don't go?"
The angel smiles the inscrutable angel smile.

"Why the hell would I go to such a thing? What if I just don't go?"

The angel darkens, everything around him darkens, no more golden rainbows, and his expression becomes grim. Now, in a blink, the angel turns into the Italian bookie his uncle works for on the east side, mustache, sunglasses, the whole bit. Vincenzo. Went to school with him. And they call him Vincenzo, too. He gets pissed if you call him Vinny.

Vincenzo takes off the dark glasses, lowers his head, fixes Daniel with a stare, raises a leather-clad arm and points at Daniel like a threat.

"Don' even *think* about it."

Daniel wakes instantly, completely lucid, and repeats to himself the dream message, and then does it again. His chest hurts, as it sometimes does when he is very anxious, and he opens the bedside drawer to pop a pill which lends him instant relief. He knows that won't always be the case. He's afraid he's going to forget what the angel said so he stumbles out of bed, goes to the desk in his living room, finds a pen and scribbles on a pad the dream message, which he still recalls perfectly. He finds this odd, since he generally forgets his dreams almost instantly, and the message is a long one. He renders the last line, puts the pen down and stares into space.

"What the hell was that?" he says to the room.

He looks down at the scribbled pad.

"St. Stephen," he reads. "O'Connor."

Daniel checks the time, 7:30 in florescent blue numbers. *Too early to call the church and check this out,* he thinks. *Anyhoo, there'll be no such event scheduled and that will be that. End of psycho episode.* He'll call from work when he gets in. He doesn't shower or shave this morning. He pees, eats two pieces of cold leftover pizza, dresses, and leaves for work.

Daniel LaRue was born and bred on the west side of Detroit and grew up there when the city was at its worst. He lost both parents before he was three in a car wreck on I-94, passed around till he was 17 to various family members, none of whom cared terribly much for him, and since little Danny

102

kept to himself and offered no more affection and regard to them than they to him, they were always relieved to see the back of him when he was passed to another relative. He got a job and his own place at 18 and has had both ever since.

He has no wife, romance or friend in his life. He's not a virgin. Women like him because he's handsome, trim, and prosperous, but they never get to know him very well. "You put up a wall," is a line he's heard a few times. He doesn't do it consciously; he just doesn't care. When the lovemaking fizzles, as it always does, he's gone. He's given up. He hasn't had a date in almost 10 years unless you count the virtual ladies of the internet, and Dan doesn't.

At age 34 he takes solace in his mad skills as a mathematician for an international software company with a Detroit riverfront campus. He makes good money. He drinks moderately, smokes a little weed and likes movies. His only recreation is to combine all three of his hobbies on weekend evenings. By himself.

Dan has aortic stenosis and stable angina. His heart sometimes doesn't get enough blood and when stressed he gets bad pains in his chest and neck. This scares him. Though it's happened a hundred times by now, he can't shake the panic when it hits for long minutes even after the pill takes the pain away.

He lives now in a small condo downtown, right on the waterfront, and he got in when the gettin' was good, right at the start of gentrification. Now there are high-rise condos and apartments springing up with construction everywhere. On the way to work, a short and wildly windy walk west to the office, he notes the massive crane being assembled a few blocks away, hundreds of feet high, in service to a new high rise on the banks of the Detroit River.

Arriving at the office promptly at 8 o'clock, he unloads his gear and calls the church, and a woman picks up.

"Good morning! St. Stephen's. This is Mary."

"Yeah, good morning. Ahh, is there something going on in the hall tonight?" he asks the voice.

"Tonight…" he can hear papers rustling. "Well, let's see now… no. No. Nothing listed."

Dan breathes a big sigh and presses his forehead to his desktop. "Okay, well, thanks for your help."

"Did you want to use the hall?" she asks.

"No not rea-"

"That's tonight, so it's short notice but depending on what it is maybe we can… wait a minute. You know… I ought to check the spreadsheet on the computer. Let me click on that to make double sure there's nothing going on in there this evening."

Dan lets it play out just to be certain. A minute passes during which Dan can hear keyboard clacks. This reminds him to boot his own PC to life while he waits for the clerk to clarify.

"Actually," she pipes, "we do have something there tonight. I don't know why it's not on the sheet but it isn't. Dammit. Sorry."

Dan stiffens in his chair. "May I ask what the event is?"

"Certainly it's… it's an 80th birthday party. That sounds nice."

"For whom?"

"I'm sorry?"

"For who!"

"Oh! I'm sorry! It's umm… for a mister Kevin O'Connor on the occasion of his 80th birthday. And that's at 7 p.m."

Dan hangs up the phone without a word, turns in his chair and for long minutes stares blankly out the window down onto the city below. He can see the church from here. He decides to go home. He spins back around and turns off his PC. He has a million sick days coming to him and he's too freaked out to work. He thinks it through and decides if he goes home, he will climb the walls with anxiety and boredom and start drinking early. He turns the computer back on and decides to work his ass off today for the sake of his sanity.

He vacillates as the morning progresses, between doing what the 'angel' ordered and ignoring the entire thing, as any sane person would likely do.

Then he thinks about death. He wonders what is the power of it? What would it take away? His job? His condo? His bills? His health problems? His boredom and ennui, which is a sort of death-in-life? Though Dan is not the suicide type, there have been times when death would have been welcome, would have called a blesséd halt to life's routine, which had become psychologically (spiritually?) corrosive. And again, he wonders, *where, precisely, is Death's Sting? Who,* he speculates sadly, *would even mourn my passing?*

At lunchtime, Dan gets some Thai food, and on the way back he ducks inside the party store for a bottle of Redbreast, just in case, and a pack of smokes, impatient because he's almost late from lunch and there's a guy in front of him buying lotto tickets. Daniel considers lotto to be a tax on people who don't know arithmetic, and the state taking advantage of the stupid and the poor, and so he adds disgust for humanity to his impatience. While waiting for the fellow to conjure up his 'lucky' numbers, Dan thinks about tonight. He's never liked being told what to do, not even by dream angels, and he starts to resent the whole situation.

I'm not going, he concludes to himself. *If I die I die, I don't care about that. Hell, bring it on. I've been one of the walking dead for 10 years.* The annoying lotto customer starts rattling off strings of one and two-digit numbers to the clerk in sets of six, then, to Dan's growing disgust, starts another set, then after that another. *But I'll be goddamned if I'm going to crash some poor old son-of-a-bitch's birthday party. Death? Fine. Another uncomfortable social situation in my life? No. Not going to happen. I ain't going. Fuck this.*

And angry Dan decides to leave the store, but at last the lotto-buyer finishes his business and turns around, and Dan's heart skips a beat.

"Vincenzo!"

Vincenzo takes off the dark glasses, lowers his head, fixes Daniel with a stare, raises a leather-clad arm and points at Daniel like a threat.

"Don' even *think* about it."

Vincenzo muscles out the door and Daniel grabs hold of the counter, suddenly so dizzy that he sits himself on the floor, his breath coming in short bursts and his chest starting to cramp. He fumbles for his wallet and isolates a little pill. *Two in one morning. That can't be good.* He swallows and sits, head down, waiting for relief.

"You know Vincenzo, eh?" the cashier says to Dan. No response. "Hey pal, you okay?"

Dan looks up and forces a smile. "I'm good. I'll be all right."

"Whaddaya owe Vincenzo money? I'd be down there too if I was you," the counterman quips with a mostly toothless grin.

Daniel gets slowly to his feet.

"So, can I get ya' somethin'?" the clerk asks. "Lotto?"

Dan shakes his head. "No." Takes a big breath. "No fucking lotto. Pack of Camels and a bottle of Redbreast."

Danny wheels his big old Buick into the churchlot and decides to park far from the close clutch of cars surrounding the entrance. He lights a smoke, sits for a minute and watches the doorway. Lots of pretty girls, some smoking on benches where it's permitted, some with funny-looking Irish boys uncomfortable in their Sunday suits. Lots of old people. He is half an hour late – the better to study the situation and slip in with the crowd.

He flicks the butt out the window, grabs his clumsily-wrapped package of good whiskey, gets out, locks the car, sets the alarm (church parking lots being a favorite theft arena here in the Motor City), tightens his belt a notch, and starts toward the door. The wind is intense, blowing hats off a couple of the women.

He feels a little as though he were walking the plank, but oddly calm and resigned. The late summer eve is still bright, and the colors seem more alive to him than they ever have, the smells more vivid. He has to turn his face away from the wind to avoid the dust and dirt that is stinging his eyes. He stops halfway across the lot to take it all in. Suddenly he realizes that he will maybe never see the outside again if the predictions are true, and he starts to cry where he stands.

"Hey man, you alright?" It's a young man comes up behind him and stops next to him.

Dan quickly wipes at his eyes with his free hand and forces a smile at the fellow. "Oh, I'm fine. It's... it's nothing," he dismisses. The young man nods, cautiously returns the smile and heads toward the door. Daniel takes a big deep breath and follows behind, letting go of the experience, and trying to let go of the world.

Through the double doors of the rickety ancient building is a large lobby with about a dozen people of all ages milling about and chatting as a large family does when occasions like this bring them together. Dan, of course, knows no one, smiles at everyone and makes his way into the hall proper.

He takes the place in with a panoramic twist of the head. About 30 more people, ten or a dozen tables, a small stage, bare but for a lectern and an old upright piano, and along the wall near the door is the mandatory bar. An old fellow in a wheelchair sits by the big window opening out to the back of the churchyard, surrounded by well-wishers, chatting lively and watching the wind bend the trees. Obviously, this is the man of the hour.

Dan feels clumsy with the wrapped liquor in his hands and looks about for the gift table. He spies it, but before he reaches it, he once again encounters the young man from the parking lot, and this time he has a companion. Big, tall, redhaired, the map of Ireland on his face, about 25 or so. The pair exchanges mumbles and intercepts Danny with cautious hellos. They introduce themselves.

"I'm Sean," the big red-haired one says, "and this is Kevin."

"Danny," Danny said, and they shake hands.

"So how do you know grampa?" Sean asks, still friendly.

Now, Dan might have considered how he would respond to this inevitable query, having a whole day to prepare for it, but he did not.

"Umm… I don't, actually. I ahh…"

"You see," Kevin offers, "we don't recognize you. Nobody does. We don't know you."

"If I told you why I was here, you'd never believe me." Dan isn't nervous. He believes, after all, that he is prepared to die here, and is really quite calm about all this. The two lads are not.

"Well now, you see," big Red says, "we'd like to know why in hell you would be wanting to crash an old man's birthday party." Red lays a large paw on Danny's shoulder.

"I didn't! I don't!" Danny stammers. *So, this is how it ends?* he thinks. *I'll be pummeled to death by some giant Irish goon?*

At that moment the most beautiful woman in the entire world walks up to Danny, ceremoniously lifts Sean's paw off of Dan's shoulder and stands between Sean and Dan and glares at the large one.

"What. The hell. Is the matter. With you?" she asks Big Red, who takes a step back and chuckles.

"Mara, relax," Kevin said.

She turns to the other lad. "You relax yourselves."

Big Red tries to explain to the beautiful girl with pleading upturned hands. "He's crashing grampa's party!"

"He's dressed nice and he brought a gift!" she snaps at him. Her brow furrows and she looks up at Dan with a smile. "And who the hell are you anyway?"

Dan cannot help but smile back. "My name is Daniel LaRue. Nice to meet you."

"Lah-roo," big Red mumbles. "What the hell kind of a name is that?"

Mara returns Dan's smile. "I'm Mara O'Connor. Nice to meet *you*." And they shake hands. Daniel is enchanted. "So, Daniel," she says brightly, "what is it that brings you here tonight?"

The three from the family clan stand waiting impatiently for an answer, but again, Daniel is flummoxed and tongue-tied. What exactly can he tell them? *Well, see, an angel told me to come and meet my Death here.* Somehow, he balks at that.

Patience frayed, the big man has had enough. "For Christ sake, Mara, this guy needs to go."

But Mara's interest is piqued, Danny interests her, and she's the kind of girl that will have her way. "Give Daniel a chance to explain."

"Explain my ass," Sean hisses and as he reaches out to take Dan's lapels in hand, Mara slaps at his hands. Sean releases him and a shouting match ensues, and in a matter of seconds the old man in the wheelchair has his hand on Sean's belt and yanks him away smartly, nearly causing big Sean to stumble backward. He recovers, wide-eyed at his grandfather, then wilting under the old man's glare.

"What's the matter?" the old man demands.

"I'm trying to get a party-crasher out of here," Sean says defensively.

"Sean, you great nitwit," the old man observes. "Why would someone crash an 80 year-old's birthday party?"

"I dunno grampa! Ask this guy!"

The old man fixes Danny in a glare. "Are you crashing my party, boyo?"

"Well…" *what* can he say here? "Yes and no, I suppose." He points at Sean. "Not like Sean thinks. Not to be rude or annoying or get anything from you."

"How do you even know who he is?" Kevin asks Danny. The old man puts his finger to his lips. "Shutup, Kevin."

Interloper Danny looks down at the floor, waiting for judgment.

"Look at me, you," the old man orders. Danny meets his eyes, no longer glaring, but as neutral a gaze as he's ever seen.

He studies Danny's eyes for long seconds, then nods. "What's under the wrapper?"

"Ahh… a gift. For you."

"Open it."

"Me? Open it?"

"Yes. Open it. What is it."

Dan rips artlessly at the wrapping, freeing the fifth of Redbreast whiskey. He holds it up and slowly proffers it to the old man, who receives it from Daniel as if it were a newborn babe.

"Sweet Mother of Christ," he pronounces gravely. "It's me own favorite and I so rarely dare to indulge it." The old man looks crossly at his grandchildren and brandishes the revered object. *"Is this what an enemy brings?"*

"Silence.

"Do you know the swill you've all got me drinking over there, and on this me own birthday? Canadian – what is it?"

"Canadian Club, grampa," Kevin said.

"Canadian Club! Jesus, Mary and Joseph. That's enough to kill you."

Mara gets defensive. "We didn't know, grampa, we don't drink it."

"It's imported," Big Red assures him lamely.

"From *Canada*, you great jackass! You can see the distillery across the river out the window!"

He turns again to Daniel and studies him. "I don't know you, and I don't know why you're here, but I'm going to find out. Now, listen to me," and he points to the table nearest the stage. "My table is there. Put this whiskey on the table and sit your arse at it. And wait for me." And with those instructions the old man wheels away but stops and turns back his head. "And Mara, dear."

"Yes, grandpa."

"I'd appreciate it if you'd also sit with me at my table tonight. Your grandmother is driving me nuts. Let her play with the baby."

The three grandchildren laugh, and Mara agrees. She'd be honored, she says. The old man puts it in gear but doesn't get ten feet before he is instantly engulfed by a new set of well-wishers. Daniel starts toward the table as instructed but is stopped by Sean with a finger to the chest.

"Danny-boy."

"Yes, Sean." Dan does not like that nickname.

"Your fancy booze means nothing to me. I'm watching you."

Dan nods and starts to the table when he feels Mara take his arm, and they begin to walk together.

She smiles up at him. "Well, aren't you mysterious."

He feels her breast against his arm as they stroll. He hasn't been this close to a woman in a long time. Her eyes are blue magnets to his own. They are intelligent and gentle and bright. She is such a beauty. Black curly hair, just the right side of plump. About his own age. She says something, but Danny is too much in her spell to have heard her.

"I *said*," she repeats, pretending impatience but secretly thrilled to have her power honored by him, this handsome stranger, "that you are mysterious."

"Oh, no," he replies. "I'm really not. I'm a mathematician. I'm probably the most un-mysterious type of person there is. Well. Usually, anyway."

Danny puts the whiskey down in the middle of the round table set for six and has his wits enough about him to pull a chair out for Mara, and she smiles at the courtesy and sits gracefully. He is about to take the seat next to her when a child, about two maybe three, runs up to Danny and grabs hold around his leg, hugging it like a little tree. Daniel stiffens and stares at Mara with his wide eyes pleading for help.

Mara laughs and reaches out to the child. "Oh, Shannon," she beckons. "Stop that and come to mama." She does, and Mara takes the child in her arms and gives her a hug. "She never does that, you know," she explains to Danny. "Since her Daddy passed last year she's shy of men, even though I can't believe she remembers her father. She was only one."

"Oh." Danny watches as she dandles her baby on her lap. "I'm sorry about your husband." He doesn't know what to say so he says that.

"Car wreck," she offers.

"Really? Me, too. I lost both of mine when I was her age. I have no memory of them." He studies her as she plays with the child. "Who is the relation, you or your husband?"

"Me!" she beams. "I changed my name back to O'Connor. I'm his true grand-daughter, and this…" she arranges the baby on her lap for display, "is the first of the great-grand-children."

Then the most beautiful thing Daniel had ever seen begins to unfold. Mara has on one of those long dresses (dark green with lacey embroidery) that has buttons from the neck to the hem, which is almost to her ankles. She unbuttons the top four, almost to her waist, and sweeps aside the left half to expose her breast and brown nipple, which is soon, too terribly soon, obscured by little Shannon's blond curly head as she positions herself to breastfeed. Mara's gestures are artless, but graceful and practiced, and after a few moments when the pair are finally settled in, Mara looks at Daniel, does a double-take, and though she tries to suppress it, cannot but laugh at him.

He is completely lost in it all. He has never seen anything remotely so exquisite as this in his entire life. Her white breast and long brown nipple, and is there a faint net of small blue veins glowing underneath? Did he really just see that? He knows women do this sort of thing of course but never witnessed the act. *So this is what can happen at a family party,* he thinks. *Was I breastfed? Why don't I know that? God, she's perfect.*

"Daniel, close your mouth, please, you're making me embarrassed!" she stage-whispers sternly at him with another little laugh. A couple of the older women glide by, kiss Mara on her head and tell her how adorable she looks, nodding politely at Daniel.

Daniel is in love. Mara has him absolutely. He knows he would kill or die for her at that moment. If there were anything in life more lovely or perfect than Mara he has no interest in knowing about it, and then he remembers why he is there in the first place, and it shakes him.

His walls crash down, and he looks pleadingly at Mara. "I don't want to die," he whispers. "Not anymore. Not with you in the world." Daniel is bound by none of his natural shyness or reserve, for he's now somehow convinced that Death really is coming for him at this very place, and soon.

She naturally looks alarmed and puts her hand on his own atop the table. "What are you talking about, Daniel? You're scaring me. Listen. Danny." She puts it in perspective. "You're a total stranger here, and I'm breastfeeding my baby and you're... making love to me, talking crazy, and surrounded by my entire family, some of whom would like to beat you."

He shakes his hand free, coughs, squirms in his chair and looks about cautiously. Big Red is across the hall telling stories to some laughing old man, and no one else seems too interested in Danny or Mara.

"Danny," she pipes.

"Yes, Mara."

"I like you, too." She smiles. "And what's all this nonsense about dying?"

"Are you enjoying my granddaughter's breasts, young Daniel?"

"O grampa, stop it!" Mara is annoyed and embarrassed. Dan has no reply. The old man had wheeled up silently between them.

"Relax, for Christ's sake. It was a simple lighthearted question."

"And at my expense!" Dan notes that she speaks with a touch of the brogue when she talks to her grandfather.

The old man lets that pass and points at the bottle of whiskey. "That's the breast I'm interested in. A little daddy's milk. Pop open the Redbreast, lad." He settles in at the table on the other side of Daniel. "And pour me half a waterglass."

Dan does as bid.

113

"And yourself. The same." Dan pours another healthy dose. "And none for the lass. She won't touch it."

"And well you know why," she answers sternly.

"I do and I'm sorry I brought it up." The old man reaches across for Mara's hand, and he takes it and kisses it. Dan's intuition flashes on Mara's husband, that his wreck might have been due to the Irish weakness.

Danny almost misses it, but thanking God, he has not. (Or was she waiting for his attention?) Mara reaches down and lovingly detaches the little lips from her nipple and caresses the now-sleepy baby onto her lap. Dan notes the well-suckled nipple, swollen and long, and this takes his breath away. He sees tiny flecks of pale white milk on her nipple and on the babe's little lips. Sensing her effect, she smiles at him and shakes her head. She dabs at the baby's lips with a spare diaper, pats her breast dry, and buttons her dress. Grampa never took his eyes off of Danny's face the whole while, and while she buttons up, he laughs softly and holds up his glass to Danny, who nervously mirrors the gesture.

"To Life," the old man pronounces. "Like the Jews say."

"*L'Chayim*," Dan responds. (He had to say that many times last week at a co-worker's wedding.) They nod at one another and drink. The old man puts away half of the half-glass, raises his chin high and closes his eyes. "Sweet... sweet... Jaysus." he whispers. He suddenly opens his eyes and looks at Dan.

"You're not a Jew, are you Danny?"

"No, sir." Silence. "Umm... mostly French. I guess."

"Ah," the old man says. "Doesn't matter."

"Where's gramma?" Mara asks.

"Oh Jesus, let her alone. She's busy and she's happy."

"Who else will be at our table?" she asks.

The old man huffs. "Nobody. If we're lucky." And he winks at Danny.

So for the next hour, the four of them sit, with minimal interruption, and talk. And drink. And Danny holds the baby and actually enjoys this novel activity, and Mara watching him

114

enjoying the baby, and this makes her happy and stirs in her something warm that has not been felt in a long time. Danny tells them about himself, and he listens to their stories and outrageous tales of various family members who are pointed out to Danny when the telling is over. You'd never have known what mad capers some of these perfectly normal-looking old-timers were capable of back in the day.

The old man's wife, Edna, comes now to the table to share the dinner with her husband, Mara and the baby (now in a highchair) and Danny, with whom she gets along famously. All through the meal old Mr. O'Connor holds court with many who pay their respects, with Danny being introduced now to all as an "old friend of the family." And all the while the Redbreast flows exclusively into the gullets of Dan and the old man.

This was almost tragically not the case! An old pal of grampa stops by to wish him well and spies the bottle of Redbreast. "Ah, so there's whiskey!" the pal says. "I thought just beer and wine at the bar."

"Oh Christ, no," Old Kevin says. "Go ask for some of that Canadian Club they got over there. Now *that's* some good whiskey!" The old fellow is off to pursue the hot tip and grampa looks at Danny with a bug-eyed expression eloquent of a catastrophe just barely averted! They laugh and pour more.

And after dinner there is dancing. Mostly old-timer stuff, so Danny dances (!!) with Mara, wanting and deeply enjoying so many slow dances with her that she is again embarrassed, and has to tell Dan to "cool your jets!". There is a moment on the dancefloor when big Sean threatens to rip Danny's throat out for "gettin' way too close there," but the threat is empty, as Danny is so obviously under the blessing of the patriarch himself.

Having Mara in his arms is the best feeling Danny has ever had, and for a couple of hours he forgets why he's there, with not a thought to his fate or future. By now, it is not only just

Mara with whom he has fallen in love, though he is so deep into Mara's spell that he knows he will never come out again.

The old man is scheduled to address the gathering in a few minutes. Old Kevin does not care for public speaking, but he knows propriety demands he says a few words. The sound man takes the opportunity while setting up the lectern microphone and speakers to let everyone know that high wind warnings were issued until 8 a.m. next morning, and many power outages were plaguing the city.

"Daniel," the old man whispers. "Grab the bottle and come with me."

They both rise, and old Kevin seeks out an empty table near the rear and wheels over. Danny sits, and the old man pours two more shots into clean glasses, and the bottle is empty.

He turns and looks at Danny, who is quite drunk, but contained. "I want you to tell me why you're here."

"Oh God…" Danny shakes his head. "It might not happen. Maybe nothing will happen. God I hope nothing happens to me. Not now. Not tonight after all this. How could it?"

"Now calm yourself and listen to me. Just tell your story. Don't worry that I won't believe you," and he throws half of the shot back. "But don't lie to me or I'll know. And I'll think poorly of you, and that'll be the story of us. But you will tell me now. And not a word from me till you're finished."

And so, Danny tells him.

"I had a dream." He looks at the old man, who nods patiently. Danny closes his eyes and braces himself and takes a deep breath, opens his eyes and looks at the old man. "An angel told me that, tonight, at this place, with the O'Connors, that death was coming for me, and if I showed up with a bottle of Redbreast I could get in, and I was to prepare myself because tonight I am supposed to finally fucking die."

Old Kevin nods. "Go on, lad."

Danny sighed. "And I tried to say no, and I tried to wake up, but the angel wouldn't let me, and finally turned into this guy, Vincenzo, you don't know him..."

"Vinny the bookie?" Kevin asks.

"Yeah! You know him?"

"Let's just say we've done business. Go on."

"Yeah, so the angel turns into Vincenzo. I can't believe you know Vincenzo. And threatens me and says don't even *think* about not coming tonight. And then I see Vincenzo at the party store! and he yells at me the same thing! How the hell weird is that?"

A minute passes in silence. "Are you afraid, Danny? You know, there are worse things."

"Well, I wasn't all night tonight. But I am now." And he pours his heart out to the old man. "I've lived more tonight than I have in all my years put together. I never cared about dying, see? What the hell – I think I've wished for it. But not *now*! To know that she's out there. And you. And Edna and the baby. And to die now?" And for the second time that day, and for decades, now that he thinks about it, his eyes fill with tears.

"You get along with everyone. You had fun. You danced with my Mara and, if you don't mind me sayin', it was pretty obvious that you're just about completely unpracticed in the art."

"Oh, but just to have held her," and he spaces out a little in a drunken reverie, then snaps back in a start to the old man, who is looking on him kindly. Dan relaxes and wipes his eyes with his palms.

Old Kevin smiles a kind smile. "I never thanked you for the whiskey. Thank you."

"You're welcome."

Then they hear the strangest sound. Loud. Like a metal whine. It stops.

"I know you're telling me the truth, lad. But I have one request."

"Name it."

"I want to know *exactly* what the angel said. The exact words. There's something bothering me about it all. You do remember, right?"

"I remember exactly," Dan says. He clears his throat. "Death is coming, Daniel, and Death is coming especially for thee. Saturday at St Stephen's Hall is the appointed time and place. The O'Conner clan has not invited you but bring a gift of Redbreast and thou shalt be welcome there. Prepare thyself, as well as such can be done, for tomorrow night, though the Lord holds all the others in His hands, thou shalt fully and at last know Death. Can you believe I remember all that? I can't even remember my own phone number."

"Again." the old man orders and Danny repeats word-for-word.

The metal whine, now louder and longer, wails again. And stops.

"What the hell is that?" Danny wonders aloud. The hall quiets noticeably.

The old man picks up his glass, puts it to his lips and stops right there. All the color, all the red drunken Irish ruddy blush, drains from his face in seconds and he puts the glass down.

"Danny. At no time were you told that you're going to die tonight."

The metal whine again. Now turning into a metal scream. The crowd is getting alarmed. The old man grabs Danny's hand. Danny stands up, panicked.

"But the dream!" Danny cries.

"Son, the dream isn't all about you! Oh God. Oh sweet Christ!" And then old Kevin yells for his wife and turns back to Dan. "Danny! It isn't you, son! *Edna! Edna!*" but she doesn't hear him. Now the metal screams one last deafening shriek.

Channel 7 has confirmed that the Detroit Fire Department is investigating claims the crane was not properly secured and broke free from its mooring during final assembly in these record-strong winds and the ensuing power-failure affecting most of the midtown area. Foul-play has not been ruled out. The death toll stands at 32 but the count is likely to increase as rescue workers continue their search for survivors. A nearby neighbor, whose home was untouched, was witness to the event. "The wind was quite strong, like it still is now, and right in front of my eyes the crane started rolling down the rail towards the house. It drove for about 100 yards and then hit the... what do you call it... the limiter thing, and fell onto the church place. It fell so hard! First the hall was there and then it was just... gone. It also fell on all those cars in a long line there, see?"

Dan has no memory of the moment of impact. He remembers no sound. He smells no gas. Just a before, and an aftermath. He remembers that he is still holding the old man's hand, but he looks down to see there is just a hand and a forearm, the rest detached at the elbow and under cement rocks. Dan looks around. He hears none of the sirens. He is the only one standing, covered in grey dust but completely untouched, and everyone not buried under steel and wood and concrete is obviously beyond saving. Every single one of them. There are no cries or murmurs for help. He thinks of Mara and the babe. And he walks like a zombie through the smoking rubble until he finds their twisted bodies, past suffering.

And perfectly as promised, Death came this night for Daniel LaRue, and fully, and at last, he knew Death.

༄༅

My Saturday Morning Coffee

A true slice of my life

The medications I have been on since a recent brush with death have had an annoying and kaleidoscopic set of side-effects. I just got off a drug that made my already Irritable Bowel Syndrome (IBS) much worse and I have enjoyed relief for a week now.

It seems, though, that caffeine has always had an almost allergic effect on me, causing skipped heartbeats, anxiety, and yes, an un-soothing effect on my intestines. You'd think I could just lay off it. Well, today, to reward myself for not being dead, and to celebrate my slow return to life's rich pageant, I decided to indulge myself with a nice *café mocha*.

The only thing worse for me than caffeine, is chocolate. It turns my IBS into what I call EBS, or *Enraged* Bowel Syndrome.

I picked the *mocha* up near my house in one of those coffee drive-throughs, enjoyed it immensely on the drive back, and then thought I'd cruise to Dearborn to see me old mum. But by the time I got to Ann Arbor I realized that I was not going to make it. Trouble was percolating down below in a very urgent way. I reckoned that *Nicola's* was my best bet and have after all patronized her bookstore enough over the years that I wouldn't feel guilty not buying anything after obtaining relief.

I wrenched myself out of my car, hobbling in intense pain due to a botched procedure at U-M Hospital. (I was released a week ago after an eight-day stay.) I entered *Nicola's* and noted with relief but a single customer in the whole place, chatting it up at the register with one of Nicola's creatures. It was a clear shot through the store and then down the long aisle to the backmost room where the blessèd male's toilet waited patiently for my arrival.

Near tears from the pain, I walked very slowly but purposefully, trying as best as I could not to look like some frantic spaz about to shit in his pants, which of course is exactly what I was. About halfway to my goal I hear rustlings behind me of the guy I saw on the way in. He brisks on by, and I watch in dread as he enters the men's room, and a moment later, I hear the hollow echo of the toilet stall door being shut and secured.

Shaky and confused at the end of the hallway, I realize I have absolutely no choice. I turn to the Ladies Room door. Urgency rules and I push my way in, not knowing what I will do if I encounter some woman (or worse, a girl with a mom or dad somewhere) whom I will surely panic. But the coast is clear, and here I am in an actual Ladies Room for the first time in my life. I am relieved to see there are no strange machines on the wall or odd appliances sticking out of a bin, and I mince over to the farthest of the two stalls, enter, lock the door, sit, and sigh—safe at last.

But before relief can be had the Ladies Room door opens and I have company.

When my partner is settled in, I peek beneath the divider and see a cute little plaid tennis shoe. As she tinkles away, I realize with a shock what my own gigantic be-sandaled foot, with its Sasquatch toenails and attached hairy leg would look like to her. I zipped it out of her line of sight and hoped I was not too late. But now I can hold back no longer for the moment is upon me.

Now, the entire event, without benefit of fanfare or postlude, lasted about a quarter of a second. But what a sound! It was a gut-clearing detonation of Homeric proportions. I was sure that my cube-mate knew now that it was not a woman sitting next to her, but a monster. I was certain they could sense the event up at the checkout counter, sharing concerned looks and asking, 'My God! Did you *feel* that?'

Within seconds, my partner had tidied up, flushed, and vacated the room. I struggled to do the same, cracked open my stall door, scurried to the Ladies Room door, slipped out into an empty hallway and no one the wiser. Cross-eyed with relief I dabbed the beaded sweat from my forehead with my sleeve and paused to collect myself.

The post-op pain was much easier to ignore as I moseyed back down the aisle, and while headed toward the exit decided to scout for the cute pair of plaid sneakers, presuming the girl attached to them had not already fled for her life.

And there they were. Unmistakable. And I looked up, and they were attached—to a man. A wispy-haired elfin fellow skimming a car magazine who must have checked the Men's Room, found it occupied, and with much less apprehension than I, did exactly what he needed to do.

ԶՍՅ

Love Story with Flute

a little fable
for Rosemary

J ohnny Long Night Moon Jones sat in the sand with his friends Ralph and Ben, peering over the sandy ridge to catch a glimpse of his beloved.

"She's a total babe, all right," Ben said, straining for a better view.

"But there's too many guys that like her," pessimistic Ralph put in. "And they're older."

"And cooler," Ben observed.

Johnny punched Ben in the shoulder. "Shut up." Then he turned back to watch, totally absorbed by the sight below and unaware of the taunting of his friends.

The three boys stayed on the sand ridge for a while, peering down, watching Julie and her friends swimming in the quarry pond almost 200-feet below. In truth, all the boys loved Julie (what was not to love?), but Johnny was the only one of the younger lads to give voice to his lovesick fantasies. Johnny was like that, lacking the natural reserve about the subject of love that was innate to other boys. He wanted her badly. The thought of swimming naked with her on this hot, humid afternoon was almost too much for him to bear in the company of others.

But it wasn't just that kind of thing. Johnny liked everything about her, the way she talked, how smart she was, how she danced, the way her sharp tongue would cut a man's pride to ribbons if he dared to make fun of her or belittle her or her friends in front of others. Even the older guys with good jobs and nice cars were very careful about what they said to Julie. And what they said *about* her.

"It's really creepy being watched like this," Rachel said to her companions, popping up from a dive in the springfed pond and squeezing the cool water from her long jetblack hair.

"Just ignore them. If you pay attention to them, they'll start to bother us. But if you ignore them, they'll be happy just to spy on us," Julie counseled. "Just keep your tops on, though."

The girls laughed. "That's what they're *really* hoping for," Rachel said with mock disgust.

"Who are they, anyway," Sharon wondered aloud. She strained to see. "Can anybody tell?"

"Don't be so obvious!" Rachel warned, and Sharon looked away.

"It looks like those young guys," Marie observed disdainfully. "You know. They're 14 or 15 and they hang out together all the time. My sister likes one of them. Ben, or something like that."

"He hangs out with Ralph and Johnny," Rachel said. She turned to Julie. "You know those boys. That Johnny is the one that follows you around all the time like a puppy."

The girls laughed, and Julie smiled, nodding her head in acknowledgment. "He's kind of sweet, and he doesn't pester me," she said. "But he's just a boy."

"I wish they'd go away," Rachel said, annoyed.

Johnny, in fact, was 14 to Julie's 18, a great, yawning breach of years at that age. *But if we get married*, Johnny reasoned privately, *and when we get super old, then like one day I'll be like 44 and she'll only be 48.* The thought was almost comforting to the lovesick boy as he craned his head to get a better view of Julie.

"What's so interesting down there, eh?" The boys slid down the sand ridge to greet old White Crow. Everybody, even the white folks, called him Grandfather. "Could only be one thing," the ancient medicine-man laughed.

"We're just watching the girls swim," Ben explained, dusting off his jeans.

"Does the heart good," the old man nodded. "Are they your sweethearts?"

126

"Johnny has it bad for Julie," Ralph said. Johnny looked away.

"Julie Red Feather is like the full moon on a cold winter night, Johnny," the old man said. "Beautiful to the eye, and she casts a spell on all the young men. But like the moon, you cannot warm yourself in her glow. Trust me. I knew her grandmother."

"He'd like to try, though," Ben laughed.

Johnny punched him on the shoulder. "Shut *up*."

White Crow looked hard at Johnny, who squirmed a little under the old man's scrutiny. Finally, the old man spoke. "Do you have a plan?" he asked.

"To what, Grandfather?" Johnny replied.

The old man looked disgusted. "To make Red Feather love you. What the hell did you think I meant?"

"Not really…" Johnny never actually considered this.

"What kind of love is that?" the old man asked. "You're young. You should be in love all the time."

"Julie's older, Grandfather," Ralph explained. "She's going to college next year."

White Crow snorted. "That's crap. If you love her, go after her. But remember – it takes the man in a male to bring out the woman in a female."

"What?" Ben asked.

"I know what you mean, Grandfather," Johnny said. "I think."

White Crow sat in the sand and lit a cigarette. The boys sat, too. "I'm an old man. Soon I will be gone," he said. "I wish I knew everything I know now and was still as young as you boys." He breathed in the smoke deeply and blew out rings in the calm, hot air. "I don't regret too much. Only two things: that I didn't love more women, and that I didn't take better care of my teeth." He grinned, and the boys smiled at his two remaining tusks.

"But the main regret is the women," he continued. "You boys need to love the girls. And you know what? You'll be surprised. More than any other thing in the world, that's exactly what they want, too. So, see? It works out good all the way around."

"So, what should I do?" Johnny asked.

"Does she like you?"

"I don't think she knows I'm alive."

"Hmm…" the old medicine man considered this new datum.

"The real problem, Grandfather," Ralph said, "is that the really cool girls are a lot older and they think we're just kids." He laughed bitterly and looked over at Johnny. "There's no way that somebody like Julie is going to fall for Johnny. All the other girls would make fun of her."

Johnny looked pained.

"You're right. That's a problem," White Crow agreed. "But there's medicine for every difficulty."

Johnny brightened. "So, what's the medicine for this?"

The old man stood up and flicked his half-smoked cigarette butt away. "Stay here. I'll be right back," he said and walked to his shack.

When White Crow was out of earshot, Ben shook his head and laughed. "This is really nuts," he said, looking at his friends.

"Aren't you curious?" Ralph asked Ben.

"I guess so…"

A moment later the old man emerged from his house carrying a stick.

"What's that?" Ralph wondered aloud.

"Looks like a stick with a feather," Ben said.

"It's a flute," Johnny said, and so it was.

White Crow stopped in front of the seated boys and held up the flute with formality. "I got my wife with this," he said proudly, turning the flute around in the air so it could be appreciated from all angles.

"How did that get you a wife?" Ralph inquired.

White Crow thought the question inept and scowled at Ralph. "How do you think? I played her a love song."

Johnny moaned and fell over onto his back. "Grandfather," he said squinting to the bright sky, "I can't play the flute, and I don't know any... love songs."

The medicine-man shook his head in bewilderment that young people are so stupid. He sighed. "Never mind then. But one day, Long Night Moon, you will be so in love that you will be willing to do whatever it takes to get your woman. Instead of playing at it like a boy." He turned and started to walk back to the shack, but his parting words were like an arrow at Johnny that found its mark.

Johnny jumped up. "Wait!" White Crow stopped and grinned, then turned. "I see what you mean, Grandfather. Tell me what I need to know about the flute."

His companions stood up and White Crow faced the three boys, holding the old flute aloft. "There isn't much to it, really. Except that you have to make it yourself and the song you play must be yours alone, not something you heard somewhere. Decorate the flute like you know it should look, and then play outside her house late at night. See, here is the medicine: *even if the one you love does not love you in return, she cannot resist the love-song of the flute.*"

The boys, who knew that the old medicine-man was wise and didn't waste words, were enchanted in spite of themselves at the idea of the flute's magical power over women.

"The medicine is so powerful that the fathers made the young men go outside the village to play their lovesongs, because the young girls found the music impossible to resist. It's old medicine. Young people make fun of the old medicine, but they have no idea," White Crow said.

"But..." Johnny knitted his brow, "I don't..."

"I'll teach you how to find the wood and carve the flute," White Crow said, anticipating Johnny's problem. "Come tomorrow, unless it rains. Then come the next day."

"Thank you, Grandfather," Johnny said, filled with optimism. "I'll be here."

White Crow retired to his shack and the three boys scurried back up the sand ridge. Johnny couldn't resist another peek. But all was quiet, and the girls were gone.

"A flute? That's stupid," Margaret was disgusted. "How stupid do you think girls are?"

Ben was flustered. "I'm just telling you what White Crow said. He said that..."

"So that *was* you watching my sister swim this afternoon," Margaret inquired. The waitress arrived at their table with cinnamon rolls and coffee.

"Yeah. That's because Johnny wanted to look at Julie."

"Right..." Margaret was skeptical.

"*Anyway*, so Johnny's going to do the old Indian thing and serenade Julie." Ben took a bite of his cinnamon roll and watched for Margaret's response.

She smirked. "That's just old storybook stuff," she said. "Do you know how old Julie is? And if a girl doesn't like a guy then some stupid flute thing in the middle of the night isn't going to make her change her mind. *You* don't believe that stuff, do you?" She waited for an answer.

Ben considered, and his admission pained him. "Well... No. I guess not," he said. "Anyway, don't tell Julie. You promised you wouldn't tell and you better not. Right?"

"I said I wouldn't." She sounded like she regretted the promise. "So, when's the big night?"

"Tomorrow night," Ben said. "White Crow taught Johnny how to make the flute. Then he decorated it. Today he's learning how to play it."

"In one day?" she scoffed.

"Yeah." He laughed softly. "It looks pretty cool, actually."

"Well, no matter how 'cool' it looks, Johnny's in for a big surprise," Margaret said through a bite of her roll. "I can't believe you guys are so stupid. Plus, what about her dad?"

Ben chilled at those words. Nobody even considered that. Johnny might need to re-think all this. Ben stood up and looked at his watch. "I gotta go to the casino. My shift starts in ten minutes." He paused and looked at Margaret. "Anyway, I think it takes some balls for Johnny to do something like this. And I don't care how wonderful she is. If she hurts his feelings, she's a real bitch." He started out of the restaurant and turned back when he got to the door. "And don't forget," he hollered. "Not a word."

She made the cross-my-heart sign and sulked when Ben left. How could she not tell Julie? There was no way for her to wiggle out of her promise. If Ben ever found out, that would be the end of them. She brightened, though, when she realized that she had made no such promise not to tell the other girls.

The door burst open again and it was Ben. "And one more thing!" he called across the café to Margaret.

"Hey, pal," the guy at the cash register said. "Get in or get out, eh? The air conditioning costs money."

Ben ignored him. "Don't tell any of those other gossipy girls, either."

Margaret just sat, expressionless. She didn't have to agree to everything Ben said *all* the time.

Ralph stood at the door of Johnny's house and listened to the thin tones that Johnny was coaxing from the wooden flute. He looked at the sky. Tonight, he mused, would be an excellent night for the sort of undertaking that Johnny had planned. It would be too hot to sleep, the sky was clear, and the halfmoon would rise about midnight. The music stopped.

Ralph clapped maniacally. "That was beautiful!" he cried. "I think I'm in love with you myself! Oh God! PLEASE let me in!" he cried as he pounded madly on the door. "Let me in! Kiss me you fool!"

The door opened and there stood Johnny's father. Ralph gulped.

"What the hell's goin' on, Ralph?" Johnny's dad demanded.

"I'm sorry. I… was…"

"You was what?"

Ralph coughed. "Is Johnny home?"

Johnny's father shook his head and walked from the doorway. "Johnny!" he barked. Ralph heard a door open and Johnny came into view. He looked out the door and saw Ralph.

"Hey, Ralph."

"Come on out," he whispered. "I think I pissed your dad off."

"He was laughing, actually," Johnny said as he joined Ralph outside on the porch. They sat.

"You sounded pretty good in there," Ralph said.

"You're not supposed to listen," Johnny scolded. "If you do then the medicine won't work."

"Gee. Sorry."

"That's okay because I wasn't playing the lovesong."

Ralph was relieved. "Can I hold it?" he asked.

"No."

"Just to hold it."

Johnny considered the request for a few seconds, then handed the flute to Ralph. "White Crow didn't say anything about not letting somebody else hold it. Keep your slimy lips off it though."

Ralph examined the instrument carefully, with great reverence. "Wow…" he whispered, most impressed by the care and craft that went into the flute. It was about a foot-and-a-half long, of cedar, with seven finger holes in a neat row. Johnny had painted it red and illuminated it with swirly designs in various colors. Here and there a red heart could be seen, and some black arrows along the length. The crowning glory was the feather – an eagle feather given to Johnny by the medicine-man – that was attached near the top with a red thread. It fluttered softly in the warm afternoon breeze. "Wow…" Ralph repeated and returned the flute to Johnny.

They two boys sat in silence for a while, absorbed in the seriousness of the impending deed.

"Tonight the night?" Ralph asked.

Johnny nodded gravely. "Tonight's the night."

"You really think it'll work?"

"Well… It better." He counted on his fingers. "One, she doesn't know I'm alive; Two, I'm way younger than she is; Three, all sorts of other guys are after her…"

"That have cars and are cooler than you," Ralph observed. Johnny glowered at him.

"Ah, hell." Johnny rubbed his face, looking resigned. He looked like a man about to go into battle. "I guess this flute medicine thing is my only hope."

Ralph told him that the moon wouldn't be up till after midnight, so he waited until 2 a.m. when it hung, a fat neon half-circle, low in the sky. He needed all the help he could get.

He sat under Julie's first-floor bedroom window in her family's little bungalow and listened to the dogs barking in the distance. A porcupine bumbled through the bushes near the strip of woods on the side of the dilapidated old house. The night was warm and the little breeze that brought some relief from the summer heat of day had vanished, making the night warm and muggy.

Johnny's only real worry, aside from having his heart smashed to a pulp and being humiliated forever by Julie's rejection, was being discovered by Julie's father, whom the oldtimers called "Iron Shirt." He was by consensus the biggest Indian in the county, did a stretch in the rebar hotel for manslaughter, and his disposition was rarely a sunny one.

All at once Johnny began to have doubts about the entire enterprise. After all, love would come to him again. Wouldn't it? He was young. He stood for many minutes staring at Julie's moonlit bedroom window and at length decided that there was too much to lose to go through with his plan, which suddenly seemed quite mad to him. After a lengthy meditation along these lines, Johnny stood up and took a few steps out from the shadows through Julie's yard when the flute in his hand caught the moon's white glow. He stopped and raised it up into the light.

The sight of the flute took Johnny's breath away. This could not have been the piece of common cedar he struggled with in the daylight, boring holes and clumsily detailing with his old latex paints. In the moonlight, it positively glimmered, and all the many outlines and patterns so carefully arrayed along its length came shining to life before his eyes. The black arrows moved along the shaft, and the red hearts quivered with bright bloody passion. This was no simple stick of wood, he realized. It had become a magic wand that needed only his breath to bring itself to life.

He hurried back under Julie's window and paused there, heart pounding, to catch his breath and collect himself. At length, he placed his fingers over the holes and brought to mind the song he had written to capture Julie's heart. This flute was the bow, he thought, and his song would be the arrow. He brought the flute to his lips, closed his eyes and played.

It was a very simple song, but it was his own. White Crow assured him that the situation called for nothing fancy. In fact, the simpler the song was, the stronger the medicine would be. When the song ran out, he paused and listened. Hearing nothing stirring in Julie's room he started to play it over again. After a few seconds, Johnny heard a rustle in the bedroom and saw the curtains pull apart. He stopped playing when he saw Julie lean out of her window to see who was there. Johnny stood where the moonlight fell on him and the two looked upon one another.

Julie squinted, bent lower and turned her head like a doe might when it's looking at a hunter standing very still.

"Johnny?" she whispered.

Holy crap! he thought, *she knows my name!* "Yeah. It's me. Hi, Julie." To his own surprise, his voice was calm and confident.

"Johnny, what are doing here?" she asked, not angry, but it was too dark for him to make out the mood on her face. He had not anticipated this question but decided to be direct and honest. He didn't think the medicine would work if he got clever.

"I… I love you, Julie."

In the darkness he struggled to see the expression on her face, and his imagination was running wild. Was that a look of horror? Repulsion? Was she mad at him? Or worse, was she laughing? It seemed like an eternity before she spoke.

When her voice came it was gentle. "What's with the flute?" she asked.

He held it up in the moonlight. "I made it myself," he whispered.

Julie had heard of such things. Her people did that sort of thing a century ago. She was touched by this. It was sweet, and terribly naïve.

"Listen," Johnny said, determined to pierce her heart with one more well-aimed arrow. He played his tune again from start to finish. In his nervousness, he made a couple of mistakes but disguised them so artfully that this new song sounded even better than the original.

Julie did not interrupt. She listened with half an ear while she wondered what Johnny expected her to do. As he played on, it occurred to her that she had been courted in many inventive ways by all kinds of popular guys, and even college men, but no one had ever approached her with this sort of purity. The kid was putting it all on the line. No one had ever done anything like that for her before.

Johnny finished playing and stood starkly before his beloved in the moonlight, looking on her with a strange mixture of pride and affection, well beyond, thought Julie, his boyish years. Johnny couldn't see, but she was smiling.

"Come in," Julie whispered and beckoned him to climb into her window. With a deep sigh, he carefully lay down the flute, which had possibly acquitted itself quite well, in the dirt under Julie's window and climbed on in.

Once inside she put her hands on his shoulders and warned him, "If my father catches you in here with me, he'll hurt you," she explained quietly. Johnny nodded, and Julie could see that he understood. "Sit down next to me, okay?" she sat on her bed and patted the mattress. Johnny sat.

It was still too dark to see her face or to notice what she was wearing. Julie took his hand in hers. "Tell me about the flute," she whispered.

Her hands were warm, and his leg was against her own. He was intensely stirred and cursed himself for wearing tight jeans on such a warm night. "Well, I needed big medicine because I love you so much," he explained slowly, letting Julie play with his fingers. "So White Crow told me that if I made my own flute, and decorated it just right, and made up a good lovesong, then you'd fall in love with me. Even if I'm younger than you, and even if cool older guys with cars are after you all the time."

Julie was nearly moved to laughter by both the sweetness and the simple-mindedness of the idea, and she was glad that he couldn't see the expression on her face. She raised his hand to her lips and kissed it, then fell on her back and sighed.

"Well, Long Night Moon," she said, using his Indian name for good measure, "your medicine is strong. Your Red Feather is at your mercy. The song from your flute has stolen my heart."

Oh, man! Johnny thought, *Oh, man! Oh, man! Oh, man! Oh, man! it's just like the medicine-man said it would be!* Johnny didn't know where to begin. He lay next to her on the bed and reached out his hand in the darkness. He touched her stomach and felt her warm, bare skin. Julie sighed. Johnny thought he was going to burst. His hand went its own way, as if it had a mind of its own, moving slowly north over the flimsy fabric of her nightclothes, resting on the soft mound of her breast. He wanted to feel her naked skin and moved his hand under the negligee, but then Julie began to cry.

Johnny pulled his hand away. "What's wrong, Julie? What did I do?" She continued to weep softly for a space before she could speak.

"Now that I'm at your mercy, what's to become of me?" she sniffed plaintively.

Johnny was terribly flustered. He sat up. "What do you mean?"

"Well… after you have your way with me, my life will have to change completely."

Johnny thought that he should understand what she was talking about, but he had no clue whatsoever. "How will your life change?" he asked quietly.

"Well… my friends will make fun of me for being under the spell of a boy so young. My family will be embarrassed. My father will be so *angry*… I don't know what he'll do."

"Oh," Johnny said.

"He'll probably make you marry me."

Johnny's eyes widened.

"He probably won't kill you, though."

"That's good…" Johnny whispered.

"He might beat me. But your medicine is strong. So, you could probably rescue me."

"Yeah," Johnny muttered, "probably…"

"I won't be able to go to college, because all I could ever think about would be you. All the time, and nothing else. Plus, there would be all the babies…"

"Oh," Johnny repeated. "Right. The babies…"

Julie sighed a deep sigh and started to cry again. "Oh well, I know it will be worth it! Come and take me, Long Night Moon. Your magic is too strong for me to resist." And she put his hand back on her naked belly.

Johnny's hand froze and looked to him in the waxing moonlight like the hand of a marble statue, and he slowly withdrew it to his lap.

"What's wrong?" Julie whispered.

"I guess I didn't think about any of that stuff," he whispered as to himself. "I should've thought about it… How could I never have thought about any of that stuff?"

In a gesture both naughty and generous, Julie pulled his arm to her and moved his hand back over her soft breast, panting softly. Johnny could feel her nipple under his thumb and his mind raced. After a few seconds of confused bliss, he pulled his hand away. Julie sighed and after a moment slowly drew herself up, sitting now again leg-to-leg with Johnny on the side of her bed. "I'm just so completely under your spell, Johnny. You'll have to think for the both of us, I guess," Julie said softly and took his hand in hers.

BANG! a pounding on her door. *"Julie! What's goin' on in there?"*

Johnny, terrified, dove down silently between the bed and the window.

"I'm okay, Dad. I'm just listening to the radio," Julie said cheerfully.

Iron Shirt shouldered the sticking door open and stood glaring down at his daughter. "What radio?"

"That NPR show, you know. I just turned it off."

"That stuff's crap." Iron Shirt surveyed the room suspiciously. "Well... go to sleep or you'll be tired in the morning," he grumbled, pulled the door shut and tromped heavily back to his bedroom.

The coast clear, Johnny stood up and wiped sweat from his face. He pulled Julie to her feet.

"Listen, Julie. I guess I just can't... you know... I didn't think..."

"You can't make love to me?" She put her hand over her heart and sighed. "Oh well... I suppose you know best." Then she put her arms around him and hugged him to herself tightly. When she released him, she touched his cheek with her hand.

With easy grace, Johnny turned and hopped out the window, then bent down to pick up his flute. He regarded the magical object for a moment, then offered it to Julie.

"You better keep this," he said to her, and she took it from him. "I still love you, you know?"

Julie bent down and cradled Johnny's face with her hand. She kissed Johnny, his first real, long, deep and wonderful kiss. When she released him, he stood a moment with closed eyes, then became unsteady, and had to brace himself for a dazed moment against the house.

"This will be our secret forever," Julie said to him. Johnny, snapping to her words, recovered, waved goodbye and scampered away into the dark, moonlit woods.

Julie leaned against her windowsill and listened to the fading sounds of his retreat. She held his flute out the window, turning it about in the light of the moon, marveling at it, smiling, and lazily spinning with her moonlit finger the feather on its invisible thread.

Julie was extremely annoyed by the badgering of her girl-friends the next day, but being Julie, she was careful not to show it. She wondered how it was that her friends knew about Johnny's visit but decided not to get into all that.

"He was very sweet," Julie said to Rachel.

"Well, what did you do? Tell, tell, tell!" Marie did little hops of impatience.

"C'mon, Julie. Just tell us what happened," Sharon cajoled. "Did he make a complete idiot out of himself?"

"I told you," Julie said patiently, "he was very sweet to me, and I won't have him put up to your ridicule."

"Omygod!" Marie exclaimed, and then she put her hand over her mouth, made her eyes as big as she could make them, and gasped. "Did you let him…"

Julie looked on Marie with a threadbare tolerance. "Marie," she said, "how old is Johnny?"

"14," Marie answered.

"That's right," Julie agreed, as if that settled the whole thing. The girls looked at one another and realized that this conversation would not bear fruit.

"But did… oh, nevermind," Rachel moped. "This is stupid anyway."

There was no sleep for Johnny that night, and the next day his friends noted a peculiar aura about him, a certain gravitas and secret melancholy that they had never sensed before. Ben and Ralph sat with Johnny at the sand ridge, waiting for White Crow to come back from his morning fishing trip. Johnny's companions were likewise dying with curiosity and waited impatiently for Johnny to fill them in about last night's adventure.

"Looks like it's gonna rain, finally," Johnny observed, poking at a purple flower with a willow stick.

"Yep," Ralph agreed.

After a few more minutes of this torture, the situation became unbearable and Ben was the first to break, using the time-honored 'concern for the friend' method.

"Say, umm, Johnny? Are you okay?" he asked.

Johnny looked at Ben and laughed quietly. "Yeah. You guys wanna know about last night. Right?"

"Well, only if you want to tell us..."

"I guess so... you know..."

Johnny stood up and faced the two lads. "The medicine worked."

"WOW!" This was awesome news to the boys, and their eagerness for the details was savage.

"So, what was it like? You know? With Julie?" Ben was notoriously direct.

Johnny answered with a serious look. "We didn't do anything."

"*What?!* What do you *mean* you didn't *do* anything? I thought that the whole *idea* was..."

"Hello, boys!" White Crow, empty bucket of fish in one hand and a cigarette dangling from his lips, interrupted the interrogation. Just in time, too, thought Johnny. "You two!" the old man pointed at Ben and Ralph.

"Yes, Grandfather?" they answered.

"Go and let me talk to Johnny alone," he ordered, and the boys, annoyed and reluctant, obeyed.

White Crow looked at Johnny and smiled. "I can see in your young face, Long Night Moon, that the medicine worked," the old man said.

"The medicine was too strong," Johnny confessed.

"If the medicine is real and strong, then it gives us what we need, which is maybe not what we want. Go home and sleep."

The old man flicked his cigarette away. "And don't worry about your friends. You should protect Red Feather by telling them nothing."

Johnny nodded. "Right. I'll do that," he said.

The old man turned and started to walk to his shack. "Just like her grandmother..." he said over his shoulder, shaking his head. "Come again tomorrow. I'll tell you all about it."

Now Johnny stood alone on the hill, looking with blank, sleepy eyes at the thick clouds over the lake that were blowing in from the west. He heard the familiar enchanting laughter of girls, clambered up the sand ridge and peered over the edge. It was Julie and her friends swimming again. He stood up on the edge of the sand in full view of the girls far below. No more hiding; no more spying.

They stopped their swimming and laughter to look up and see Johnny standing so proudly on the ridge. He waved to Julie, and she waved a big wave back at him, smiling her beautiful smile. Johnny turned, slid down the sand to the road, and started home, a young man longing for sleep.

80CR

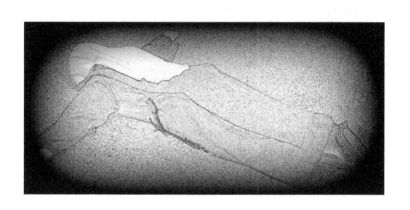

nun

It's not generally known that it takes as long to become a nun as it takes to become a surgeon.

In the case of the Sisters of the Consecration order (the ones who taught Dolores for 12 years of school), that is at least an eight-year investment, often longer.

- When a woman is 18, she may become an Aspirant, staying within the convent, learning and doing all the nun things with the other sisters. This is usually a two-year bid.

- If and when she is deemed ready, she may become a Postulant, donning a simple jumper and veil she is introduced to the sisterly way of life. This, too, usually takes a couple of years.

- After that she may become a Novitiate, which is another two-year sentence. She receives the habit, different veil, and a shiny new religious name in a simple ceremony. Now she shall receive some serious instruction in scripture, doctrine, general rules of the order, monastic spirituality, liturgy, Gregorian chant, Latin, and related subjects.

- If she persists, she takes her Temporary vows, commencing a trial of *at least* three more years. These are vows of poverty, chastity, and obedience, while continuing her studies in preparation for her final vows.

- Then may come the big day at last when she is eligible to take her Solemn or Perpetual vows: The nun 'marries' Christ, sometimes actually dressed as a bride, receiving the cowl, ring (yep—left hand, fourth finger), the *black* veil, and a psalter, symbols of her spousal relationship with her God and her mission within the Church.

Dolores is 22, and about to become a Novitiate. She shall become Sister Mary Dolores at last, after two long years of being a mere Postulant. Dolores doesn't seem like the nun type unless you really get to know her. She is of average intelligence and has no especial talents.

But there is one thing about her that everyone notes immediately and that becomes unforgettable—*she is likely the most spectacular natural beauty that you shall ever see in your life.* She has skin like a baby. Her angel face and long-limbed body are unblemished and perfect in proportion and symmetry. She has the natural poise and grace of a supermodel. She has short brown hair and blue eyes that are luminous. She is, quite physically perfect. But she sees this as a burden, not a blessing. It has been the cause of most of her heartaches. She doesn't see it; she doesn't get it.

The ceremony of her Novitiate status has just begun in the small chapel of the SC mother house. A pianist sits at the small grand and sings a pop-style hymn. The congregation features all the sisters of the convent, a few friends, and Dolores' older brother Jason. Her father is absent, having left his family when Dolores was 17. Mom isn't here, either— they never did get along.

It took Dolores till she was 16 to realize, with her loving brother's help, that mom was jealous. Mom tried hard to look good—exercise, weightwatchers, loads of makeup and hair treatments, and finally, surgery. But no matter how hard she tried, the pig's ear would simply not transform into a silk purse. When mom noticed that hubby in his cups was ignoring her in lieu of leering unabashedly at his only daughter, mom started to lose it. She could delude herself up to a point that she was still an attractive woman, but one glance at the perfection of her daughter would bring her crashing earthward. She was not proud of her daughter's beauty; she feared and loathed it.

"You're a little slut, is what you are," mom would rant at Dolores after a few Manhattans on one of the many nights when dad had to 'work late.' Dolores would try to explain that she would never submit to any of the awful things that boys wanted to do to girls, but to no avail.

"Mom," she would plead, "I'm a good girl."

"You're a lying little whore, is what you are. I seen the ways boys look at you."

"But mom!" Dolores would explain tearfully, "I've never even *kissed* a boy!"

"Don't lie to me." Mom would look her over, disgusted. "Showin' off them tits."

"Mom, you *gave* me this dress."

This theme was played with variations for two years on a pretty much weekly basis.

The song was almost over, the earnest amateur croon of the young woman giving it her best shot. Dolores wasn't paying attention, losing herself in her reveries of the past as her new life was unfolding before her. The stirrings of Mother Superior standing beside her broke Dolores' skate down memory lane.

Mother Superior headed to the podium for the first address, where she welcomes all and does a little summary of Dolores' life, leaving out the creepy stuff and concentrating on her many virtues. She welcomes her to the ritual. Next came a reading from Isaiah, then the sister 'in charge' of Dolores for the past few years gave a little speech attesting to Dolores' readiness. It was a bit lengthy and droning and it shuffled Dolores back into her reverie.

One Saturday night when mom and dad were tying one on and seemed to actually be getting along for a change, dad suddenly went to bed. Mom followed soon after and the house was quiet and dark. Hours later, Dolores woke suddenly and there was dad in his PJs standing next to her bed. He sat on the edge of her mattress and started to stroke her hair, which before her convent days was long and luxurious. Dad reeked of booze.

Dolores intuited right away that this 'loving' gesture did not feel at all affectionate. There was something else at work here, something dark and nasty and unsavory. She was frozen with fear. Dad's stroking hand slid down her cheek, down her neck and onto her sheet-covered breast.

At that moment the door, which was only partially closed, sprang fully open to reveal her brother Jason. Dad stood in a panic and Jason wound up and expertly bashed dad's nose so hard with the heel of his hand that dad bounced off the wall, fell flat on his back and stayed that way. Jason had wanted to do that for several years.

Terrified Dolores sat up and Jason embraced her shaking body until he was assured that she was all right. Next through the door came mom. Jason tried to explain but to the confused astonishment of both son and daughter, mom began to scream at Dolores, wailing hysterically and calling Dolores all sorts of filthy names. Dad, bleeding from his nose like a stuck pig, started to choke on his blood and sprang back into consciousness with a fit of violent coughing. He rose up unsteadily, hugging the wall.

"Fuck this," dad said to the three of them, spitting blood onto the bed and floor. "Fuck this completely." He looked daggers at Dolores. "You little bitch."

"You want me to knock the rest of the shit out of you, you fucking pig?" Jason asked calmly. "I've seen the way you been lookin' at her. I was waiting for this."

"It's not his fault!" mom wailed. Dad marched from the room. "Where are you going?" mom called after him. *"What are you doing?"*

And just like that, dad took his wallet, keys, and the family car—and was gone. A month later he returned for his things. Soon after, papers were filed for divorce.

Dolores has missed her cue. Mother Superior was back at the podium waiting for Dolores to join her. Another sister had to give Dolores a good couple of pokes to get her back to reality. She blushed with embarrassment and moved to attain the podium as fast as she gracefully could manage. The pair commenced a scripted Q&A session about Dolores' aspirations and intentions. After that there was another religious pop song from the piano.

More prayers and readings, then Mother Superior, flanked by Dolores and her 'handler' do another scripted Q&A to which Dolores was required to say "I do" after each query. Then Mother Superior gave Dolores the 'official' welcoming speech, and at the close she handed Dolores a copy of the *SC Constitution* for her edification and instruction.

She is no longer 'Dolores' but Sister Mary Dolores, one of the many thousands of chaste wives of Jesus throughout the centuries. It's still a long three-year climb before she is eligible for her temporary vows. In this still-early stage she will maintain contact with her brother and her few friends, while giving priority to her new and developing relationships.

They sing a closing hymn, everybody claps, and that's that.

After dad flew the coop, living with mom had become practically unbearable and psychologically oppressive. Her loving brother Jason, a software designer with a good starter income, left home soon after the blow-up, secured an apartment and invited Dolores to share the space, rent-free. She jumped at that, having no job, hating her home, and having no other option.

Dolores had several easy acquaintances but only one real friend. Hanna and Dolores had been besties since 4th grade. They met for coffee, greeting with a big hug.

"Hey Dolores-asaurus," was her standard greeting to her BFF, and it required the customary response-

"Hey Hannabanana." They giggled and took a table at the back of the café. The server already knew what they wanted. They wanted the usual. They sat but Dolores was quiet and looked pensive.

"Something wrong, D?" Hanna asked.

"I was just thinking about my stupid name," Dolores replied. "I mean, who names their daughter the Latin word for 'sadness'?"

"It is?" Hanna asked. "Really? Dolores means 'sadness'?"

Coffee and pastry served, and Hanna dived in, but Dolores just sat there looking annoyed.

"Yeah, really. I found out in first year Latin with Sister Ethel and went home and asked my mom why she named me 'sadness.'"

Hanna took a big bite of her Danish and mumbled, "Wud she say?"

"She said it did *not* mean sadness and that I was rooting around for new ways to hate her," she seethed. "Can you believe that?"

"Your mom? Yeah, D. I can believe it." After a beat she added, "I'm glad you're out of there."

Dolores sipped coffee. "Yeah. Me too. Although…"

"What?"

"It might actually be an accurate name for me," she moped.

"Oh—here we go…" Hanna moaned. "You need to snap out of it, girl."

"Easy for you to say," Dolores whined. "You're headed for pre-med! Gonna be Doctor Hannabanana. I have no clue, no actual talents, no big brain like you." Big sigh. "What have I got?"

"The most beautiful face and the most perfect body and the most loving nature in the entire Midwest."

Dolores huffs derisively.

"And I've been jealous of you since… since… *I still am!*"

Dolores waves her off. "Oh, cut it out," she said. She slams her palm on the table. "You know what? It's actually been a curse."

"You've been saying that since-"

"I'm almost 18 and I've never kissed a boy. Did you know that?"

"Yes. You never shut up about it. It's not like there have been no opportunities."

She made a face. "They're all so clumsy and gross."

"They're *intimidated*," Hanna said. "Most can't believe that you're actually in their company."

"Oh, come on-"

"No, really. Listen to me. You can't see yourself as others see you. You never could. And your attitude about yourself just makes you more attractive. You have no conceit, no guile, no defenses, no bitchiness… you have a sweet and loving nature. Anyone can feel it just by being near you."

"Well… thanks, but-"

"And I'm not blowing smoke, girlfriend," Hanna said. "You know I don't do that."

Dolores giggled. "I know."

"And I know why you're like you are. That monster prick dad of yours. Your jealous and hateful mother—I don't know how you've avoided the nuthouse with a past like yours."

"Thanks."

"But you do need a little lovin', D. You need to make yourself at least somewhat available for the rest of humanity to know and appreciate. Find something you like to do. Get some life experience." Suddenly Hanna burst out laughing.

"What's that all about?"

"Maybe… oh dear…" still laughing, "maybe you should become a prostitute."

Dolores was not amused. "Well, that would certainly get me some experience."

"Yeah but, and here's why I'm laughing: I realize you would never *charge* anybody!" She laughed again, and Dolores joined her this time.

"Either that," Hanna's spasm of mirth finally ended, and she dabbed at her teary eyes with a napkin, "or a *nun.*"

Dolores is now 23 years-old, a novice sister of the SC order. Her one-year anniversary is tomorrow but there shall be no cause for celebration: after five years of her nine-year trial, Dolores is leaving the order.

"I can't serve this way, Mother." Dolores couldn't stop crying though she swore she would not let her Mother Superior be burdened with the anxiety of her decision. The much older and wiser woman knew she had to step carefully with this troubled girl.

"How do you know this, Dolores?" Mother Superior whispered.

"I feel useless and empty," Dolores answered. "I know nothing of the world. I've accomplished nothing. I feel like I'm... I'm *hiding* here. Here in the convent. Away from the world that I have been too cowardly to ever have bothered to know anything about."

"Some of us aren't meant for the world. You've been an exemplary Novice," Mother said softly. "Are you perhaps being a little hasty in your decision?"

"No. The feelings started when I was still an Aspirant." Dolores sniffed and wiped her nose with another tissue from the box. "I want to serve God and my community, but I know nothing of my community! I've never had a boyfriend, or a job, or... or *belonged* to anything."

"Do you not feel as if you belong with us?"

"Well, I-"

Mother Superior held up her hand. "Stop!" she said. "Think about your answer. Your next words will be very significant. I call on your heart and head to summon all your honesty and eloquence."

Dolores was silent with eyes closed for a whole minute during which interval she said a heartfelt prayer. She opened her eyes and lovingly regarded her mentor.

"I know in my heart, Mother, *in my heart*, and of this I am certain—that I am not worthy to live a life among you all, and that I should not have come to you so green and naïve. Coming here was an *escape*. A gesture of weakness and... and *cowardice*. So, you see... that I must go."

The pair sat in silence for a space and finally Mother Superior spoke.

"I see," she said. "Well, then... I release you. But if you feel the Lord tugging you back here at some time during your worldly sojourn, do not deny yourself that option. Do you understand?"

"I do, Mother."

"What will you do? Where will you go?"

"My brother has agreed to give me room and board until I figure out how to make a go of things on my own. I'll ask him to pick me up tomorrow after Mass."

Mother Superior stood and this was Dolores' cue to do likewise. Mother reached for her, and they embraced fervently.

"I shall miss you," Mother whispered, "my dear sad one."

Dolores chuckled and straightened, now holding both of Mother's hands in hers.

"Ah, yes. My *name.*"

"You can always legally change it," Mother said with a sad smile of her own. "But most important?" She gently touched the space between Dolores' breasts. "Change it here."

"I don't want you to just jump at any job you find," said big brother Jason on the ride from the convent the next morning. "I got plenty of money and plenty of room in that house. Relax into it. See some friends. You'll be working soon enough but I want it to be something you'll enjoy. Okay?"

Dolores leaned over and kissed her brother on his shoulder. "You are the best brother in the history of brothers," she declared.

"Aw, shucks," he clowned. They drove in silence for a space. "Have you thought about what you'd actually like to do?"

"I need to serve," she said. "In real, concrete ways. I'd like to relieve suffering. Bring what joy to the joyless that I may."

"You could be a model," he suggested.

She looked askance at him. "Did you hear what I just said? No modeling."

"But what about you, D? What about *your* joy?"

"I think that what I *said* would bring me joy. Helping others by taking their cross and carrying it for a while."

Jason looked skeptical. "Something bugs me about a plan like that." He smiled. "Then again, you're such a strange bird that it just might work for you."

"Your confidence urges me onward," she said, most sarcastically.

The first six weeks or so of her new arrangement went very smoothly for Dolores. She renewed relations with a couple of old friends. These were "lower case 'f'" friends, as she called them. She felt lucky to have Hanna, her only true "upper-case 'F'" Friend. They went to movies, lunches, even a bar or two that Hanna liked. Both enjoyed a few glasses of wine, but Dolores was constantly "pestered," as she would say, by men trying to hit on her. Occasionally two guys might pop by their table. Hanna would be friendly, sometimes frankly interested, but Dolores would never let any of them get close, often to Hanna's annoyance. This was getting to be a sore spot.

Dolores did all the shopping, cleaning and cooking and enjoyed doing it. She even did Jason's laundry, for which he was almost tearfully grateful. She was content for the first time in many years. But she still had no idea of what she might do for a living.

Until one late night, her brother long gone to bed and Dolores getting droopy eyes in front of the TV, her attention was roused by a late-night news feature. She jumped from her recliner and grabbed an envelope from the trash, snatched a pen from the kitchen drawer and raced back to her chair just in time to record the name of the woman featured and where she worked. The idea was almost insane, but there was something to the concept that stirred Dolores deeply.

She switched off the TV and headed for bed, too excited to sleep.

It was late afternoon the next day when Dolores borrowed her brother's Mustang, (which he always pretended did not annoy him but actually did), hit the freeway from Dearborn and headed to nearby Livonia. She remembered the area well enough that no map was needed. When she hit Plymouth Road, she simply watched the addresses go up until she arrived at her destination. It was, as expected, a nursing home. A very large and very *nice* nursing home.

She parked in the visitor lot, said a prayer to the Virgin, and headed for the front porch. This was the main entrance and there were many... patients? residents? inmates?... she didn't know what the proper term was but there was about a dozen mostly elderly men and women, some in wheelchairs, enjoying the sun on this warm spring afternoon. Like typical younger and healthy people, they stared at Dolores, briefly paralyzed by her beauty, recovered, and smiled. (Only babies and the blind were immune to her visage.) She was well-used to this. She smiled in return, made her way to the front door where a gallant old gent in pajamas and sporting a metal cane beat her to it and held the door open for her. She smiled her thanks, which felt as a precious blessing to that old guy.

She entered into a large reception area, and it was extremely well-appointed. And so was Dolores. She hasn't had many business appointments in her experience, but she was appropriately decked out. (Her fashion sense, for all her dismissive attitude about her stunning looks, was well-developed.)

The enormous mahogany reception desk was unpopulated save for a stout redheaded woman dressed in white. She was giving Dolores an appraising look and Dolores realized that this was the guardian with whom she must establish a pleasant rapport. She stepped her way but was interrupted by the sight of a woman who appeared in the hallway leading to the right wing of the facility. It was her!

Dolores forgot all about the authority figure at the desk and started down the hallway when a voice boomed and stopped her in her tracks.

"*Excuse me!*" she stood and shouted at Dolores from the desk. Dolores turned to face the desk, vaguely frightened. "You must see me before you do anything else."

"Oh. Yes. Of course. I'm sorry. It's just that the person I'm here to see just stepped into the-"

The formidable receptionist said not a word. She simply beckoned Dolores with a come-hither index finger and Dolores approached her as if in a trance.

When they were face-to-face the receptionist handed Dolores a pen and pointed at the book on the desktop.

"Sign in with name and time, and then we'll have a chat," the big redhead said with a smile. Dolores did as ordered. "Now, who are you and what is your business here today?"

"I'm Dolores," she said, holding out her hand.

"I'm Gretchen," she said with exaggerated friendliness, taking her hand briefly.

"Well, Gretchen, I'm here to see Agnes Woods. I understand that she-"

"So, you saw the thing on the TV last night, right?"

Dolores nodded. "That's correct."

"May I ask why you want to see Agnes?"

"I'd like more information about what she does."

"Uh-huh. May I ask why?"

"Because…" a little uncomfortable here. "I might want to do what she does."

Gretchen could not hide her amusement. "Dolores," she said, "do you have any experience as a sex-worker?"

She was flustered. "N… no."

Just then who comes traipsing down the right-wing hallway but Agnes herself.

Sensing the opportunity, Dolores turned and called out, "Ms. Woods! May I speak with you a moment?"

Agnes looked to the receptionist for a hint about this curious stranger, but the big redhead threw her hands in the air in a frustrated gesture and sat back down, content to observe.

Agnes smiled. "Yeah, sure hon. What's up?"

"Can we talk in private?"

Agnes looked to the receptionist, who nodded, and off the pair went to a small consult room at the head of the hallway.

Dolores closed the door and they both sat at a small round table.

When they were settled in, Agnes smiled and shook her head. "My god!" she said. "You are amazing."

"Amazing?"

"I've never seen anyone like you," Agnes said. "You're... you're perfect. You're a model, right? Actress?"

"No. Never. But I understand that I'm... I'm physically gifted."

Agnes laughed out loud. "D'ya think?" She paused and shook it off. "Dolores. What can I do for you?"

"I just left the convent after five years," she said matter-of-factly.

Agnes closed her eyes and shook her head. "Oh my god. What are you doing here with me?"

Dolores screwed her courage to the sticking place. "I want. To try. To do. What you. Do." Big sigh.

"I'm sorry, but... are you crazy?"

"That's kind of rude," Dolores said.

"Okay, okay, sorry." Agnes backed off sincerely. "But lemme get this straight. You were going to be a nun, but your *real* passion is to be a prostitute, that caters to feebs, geezers, cripples, and the terminally ill. Is that right?"

"Yes." She studied Agnes. "Now, please get *this* straight. I've been five years in a convent. I am smart and well-educated. I've been taught to be capable and resourceful in many ways. But this is the only thing I know for sure: I am perceived as *beautiful*. I don't feel it, myself, but there it is. It's the only thing I've got. I have to use my gifts, my *only* gifts, to bring joy and comfort to those about me who suffer."

Agnes blinked and looked stunned. "Holy fucking shit, are you for real?" she said. "You're serious! Are you actually as beautiful inside as you are outside?" A little sarcasm there but not much. "Next, you'll be telling me you're still a virgin."

"Well, I wasn't *going* to tell you, but yes, I am. I am completely inexperienced. I've never... I've never even kissed a man."

155

Agnes was just amazed. "Wow," she said. "Excuse the intimacy of the question, but—do you masturbate?"

Dolores was obviously startled by the question. "No," she fidgeted. "I tried once but... but it didn't feel right. It felt weird."

They just sat in silence for half a minute, Agnes staring off into space. "Would you mind... standing up?" Agnes asked. "Let me look at you?" Agnes complied. Dolores wore a modest summer dress, the cornflower blue a perfect match to her eyes. "Would you turn around, please?" She did. "Well, I see one problem right away. I mean besides the fact that," laughing now, "you're an ex-nun, and a virgin who has never even been kissed or touched herself, who wants to be a sexworker for the most physically unattractive people in the world."

"I don't see it quite that way, but what's the other problem?"

Agnes hesitated, head down, eyes closed. She perked up. "I don't know how to put this, so I'll just lay in on you straight," Agnes said. "I'm pushing 40. So are the other two women who are contracted here. We look like normal, above-average women who take pretty good care of ourselves. *You* will put us out of work or at least drastically reduce our client list. One look at you from any of these geezers and you will instantly have a huge caseload and hurt our business."

"That sounds so unlikely to me," Dolores said. "You're very pretty and-"

"Honey," she interrupted, "nobody is going to want a piece of this after they get a look at you. One thing about being a working girl—you don't have many delusions about your physical self."

"May I ask why *you* do this kind of work?"

"Sure. We're being honest," Agnes said. "I've been a sexworker for almost 20 years. Standard call-girl. Never had a pimp. Handled my own business. I did all right. But I wasn't getting any younger and the client list got thinner. And weirder. So, when Michigan changed the sex laws, I thought

I'd give it a spin. So, I applied here. That was last year. I was one of the first and the media picked me as kind of a... like a spokeswoman."

"Is it very different here from before?" Dolores asked.

"In essence, no; in the details, yes, very different. See... life is getting tougher on the streets, and at least half of the women I know want to leave the sex business. The idea that all working-girls are in the biz because we we're so thrilled to be fucking a parade of sleazeballs who need to pay for it is complete male fantasy. It's a *job*. But there's physical and financial *security* here. No methheads are going to beat and rob me, and if I take care of myself, I figure I got another 10 years, at least."

"So, the, umm... *skills* you developed carry over well?

"Well, let's see... an experienced sex worker has to have good people skills, isn't easily disgusted, and has zero fear of physical contact. All that carries over. When I started looking after old men instead of young men, I found there were many similarities. Most of these men just want a nanny. All I really had to change was the outfit," she laughed.

They sat for a space in silence again, each trying to sort their own uncertainties. Finally, Agnes asked, "So... are you still interested?"

Dolores smiled. "Yes. I am. Will you help me?"

Agnes laughed. "Will I help you to put the three of us out of business?" Dolores looked down at her shoes with a sad face. "But, yes, I will help you get started. Helga is leaving the business and I have to replace her, so this is kind of kismet. And besides, if I have to worry that badly about the competition, I need to find a different career. Plus—I have a feeling you may turn out to be a miserable failure at this sort of thing. I think that's where the smart money is. But, that said, I promise to do my best to help you, and you have my word that I will do nothing to sabotage you. I can't say the same for Cathy. One look at you..."

She stood and so did grateful Dolores. She stepped to Agnes with a genuine smile, and they hugged briefly.

"Now listen, Dolores. Some of your clients will pay cash, and insurance covers the others. They cut a check to you once a month on the insurance payments. They take a cut. For 'administrative purposes.' You charge your cash clients whatever your rate is. You decide. I suggest $100 a pop. The home takes 10% of that, too. Kind of like a benevolent and trustworthy pimp. Tomorrow's Saturday and that's a good day for your orientation. Be here at 10 a.m. I'll get you registered, fill out a hundred stupid forms, you'll take the first of your weekly STD tests, get you acquainted with the boss, introduce you to Cathy, give you the nickel tour, and maybe pop your cherry."

Dolores winced at the vulgarity.

"Sorry, Sister Dolores," she laughed. "But tomorrow will be a big day."

"Thank you so much for this opportunity," Dolores said.

"Don't thank me yet," Agnes said. "You have no idea, no *clue*, of what's about to happen to you. And though I promised to help you wholeheartedly—I can't imagine you'll be back with us come Monday."

There would be no cherry-popping on Saturday. But for two interactions, the day was unrelievedly boring. Filling out forms, meeting the bureaucracy, etc. But, as stated, there were two signal encounters.

Xenia

Xenia ran the place. She had a Ph.D. in Nursing and a masters in Hospital Administration. She was well north of 200 pounds and carried it well. She looked like she *ought* to weigh 200 pounds. Xenia was large and in charge. She had little patience for dissent and was completely intolerant of stupidity. If you were good at what you did and showed her the proper respect, she would be a powerful ally, an intensely loyal advocate, even a friend; if you were sub-par or insolent, she would make your life miserable until you quit, or just fled from the building.

When Agnes introduced Dolores to Xenia, Xenia laughed.

"I'm sorry," Xenia said, holding out her hand in greeting. "That was a poor reaction on my part." Dolores took her hand, cautiously. "It's just that... well, let me just say that you don't exactly look the part."

"I know, right? She's fresh from three years in the convent," Agnes said, "has never been kissed or had an orgasm."

"Agnes!" Dolores was shocked at her bluntness.

Xenia was baffled. "Then why is she here? How can she... what the hell are you up to, Agnes?"

"Hey, she'll work out or she won't," Agnes said. "And you know... funny thing... Helga gave notice, and I was just about to get started on looking for a replacement—a real pain in the ass proposition—and then this one walks in the door asking for Helga's job. So, I figured what the hell."

Xenia laughed again. "Okay, but you must have figured out that if she does work out, I'm not sure you or Cathy are going to have enough work."

"Yeah," Agnes said. "I get that. She's amazing. But I gotta give her a chance."

"That's very generous of you," Xenia said, "But Cathy is going to hate her. You know that, right?"

Cathy

"Oh *fuck!*" was Cathy's response to Dolores' friendly greeting. "Who are you supposed to be? God's gift to horny geezers everywhere?" She looked daggers at Agnes. "You really going to hire her?"

"Why not?" Agnes was going to make her say it.

Cathy smirked. "You really gonna play dumb with me?"

"Look. It's a done deal. She'll work out or she won't. And I knew you'd be a bitch about this, and I won't tolerate you making it hard for her. When you started here, we did everything we could to make it as easy for you as possible."

Long pause here while Cathy narrowed her eyes in an angry squint. "You called me a bitch."

"Well?"

"You're not the boss of me."

"Actually, I kind of am. And you know it."

Another uncomfortable space of silence. "And?"

Agonizing seconds passed and at last Agnes played the sensible boss. "And I'm sorry I called you a bitch."

"Okay then."

"So, let's go back to the beginning," Agnes said. "Cathy, this is your new colleague, Dolores."

Cathy extended her hand and Dolores took it with a cautious smile."

"Hello," they said simultaneously.

Dolores did indeed arrive to work Monday. The hours these women kept were strictly their own, subject only to negotiations with their clients and supervisory approval. They would often take weekends off, and by Monday, many of their regular clients were eager for their reappearance. There were two special rooms outfitted for the assignations that the home provided, and it was private and secure. Clients were ported to these well-maintained rooms for their meetings with the women.

Agnes asked Dolores to be at the home by 10 a.m. on Monday. Cathy decided to also be present for the debut of their new colleague.

Agnes summoned Cathy to her small office. Dolores was already present.

"Cathy, I want you to arrange this first encounter for Dolores. I'm thinking of Rodrigo. He's one of mine and he's a darling man. You know who I mean. He'll be good with her. The room is ready, so please have him in there by 10:30. I'll send Dolores up, you introduce them, show Dolores how to secure the room, then you scram, and then we just have to let this little bird try her wings. Understood?"

"I got it," Cathy affirmed.

"Good." She nodded to Cathy. "Off you go."

Agnes turns attention back to the new girl. She opens her desk drawer and extracts a small purse. "I've taken the liberty of packing a small kit for you, in the unlikely event that this crazy idea of yours works out."

Dolores sighed. Agnes gave her a little nudge.

"Oh, lighten up, Dolores. Just kidding."

She unzipped the little purse and extracted a half-dozen condoms, and a small squeeze bottle of lubricant, and laid them on the desktop. "Do I have to explain either of these items?" she asked.

Dolores looked anxious and puzzled.

"Oh jeez," Agnes said. "Okay then. I presume you do not take birth control pills."

"Correct."

"Any man who penetrates you vaginally *must* wear a condom. *Must.* Understand? They're supposed to have their own, but they sometimes don't. Some of these old fellas, you're going to have to help them with the putting on of it."

"Umm... okay..."

"You'll get the hang of it. It's tricky with the old guys, though. And this," Agnes holds up the little bottle, "is lubricant. Use it if you are too dry to accommodate them. If you are aroused, you are unlikely to require it. But... well... just in case. Most of these guys are pretty much the opposite of arousing." She put the bottle back in the little purse and zipped it closed. "Nervous?"

"Maybe... *panicking?*"

Agnes laughed. "Again: lighten up. You'll get through this. Plus... there's still time to change your mind."

Dolores sighed and shook her head in an emphatic negative.

Agnes reopened the drawer and extracted a small transceiver, a tiny walky-talky. "We use these to communicate. Only me, you, Cathy, and Helga can use this frequency." She held it up to demonstrate. "Just press the button to talk. Here's volume, and here's the power switch. Just leave it on. Clear?"

"I got it."

"Keep it in this little purse. It also clips on to your clothes," she giggled, "when you're wearing any. Don't lose it."

The device crackled. *"Agnes? We're ready up here."*

She pressed the button on Dolores' unit. "She's on her way."

"You know where the room is," Agnes said with an encouraging smile.

"Right," Dolores said. "Thanks."

"You forgot your little purse."

"Oh! Right."

And with that Dolores was off to the third floor conjugation room.

But this was as much a test of Cathy as it was of Dolores. Agnes hurried to boss Xenia's office, where they would both get an earful of the proceedings via an audio feed from the conjugation room to Xenia's intercom. They listened in silence to the entire episode.

"Hey, give daddy a little sugar, baby. I missed ya'," croaked Irving from his bed. Irving is 78 years-old. He has many debilitations, most essentially, emphysema. He is ugly as a goat, weighs 98 pounds, is on oxygen, is a rude and nasty prick of a man, but with a little chemical assistance he can still get it up once a week for his sex session, which is covered by his lavish insurance. The operative word in this paragraph is 'Irving.' Irving is not Rodrigo. Cathy thought it would be amusing to substitute a client of her own choosing to initiate Dolores into the art. Kind of like a little joke.

"Oh, I have a surprise for you today, Irving, dear," she singsonged.

"What? I don't want no surprises. I want you. Now! Climb aboard you nasty little girl!"

At that the door opened and in stepped Dolores. She wore a yellow dress almost to her ankles cinched with a red cloth belt, and slippers. Underneath she wore panties.

Irving gawped for a moment and then thrashed about furiously for his glasses. He put them on and just stared in silence.

"Who'r you?" he croaked softly.

"I'm Dolores."

Irving looked at Cathy. "Is this for me today?"

"Yes. There was a little mixup. Is this okay?"

"Uh-huh," Irving was trying to work himself into his usual vulgar teenager impression but just wasn't coming.

"Well," Cathy announced, "I'll leave you two to it!" Cathy closed the door, Dolores secured it and then approached Irving's bed with a smile.

"You are Rodrigo?" Dolores asked.

"What? No. I'm Irving."

This unsettled Dolores. "Oh! Must be another mixup."

"What? You gonna run out on me?"

"Well... no. Not if you want me to stay."

"Damn right I want you to stay!" Irving was starting to feel more like himself. "Why dontcha lose them clothes." He snapped his fingers impatiently.

Dolores stiffened at the inevitable suggestion but was determined to see it all through. Off came the yellow dress in a single graceful movement. Irving was entranced.

"Wow. Yeah. Now them panties."

Off they came, and Dolores stood naked in front of a man, if you could call him that, for the first time in her life.

Irving whipped the sheet down revealing that he was ready for action, condom already in place. "Climb aboard!"

Dolores had never been so unsettled in her life and was considering bolting from the room, but she gritted her teeth and moved to the bed, climbing aboard cautiously and straddling skinny Irving. She sat on his stomach. He grabbed at her breasts and squeezed them as if they were party balloons, kneading them painfully, all the while making the most obscene comments and observations, nearly bringing Dolores to tears.

"Okay! Now climb on! *Climb on!*"

She moved to comply, but he stopped her, "No! Not like that! Goddammit. Didn't Cathy tell you nuthin'? Turn around and face the other way. It took her a tearful moment, but she was finally turned away from him and hovering. She finally came down on him and he stopped her again.

"No! Not there! The other hole! I swear that bitch didn't tell you nuthin'!"

Dolores finally understood what Irving demanded and she fairly leaped from his bed.

"You want to put it where?! Are you serious!? What's wrong with you?" And she started to cry hysterically, throwing her dress back on, stepping into her sandals and snatching up her panties from the floor she bolted the room.

"Hey! Come back here!" Irving yelled. *"I demand satisfaction! . . .* crazy bitches."

Dolores ran to the stairway, not even knowing where she was going. Cathy, meanwhile, stepped from an adjacent doorway in the throes of a laughing fit. That went *so* much better than she had even hoped!

As her laughter subsided her transceiver buzzed to life.

"Cathy, this is Xenia. Come to my office immediately."

"Shit!" Cathy said aloud. She pressed the button. "Be right there."

"Dolores? Report to my office also, please."

As Cathy stepped into the elevator and pressed for the main floor the situation was becoming disquietingly clear: Xenia must've heard the whole thing. *Shit!* She thought to herself. *How could I be so stupid?*

Two security guards were standing outside Xenia's office. They greeted Cathy as she approached.

"Hey, Cath, lookin' good," said the tall one. "How you doin'?"

"I've had better. What's up?" Cathy asked.

The two guards shook their heads. "Dunno," the even taller man said. "Just told to report." He held open the office door and Cathy stepped inside. The guard closed the door. Cathy turned and noted Xenia enthroned behind the center of her big mahogany desk, flanked by Agnes on her right and Dolores on her left. Dolores was *still* crying.

Cathy faced the three, stood erect, and coughed. "Yes?"

Xenia shook her head in disgust. "You're fired. Get out. Your check will be mailed to you. Don't come back."

"Can I at least *explain?*" Cathy was wringing her hands.

"Xenia, please," Agnes said. "I gotta hear this."

Xenia laughed and turned to Cathy. "Sure. Go ahead. Let's hear it."

"I just meant it all to be kind of like a little initiation ceremony. You know? Like... if she could do Irving and... get through it okay, then she... she could handle *anybody*, right?"

Agnes looked disappointed. "That's your excuse?"

Cathy could only nod.

Xenia made a disgusted noise. "That won't work."

"Is there *anything* I can do?" Cathy pleaded.

Xenia feigned thoughtfulness. "Hmm... Well, I suppose if Dolores and Agnes want to give you another chance, then we could maybe put you on probationary status-"

"Oh, *thank you!*" She turned to Dolores and pulled a remorseful face. "I'm sorry, Dolores. Really. I didn't know it would go like it did. I didn't think you'd be so upset." Cathy turned to Agnes. "And I'm sorry, Agnes. I disobeyed but I promise never to do it again."

"Uh-huh," Agnes said and turned to Dolores who had at last regained her composure. "What do you think, Dolores? Shall we let her come back?"

Dolores wiped at her nose with the back of her hand and sniffled. "If she promises never to do anything like that to *anybody* ever again, then maybe we should forgive her and take her back."

"You know, Sister Dolores," Agnes said, "that's exactly what I thought you'd say." She touched Xenia's arm and said, "Thanks for this, Xenia." Agnes shouted, "Security!" The door opened and the two guards marched in. "Escort this bitch off the property."

"What?!" The two guards came forward and touched Cathy on each shoulder. She shook them off. "It wouldn't have mattered what I said, would it? You getting off on this, Agnes?"

Agnes smiled. "Don't forget to contact me if you need a reference."

"Fuck both of you!" she snapped, turned and headed out the office door, security close behind.

The smoke finally cleared, Dolores stood. "I suppose I should just call it a day."

"Still upset?" Agnes asked.

"Very upset. Yes."

"I don't want you to leave."

That did not compute. "But-"

"If you do, then I don't want you back tomorrow."

This verdict struck Dolores as most unjust.

"I need you to get back on the horse, not moping and licking your wounds at home," Agnes explained. "I want you to freshen yourself, have a bite of food, cup of tea, whatever. But I want you to visit Rodrigo today. *Then* you may go home."

Xenia sat back, observing. Agnes waited while Dolores considered her fate.

"I brought a sandwich," Dolores said. "I'll have lunch and then report to you. That okay?"

"Perfect."

Dolores left the two ladies alone.

"I like her," Xenia said.

"How could you not? It would be like hating the Easter Bunny."

Xenia laughed. "Part of me hopes she'll work out; another part wants her to do something else for a living."

"I feel the same way," Agnes said. "I never saw or met anyone like her."

"She's incredibly beautiful and sweet-natured," Xenia observed. "Why is she doing this? She tell you?"

"It sounds crazy…"

"Tell."

Deep breath. "She believes that her looks are all she has, that and her beliefs and caring nature, and that she needs to serve people who need her most as best she can. How did she put it? Something about… carrying another's cross for a while. Bring joy to the needy or some such."

"I don't know how much joy will be in it for *her*," Xenia said. "It's like the spirit that animates that body… you know? I wonder if we would find her as physically beautiful if there were a different person inside her? She's just so… other worldly," she said, then was silent for a long space.

"What are you thinking?" Agnes asked.

"We have to *protect* her," Xenia said. "If and when she fails it can't be because *we* failed *her*. I would find that hard to live down."

"I've been as gentle as I can with her."

"I know, you've been good. This Rodrigo idea. That's good."

Agnes nodded, rose, took her leave, and went back to her office to wait for Dolores.

"I'm ready." And there she was in the doorway all freshened up, no sign of the recent turmoil on her face or in her demeanor.

Agnes regarded her new girl. She wondered if she'd ever grow used to the splendor of this young woman. After 20 years of whoring, seeing how a real naturally beautiful woman looks and behaves. She pressed that feeling down. "Nice recovery. You look good." She stood. "Let's go meet Rodrigo. Got that purse?"

Dolores held it high.

They were silent on the elevator ride to the third floor and then the short stroll to the conjugation room.

Agnes gripped the door handle and turned to Dolores. "Ready," she asked.

Sweet smile and a nod. "Mm-hmm."

Agnes pushed open the door and stepped right to Rodrigo's bed while Dolores stood back near the door.

Rodrigo gave Agnes a big smile. "Agnes, my dear, hello. I been waitin' for you." His voice was soft and weak. Rodrigo was 74 years-old with a long list of chronic health issues. Sparse white hair and rheumy brown eyes, and a nice smile that rarely left his face when Agnes was present.

She took his hand. "Rodrigo, something has come up and I won't be with you today, but I'd like you to meet my friend, Dolores."

"Oh, no," he frowned. "That's too bad." Dolores stepped forward and Rodrigo squinted. "I better get my glasses." Agnes fetched them from his tray and put them on his face. His eyes got big. "Oh my gosh! Look at you!" he said.

Dolores stepped to him and took his hand in greeting.

"Do you mind if Dolores takes my place today, Rodrigo?" Agnes asked. "Umm… *Rodrigo?*"

Jarred from his appreciating trance, he affirmed the arrangement. "Wha-? What? Oh! Yes. Okay."

"Dolores will take good care of you," Agnes said, as she left the two of them alone. Dolores secured the room and turned to Rodrigo.

She took a deep breath. "What can I do please you, Rodrigo?"

The old fellow was slow to assimilate his good fortune. "So, you… you're going to be my Agnes for an hour?"

"Or longer, if you would like."

"Well…" he seemed a little embarrassed. After a brief struggle with himself he blurted, "Agnes would take her clothes off and climb into bed with me." There. He said it. "Will you do that for me?"

"I can do that for you," she said. In a graceful gesture the dress was gone, and the panties were next but-

"No. Wait. Please," Rodrigo begged, and Dolores froze. "Just stand there a minute and let me look at you." She knew that he wanted, but would never ask for, the 360-degree tour, so she turned slowly, actually appreciating his honest and benign appreciation. Rodrigo sighed softly and gazed contentedly for half a minute. "My gosh but you're a true beauty, Dolores."

She smiled and thanked him and removed her panties. She stepped up right next to him. "Permission to come aboard, Captain," she said, laughing at her little joke. She was not at all nervous. She felt in control and appreciated by this old gentleman whom she liked instinctively and knew would never hurt her.

He reached out to touch her but stopped at the point of contact as if the gesture was somehow forbidden, though she would have permitted him his explorations. Noting his hesitation, she pulled up the bedsheet and climbed on in, lying on her side, putting her head on his skinny shoulder, her hand across his chest, and her leg across his lower body, and with a big sigh, relaxed into him.

Rodrigo did not relax. He was stiff and tense.

Dolores lifted her head and smiled at him, while gently stroking his arm and chest as he very gradually settled into her embrace. Neither of them was aroused in the slightest—Rodrigo lay flaccid under Dolores' long thigh.

After a minute of this gentle communion Rodrigo, finally perfectly relaxed, closed his eyes and started to weep. Very quietly. Dolores did not ask after his tears. She felt instinctively that he knew that she would acquiesce to any wish he had, but that he was doing just what he needed to do and that she was giving him exactly what he needed. She put her head back down on his shoulder and continued to stroke him tenderly. Occasionally he would reach to stroke her hair, cheek or shoulder lovingly in return. Rodrigo wept softly on and off for a full half-hour before he fell asleep. There was still 20 minutes on the clock and Dolores simply lay motionless, not wishing to perturb him in his deep reverie. His face was a mask of perfect contentment.

When the hour had expired, Dolores left the bed stealthily, but Rodrigo woke, a little startled, as if he had never seen her before. He recovered quickly and smiled. He reached out and tentatively touched her white belly. She took his hand and pressed it into her soft flesh, rewarding his courage, and she smiled warmly in return. Finally, she bent to kiss him on his lips, pale and dry but eager for that lovely blessing. She stood erect and they exchanged a fond final gaze. Dolores dressed herself, slipped on her sandals, grabbed her purse, and blew Rodrigo a playful kiss before she disappeared from the room.

The two ladies heard everything, and though they were not about to lie about it, they decided not to share that datum with Dolores.

"She certainly puts my 37 year-old ass in perspective," Agnes said.

"Apparently not. You're 39," Xenia corrected.

"Right. Thanks for the correction," Agnes said sarcastically.

"She's not exactly an ego-builder, is she?" They laughed. "Are you still worried about her putting you on the streets?" More laughter.

"Not really," Agnes said. "With Helga *and* Cathy gone? We'll both have all the work we need. Plus, I got my regulars."

"Who's next?" Xenia inquired.

"Julian, I think. You know Julian?"

"Nope."

"He's recent. Late 60s. Real gentleman. He's coming off of radio and chemo. They think they got it, but he needs rehab here. He's another one of mine. See… I needed to find someone to pop that cherry of hers." She threw her hands in the air. "She's actually a *virgin*. Can you believe this?"

They laughed. "It's hard to believe."

A knock on the door and the two ladies looked bug-eyed at one another.

"Busted!" Xenia said, recovered herself and called out, "Come in."

It was, of course, Dolores. "Were you two listening in?" she asked without rancor.

The two ladies smiled and nodded.

"That's okay. I figured. But I hope you won't always do that."

"Just till you get your wings, dear," Xenia said.

"You did well," Agnes said. "Of course, all we had was the audio. How do you feel?"

"I feel good. I actually enjoyed that." She made a face. "I feel a little guilty."

"Of course you do, Sister," Agnes said and all three laughed.

"Should I call it a day?"

"Hold on," Xenia said. "How much did you charge Rodrigo?"

"Charge?" she squeaked.

"Yes, money. For your services."

"I couldn't *possibly* charge Rodrigo for that. I enjoyed it as much as he did."

Agnes laughed.

"Oh, honey," Xenia said, "we need to talk."

The two spent a good ten minutes drilling it into Dolores' hard head that she may never again hand out a freebee inside that facility. They set her price and advised her how and when to collect. That accomplished, Dolores asked again.

"Should I call it a day?"

"Up to you," Agnes said. "Now that you have sampled the easiest and best-behaved client in the building, as well as the most disgusting and most difficult to work with sleazeball in the building, I figured it's maybe time for a more typical client that will…"

"Oh dear," Dolores whispered.

"Babe, it's gotta be done if you're going to take this job," Agnes was being cautious. "You can still walk away with no hard feelings. But if you stay, your virginity has to go eventually. You get that, right? I picked out a good man. You can go home and mull it over or we can set it up in a half-hour.

He was supposed to be my client today, but he's perfect for you if you're willing to do this now."

Agnes and Dolores stood outside the conjugation room.

"His insurance covers this so you needn't mention payment. I'm going in first, then I'll come for you, okay?" Dolores nodded her assent and Agnes entered the room and closed the door behind her.

After greetings and some smalltalk relating to Julian's health and recovery, Agnes got down to business.

"Julian," she said, "I need a favor… and I don't think you're going to mind."

Julian was a good looking man. Thin from his ordeals but you could tell he had plenty of vitality. He won a bronze medal as a swimmer in the Summer Olympics years past. He still had a full head of salt and pepper hair and dreamy blue eyes. He was one of those guys who always looked like he needed a shave—a look he cultivated.

"Sounds mysterious," he said.

"It *is* mysterious. We still can't figure it out," Agnes said.

"Well… what is it? If I can do it, I'll do it."

Agnes took a deep breath. "I need you to take the virginity of the most beautiful woman you will ever meet. And be gentle with her like you are with me. Now listen: she'll likely bleed a little, and it's not going to be terribly fun for her this first time, so don't blame yourself. And you're the type that will."

Julian just stared at Agnes with a knowing smirk. "C'mon, Agnes. Stop the nonsense and come to bed with me. I've been thinking about this all night and day." Agnes strolled to the door. "Hey! Where you goin'?"

She opened the door and Dolores appeared. "May I come in?" she asked.

"Your speaking voice sounds like singing," he said quietly, spellbound. "I mean… of course! Come in. I'm Julian."

Dolores removed her sandals, tossed her little purse on a chair, and padded over to the bedside. She extended her hand

and Julian sat on the edge of the bed, feet on the floor, and took her hand.

"I'm Dolores," she said. "Glad to meet you."

He looked at Agnes. "You were right."

"What was she saying?" Dolores asked in a playful tone.

"Nevermind," he laughed. He was still holding her hand.

"Thanks, Julian," Agnes said on the way out the door, "you're a dear."

Dolores gently pulled her hand away from Julian's gentle grip and secured the room. She turned and took a deep breath.

"How can I please you," she said.

"Come here to me," he ordered.

She approached and stood before him. He disrobed her languidly as she stood with eyes closed, breathing irregularly. He touched her, and kissed her, with soft caresses all over her body. He couldn't tell if she was enjoying these tender touches and he was mindful throughout that this encounter was not about him; it was all about Dolores and he would not fail her. He took his condom package from the tray, removed it from its package and placed it back on his tray, stood, removed his nightshirt, and embraced her.

He took her to bed and became her teacher. She was willing, but seemed almost reluctant, and she was nearly silent throughout the entire ordeal. He taught her everything she was willing to learn in that single lesson, things she heard that men and women did in bed, mechanical things she was determined to perfect to serve her patrons, but which gave her no pleasure. She would not kiss him—an intimacy that many working girls specifically avoid with their clients, though Dolores did not know this and thought that she was being deficient in her duties.

Nor would she permit him to engage in that common act which would give her body the most pleasure, riding rampant and roughshod over any objections she may have tried to conjure of the 'grossness' of the act—though she learned to serve *him* in this manner without objection. She evinced nor pain nor pleasure when at last he entered her, and when it was over, she cried softly, lying in Julian's thin but still-strong arms.

He was sure he had failed her.

When she recovered, she artlessly abandoned the bed, dressed robotically, and with a sad smile that somehow seemed courageous, kissed him goodbye—on the cheek.

Dolores made a slow beeline to Xenia's office and there they were, her two monitors, giving Dolores a little wave as she entered.

"Were you listening in?" Dolores asked. "I presume you were."

"We were," Agnes said, "but there was almost nothing to hear."

"How do you feel?" Xenia asked.

"Like I let him down. Confused."

"Why do you think you let him down?" Agnes asked. This was an interrogation, but Dolores knew it was coming.

"Because he... he wanted to get pleasure, by pleasuring *me*. As if that were more important than his own."

"It probably was," Agnes said. "Men aren't all the same."

Xenia had an idea of what happened. "And you had trouble-"

"He wanted to do something to me that I didn't want him to do," she said quietly. "I did it for *him*, and he really liked it... but... it seemed gross to let someone do that to *me*."

Agnes wanted to just name the act but thought better of it. Everyone was clear. "Did you have intercourse," she asked.

"Yes."

"Did you enjoy it?" Agnes asked.

"No, it was a little painful, and I was dry... and I bled a little and felt really disgusted about that. I mean... *what must he have thought of me?*" She started to cry.

"I told him you were a virgin, Dolores," Agnes said. "He knew to expect those things. We had a talk. I'm sure he enjoyed himself much more than you think he did."

Dolores looked away from the ladies and fidgeted. "May I go home?" she asked. "I'll be back tomorrow. 10 a.m.?"

"I need to say one thing, Dolores," Xenia insisted. "About the act that you believe you would have found disgusting."

Dolores plopped into a nearby chair. "Oh God... do we have to? Can you not just accept that I have an issue with this?"

"No, I don't think we can," Xenia said. "And I find it all very ironic. You know... you can't have it both ways, girl."

Dolores sat up straight. "What? What do you mean?"

"You believe that you are undertaking this way of life for yourself in order to... how did you put it? To give some joy to another, to carry their cross for a stretch?"

"Okay..."

"But when a man wants to give that joy back to you, to show his appreciation, you think it's okay to embarrass him by refusing to let him give a little joy to you in the way that he finds appropriate?"

Dolores was truly puzzled. "How is that joyful for me?"

"It's joyful for *him*. I thought that's what your... your *mission* was all about? Putting yourself second."

It was sinking in.

"And we know all about that act you find so despicable. And for your next encounter, if there is to be one, I will *insist* that you do not refuse your client this way of showing affection if it's offered," Xenia continued. "In fact, once you have experienced this act of gratitude, you may actually find that there is more than just self-scourging and self-sacrifice to your mission. I'm sure Agnes will agree that you will change your tune on this subject very quickly."

Agnes smiled at Dolores. "That's an order, honey. That's the job. Learn how to do it or find another line of work."

Dolores rose to her feet. "Well, just where do you draw the line?" she almost shouted. "Shall I let a man do what that animal Irving wanted me to do?"

Xenia fielded this one. "No. Many working girls will not allow this. You will never be compelled to do that."

"So, there *is* a line?"

"Yes. You are not required to do that. They aren't allowed to *beat* you either," Agnes said. "Just use some common sense."

Dolores grew sedate, and inquired softly, "What about kissing? I mean real deep kissing," Dolores asked. "I don't feel I'm able to offer that degree of… intimacy."

"I thought you said you've never kissed a man," Xenia said.

"I haven't," she replied, "but *please* tell me that's not a requirement."

Agnes and Xenia spoke at once. "It isn't." They laughed.

"Most of the working girls I know don't kiss," Agnes said. "And that's not really what most of the clients are interested in anyway."

Dolores thought about this for a space. "I'll see you tomorrow."

"You'll be welcome," Xenia said.

"Goodnight, hon," Agnes added, and Dolores was gone.

"You're doing what?!" Hanna could not assimilate this information. I mean… Dolores just came right out with it! *"Oh my God!"* Hanna said. *"Are you really okay with this?"*

"Will you tone it down?" Dolores squirmed. "Everybody's looking at us."

"And you're okay with this. Sister Mary Dolores-asaurus is now a prostitute for old people and cripples. You. Of all people. And you're okay with that."

Dolores looked thoughtful. "I think so," she said. "It's been a bumpy ride, and about to get bumpier, maybe, but I really think I need to go on with this."

"Are you enjoying it?"

"No. But that isn't the point," Dolores answered.

Hanna huffed. "Of *course* not."

"If I can bring joy to these pretty joyless people, then it shouldn't be about me."

"Does Jason know? I can't believe that he would-"

"I haven't told him. I told him I got a job at the nursing home. I didn't specify."

"Are you going to?"

"Yeah. Soon."

"Well, tell me this, how-"

Dolores held up both palms in surrender. "Please... out of love and respect for our friendship I just told you all about it. Now... can we change the subject?"

Dolores had three appointments that next day, and her initiation was complete. She abandoned herself twice to the hated act, and to her surprise, and very much against her will, she enjoyed it. She in fact experienced her first orgasm, which astonished her and shook her to her core. She also discovered the relaxing effects such an experience lends. Mercifully, her two inquisitioners spared her the usual post-game analysis, but they could not withhold their we-told-you-so smiles.

Dolores was by now pretty much the talk of the place. Everyone was charmed by her. Not just the nurses, but the aids and the housekeepers enjoyed her company and conversation whenever they were lucky enough to have it. The guys in maintenance were most enchanted with her, but none of them ever made with the usual lewd guy-talk one might expect. No obscene joking, nothing. Everyone adored her, but nobody could understand what this unearthly beauty was doing "wankin' the geezers" as one wag put it.

An entire month had passed and, as suspected, there was plenty of work for both ladies. It turned out that Agnes had many loyal customers after all. The relationship among Dolores, Agnes and Xenia was special and easy. They behaved like schoolgirls when they got together for the occasional drink after work.

The duo ceased to monitor Dolores' sessions with clients. She had gained much confidence and began to wonder, being Dolores, if she should feel guilty about how much she was enjoying her vocation. But two months into her journey a terrible event came to pass with mortal consequences.

The day began with an unexpected but quite poignant encounter. Dolores had just refreshed herself after her second client of the day and was heading down the hallway to the kitchen for a bite. As she passed one of the patient rooms, she heard a woman call out her name. She came about and stood in the doorway of the woman who had hailed her.

"Yes. You're Dolores. Isn't that right?"

Dolores looked upon a frail woman who looked mid-80s and had a thin papery voice. She was almost bald (cancer therapy?) and she looked sad.

"Yes. I'm Dolores. Do you need your nurse?"

"No, no, no. I wanted to ask you something. Please come in and sit a moment." Dolores complied and sat erect at the edge of an armchair next to the woman's bed.

"What can I do for you," Dolores asked.

"I know what you do here," the crone said quietly. "Your job. I know what you do."

Dolores smiled nervously and nodded.

"Is it just men?"

"I'm sorry…"

"I mean, do you just have customers that are men?"

"Well… yes… that's how it's worked out."

"I don't want to have sex. Honestly, that ship has sunk and I'm too weak to do that sort of thing even if I wanted to. But I just wanted to ask you…"

"Yes?"

"Would you just lie down with me? In my bed? You're so lovely and young… and perfect. Even to just have you lay down next to me would be so nice."

Dolores thought the woman was about to cry, but she didn't.

"Well… I can't lie with you in this room. We have to go to one of the rooms that are dedicated to that sort of thing." She considered her options and decided to take matters into her own hands. "Are you okay to travel in that wheelchair?"

"Oh sure," the old lady said. "I even take little walks."

Dolores took her phone and checked the room schedule for the day. She looked up and smiled, stood, and moved to fetch the wheelchair. "Let's go for a ride upstairs!"

The old woman was transformed with delight.

They arrived at the designated room, which was, as expected, spotlessly clean and sweet-smelling. She secured the room and helped the crone to the far side of the bed, positioning her comfortably. Dolores next removed her dress and panties artlessly as the old woman looked on with amazed adoration.

"You're like a vision," she whispered.

The old woman had on a full-length dressing gown which stayed on throughout. Dolores knew she was embarrassed by her wizened body but was silent on the issue. Dolores laid her body down on the near side of the bed. She was nude, uncovered, and a little chilly. The crone turned on her side, placing her head on Dolores' shoulder and her thin arm draped across Dolores' body, under her breasts.

The woman's breathing became slower and deeper. "Thank you for this," she breathed. "You are a blessing." They lay together like that for many minutes and Dolores thought that the woman had fallen asleep. She had not.

The woman shuffled her thin body down a few inches, with her head even with Dolores' left breast. To Dolores' astonishment, the crone began to suckle her. Her instinct was to pull away, but she brought to mind her mission here and instead remained frozen in place, only gradually relaxing, and *when* she relaxed Dolores discovered a deep and distinct pleasure in this act. She was becoming aroused and could sense her wetness. She was, after almost 23 years, finally discovering the secrets of her body.

After a couple of more minutes of this gentle suckling the old woman began to weep, almost imperceptivity, bringing her meeting with Rodrigo to mind. But two minutes later the crone was in a deep sleep, Dolores' nipple still in her mouth. She gently pulled free, slipped out of the bed and dressed, gathered her purse, slipped on her shoes and still the old woman slept, a serene smile on her wrinkled face. Dolores decided to slip away and let the woman rest.

What followed was in every way the complete opposite of the gentle, blissful goodness that she had just shared. As she walked down the busy hallway to the elevators, she noted a natural soreness of her nipple which was unused to the recent activity, and she cupped her breast. Turning the corner up ahead was none other than Irving the Sodomite, as Dolores dubbed him in her mind, out for a stroll. Irving saw Dolores cupping her sore breast and made a beeline toward her. Dolores froze in her tracks as Irving confronted her.

"Hey, Doris! Lemme help you with that!" he cried. He rudely cupped both of her breasts and began to twist them in his hands, apparently mimicking the act of tuning an old radio. "Hello Tokyo! Come in Tokyo!" he yelled idiotically between her breasts. Dolores was frozen in place, terrified.

The assault was of brief duration, as one of the maintenance men had witnessed this incalculable vulgarity, came up from behind and administered a well-judged kidney-thump to Irving's back—hard enough to drop him like a rock and cause great pain but no lasting injury. The fellow ignored Irving's screams of agony and protest and made certain that Dolores was okay. He ushered her away toward the elevator leaving the human pig writhing on the floor.

When Xenia found out about this (firsthand from Dolores and the maintenance guy) she hustled straight to Irving's room and bitched him out within an inch of his life for sexually assaulting an employee. Irving had countered with a threat of legal action for being violently assaulted by one of the workers.

180

Xenia sent Dolores home for the day, decided to reward rather than persecute the maintenance guy with a week paid vacation, and considered how to best handle the situation. This assault on Dolores had unhinged Xenia. She felt responsible and ashamed that this good and lovely woman could be so insulted *on Xenia's own watch*. Add to that: she realized that Irving's legal threat was likely genuine.

Irving was very wealthy, and Xenia sensed that his threats were real. She could lose her job, the maintenance guy could be fired, if not prosecuted, and the home could be on the hook for an enormous settlement. She would be damned if she would let any of that happen.

Her solution was simple and typical Xenia. She had oversedated him in his meds that evening. When Irving was nearly comatose, she entered his room, closed the door, and administered an intramuscular injection of enough Pentobarbital to kill a large bear.

The next morning Irving woke up dead.

He had a long-standing 'Do Not Resuscitate' order. There was no autopsy. No one but Xenia ever knew how Irving died. No one really cared.

"Wow!" Agnes said when she heard of Irving's demise. "We sure dodged a bullet there!"

"Yep," Xenia agreed. "We were real lucky."

Dolores had finally told her brother.

"You do *what?!*"

"I think I was pretty clear," she said defensively.

Jason sprang from his chair and began pacing the room in silent anxiety. After a space he stopped, turned and regarded his little sister. He sat back down and took her hand in his.

"Does this make you happy?" he asked.

Dolores took his hand, raised it to her lips and kissed it. "I've never been happier," she whispered.

Jason took his hand back and shook his head. But he was smiling. "Okay then," he said. "As long as you're happy."

Jason stood and went about his business in another room, leaving Dolores alone to wonder just how unexpectedly well all that just went!

Dolores' client list was now almost unmanageably large. She had four encounters per day, took every weekend off, and was taking in well over $1800 of 2022 dollars per week. After the third month, she had moved from her brother's home into a small house in Livonia not far from work. She still saw Jason and her BFF Hanna at least once a week and her relationship with Agnes had become close enough that Dolores now considered her a good friend.

Still, she never dated. Guys from work were fairly swarming her with invites to this and that but she could not get past the wall that kept her from a loving relationship with a man. She considered this 'the final frontier' in her development as a woman. She had come such a long way, but despair filled her heart whenever she considered the topic of Love. Hanna had actually convinced her to go on a blind date with her and her current beau, and it went so badly that Hanna never tried that strategy again.

When it came, it came out of nowhere.

Xenia called Agnes to her office to discuss a new admission named Evan Townsend. It was Agnes' turn to add a new client to replace one that she lost to death the week before, but Xenia asked Agnes if she would forego her turn and allow her to offer the new client to Dolores.

"I presume you have a good reason to ask this," Agnes said.

"I think so," Xenia replied. "He *asked* for her."

This was baffling. "How… how did he know how to do that?"

"So, his name isn't ringing any bells."

"What was it again?"

"Townsend. Evan Townsend."

Agnes thought hard. "That Townsend from… about five years ago? That zillionaire playboy who bought half of downtown or something?"

"Well," Xenia laughed, "not quite half, but you know who I mean."

"Why's he here? He's a young fella'."

"ALS."

"Oh, jeez…"

It's an unseasoned nursing home worker who hasn't encountered Amyotrophic lateral sclerosis, or ALS. It's a disease that affects the parts of the nervous system that control voluntary muscle movement. Eventually, ALS takes away the ability to walk, dress, write, speak, swallow, and even breathe. The average age of onset is 55, but Mr. Townsend was diagnosed at 43. He's 46 now. ALS is invariably fatal. This disease is probably better known as Lou Gehrig's Disease, named after the baseball great, and only half of victims survive longer than five years.

"Late stage?" Agnes asked.

"No," Xenia said. "It doesn't seem. He's lost a lot of function, but it doesn't affect involuntary muscle groups."

"Like?"

"Like those that control the heart, GI tract, bowel and bladder function, and sexual functions. So, I presume he's still able to enjoy sex. As much as he can enjoy much of anything."

"But how is it he knows about our Dolores?"

"I wondered, too. So, I just came out and asked," Xenia said. "Turns out he hired investigators to evaluate our home here. He can stay anywhere, hire a slew of healthcare workers, and live in a mansion if he wants—but he doesn't want to do that right now. I'm guessing he's planning something like that and he's here on a transitional basis.'

"So, Dolores?" Agnes pressed.

"When he found out about our program here, he studied as much as he could about you and Dolores."

"And she won."

"Well… I don't know if 'won' is the right word. We have no idea what he's actually like. Maybe she lost."

Agnes looked away and was thoughtful. "Anyway, of course I don't mind deferring to Dolores on this."

"I knew you wouldn't, but I had to ask."

The home converted one of the luxury patient suites to accommodate the intimate sessions so that Evan would not have to be shuttled back and forth to one of the two conjugation rooms. On day two of Evan's stay, Dolores was to make her first visit. She was briefed by Xenia that morning, and he was her first appointment after lunch.

Dolores knocked on the door of the suite exactly on time. It was answered by a tall, thin man who looked about 50, impeccably groomed, obviously of the butler species.

The sleek man smiled and gave a little bow. "Good morning," he said. "You are Dolores, I presume?"

Dolores smiled and assured him that she was indeed herself.

"I am Benson, Mr. Townsend's valet." He stepped aside and bade her to enter. "Please come in." She entered and Benson closed and secured the door. "Please follow me."

They walked down a short hallway with doors on either side, at the end of which was a single door. Benson knocked.

"Come in, Benson," came a call from within. Benson opened the door and bade Dolores to proceed him into the room. "Thank you, Benson. You may leave us."

What Dolores saw: was a man mid-50s, good-looking but thin, thin in a deteriorating way, not in the good way. He was sitting up in bed, uncovered, wearing casual clothes and slippers. He was gazing at her adoringly. She had seen this look a hundred times. He was just another client, and she would give it her best.

What Townsend saw: that the photos did not do her justice.

"Good morning, Dolores," he had a fine bass voice. "I am Evan Townsend. Please call me Evan."

Dolores smiled. "Good morning, Evan."

"The photos I've seen of you give little indication of how... stupid overused word... how *beautiful* you are in person."

"Thank you."

"I suspect that the true beauty is an inner one that animates the outer. That's why a picture just won't do."

"Again, I thank you," Dolores, who had been praised for her beauty all her life was actually moved by the testimony of this well-spoken man.

Evan snorted. "You get that a lot, though, don't you?"

"No," Dolores said. "Not like that."

They were silent for a while, comfortable in each other's presence, smiling.

"What can I do to please you, Evan?" she said at last.

He motioned her to a large, overstuffed chair next to the bed. "Please. Take a seat."

She complied, and for the remainder of the assigned hour, *they talked.*

"You *talked?* Agnes was skeptical.

"That's right," Agnes confirmed. "He's really a fascinating man."

Agnes considered this. "You going to see him again?"

"He wants to see me twice a week. *For two-hour sessions*," she added.

"Can you handle that?" Agnes laughed.

"Let's just say I'll make it work."

"You sound a little... smitten?"

Dolores blushed. A prostitute who can still blush. "I don't know. Maybe. I've never met anyone like him."

Agnes studied Dolores carefully. "Careful, honey," she said. "He's an ALS patient."

Dolores looked anguished. "Yes. I know. He talked about it. He gets these things he calls contractures; his joints get rigid and painful. He fell last week and he couldn't get up by himself. That freaked him out. And he can never lie flat because it's hard to breathe that way."

"Oh dear," Agnes said. She pointed to her lap. "Is his equipment still working?"

Dolores laughed at the mild vulgarity, grateful for the mood change. "Yes. I guess in ALS patients that's not so much affected."

"But... really? You just talked?"

"Yes, and please don't ask me that again."

"Is he here for the long haul?"

"No," Dolores said forlornly. "He's setting up a conversion of his home and putting a staff together. He says he'll be here for a month or so."

They were silent for an entire minute, Agnes staring out the window with a sad, furrowed brow.

"Be careful, honey."

A full hour into their second session, all spent in happy, often laughing conversation, Evan took on a suddenly serious, silent and determined aspect.

"Evan?" Dolores said carefully. "Is something wrong?"

"You know," he said, looking away from Dolores, "I used to be quite a womanizer."

"Yes, I remember. I read the papers," she laughed. Evan didn't laugh. He looked embarrassed and contrite.

"And I know what you do for a living... and..."

Dolores sat next to him on his bed and put her hand atop his. "Just say whatever you need to say, Evan. It will be okay. I promise."

"I made a mistake," he blurted, pulling his hand away. "I'm not... worthy of your company and I feel bad that I brought you here for the reason I bought you here. Do you understand?"

Dolores shook her head. "No."

Evan looked so anguished. He took her by the shoulders. "You are the beauty of the world to me. No. Strike that. That's crass. You are the beauty of the *earth*. I never saw that

186

coming or could even imagine it. Just walked into my room
and BAM! Just like that. And I am a man in decay with many
sins. I am… the *opposite* of you."

"Opposites attract," she said, and winced. "That sounds
lame but it's true. I don't care about your past. My job is to
bring joy to people who have lost their joy. This pleases me
and brings *me* joy. A man like you will never understand that.
I don't need… *we* don't need you to understand. We need
you to simply accept me. As I accept you."

Evan touched her cheek. Something changed in Dolores
when he touched her, and she choked up a little. "And I have
never met a man I so enjoy being in the presence of. So don't
think it's all so terribly one-sided. I feel lucky to have met
you. And I'm grateful for you."

And of course, after all that, how could they not have
kissed? Evan gave Dolores the first real kiss of her life. They
kissed again and she felt herself melting. This kissing was better than any sex she had ever had. After who knows how
long, she pulled away and stood. Evan was baffled.

"Did I do something wrong?" he asked.

"Oh! No!" she smiled. "Just watch."

She stepped to a space beyond the foot of the bed and,
more seductively than usual, removed her modest saffron-
hued summer dress. She stepped out of her panties with conscious grace and slowly turned, hoping that Evan was taking
in everything she physically had to offer him. For once she
did not take for granted the idea that he would obviously appreciate what she had to offer.

She returned to his bed and together they removed his
clothes. And at last, Dolores came to understand the loving
and passionate nature in the union of intercourse with a truly
beloved partner. It changed her life. By the time the two-
hours were up, Dolores had been convinced to quit her job.
She would only have one client, but client isn't quite the right
word. She resolved to visit him daily, at his request, and
agreed to move into his remodeled home in a month, to live
with him and be his Love. As his companion, she would have

her duties (so far unspecified) and he insisted on compensating her with a stipend that was far more rewarding than the home was paying her.

The home was upset with the news. Dolores had made herself, through no conscious effort on her part, an indispensable member of the family of employees and of the many long-term patients. If one was having a rough day, just the simple sight of her lifted one's spirits.

One old Italian fellow, a janitor, used to call her 'Benigna,' (which he pronounced bay-NEEN-ya). He explained to Dolores that it meant, 'a woman incapable of causing harm.' She gave him an unforgettable peck on the cheek for that consideration and his pale, old face blushed scarlet.

Agnes could not be angry at her friend's decision to leave the home. She was a good friend and was happy for her but sounded again her wish that Dolores would exercise care and caution for the sake of her own well-being. But Dolores was not capable of this. She would never put her own needs before the welfare of someone she loved, or for that matter, someone whom she did not.

Xenia pretended to be angry but couldn't make it stick. She, too, was delighted at this wonderful opportunity for Dolores, but, like Agnes, counseled her to face the obvious facts that he could not be with her for long.

For the next three weeks she was with him in his rooms as often as she could spare. They made love frequently and were as close as two hearts can be.

This put Hudson's nose a bit out-of-joint, as he well realized that he was playing second fiddle in the household now, and it was bound to get worse when she moved into the remodeled mansion. Evan had a firm but gentle sit-down with his valet, asking that Hudson accept the situation to make Evan's final years (he hoped) as happy as they could be. Hudson acquiesced, and there was never any friction between him and Dolores.

In these three weeks Evan's condition had deteriorated noticeably. The course of ALS is not one of consistent decline; rather, there are often long periods of a steady plateau of the symptom picture. Dolores prayed for this to happen. Evan was having trouble eating, and his legs were becoming weaker, it seemed, by the day.

She felt guilty that she was ignoring her brother and she stayed home an entire day to go out to lunch with him, do his laundry, see a movie, and make him a nice dinner.

When she returned to the home early the next morning, she was met at the front desk by Agnes and Xenia. They could not stop their tears as Xenia informed Dolores that Evan had choked to death at his early breakfast as she was on her way to work.

Dolores was inconsolable for almost a month before she would even come out of her room. She emerged only to eat. She refused calls and visits from Agnes and Hanna. She alternately wept and prayed. After more than three weeks she emerged from her chamber and had a long talk with her brother. Jason was patient and accepting, offering no advice or stale platitudes that he was certain would annoy Dolores to the extreme. He just listened. He was a great brother.

Dolores had something else on her mind. Her period, regular as a stopwatch, was two weeks late. That evening after she had talked with Jason, she called a midwife that she knew and liked who was also an ex-nun candidate. She set an appointment but knew in her heart as some women do, that she was pregnant with Evan Townsend's child. She was excited.

She was terrified.

Her research revealed that about 90 percent of ALS cases are sporadic, meaning the cause is unknown. The remaining 10 percent of ALS cases are familial and inherited through a mutated gene. In those families, there is a 50% chance that each offspring will inherit the gene mutation and may develop the disease. She was determined to have the child in any case and pray for the best outcome.

The midwife confirmed the pregnancy, estimated the due date, and they set a schedule of visits. Jason was thrilled with the news. Likewise, Hanna and Agnes but neither could hide their anxiety over the ALS possibility (which they did *not* discuss) or just the idea of Dolores being unemployed and single.

The next morning Dolores got a call from one of Evan's legion of attorneys. There was a will and Dolores was in it.

The next week, Dolores discovered that she was entitled to 10-million dollars from Evan's estate—a drop from his bucket. His small family was well provided for in the will and they did not protest Dolores' share, though no one had so much as heard her name before that day. Dolores was grateful for the gift, but she would have given it all away for one more day with her beloved Evan. The money confused her, and she felt that she had no energy to sort the matter yet.

Her trials were not yet over, for three weeks later, Dolores miscarried. This was another death and again she sequestered herself for days. When she emerged, she was struck down with a terrible despair that lasted for months. She refused any counsel and would take no treatments. Again, she wept and prayed. She lost weight and her youthful physical perfection was being sanded away by the gale force winds of her misery. She was pale and had a hollow look. Her eyes seemed haunted.

Finally, at her lowest point of despair, Dolores had a crisis of faith. She prayed and wept so long and hard that the emergency solace of sleep rushed to her like a balm.

She dreamed of Evan.

In her vision Evan was a hale and hearty man in his prime. He was dressed in a grey three-piece suite, with a white shirt and a red tie. He looked like the billionaire he had been. He was holding an infant, swaddled in a white blanket. He offered the child to Dolores who received the baby with infinite gentleness. She held him up. The baby was so beautiful! She kissed the infant's face and held the baby tightly to her breast. She tried to focus on Evan, smiling before her, but her tears distorted his visage. Evan pointed at a tiny cradle next to them that was not there before. Dolores stooped to place the infant therein. She stood and they embraced, he enfolded her in his strong arms and pressed her into himself.

When at last they untangled, he pulled her hair to tilt back her head and he kissed her. It was her first kiss all over again. It was the kiss that was stolen from her, that she had never had a chance to give him before he passed. When the kiss had finally run its long and languid course, Evan held his true love at arms' length.

"Do you understand?" he asked.

She nodded and tried to speak but she was choked with tears. Finally, she found her breath.

"Yes," she breathed. "I understand."

She awoke immediately and lay calmly; the rising sun had tinted her window shade to a dull gold. She bathed in serenity for long minutes with no desire to move.

She sat on the edge of her bed and breathed deeply, filling her lungs with a renewed spirit. She smiled to herself, for the first time in months.

There was much to be done!

There is no tax on inheritance in Michigan. Dolores gifted her brother five-million dollars. She gave a million to Xenia, Hanna, and Agnes. The remaining two million she apportioned to favorite charities and organizations that she liked. That was fun!

There was nothing left.

That suited Dolores just fine.

Sunday is a special day for her. Today she turns 32 years-old, and she will take her final vows as a Sister of the Consecration. She is no longer Dolores. No longer the personification of the Latin word for sadness.

She took the long way home, starting from the beginning, reliving the Aspirant and Postulate stages. She was offered a faster track, but she explained that she was a different woman than the naïve girl of a lifetime ago and she needed to start at the beginning.

The ceremony is nearing its conclusion. She prostrates herself face down in the form of a Cross on the chapel floor while the choir sings the *Litany of the Saints*.

At its conclusion she rises and lights her special candle from the flame of the baptismal candle, kneels before the Rev. Mother, places her hands on the Gospels, and makes her vow to keep forever the vows of chastity, poverty, and obedience.

Mother Superior places a simple silver ring upon the young woman's finger, the first Sign of Consecration. "Receive this ring," Mother intones, "for you are betrothed to the eternal King; keep faith with your Bridegroom so that you may come to the wedding feast of eternal joy. Amen."

The second sign is a crown for the new sister. Of thorns. "Receive the crown of excellence, that as you are crowned by us on earth, so may you merit to be crowned by Christ with glory and honor. Amen."

And finally, "In order that your life may be one act of perfect love, accept this crucifix as a symbol of your offering of yourself as a victim to the Merciful Love of Jesus. In the name of the Father, and of the Son and of the Holy Spirit. Amen.

"By the authority entrusted to me, and in the name of the Church, I receive the vows you have taken." Mother Superior concludes. "By this perpetual profession, dear Sister, you are now fully and definitively a Sister of the Consecration and incorporated into our Congregation with all its rights, favors and privileges. Amen."

She turns and the woman formerly known as Dolores takes Mother's hand, stands straight, and smiles regally at the congregation.

"Please welcome," Mother says, "Sister Benigna."

ಬಿೂೕೕ

Royal Delusion

She looks out of her skylight and sees stars. She wipes away a tear and curses herself for her weakness. She looks awkwardly at her brother who sits next to her on the shuttle. He shares her sorrow but will stay strong for her sake.

"Now he thinks he's the King of Denmark," she whispers. "Did you know that?"

Her brother reaches over and strokes her cheek tenderly and coaxes a small smile from his own sad face. "That's a new one. What will it be next week?"

She matches his little smile and turns away to get down to business. Their shuttle must depart in minutes and there are still a few details to attend to before lift-away. Their trip will take but a fraction of an hour.

So many moons of Jupiter!

Europa is their base. From Europa there are 78 more 'official' moons and many of these have been colonized for decades, some terraformed, some 'specialized.' Himalia is such a one, a planet consecrated to the rehabilitation of psychotics, system-wide. At 170 kilometers in diameter it is one of the largest of Jupiter's moons, and to Himalia this day the two pilots, Telma and her brother Odis, fraternal twins, will usher their troubled sibling, Santos, to his new home.

Telma is impatient. "He's late."

"No, he isn't," Odis says. "Here he comes."

Telma touches a switch and the hatch slides open. They behold two uniformed guards, and between them, their beloved brother Santos. He smiles at them, genuinely glad to see them, and climbs aboard. Odis helps to secure him while Telma dismisses the guards with a nod and closes the hatch. They are ready to depart.

Coordinates entered, systems checked and cleared for lift-away, the three feel the thrust and know that they are

Himalia-bound. Full autopilot engaged, Telma turns away from her panel and settles in, with no further duties until they are about to arrive at their destination.

"ETA is 13 minutes," she says to her brothers. Against her best efforts her brow darkens and, realizing that this may be the last 13 minutes she will ever spend with her brother, she puts her head down and weeps.

Both brothers stretch out to her from their belted chairs, Odis next to her and Santos just across. Each a loving hand caressing one of her knees. She wipes her eyes with both palms and laughs softly.

"I'm alright."

The brothers straighten in their chairs, obviously upset. They regard one another with sad affection.

"Do you know where we're going, Santos?" Odis ventures carefully.

Santos looks confused.

"Don't agitate him," Telma pleads in a whisper.

"I'm not agitated," Santos says. "I'm okay. And yes. I know where we're going."

"And you're okay with this?" Odis asks.

"I... I'm..." Santos covers his face with his hands. "No! I'm not okay. It's the saddest thing that's ever happened to me. Why must this be?"

"It's the saddest thing that's ever happened to us, too," Telma says.

Santos uncovers his face and pleads with his siblings. "Does it really have to be this way?"

Telma and Odis exchange a sad look.

Odis asks, "Santos... who are you now?"

Santos breathes a sigh of exasperation. "Why must we-"

"Please. Just answer."

"I am Waldemar the Fifth, King of Denmark."

"King of Denmark. Like, Hamlet's father? And who will you be next week?" Odis asks.

"I will always be King Waldemar the Fifth, of Denmark." He waits while his two siblings, looking away, gather their composure. "Don't you remember? Don't you? Growing up in the palace together? All the fun-"

"*Santos!*" Odis barks. "Listen to me! There hasn't been a Denmark in two centuries!"

"Two and a half," Telma whispers.

They sit in silence as the minutes pass, none of them knowing what to say.

The shuttle vibrates harshly, settles down and shudders again. Telma turns toward her panel and holds her hand over a small lighted area. Soon the quivers cease. She turns back to her brothers.

"It's nothing," she assures them. She gives the panel another quick glance. "ETA is four minutes."

They sit in silence for another space. Is there even anything left to be said?

"I'm sorry about all this," Santos says.

"We know that these things are beyond your control, Santos," Odis says. "We know you're trying, and we don't hold you responsible for how you're behaving or the illusions that bedevil you. We will always love you. We're just doing what we know is best for you."

Their older brother promised himself he would not weep. He took a deep breath instead and waited until he was settled. "I don't blame you for your actions. I love you both and always shall. Don't worry about me. I'll be fine. I know how to get along."

"We aren't sure..." Telma chokes up again and takes a breath to calm herself. "We don't know when... or *if...* you will be permitted to have visitors. If this were Europa, we could find a way, but we have no special status in Himalia." She starts to cry. "That's what's so hard."

"*Love* will find a way," Santos says tenderly. "I promise."

Deceleration has begun. Wiping her tears away, Telma turns toward the panel and nudges a single switch. The lights in the cabin brighten and the shuttle eases to a landing.

Powered down, the trio unbuckle, and sit, reluctant to open the hatch and suffer the pending separation. At last, with a heavy sigh, Telma switches the hatch to opening position and it swings free.

Six uniformed guards are arrayed outside the shuttle.

Telma touches her brother's hand. "Santos, these men will usher you to your new home. We are not permitted inside. I'm sorry."

Santos takes her hand and bring it to his lips. "Goodbye, Sofia." He kisses her hand.

The three rise and 'Santos' is the first to step out of the back door of the big black government van.

"Is everything in order, Your Majesty?" asks one of the men with a small bow.

"Yes, fine. Thank you, Johann."

The two siblings step down to the pavement and two guards rush to flank each of them, holding their arms gently but firmly. They are being led away toward a private entrance to Copenhagen's Amager asylum, for a very discreet and very thorough evaluation.

"*What are you doing?! Odis! Odis!*" Sofia cries, twisting from her captors. Karl, too, struggles with the two men at his side but soon slackens as he realizes the futility of resistance.

"It's okay, Telma," Karl rasps. "It must be some sort of mistake." He looks about him His eyes are bugging out in terror. "What sort of primitive world is this? *Where are we?*"

As they are being tugged away, they look back in bafflement at their brother and the two uniformed men waiting upon him. That trio stands respectfully until the two captives disappear inside their new refuge, while King Waldemar V forces himself not to look away in his agony.

At last he turns to his aide. "My god, Johann, I love them so much." And the King starts to sob.

These are not good optics, Johann muses, scanning about for paparazzi and spotting none. He puts a hand on the King's shoulder. "This is not good, Your Majesty." Johann turns and bids the big old Daimler limo come hither. "Your car will take you wherever you wish. I'll send the van back."

"Yes," the King says. "Have him take me to the Palace. I told my mother I'd report to her as soon as I could. She'll be in a bad way, I'm afraid. The family has had its ups and downs for years but nothing like this."

Johann opens the back door to the limousine. "Begging your pardon, Your Majesty, please never do this sort of thing again. Not without an escort. It has created so much anxiety."

The King laughs. "I was never in danger, Johann, it's just Karl and Sofia. I needed to be with them at the end. Come now—I'm their older brother, and you've known them as long as you've served our House." He slides into the back seat next to a burley special agent, greets him and turns back to Johann to assure him. "But I take your meaning."

His Majesty's faithful aide presses the car door closed and King Waldemar V of Denmark is on his melancholy way to the Palace.

ဆာ႗

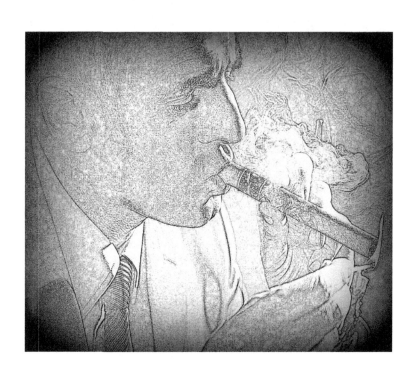

Blowing Smoke

"He'll never guess." Henry Ballentine whispered to Maia, his wife of ten years, and he dropped sugar cube number five into his cup of espresso and stirred. "I'm telling you. Never in a million years."

"But if he's as good as they say..." Maia frowned, unconvinced.

"It doesn't *matter* how good he is. Christ." Henry was irritated. "I'll explain it again. This time pay attention: My dad bought a bunch of those cigars in Cuba in 1950, right?" Maia nodded, and Henry dropped in the last of the sugar and stirred automatically. "The plantation, or whatever the hell they call them, only made cigars that one year and only a few of them were banded and stamped for export. The next year that little plantation was absorbed by a bigger plantation. There's no record of those cigars, I'm telling you." Henry sipped noisily.

"Now," he continued, "here's the kicker: the boxes were all stamped for export, but none of them left the country because my dad and his buddies bought 'em all! Don't you see? Even if he's heard of 'em – which is almost impossible – there's just no way he could know what they taste like. See? And my old man told me he and his buddies smoked them all up! It took them 20 years, but they're all gone now. They were my daddy's pride and joy. He only smoked them on special occasions. Sometimes a whole year would go by and he wouldn't smoke any of 'em. When he died, he left the rest of them to me, and I got the only three boxes that are probably left in the entire world."

"Well... you seem to have it pretty well figured," she agreed, squinting a little as the afternoon sun descended into the window of the café. She moved her chair around to where her husband sat. "Still, it's pretty complicated. And he's the best there is. You know he's famous for knowing everything," she chuckled. "Like that guy in Las Vegas we saw that when you say a zipcode he could tell you what city it is, and how many people live there? Remember that?"

Henry remembered, all right. He thought it was a scam until he tested the man with the zipcode of his boyhood home. Not only had the savant instantly reported the right town (an obscure village in the Pocono Mountains), but the names and populations of the nearest five villages. Henry was convinced the man was genuine, recounting the miraculous deed to everyone who would listen for weeks afterward. But they found out a few months later that it was indeed a scam, for the fellow had a transceiver in his ear and worked in tandem with a fellow in the parking lot who simply entered the zipcode into his iPad, reporting back the results in seconds to the entertainer.

"You really had his number, huh honey?" Maia teased, poking Henry in the spare tire hanging over his belt.

"Cut it out." Henry was not amused. "And keep your voice down. Hey. Are you with me on this or not? What the hell?"

Maia leaned over and kissed Henry on the ear. "All right," she whispered, "I'm with you. But you'd better be right. Some of those things you want me to do... I'm your wife, remember."

"You'll see. And don't mention the car. When he mentions it, act surprised." Henry cleared his throat. "Excuse me!" Henry called over to a nearby table in the café where sat a lonesome gentleman with his back to Henry, impeccably dressed in an Italian silk suit. "You're Ruiz Cortez, aren't you?"

The man twisted slowly in his chair until he faced Henry. He did not smile. "Yes," he said simply. "Good afternoon." He twisted around a bit more and noticed Henry's wife, Maia. He smiled and nodded, and turned again to his cup of espresso, sipping and savoring with the air of an aristocrat.

"We saw your demonstration at Panella's," Henry called out again to Cortez' blue silk back. "It was pretty amazing. I never would have believed it if I didn't see it with my own eyes."

Cortez turned again and smiled. "Thank you."

"Why don't you join us?" Henry asked.

"Yes, you look a little lonesome over there," Maia chimed in, holding up her menu. "How about a snack?"

"On us," Henry added, rising to pull another chair over to the table, next to Maia.

"Oh really, I am not very hungry," Ruiz rose and protested in an English heavily tinted with the accent of his Caribbean home.

"Oh, please join us!" Maia pleaded. "You are such an amazing man and it would be such an honor." Henry remained standing, eyeing Ruiz while holding the back of the extra chair, beckoning him to sit and join the pair. Ruiz, a little flattered and far from his familiar haunts, accepted graciously and soon the trio sat looking at their menus in the bright early afternoon sunlight of Miami.

Ruiz Cortez was a prodigy, and a real one. At age 47 he was the undisputed king of the cigar connoisseurs. It was rumored that he had smoked every sort of cigar made in this century and could differentiate each with a memory as unfailing as his palate. He could tell you not only what brand a cigar was, but the year it was made. He could not only tell you *where* it was made but from what *vega* the tobacco was procured, no matter how complex the blend. He was the Mozart of the cigar, and there was no one in the world like him, now or on record.

Born on the island of Guadeloupe, he still spent many months of the year in that idyllic place. A playboy in his youth, Cortez had squandered his part of the magnificent Loria wine fortune left to him, then turned and made a fortune of his own in wine and real estate speculation. But it was his love of the leaf that made him famous, and there was not a man alive who could match Cortez in the theory and practice of fine cigars. Though many had challenged his abilities, every one of them had regretted it, for Cortez had a gaming spirit. But he never gambled, he said – he *knew*.

Panella's restaurant was one of Miami's finest, perched in the same high-rise complex high above the café in which the trio sat. It was there, an hour earlier, that Ruiz gave a demonstration at a benefit party organized by Miami's cigar barons for some of that city's poor children, the sons and daughters of Cuban immigrants. The demonstration was a breeze for Ruiz, who correctly identified three cigars, all pre-embargo Cuban brands that were no longer made, but not hard to find even in the aging rooms and humidors of the connoisseur of means. The fourth cigar was a ringer, rolled just for the occasion, of a blend of two Honduran leaves and a Dominican leaf. Ruiz could not identify the brand because it did not exist and insisted that it must be a new cigar. He then identified the filler leaves by the *vega* from which they had been procured for this unique cigar. He further stunned the assembly by identifying the binder and wrapper by country and plantation. Truly, there was no one in the world now or ever like Ruiz Cortez.

The trio shared a light repast of cheeses and breads. Henry was on his best behavior and Maia was, as she always was, charming. When the talk moved around to Ruiz' accommodations for the week, Ruiz made a gagging sound. "This city…" he shook his head. "All right to visit, but for a short time only."

"You must get tired of the hotel scene," Maia ventured.

Ruiz laughed. "As a matter of fact, I do. And I am sick of Miami. I want very much to have some peace and quiet by the sea. No crowds, no noise." He sipped at his coffee. "I hate this city, but I need to stay close because I must be at the port tomorrow at three o'clock."

Maia frowned. "You must have big plans tonight with all your friends here. They seemed so glad to see you at the demonstration."

"Oh…" Ruiz laughed and waved a hand, "I am a little weary of the same company for the last three days."

"Stay with us," Henry said through a mouthful of Camembert. "We got plenty of room and we're only a few miles from here. Right on the ocean. Good and quiet. You'll love it."

"That's very kind but I could not impose."

"Oh do!" Maia said, turning up the heat. "It would be a pleasure to have some company and we do have a lot of room."

"What the hell," Henry said. "We'll have you at the port tomorrow in plenty of time."

"Oh," he laughed. "Actually, it is not I that am sailing back tomorrow, it is my car that I must take to the port. I fly back to Guadeloupe on Tuesday."

"Your car?" Henry asked.

"It was my real reason for coming to the States this month. I bought a car and I must have it shipped home tomorrow."

"It must be nice," Maia cooed.

Ruiz brightened at the sweetness of her smile. "Oh yes, it is very nice indeed. It is a Ferrari, a 250 GTO from 1963. It will enhance my stable significantly."

Henry's eyes were like saucers. "You're kiddin' me. A 250 GTO? And you have more Ferraris, too?"

Ruiz smiled at Henry's boyish enthusiasm. "Yes. I now own four Ferraris. An F-50, a little Dino, and a 512 Boxer that needs constant and annoying attention. I also have a Porsche Twin Turbo and a Bentley convertible that I just adore."

"My God." Henry was astonished.

"And a Mercedes 600, and a Jeep. That little Wrangler Jeep. It is very entertaining," Ruiz laughed. "Very American."

"Hey! I got me one of those!" Henry gushed. "Me and Maia took the Jeep here today!" He looked at Ruiz with admiration. "Ah, hell, Ruiz, come on back with us for the night. I got a hell of a collection of single malt Scotches. You don't wanna stay in this hotel again tonight, anyway. What do you say?"

"Yes, Ruiz. Please come back with us," Maia chimed and tugged playfully at the sleeve of his coat.

Ruiz considered a moment. "All right. I will follow you in my car..."

"The GTO?" Henry enthused.

"Yes. And I will meet you there." Ruiz then read Henry's mind. "Perhaps you will accompany me, and Maia can show us the way back?" He turned to Maia. "I am sorry, but she only has two seats."

"Hell yes!" Henry slapped his thigh. "Okay, honey?"

"Okay," she said, rising with a smile. "See you there."

Henry grabbed the check before Ruiz could snatch it up, looked at it and laid a $20 bill on the table, and the two men left the cafe right behind the willowy Maia, long blond hair and loose print dress fluttering in the seawind, a sight appreciated keenly by Ruiz but long since lost on Henry.

After dinner it was Craggenmore for Henry and a dram of the Oban for Ruiz. From where Ruiz sat he had watched Maia on the patio grilling hamburgers. Where was she now? *Maia is a very supple woman*, Ruiz thought. She had a natural beauty that many of the women Ruiz knew would spent thousands of dollars to not attain. She was a casual vegetarian (fish and cheese was okay) and had not joined them for burgers, nibbling instead on vegetable snacks and dip.

"Ruiz, I want to challenge you," Henry said.

Ruiz glanced at Henry, looked away and shook his head slowly. "Oh, I see now. Is that what this was all about?" Ruiz was disappointed. He smiled, as he often did when he was disappointed, unbuttoned the top two buttons of his shirt and let out a long sigh. "Ah, Henry. Put all that out of your mind. Let us just enjoy the evening air."

"I ain't kidding, Ruiz." Henry rose from his couch and began to pace. "I got some cigars that you'll never guess.

That's all I'm saying about 'em.'" He stopped pacing and stood in front of Ruiz. "What do you say?"

Ruiz had heard it all before and was not in the mood for this, especially after the trivial and circus-like demonstration for the public that morning. He looked up at enthusiastic Henry and smiled only with his mouth, his brown eyes betraying only tolerance. He was about to speak when Maia entered the room, barefoot and fresh from the shower, wearing a thin, grey – what was it anyway? A dressing gown? Two graceful spaghetti straps over her white shoulders held the frock in place. She was drying her hair with a checkered towel.

Ruiz rose from his seat as Maia entered. This took her aback, for she was evidently not used to such deference. She stopped drying her hair in mid-rub and smiled at the courtly Ruiz. Henry looked and laughed, then stood up himself.

"Sorry, honey. Guess we've been married too long for the formalities," he said.

"Really," Ruiz smiled at Maia. "How could one ever get used to such a lovely sight?"

"Oh!" Maia blushed. "Thank you." She knew she should shrug that off as a sophisticated woman might do, but her easy blush would always give her away.

"Yeah, well. Want a Coke, honey?" Henry asked, walking over to the table and putting some ice in a tall glass.

"Yes, please," she said, pitching her towel over the stairway railing and giving her tangled blond tresses a final toss through her fingers.

"So me and Ruiz was talking about that test I was telling you about," Henry said as he poured Coke, his back to the pair. "He don't wanna do it."

"Frankly, Henry, I feel a little like a carnival act," Ruiz said. "Can you not understand that?"

"Maybe you should forget it, then," Maia said in a tone of warning.

Henry turned and handed the drink to Maia. "Nah. Listen, Ruiz: I got it figured pretty good to make it worth your while." Henry moved to the big red leather chair and sat. Ruiz and Maia took the cue to sit also, across from Henry on the matching sofa. "So how are these things set up, anyway?"

"Henry..." Ruiz was getting annoyed.

"Just humor me. What the hell," Henry said. "Just tell us how these things work."

Ruiz nodded wearily. "Of course," he said, "there are certain, standard conditions for such an ordeal."

"Like what?"

"Reasonable and logical ones. The cigars must be of the past 75 years; they must be from a sealed box and there must be at least one other box identical to the opened box that is likewise sealed with the original, unbroken government stamp. At my request, I may witness the breaking of the seal of the second box to confirm that they are indeed of the same pedigree. I may smoke from the second box to confirm that they are from the same vintage of cigars."

"How do you know nobody's pullin' a fast one on you?" Henry asked him. Ruiz made a face. He didn't understand. "You know, like, how do you know everything's on the up and up?"

"Oh." Ruiz understood. "Well, there is always a moderator present. Someone that both parties can agree on. He, or she I suppose, examines the boxes and seals, breaks the seal on the first box, and presides over every stage of the test. His word is always final."

Henry thought this over. "Hmm... all that makes sense, I suppose." He narrowed his eyes and looked hard at Ruiz. "I want that red car of yours, Ruiz."

Ruiz laughed heartily. "That car cost me many millions of dollars, Henry! Already I can sell it for much more because I know better how the market works than the man who sold it to me. I don't mean to be rude, but what do you have that can compete with such splendor?" Ruiz paused. "Anything?"

Henry looked at his shoes. He thought for a moment and whispered, "Naw. I guess not."

"Well, let us examine this." To his relief Ruiz now considered the subject closed but decided, in the glow of Henry's good Scotch, to humor Henry, in the manner of a thought experiment. He cut the end off of an Upmann corona from Henry's little humidor-closet and rolled it in his fingers. "What in the world is most precious to you?"

"Maia."

She let out a gasp as her name left his lips. "What's the matter with you?"

"Relax." Henry said, "He asked what was most precious to me, and you are."

"What do you mean by that!" Maia exclaimed, looking over to Ruiz. "What does that have to do with all this?"

Ruiz laughed. "I'm sure he is joking. Don't worry."

Henry rose from his chair and stood in front of Maia. "Listen, honey. It's a sure thing. I can play by his rules and beat him. I already told you all about it." Maia looked at her husband with an unbelieving face, as if waiting for her Henry to betray the fact that he was just joking.

"There's just no way he can win this one," Henry said to her, searching her face for some hint of consent.

Ruiz' lighter snicked into life and he pulled on the Upmann, releasing a long thin jet of fragrant smoke into the den. He turned to the couple. "Don't do this to her. If you must continue this game then let us make a new wager. Something small. Like my Rolex," Ruiz pulled up his sleeve and laughed. "Or better yet, let us just forget..."

"I want that goddam car and I can get it." Henry snapped and turned back to Maia. "Listen to me: do you think I would play with you like this if I wasn't absolutely sure in every single particular that I can beat this guy?"

"What about me?!" she squealed in a high-pitch whisper. "You would bet me on a *car*?"

"It's not a *bet*, goddam it!" Henry got on his knees in front of her. "And it ain't just a car, neither. I'm telling you it's a sure thing." She stared blankly at him. "Listen to me! I can beat him!"

Maia moved to rise. "Excuse me, but I can't sit and listen to this."

Henry grabbed her by the shoulders and sat her back down, firmly but gently into the leather cushion next to Ruiz. "Just stay here and hear me out," Henry said. "Okay?" Maia sat quietly. "Just listen." He turned and saw Ruiz blow twin ribbons of smoke from his nose, above smiling lips. "Listen, Ruiz. If you guess the cigar, you can have Maia for 24 hours. How's that?"

Ruiz said nothing and simply stared at the cigar between his fingers. Seconds passed, and Henry noticed that Maia had her head down. He wondered if she were crying. She did that sometimes. Finally, Ruiz spoke.

"Your lovely wife is certainly a treasure, Henry, but—"

"Oh, I see. But she ain't worth a million, right?" Henry ran his fingers through Maia's tangled hair, lifting her head up against her will and her eyes met Ruiz'. "Well, I think she is. Look, Ruiz, we have a good marriage, see? We don't mess around. Ever."

"I'm sure that's true, but—"

Henry stood. "For Chrissakes, I thought you were a man of the world. I thought you knew you were the best."

Ruiz had had enough, and said loudly, "Henry, *I don't want this bet.* You cannot beat me at this." He took a breath and calmed his voice. "I have seen your humidor and it is very unsophisticated, even naïve in its contents. You are hardly a... well, a man of means. You yourself are an amateur with little experience. You have read about me and you have seen me give a demonstration – which, by the way, was juvenile and undemanding – and you are impressed by that. But you know nothing of my powers in this arena. I appreciate your hospitality, and that of your gracious and lovely wife, but I would be taking advantage of the two of you in a most terrible way if I were to accept your challenge. Understand this."

"You're a coward." Henry stood there, looking down at Ruiz, who met Henry's eyes with a threatening glare.

"Henry, stop it," Maia whispered.

"No. I know! You're a wimp. A homo!" Henry turned to Maia. "That's it! That's why he won't do it. Right, Ruiz?"

Ruiz rose and stood close to Henry, his fists stiff at his side. "Henry, this is not good of you." His anger was no help to his English. "I... *I take offense at you!*"

"Those contests of yours are all phony, aren't they? They're set-ups. Like wrestling."

Maia was afraid, and she turned to pleading. "Henry, that's rude. Please stop it. I want this to stop!"

"You would bet your wife," Ruiz said, "as if she were a... a poker chip. Or a trinket."

"There's no way you can win this one, Ruiz," Henry said, wagging a finger at him. "It's not a gamble for me."

"You are a fool, Henry," Ruiz said.

Henry stiffened. "I don't know if I like being called a fool in my own house."

"I trade you insult for insult." Ruiz looked at Maia and smiled, then back at Henry. "And I *accept* your challenge."

Maia's eyes went from Ruiz to Henry and back again, then she stared at the floor. "You want to gamble with me, Henry?" she whispered.

He turned to Maia. "Never, baby." Henry squatted next to her and put his hand on her bare shoulder. "If it wasn't a sure thing there's no way I'd do this. You'll see how right I am tomorrow."

Maia stood up and got her distance from both men. She turned to Henry, carefully weighing her words. "If you win, you get your car."

"We, baby, *we*."

"Shut up." She turned to Ruiz. "And if you win, you'll get a day out my life that you won't forget," Maia said that with a touch of bitterness that did not become her. She stood silent for a moment and then turned back to Henry. "If you lose this stupid bet, then I don't know what will happen to us." She waited for a reaction which, to her growing discomfort, did not come. "Even if you *win!* Henry, *did you hear me?*"

Henry nodded solemnly. "Trust me, honey. You'll see. Tomorrow it'll all be clear to you. You're doin' the right thing, Maia. You'll see, honey. And we'll be rich!"

Throughout this exchange Ruiz watched Henry closely, amazed by the man's recklessness. He sat back down. "You would bet your wife of many years, your faithful wife, against me so that you might win a *car?* Is that correct?"

"That's right. Are you in or out?"

Ruiz smiled and shook his head. "I never thought I should see such a thing in this lifetime." Ruiz paused a moment to again look fondly on Maia and puff sensuously on his corona. "If it is permissible to Maia, then I accept your proposition."

Maia simply nodded and looked soberly at her husband. "Okay, Henry," she whispered.

"Tomorrow at noon. How's that with you, Ruiz?" Henry asked with an edge of excitement on his voice.

"That is acceptable to me." He looked at his watch. "That is 16 hours from now."

"Then how 'bout a drink?" Henry hopped over to the table and poured more of the Oban. "A little water, right?" He took the drink over to Ruiz and extended the glass. "No hard feelings, eh?"

Ruiz took the glass and squinted up at Henry. Everything had changed between them. "No hard feelings. For us, and, I hope, from Maia." He raised his glass in the gesture of a little toast and Maia smiled wanly.

"No hard feelings," she said, almost inaudibly, her face a mask.

The two men drank.

Ruiz had agreed to accept the hospitality of Henry and Maia until the noon trial the next day. The Scotch flowed freely for most of the evening, and Maia stuck to her usual Coke, for she rarely indulged in spirits. Henry chain-smoked the best cigars in his humidor gluttonously: one of the Upmann coronas, a big Romeo & Juliet that he had been saving for a special occasion, and a Punch Double Corona. Ruiz, who wondered how a man could smoke so much in so short a time, smoked nothing and had to assure Henry that it was not his humidor that was lacking in appeal (though it was) but that he needed to give his palate a rest until the noonday trial.

Maia was mostly silent during these few hours before bed-time in the company of the men. She was fascinated by the elegance and charm of Ruiz and put off by the boorish be-havior of Henry. She had grown accustomed to his coarse-ness over the years, but somehow, tonight, Henry's unrefined manner seemed to stand out in high relief. She found herself smiling at Ruiz and was fascinated by his tales and travels, and his courtesy and attention to her. Henry felt left out and pulled Maia aside twice during these hours to chide her for overplaying her role as hostess. Ruiz overheard these exchanges.

Around 9 o'clock, Maia asked for a drink. "Not a Coke."

Henry narrowed his eyes at Maia and studied her. "You don't drink. Remember?"

"I would like some rum in my Coke, please," she said. "You know I don't have rum & cokes very often, but I do want one now."

Henry stayed put. It was Ruiz who rose to mix the drink. Henry glared at Maia. "No, you don't drink very often, but when you do you make up for it."

"I'm not a child, Henry. Thank you, Ruiz," she singsonged as she accepted the drink, like a little girl at a tea party, drank half of it, and put it on the coaster in front of her. Her eyes widened a bit. "Oh dear!" she said with a smack of her pink lips, "I'd forgotten the taste!" She picked up the glass and sipped. "It's good!"

And so the three drank and the men talked about cars, food, and cigars. Except for a passing interest in food, Maia had little interest in the topics of the evening, but the rum & cokes rendered her giddy by degrees.

Around 10:30, Henry asked for the keys to the Ferrari. Henry was a big man and could hold his drink, and he had a lot of practice. Ruiz, to Henry's surprise, threw him the keys without admonishment. He didn't make a face, or warn Henry about speeding, or offer advice – he simply threw him the keys. Henry tried to contain his enthusiasm but failed to do so, for he was as excited as a schoolboy, sprinting to the garage as soon as he stepped outside. Ruiz rose and refreshed Maia's drink.

"He likes cars," Maia said as she took the glass.

"More than he likes you, maybe," Ruiz said thoughtlessly. He was smaller than Henry but had matched him drink-for-drink all evening, though usually moderate in all of his vices. Maia looked away. Ruiz touched her hand. "I'm sorry. I didn't mean it that way." She looked at him with a little smile, and he went on. "I am just a little surprised that Henry would make such a bet. I didn't want to take it, *but he pushed too far,*" Ruiz said with a touch of that Latin *machismo* that was augmented from the drink.

Maia sipped from her glass. "*You* were surprised. What about *me?* That really came out of left field."

"Sorry?" Ruiz missed that one.

"I mean he never did anything like that before." She laughed nervously. "He must really think that he can win that stupid bet," she said into her glass as she sipped again, then looked at Ruiz and asked suddenly, "What do you think of American women?"

Ruiz laughed, relieved by the change of subject. "They are not all like you," he responded without hesitation.

"What does that mean?" Maia asked, a little worried. "Is that bad or good?"

"That's bad," he said. "If they were more like you then I would spend more time in America." He saw that such words, that can be so quickly thrown off in the company of high society women with no effect, actually caused Maia to blush. Her naiveté and guileless charm had cast a spell on him. "Well, I suppose that women are the same everywhere, but when you travel so much as I, well, one appreciates the differences, too."

"How are women different where you come from, Ruiz?"

214

"Well, they are more natural, I suppose." And then, sensing again that he may be giving offense, "In some specific ways, I mean."

"Well, like how do you mean?" Maia asked, putting down her drink and leaning forward.

"Well, for instance, last week I read that here in Florida three women were arrested for only wearing the bottoms of their bathing suits." Ruiz laughed and took a sip of his Scotch. "Where I come from female bodies are not so much a subject of offense."

Maia looked away, frowning. "I know. When Henry took me to France it was a little shocking. Everyone acted so free and, well... uninhibited. So much more than I ever realized. We went to the beach every day, but I couldn't bring myself to, you know... Henry tries to get me to do that sort of thing, but I just can't!" Maia's eyes returned to Ruiz and she looked searchingly at him. "Do you miss the women of Guadeloupe when you go away?"

"Sometimes," he replied quietly, smiling at his hostess. "But not right now."

Maia blushed at this, too, then stood up and walked to the window. She noticed that the red car was nowhere in sight. She turned to Ruiz and took a deep breath. Ruiz himself stopped breathing as Maia crossed her arms and pulled both thin straps of her gown off of her shoulders, then slipped her arms free of the loops. She tugged at the dress and her pale breasts swayed free, the soft grey top of the dress now bunched at Maia's tanned waist. She stood there, still blushing with her breath coming in little spasms, she met Ruiz' steady eyes and watched him watch her.

"I couldn't do this in France," she trembled, "but I can do this for you."

Ruiz had been in the presence of naked women on countless occasions, but never had it rendered him speechless. He could only look at Maia, and after long seconds cleared his throat and whispered, "Thank you. I... I'm honored."

Ruiz heard the roar of the Ferrari as it pulled into the drive and the spell was broken. Maia darted from the room with a little gasp, tugging on her dress while Ruiz rose and numbly walked to the table to poured himself another Scotch, no water this time, and threw it back hard. He resumed his seat and while he waited for Henry to rejoin them, he wondered if he should call off this crazy bet once and for all and go home. At the same time, he wondered what was the matter with himself, this man of the world who had become unnerved by the sight of a common housewife's breasts. He realized at once that it was not Maia's body, but Maia herself who had so completely disarmed him.

Henry came in through the garage door and bounded right into the den. "Jesus! What a machine!" He threw himself into the leather chair as if he were physically spent by the ordeal of driving the Ferrari. "My God." He let his breath out in a great huff, looking around the room. "Where's Maia?"

"I don't know," Ruiz said.

"That's one hell of a hostess, eh? Maia!" Henry shouted, and she returned his call, and in a few moments returned to the den.

"I just had to powder my nose," she said with a smile, but Ruiz imagined he could still see a faint, rosy blush on her pretty face, and more of the pretty face to admire with her hair up like that.

"Honey, pour me some of that Oban with a little water, will ya? You wouldn't believe that car. That was the most amazing thing I ever did." Henry looked at Ruiz, "I need that car, Ruiz. You can't back out on me now."

Ruiz let out a sigh and smiled weakly. "No, Henry. I will take up your challenge."

"And you will lose, my friend." Maia handed Henry the Scotch. He took it, drained the glass and handed it back to her, wiping his lips with the back of his hand. "Whewww!"

"What about the referee?" Ruiz asked. "Whom shall we procure for that duty?"

"I dunno. Who do you suggest?" Henry replied.

216

"I will call Hector in Miami tomorrow. He will be amused by the ordeal."

"So, who's Hector?"

"He owns *Almost Havana* – surely you know the place?"

"Yeah, sure." Henry didn't. "He'll do fine, I guess."

Ruiz lay in bed clad in jockey shorts with no blanket or sheet, letting the humid seabreeze waft over him as it blew through the large open window of his room. It was a warm evening, but not warm enough for these Floridians to put the air conditioning on, apparently. Sleep did not come at once, as it usually did to him. He lay there feeling the breeze for a long time until he sensed that his door was opening, and he watched a sliver of light from the hallway spread slowly on his bed over the middle of his body. He turned his head and saw Maia, making the shush gesture with her finger over her lips. Ruiz looked around for a sheet to cover himself, but it was quite out of reach. Maia had on a white kimono, cinched tightly. She entered noiselessly, bent her head, and with her lips to Ruiz' ear whispered softly, "Good night, Ruiz." Then she pressed her lips to his and kissed him deeply, for a long time, then vanished as quickly and noiselessly as she had come.

It took many minutes for Ruiz to recover from the buzz of that kiss. He lay there in the glow of it. A half-hour later he remained awash in a warm confusion as he meditated on the events of the day. His trips to America were never this interesting. Though he was always in the company of the elite and the jet-setters when he came to the States, here he was with a couple of rubes and having the most interesting time. As boorish as Henry was, Ruiz almost enjoyed his company, and, in any case, he could endure any of Henry's nonsense as long as Maia was near. Ruiz was not worried about the guessing game; he knew he would triumph as he always did. Even if the unthinkable happened, it was only a car, after all. But now he wanted to win very badly because he wanted Maia. He wondered, *who did she really hope would win the bet?*

217

In the midst of such musings, Ruiz drifted off to sleep, and dreamed a dream…

"I can do this for you, Ruiz," Maia said, standing in the middle of the living room with her top pulled down around her waist, breathing fitfully.

"Well? What is it?" Henry asked him, and Ruiz noticed that the contest was under way, for he had a strange cigar in his hands, all cut and lit. He brought it to his lips and filled his mouth and sinuses with the fragrant smoke.

"Well? See, he don't know, honey!" Henry said, and laughed.

Ruiz had no idea what this cigar was, and he filled his mouth with more smoke. Henry was still laughing, and Maia fell to her knees in front of Ruiz. She pressed herself against his legs and pleaded, "Tell him what the cigar is! Hurry, Ruiz!"

Henry grabbed Maia by her hair and threw her into the air, and she landed in a chair on the other side of the room. "We're gonna win this one, honey! I beat him!"

Frantically, Ruiz filled his head with more smoke but could not identify the cigar for the life of him. Henry bellowed out, "I'll melt down that golden horse and we'll be rich!" and he danced drunkenly around the room. "I'll go get the golden horse!" Henry cried and turned cartwheels on his way out of the house. Maia lifted Ruiz' face with delicate fingers and their eyes met. "You're running out of time. You must tell Henry, that the name of the cigar," she said, "is …"

And she said the name, but Ruiz did not understand her. She said it again, but again it was unclear. She scowled at him with a suddenly ugly, heavily made-up face and pulled up the straps of her dress. "You idiot!" she screamed at the top of her voice, and she turned to the beverage table, grabbed the big bowl of melted ice and heaved it at Ruiz, soaking him from the waist down.

Ruiz awoke, cold. The cold heavy rain that was suddenly driving through the opened window had drenched his bed.

"He insulted me and needs a lesson," Ruiz spoke into the cellphone which he took into his guestroom after the three had shared a light breakfast. Well, light for him and Maia, heavy on the pork products for Henry.

On the other end of the line, Hector laughed heartily at Ruiz' predicament. "How do you get yourself into these things, my friend? We missed you at *The Surf* last night. If you had just kept to your schedule, none of this would have happened."

"Anyway, can you come, say, 11:30?" Ruiz asked impatiently.

"So what does this Maia look like, eh? Is she worth the trouble?" Hector laughed.

"Maia should not be living with this pig of a man," Ruiz hissed. "I don't think she is enjoying it very much."

"Now that she has met a *real* man, eh, my friend?" Hector laughed.

"*Madre de Dios*," Hector always exasperated Ruiz. "Will you come?"

"Yes, yes. How could I miss this? I should sell tickets!"

"No! Listen to me! Just you. No one else!" Ruiz fumbled for the piece of paper in his shirt pocket. "Yes... come to... 2442 Coral Court. It is not far—"

"Yes, yes, I know the neighborhood. You are slumming, Ruiz!" Hector laughed again, and Ruiz pressed the off switch. *The fat bastard*, Ruiz thought, *wait till I see him.*

"Is everything all right?" Her soft voice made him jump.

"Oh, Maia. You startled me," he said as she entered the room, wearing the white kimono.

"Was that that Hector fellow?"

"Yes. Yes, he will be here at about 11:30," he looked at her with a penetrating look which she met with her little smile. "I guess that you will not be wishing me good luck."

Maia stopped smiling and looked away, staring out the window for a few seconds. "I have to get dressed," she said and walked out.

Hector was a bearish, big man, a Cuban expatriate, and he gave his friend a bear hug in which Ruiz almost disappeared.

How can I be angry at this hairy ape? Ruiz thought. *He is always here for me.*

After introductions were made and the specifications of the contest were written and signed in Hector's presence, the four adjourned to the den, where a little smoking nest was arranged to Ruiz' specifications. It consisted of the leather recliner with a small oak table from the library placed alongside it. Arranged upon were an ashtray, and a cutter and lighter which Ruiz refused, opting for his own lighter and requesting an Exacto knife with a fresh blade, which Maia provided. The blinds were adjusted to the correct light level and a bright floor lamp was placed next to the chair.

"What would you like to drink, Ruiz? Water? Scotch?" Maia asked.

Ruiz noticed her blood-red dress, the same color as his Ferrari, and how lithe her body was underneath it. "Tea," he said with authority. "Weak black tea without sugar. Please make a pot now, Maia." She turned to do as she was instructed. Ruiz sat in the chair and adjusted himself for comfort. "Well? Let us begin," he said, closing his eyes and breathing deeply.

"Where are the cigars, Mr. Ballentine? Let us examine them." Hector said gravely. The two men entered Henry's library and Henry opened the humidor closet to reveal his modest collection. Hector's eyes scanned the shelves quickly and he shook his head. He was not impressed. He rarely was. *How does this novice think that he will fool Ruiz?* he thought to himself, as Henry opened a drawer built into the wall. Carefully, and with the reverence afforded a saint's relics, Henry extracted three boxes of cigars, closed the drawer, and ushered Hector from the closet. Hector closed the door behind him while Henry laid the boxes out on an empty shelf of his big mahogany bookcase. Hector's eyes widened at what he saw. He whistled between his teeth as the kettle whistled in the kitchen.

"What is this?" Hector whispered.

"That, my friend, is what Ruiz will be asking himself in about ten minutes," Henry said.

From the opened box Hector, with graceful and practiced fingers, removed one of the cigars and held it in his fat, open hand. He read from the band on the cigar. "I have never heard of this cigar." He looked at Henry. "Where did you get them?"

"My father bought them many years ago," was all that Henry would allow. Hector fondled the cigar and smelled the long, dark, oily wrapper. "Mmm…" Hector hummed. He put the cigar back in the box and picked up one of the sealed boxes. He read the seal carefully and rotated the box, his sharp eye missing not a detail. "Fascinating." He eyed Henry and squinted. "This may be more interesting than I imagined."

"So bring it in," Henry urged.

"No. We must open one of the sealed boxes," Hector said.

"Bullshit," Henry said. "That ain't how Ruiz explained it."

"Well, Mr. Ballentine, that is how I explain it to you *now.*"

Henry considered the situation and Hector's serious face and lightened. "What the hell." He grinned. "Let's do it. I'll get a knife and be—"

Before he finished the sentence, Hector had slit the seal with a long, sharp fingernail kept sculpted for that very purpose, and lifted the lid. "These have been aged very well," Hector observed as he fondled a cigar almost identical to the first one. "They are also packed correctly," he observed. "We will take one from the middle, where the color is not too light nor too dark."

Henry didn't notice any difference among the set, nor did he know what the hell this fat Cuban was talking about, but he guessed it didn't matter.

"Now this band must come off without the slightest damage to the wrapper," Hector whispered as he nudged the brown and white band carefully with his customized fingernail. "There!" he said triumphantly, "not a trace left behind. See?" He showed Henry his handiwork.

Henry said, "Hmmpf. Great."

"Do you have tissue paper?" Hector asked.

"Yeah, right behind you on the TV."

Hector pulled a wad, made sure it was scentless, and nestled the cigar into the tissue. He looked up at Henry. "Let's go." Henry grinned, and they made their way to the den.

Maia was pouring tea from the pot into a big mug for Ruiz. This was the second batch, the first rejected because it was too strong. Ruiz picked up the cup and sniffed. He smiled at Maia. "This is just perfect." He looked into the doorway. "Ah, gentlemen!"

Solemnly, Hector offered the cigar to Ruiz, who lifted it deftly out of its fluffy nest.

"Wait a minute," Henry said. "There's something we need to get straight."

All motion stopped and every eye was on Henry. "Maia is right here. Right?" he said with a touch of belligerence as he pointed to his wife. Everyone agreed that, indeed, there she was. "Where's the title to your car?" he asked Ruiz.

Ruiz hesitated, then reached into his inside coat pocket with his free hand and drew the title out. Henry reached for it, Ruiz snatched it back. "Hector?" Ruiz said. Hector took the paper from Ruiz and put it in his own coat pocket. Henry eyed Hector suspiciously.

"No nonsense," Henry warned.

"There is no need for more insults, Henry," Ruiz said. Henry stared at the cigar in Ruiz' hand.

"Let this test begin now," said the serious Hector, and Ruiz drew forth his lighter and placed it in his lap. Hector fitted his great bulk into a wooden chair about ten feet from Ruiz, directly in front of him. Maia and Henry sat on his left and right, respectively, but too close for comfort. "Please move your chairs back," Ruiz ordered, and Maia and Henry complied by scooting their chairs back a foot. Ruiz nodded and turned his full attention to the cigar.

He switched on the bright lamp next to his chair and examined the cigar closely, rotating it slowly in his fingers.

"Hints of red in this wrapper, but dark and oily, too," he observed aloud. "The veins are a little course for a cigar of what I suspect to be of a premium vintage many decades old." He sniffed the cigar, and then inspected the head of the cigar carefully. Finally, after some gentle squeezing noted, "it is beautifully made and has been carefully aged." He looked up. "I think you have taken good care of these, Henry."

"Yeah, thanks. But what is it?" Henry snapped back.

"I will tell you in a minute." Ruiz turned and snicked off the bright lamp. He picked up the Exacto knife from the table and carefully trimmed the head of the cigar to a narrow opening. Drying his lips, he placed the cigar in his mouth and sucked gently. He removed the cigar and carefully enlarged the hole by an almost imperceptible diameter. Ruiz did this thrice more until a faint smile indicated that he had finally achieved the perfect draw.

Next, he wet his lips and put the cigar into his mouth, tasting the unlit wrapper. He withdrew the cigar and looked at it. "I have already eliminated 99.9 percent of the world's cigars," Ruiz said with a smile. Hector chuckled quietly. Ruiz reached for his lighter. The brilliant gold device made a bell-sound when it was clicked on and produced a blue flame with a sharp point. Ruiz rotated the cigar above the flame until the edge was just charred. He finished the procedure with a few puffs, withdrawing it from his mouth and examining the end to assess the ignition. He blew gently upon the orange glow and was satisfied.

Without delay, Ruiz filled his mouth with rich smoke, put his head back and closed his eyes. He opened his lips and the smoke formed a small grey cloud around his mouth, hovering there and rising slowly around his mustache until he began to slowly expel his breath through his nose and mouth, all three orifices liberating the fragrant billows. He sat for a moment, head back and eyes closed. Suddenly he straightened up and opened his eyes, letting them alight on Maia. "My dear," he said with a smile.

"What's this 'my dear' crap?" Henry said flatly. "What's the cigar?"

"This is not difficult," Ruiz said, still grinning. "It is obviously…" the grin vanished suddenly as if he had been slapped. Ruiz took another short puff on the cigar. "Hmm…" he tried to recall the grin but succeeded only in twisting up the corners of his mouth. In his eyes was fear.

"Hah!" Henry barked.

"Mr. Ballentine," Hector admonished with a hard glance, "please be quiet. Have some consideration."

Smug Henry smiled a malevolent smile, his green eyes shifting from Ruiz to the cigar. Ruiz leaned over to grab his mug of tea and sipped. He took a deep breath as he fell back into the leather chair. Once again, he filled his mouth with the fragrant smoke and closed his eyes.

"Cuba, of course," Ruiz said as if in a trance, releasing the smoke as he spoke. "Wrapper from *El Corojo*." He puffed again. "All the filler is from *Pinar del Rio*. There are two leaves here from *San Louis*… and another, a stronger note here… from the *Semi Vuelta*. It is bound by a leaf—"

"It ain't gonna do you any good to tell me where all the tobacco is from," Henry said. "These are boxed and stamped, and they have a brand name."

"Please, Henry," Ruiz pleaded from his trance. "Do not speak again."

Henry let his breath out in a huff and Maia, who had been on edge throughout this ordeal suddenly leaped from her chair and bolted down the hallway and into the bathroom.

Ruiz puffed again. "These cigars are from tobacco that was grown in 1949." He lifted his head and fixed his eyes on Hector. "And they are in perfect condition, Hector. It's really quite amazing. There is no mustiness, all nuts and leather, and an incredible nobility, like a great old warrior king that is still strong and full of vitality, but a vitality that has turned inward." Ruiz' eyes were glazed and though they were still looking at Hector, they were no longer seeing him. He whispered, "This cigar is worthy of the agéd Odysseus."

Hector smiled and nodded. "You are the poet of the leaf, my friend," he said softly.

"Hey. Let's have no blather between you two, eh?" Henry blurted. "What is this, some kinda *code* or something?"

Ruiz blinked and looked at Henry, the spell broken. Hector simply hung his head and sighed. Footsteps from the hallway announced Maia's return. She looked quite upset and sat down on her chair with her fists clenched. Ruiz looked at her and did not smile but quickly looked away with anguish in his eyes. He took another sip of tea, fell back into the chair and filled his mouth with smoke.

He knew all of the tobacco in this blend right down to the *vega* on which they were cultivated. All except one of the leaves. In his mind, he began to narrow down the possibilities, but in vain. He puffed again. He was always afraid during important tests, that, in his deep analysis, he might one day allow a cigar to go out. That would be fatal, for if it had to be relit a note of crudeness would obscure all the finesse of this experience. His mind then flashed a picture of the delicate Maia, in stark contrast with the crudeness of her husband. The analogy made him giggle to himself despite his predicament. He took another long draw on the cigar and let the answer come to him.

Yes! It flashed upon Ruiz at last, *it is from the vega of Valencia!* But with that realization came another note of panic, for this knowledge did him no good. He had identified all of the cigar's components but realized to his horror that *there was no such cigar!* Ruiz sat up and looked at the three witnesses as if he were surprised to see them in the same room as he. His mind raced. Ruiz put the cigar down in the ashtray and took a long breath.

"If it isn't being too rude," Henry said with quiet sarcasm, "are you ready to tell us what the cigar is?"

"No," Ruiz said. "I must think," and he leaned back in the recliner and closed his eyes. Beads of sweat had formed on his forehead. Henry looked over at Maia with a big grin, but she was looking intently upon Ruiz.

Ruiz knew that there were many cigars, often very good ones, that never left the island. But these were banded, boxed, and stamped for export. He thought again of the *vegas* from which the tobacco was taken, and he considered their histories. Valencia was small, and he knew that there was a time when it was even smaller. *Was that the secret?* When Valencia expanded its holdings did it incorporate another *vega* that had, the year before, rolled, boxed, and banded a small batch for export? Ruiz had never tasted or even heard of such a product, but that was the only possible explanation. *That must be it!* he decided. *But what was the name of that vega?* When it came to him he nearly blurted it aloud. *Raoul Menendez!* He jolted the chair to the upright position and eyed the assemblage.

"Ready?" Henry asked with exaggerated politeness.

"No," Ruiz said. "Almost." For he knew that the name of the *vega* need not be, in fact probably was not, the name of the product. He needed to know what the name on the box and band was, and to his despair he realized that he was not much closer to that knowledge than he was before. Ruiz had never before been in such a precarious professional predicament. A bead of sweat ran into his eye. He brushed it away.

Sitting on the edge of the wooden chair, Maia looked at Ruiz and in her look was sympathy and profound concern. Ruiz smiled at her and she returned his smile feebly. Henry, evidently, did not appreciate this exchange. "Hey," he called across to his wife. "What the hell's the matter with *you*?" Maia looked at Henry with sudden fear in her face, then looked at the floor in front of her.

Ruiz swallowed hard. He knew that he had only one guess and that the odds were not in his favor. He was about to speak when out of the corner of his eye he noticed that Maia had cocked her outside elbow back and opened the palm of her hand under her armpit. He looked and saw that she had marked on her palm with black marker the words *Flor de Santa Anna.*

After Ruiz read and looked away, Maia closed her palm and returned to her previous posture. A cold rush came over

Ruiz. *She is an angel, truly,* he thought, and braced himself for the critical moment. There was much at stake here. He thought of his car — a substantial investment even for him and a thing of great beauty — and his reputation, which was priceless. He glanced again at Maia and saw that little smile on her lips and — was that longing in her eyes? He knew now where her heart was. And his own.

"The cigar," Ruiz announced loudly, "is *Flor de Santa Anna.*"

Henry sprung from the chair and screamed "YOU LOUSY SON-OF-A-BITCH!" and Ruiz threw himself back in his chair at the force of Henry's exclamation.

Hector stood as quickly as his bulk would allow. Maia put her hand to her heart and drew in a deep breath. Henry looked at Maia and walked slowly over to her chair, drew his hand back and slapped her so hard that she tumbled from her seat to the floor. In a flash, Ruiz was at him and Hector, too. They grabbed Henry and wrestled him away from his dazed wife. "YOU LOUSY WHORE! DID YOU THINK YOU COULD FOOL ME!" he screamed at Maia at the top of his voice.

"Mr. Ballentine, stop it!" Hector ordered. *"Get control over yourself!"* Ruiz stumbled backward while Hector easily overpowered Henry and held him fast with both gorilla arms encircling Henry from behind.

"Let me go," Henry hissed.

"Will you control yourself?!" Hector demanded.

Ten seconds went by before Henry's muscles loosened. "Yeah… yeah. I'm okay now."

Hector cautiously released Henry from his grip, and Henry stood staring at Maia, who was now sobbing, hunched in the corner of the room.

"This is very poor sportsmanship, Henry," Ruiz said in a shaky voice.

Henry turned slowly and fixed Ruiz in an icy glare. "Don't talk to me about sportsmanship you little prick," he hissed.

"You are… you are angry, because I guess the cigar, no?" Ruiz looked sick.

"No, Ruiz," Hector told his friend. "Your guess was wrong."

"What!?" Ruiz glanced over at Maia and grabbed the arm of Hector's chair as if to brace himself.

Henry pointed to the sobbing Maia. "That little whore told you."

"What are you talking about?!" Ruiz rattled. "She did no such thing!"

"Don't you get it, you goddam spic imbecile!?" Henry roared. "Yesterday, when I told *her* the name of the cigars, *I told her the wrong name!*"

Ruiz' mind raced. He looked at Hector, who looked back at Ruiz with expressionless eyes. "What… what is that cigar?" Ruiz asked almost inaudibly.

"It is called *Raoul Menendez*," Hector replied. "I've never heard of it before, but it is genuine. There are two more boxes, both stamped, signed, and sealed for export." Ruiz' mouth hung open as he looked away.

"Well," allowed Henry, "at least *you're* for real," he said to Hector.

Maia struggled to her feet but remained in the corner, still sobbing and pressing an ivory palm to her scarlet cheek. Henry pointed at her. "You don't think I noticed the two of you sneakin' around? Henry Ballentine ain't nobody's fool, baby." Henry looked back at Ruiz. "Not hers, and sure as hell not yours." Henry grabbed the white wad of tissues and mopped his face. He gave a bitter laugh. "As you can see," he said to Ruiz, "this is about more than just a *car*." Henry walked over to Ruiz and stood nose-to-nose. "But I'll *take* it!" he barked.

Ruiz stepped back and looked pleadingly at Hector. "Hector… can this be?"

"The cigars are genuine, my friend. I cannot find an honorable way out for you." He looked at Henry with disgust. "But I wish I could."

"Well, why don't you find yourself an honorable way the hell out of my house?" Henry sneered. He looked at Maia. "This isn't over, you cheap whore."

"What are you going to do to her?" said Ruiz, suddenly chivalrous.

"That's none of your business," Henry replied, and took the cheap ballpoint from his pocket, extending it to Ruiz. "Sign the title," he said. "Give it to him," he ordered Hector, who produced the paper.

Ruiz closed his eyes. "Oh God…" he opened them again and looked disappointed as if he had hoped it was all a terrible dream. Hector looked sad, offered his friend no consolation, and could not even meet Ruiz' eyes when he looked his way.

"Sign the title and get out," Henry was firm.

Again, Ruiz had his eyes squeezed shut. He opened them and this time a change seemed to come over him. He snatched the pen from Henry and threw it to the floor. He took the title from Hector, drew his own fountain pen from his pocket and signed with a nervous flourish, turning on his heels without a glance at Maia, and started out of the room.

"The keys!" Henry demanded. Ruiz stopped, pulled the keys from his pocket and threw them onto the table. They slid off onto the floor. Hector and Ruiz filed down the hallway with Henry behind them. Ruiz opened the front door and the three men walked outside. Hector climbed into his '60s vintage Cadillac, and as Ruiz opened the passenger-side door he stopped to look at Henry.

"Don't hurt her," Ruiz called out.

"Beat it," Henry spat back, and he stood on his lawn until he watched the silver car cruise out of sight. It was now time to address the Maia situation.

He closed the door behind him and locked it, turned and entered the kitchen. She had already poured the champagne into the first glass and they listened to it fizz as she filled the second. Arm in arm they reached their balcony overlooking the ocean. It would be another sunny day. Henry touched Maia's red cheek.

"Was I too rough?"

"No," she smiled and shrugged. "Well, maybe a little over-enthusiastic."

Maia handed Henry the title to the Ferrari and he put it in his pants pocket. They touched their glasses together in a clink.

"To you," Maia said, her blue eyes sparkling.

"To us," Henry answered.

They sipped from their glasses and looked out over the rail together at the expanse of calm blue water. Maia was pensive. "He was sweet," she said with a hint of regret.

"Yep." Henry smiled and put his arm around her. "Like an all-day sucker," he laughed.

Maia shook her head at Henry and tried not to smile. "Well?" she asked.

"Well, what?" he puzzled.

"Aren't you going to take me for a ride?"

Henry turned and offered Maia his arm in an exaggerated gesture of courtliness. "My dear, if you please."

"You could have picked up a few pointers from him, you know," she smiled as she took his arm, and they descended the wooden steps to the driveway below, where a gaggle of curious boys surrounded the Ferrari.

"Hey careful, boys!" Henry called at them as he approached the driver's door. "That thing cost me a good cigar!"

A moment later the Ferrari roared off, the boys watching in silence until they could see the red car no more, and remaining still until the muted thunder died away into the oppressive heat of the Florida afternoon.

ᘒᘖ

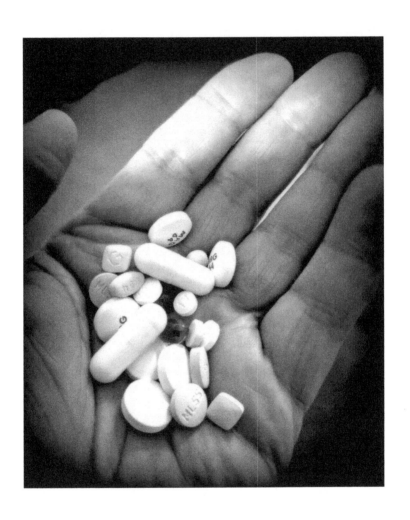

The Hypochondriac

My doctor thinks I'm a hypochondriac. Okay—my doctors, family, and friends make a more accurate list. But these people are wrong, and they disappoint me: I know my own body.

I suffer from a tragic litany of disturbing health anomalies that have been rigorously documented by health professionals over my 70 years. My medical records are testimony to this claim. And frankly, I'm a little bit put out that at the top of the official list of my many verified diseases and conditions is the word 'hypochondriasis.'

Hypochondriasis is defined as 'An illness anxiety disorder, worrying excessively that one is or may become seriously ill.' Remember the old gag, 'Just because you're paranoid doesn't mean they're not out to get you'? Well, just because you're a 'hypochondriac' <big yawn> doesn't mean you're not about to die of some awful health catastrophe, any one of many, carefully certified and as real as the nose on your face.

Briefly, a partial list of my issues includes cardiomyopathy, atrial fibrillation, chronic kidney disease (possibly), peripheral neuropathy, IBS which means Irritable Bowel Syndrome but I call my version Enraged Bowel Syndrome so that would be EBS, strange bleeds from the anticoagulants I take for my a-fib, allergies to almost everything, chronic rhinitis, chronic sinusitis, chronic pharyngitis, chronic post-nasal drip and many, many other potentially deadly issues that are sort of in a grey area of dispute with my 'expert' physicians.

The real trouble is—I don't know which <big yawn> of these things will be the one to get me, and likely soon. The smart money is on either a heart attack, a stroke, a gastrointestinal bleed, a brain bleed, or acute kidney failure. Or my neuropathy could put me in a wheelchair if it gets much worse. A stroke could do that, too, or even do worse.

Merciful sleep ends this carefully spoken monologue and similar ones, which he often summons forth in the twilight before sleep takes him. (His wife left him years ago and he sleeps alone in his small apartment.) He's retired and bored most of the time, so he's easy prey for these tortured thoughts in the morning or in the middle of the day, indeed whenever his obsession grips him. He needs to explain the Big Picture to himself (in the guise of explaining to another), to clarify, to make succinct the sum of his fears.

His merciful sleep lasts about 20 minutes. He can never sleep the night before he has to see any of his doctors, and he made an emergency appointment with his general practitioner last week, and today is the day.

And he wants some answers! He has started having panic attacks recently, vivid with the chest pains and can't catch his breath. For the first month, he thought he was having a heart attack and called 911 for an ambulance. The doctors sent him home. After the third false alarm, he decided to try the doctor's advice and breathed into a paper bag for a minute or so and discovered he could calm himself this way.

But today he must get to the bottom of things. He needs to know, with precision, which of his many maladies is the most dangerous and the most likely to end him. And he needs to know what he must do to best protect himself from this fate. He knows they're keeping something from him, and today, goddammit, he'll find out what it is they're not telling him!

He has chest pains now. Gas? Maybe but maybe heart? Also, maybe he's dehydrated. He was the last time they did labs on him. They couldn't find a vein. Poor girl poked around almost crying in frustration and finally surrendered the task to a supervisor who ended the pin-cushion torture with merciful elan. When finished she advised drink water, lots, the day before you come here, and the veins are easy to find. He grabs at the water bottle next to his recliner (he sleeps sitting up, so bad are his allergies) and slams down a pint in one draught. Hard to do when you're not really thirsty but he guesses he needs it. He grumbles as he realizes he's going to have to pee in the middle of the night.

He dozes for another half-hour, so lightly that the train blowing its goddam whistle at 1 a.m. wakes him again. He muses on the sadistic son-of-a-bitch train driver or engineer or whatever the inconsiderate bastards call themselves. The other guys cruise slowly and silently through downtown in the middle of the night, having enough consideration for people trying to sleep, but of course tonight it would be this clown. *Long-long-short-long* is the whistle code for trains barreling along, repeated *ad nauseum*. It's the 'watch out, here I come' code of the rails. He imagines his nemesis hanging halfway out the locomotive window waving a cowboy hat, whooping a rebel yell like a frustrated bronco buster.

In his sleepy wrath, he dozes again, and he dreams. It's always a variation of the same. He's been hospitalized thrice for long stays, and serious near-death experiences these were. Cardiomyopathy with congestive heart failure the first time, then a pulmonary embolism for refusing to take blood thinners.

The latest was a huge, horrible operation when he got tired of the occasional, and *terrifying,* bouts of blood in his urine, stupidly taking measures into his own hands and abruptly stopping his blood thinners. The recoil effect flooded his aorta with blood clots that seeped into his leg arteries, and he was given a choice: we cut your legs off or else we scrape blood clots and layers of muscle from *several* deep incisions into your groins, legs, and ankle. He chose the latter option. The rehab was agonizing pain for months. He dreams of these events almost nightly with unsettling technicolor lucidity.

He figures the hell with trying to sleep, grabs his e-reader, and dives into a novel he's in the middle of. Comfortable now, his mind in another place, he falls asleep almost immediately and wakes with the sun. And the birds. He hates the birds.

"Jesus Christ!" he yells to the walls. "Learn another song!" So boring! The same call for hours on end. He wishes there were nightingales in his neck of the woods. In Boston, one night, he happily stayed awake the entire night just listening to that one amazing bird spin new melody after melody, never repeating. It was so unexpected and marvelous that he rose up on that morning refreshed though he had hardly sleep at all.

He locates and pours into his hand his many morning meds, cramming the handful in his mouth at once and gulping it down with huge slugs of flat soda water.

The clock says almost 7. The appointment's at 8. He showers, dresses, and heads out to the car. He will, natch, be 15 minutes early. He's never late and has always had scant regard for the unpunctual masses.

He always arranges his doctor's appointments first thing in the morning because he hates waiting. Who doesn't? He once sent a bill for $80 to his physician for making him wait an hour. Oddly, they never paid.

He parks his Honda and heads inside. He takes the elevator to the fifth floor and makes a beeline for his doctor's office, opens the door, and steps inside. Her assistant is at her desk. She smiles. He doesn't. There's a fat lady who looks asleep and a teenage boy wearing a cast on his arm, both sitting and waiting their turn, which damn well better be after him.

He sits and as soon as he does the door reopens and his physician enters, takes one look at our man, and stops in her tracks.

"What are doing here?" she asks.

He's bewildered. "We have an appointment."

She moves to the chair next to him, sits and bends to him, and whispers in a confiding voice, "Well, that snuck by me," she says. "But again, why are you here *this* time?"

He straightens in his chair to his full sitting height and glares at her. "I need some answers," he says. "And I want them today."

"Has something changed? Are you feeling poorly?" she inquires calmly.

He looks at his shoes. "Well…"

"How many times must we do this?" she presses.

"I think you're hiding something from me," he blurts.

"That's ridiculous!"

"All these things that are wrong with me…" he's stammering now, "there's got to be a Main Thing. Something I should watch out for and… and prepare for. Is it my heart? It's my heart, isn't it?"

She slumps in her chair. "O dear."

"Why won't you tell me? Don't you understand? I can take it! I need to know."

"You have been stable since your last surgery," she whispers calmly. "You are very carefully monitored. If there were anything-"

"I need to protect myself from whatever the Main Thing is. And I need you to level with me!"

He's getting loud now, and she resolves to see him in her examining room. Again.

Another big sigh and she puts up her hands as if surrendering to a mugger. "Okay, okay. Let me get settled and Janice will call you shortly. All right?"

"That's better," he snaps. She stands and soon vanishes behind her office door.

Sitting now for 20 minutes, fuming, he realizes that he stupidly left his wallet in the car. He makes a quick exit, finds and unlocks the Honda, grabs the wallet, secures the vehicle, and starts to head back in.

In his anxious state, he never notices the panicked mom with her sick toddler racing for dear life into the emergency lane as her big SUV rams directly into him and knocks him 20 feet through the air. He lands in an unnaturally contorted heap.

He loses consciousness briefly and when he comes to, he is looking up into the faces of a gaggle of fretful gawkers and he realizes what has happened. He can't move his body. He can't feel anything from his neck down. He coughs and there's blood. Lots of blood.

He has a moment of terrific and awful clarity: *he knows his end is upon him,* and he begins blubbering.

A stretcher appears beside him on the ground, and he hears the EMTs ordering the gaggle of gawkers to stand back. Someone in the crowd, possibly the young mom who hit him, points at him and says aloud, "O god! He's crying! O my god." She buries her head in her hands.

But another spectator observes, as the poor man is being secured on the stretcher, "No!" he cries. "He's *laughing! Look!*"

And so he is. Quietly at first, but as they raise the stretcher to full height the laughing gets louder, punctuated by coughs and choking noises and now he is guffawing quite hysterically. Suddenly he stops and looks about him, and as the EMTs are rushing him toward the ER door he says aloud, as if to himself, his final words.

"A car... a *car.*"

৪৩৫৪

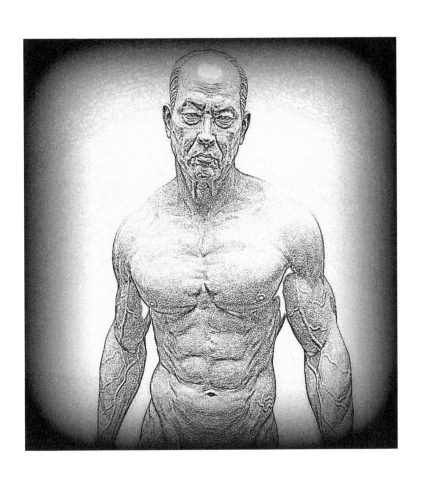

Devotion

If the prince were not fast asleep, he might notice the space next to his bed glow with a slight rosy blush for a few seconds, and then a man materializing out of thin air at the base of the reddish glow seated in a full-lotus position. If the prince were awake, he would surely note the bald, naked, slimly muscled man push up effortlessly onto his feet. He would at least react to the invader's quick advance, the snatch at his head, the deft twist. He would surely put up a struggle.

But all is accomplished and, except for the single burst of rude cracks, with hardly a stir. The prince's head, a bit crooked on his now-broken neck, rearranged nicely on his pillow so the glazed and vacant eyes of his head are turned away toward the wall. He looks like a man asleep.

Alas, the prince was Prince Elecitas, Ruler of the Six Inner Worlds of Epsilon Indi, and a good man, relatively speaking. He will be replaced in short order by a new prince, a puppet of an emerging Imperium. The assassin is Frowk bis Harsa, a Vivika priest at the height of his powers.

Frowk takes a step back into the precise spot from which he had materialized less than a minute before. With feline grace he crosses his ankles, descends to the floor and resumes his lotus pose. He closes his eyes and is almost instantly in a state of near-impeccable calm, but before he achieves this perfect state, he pauses and smiles on this special occasion – his final mission – remembering how long it used to take him to recover his serenity after an assassination in his younger days. He had been lucky. Many were the lesser and unlucky masters who, after a successful snuf, took too long to achieve perfect composure and could not quickly enough envision the home beacon to accomplish the Ting before being discovered. Naked and defenseless, they were slaughtered where they sat. He dismisses this little indulgence and within

241

seconds has vanished from the spot as suddenly as he had arrived, a deep scarlet mist in his place, fading to a rose glow quickly dissipating in the near-darkness of the now-departed prince's bed chamber.

&

The Vivika is a priestly sect of humble beginnings ages ago, not so humble now as the occult arm of diplomats, explorers and secret assassins of a Commonwealth that has ruled The Known Worlds for a thousand years. Only the explorers and diplomats are known to the worlds. The existence of the assassins is only rumored, rarely hinted at openly, and dismissed even by the ruling classes of the galaxy as a paranoid fantasy designed to keep good order throughout the worlds. A bogeyman for adults.

At any time, there are only five journeyman assassins and they represent the glorious intersection of two distinguished demographics – they are of the Elite Warrior class, and they are Vivika priests – masters of the Ting.

The Ting is the ability to disappear and simultaneously re-appear at a predetermined location anywhere in space. The apperator must take care to re-embody in a viable place, that is, not in the middle of a wall, or in water, or in deep space or under the ground. The target place must be free of other solid objects competing for space. Many have found their death in inexperienced mishap, hubris-propelled adventure, or simply poorly-drawn travel plans. Beacons guide the apperators. They allow the Ting to be executed safely beyond line-of-sight, indeed, anywhere in the universe that a beacon may be placed.

Not all elite warriors can accomplish the Ting. The ability is rare; galaxy-wide only a few dozen or so are known at present though their true number is carefully guarded. Much care is taken to detect the adept early in life before there is a malignant incident, and the gifted ones are whisked away from their families for evaluation and training. Dissent on that issue is not permitted.

Clothing, weapons, etc. do not make the trip; only the life of the naked form. Not even one's hair, as it lacks the life-force, makes the journey. Most Ting Masters are bald as a stone, many with scalps extravagantly tattooed, others with hairpieces (like Master Frowk) to sooth their vanity. They are also distinguished by their lack of finger- and toenails, for only the living tissue – the cuticles and a small crescent on their borders – will arrive with the apperator on the journey. Typically a Ting Master will have prosthetic nails when not plying the trade. There are exceptions, some who keep hair, some their nails, a few even the contents of their intestines during their mission, but they are of legendary status and occur only once or twice in a century.

The basic ability to Ting cannot be taught (one must be born with the gift), but it must be practiced and controlled, and the subtleties mastered. Otherwise, the raw gift will only bring misfortune and a tragic, early and bizarre end.

Almost all the Vivika priests are of the diplomat or explorer class, commissioned to travel the unknown reaches of space in an instant, doing the business of the Commonwealth, expanding its knowledge and influence. But it is the small band of mythical assassins who concern us here.

৪১

The reapperation is a striking ritual.

In anticipation of the reappearance of Master Frowk, there are five priests, three male, two female, all apprentices, kneeling upright around the apperation dais in bright ceremonial regalia, the chief and next-in-line rings a censer of incense and intones a quiet incantation, the other four answering in their turns. Since the missions are often quite brief, of the get-in-and-get-out variety, the potential for ceremonial tedium is absent. Before tedium becomes a factor, it is usually suspected that the travelling master has come to no good end and the celebrants will append a ritual of remembrance and eventually disband in sorrow upon the order of their Chief Apprentice. After a suitable period of mourning, the Chief will replace the departed master as a newly minted master him- or herself, in yet another extravagant ceremony. This is uncommon but not rare, for few Ting Master Assassins of the Vivika Priesthood have ever retired due to old age. It is a lavishly rewarded but most dangerous profession.

Frowk was gone for 63 seconds, two seconds shy of the estimated mission duration. His re-apperation is heralded by the reddish blush above the dais, followed by his gradual presence, in lotus pose and naked as a newborn. A bell is sounded by one of the priests as two others approach him from behind with a black silk cloak which they drape over Frowk's shoulders and clip about his neck. They retreat as he unfolds his legs, crosses his ankles and raises himself to a standing pose with perfect grace. The five celebrants bow. When they straighten up the bell is sounded one final time in formal conclusion.

That's it. Everyone relaxes and welcomes the man home from a successful mission. Frowk is hungry (fasting and co-lonics are always preparatory to an assignment) and he needs to sleep.

ಬ

"My Lady, your hair is so beautiful."

Myla, bodyservant of Lady Aracelis, moves the comb through the long black locks slowly, till it whisks clear at waist length. The Lady, seated at her marble vanity, has her eyes closed and her head tilted back. She has always loved to have Myla care for her in this special way. Myla is but a slave, but the Lady is going to change all that.

"Myla..." the Lady begins, carefully, "we need to have a talk."

Myla stops with the comb mid-stroke and removes it, now standing calmly behind her mistress. "Certainly, my Lady."

"This is so hard..." the Lady whispers, "and after so many faithful years..." Lady Aracelis stands, turns her chair around and motions Myla to sit across from her. She complies, but with an unsettled look.

"Have I done something to offend you, my Lady?" The Lady takes a deep breath, and ready now to say what must be said. She looks deeply into the eyes of her servant.

"When you are ready to leave my chambers, a host of my guards will take you to a holding cell, where you will await your fate."

"My fate?" It hasn't really sunk in yet. "What is my fate?"

"Death," the Lady says flatly. "For high treason."

Myla's eyes widen, and her jaw drops open. She looks away. "I don't understand! What could you possibly be talking about?"

"Must we go through the charade?" the Lady sighs. "I suppose we must."

Myla is agitated and moves to rise. "Sit!" the Lady orders and Myla falls back into her chair.

"I'll spell it all out, since I must," the Lady continues. "You are aware of the recent assassination of Prince Elecitas."

"No, my Lady, I-"

"That was not a question," the Lady snaps, "it was a statement."

"But what have I to do with-"

"My Lord and husband is next, and last, on the list. As leader of the Senate, he is the only real impediment to the Sovereign's ambition to turn the Commonwealth into an Imperium. Without my husband, the rest of the Senate, coward bastards all of them, will capitulate to the lies of the Sovereign. When they discover that his assurances are false, it shall be too late."

"I still don't understand why you think that I-"

"Because I have a recording of you placing a beacon in my husband's bedchamber."

"I don't know what you mean."

The Lady has had about enough. She stands. "Shall we go there and find it together, then? Where you placed it behind my picture on his desk across from his bed? Shall we view the recording together?"

Busted. "They threatened me. They said they would kill me and my daughters if I didn't comply. I... I didn't even know what the object was *for!* I was simply instructed to place it properly. I had no idea what it is! I *still* don't know."

The Lady considers this for a space. Myla looks completely crestfallen, in silent agony as she awaits her Lady's word.

"Myla," Lady Aracelis says at last, "I don't blame you for what you did. You gambled that you would not be discovered and hoped, I am sure, that the result of your actions would not help destroy a Commonwealth and give birth to a dictatorship. But you chose wrongly and have been found out."

Myla begins to weep, almost silently, and the Lady considers her next words.

"You shall die for your crime."

"But my daughters!"

"They too shall die for your treason."

Myla leaps from her chair and kneels at the feet of her Lady, hugging her legs, begging. "O please, my Lady, if ever I served you well, have mercy on my two daughters. My choice was life or death for my entire family. All I did I did out of ignorance. Can you be no better than your enemies?"

As Myla weeps, Lady Aracelis strokes Myla's hair with a tenderness that betrays her harsh words.

"There is no hope for you..." she whispers. "There may be hope for your daughters."

Myla lifts her tear-streaked face to her Lady. "I will do anything!"

"You will do *nothing,*" the Lady says. "Listen: The guards will take you to the infirmary. You will be placed in isolation, with a diagnosis of the black-pox. When my crisis is over, and if my husband lives through this ordeal, you will be executed in your isolation cell after a detailed recorded confession which will be kept under seal. Your daughters will be told that you died of the pox. There shall therefore be no thoughts of disloyalty or revenge. You will be granted a high-funeral. On the other hand, if my husband dies or is even injured in this crisis, your daughters will join you in your isolation, they will be told of your crimes, and all three of you will die by my Captain's hand. Is that clear?"

Myla stands clumsily and looks upon her Lady with an expressionless face, a deathmask of ashen grey, and nods.

"Is that *clear!?*"

"Yes. My Lady."

"Now go."

Myla steps slowly to the chamber door, opens it and is greeted by the Lady's Captain and two of his men. Courteously, but resolutely, they usher Myla to the infirmary.

ߏ

Master Frowk bis Harsa had never struck one of his concubines before, but the oldest and dearest of his harem had crossed a line. In response to his heartfelt plea to join him off-world in his pending retirement, she had giggled. Giggled! He demanded she explain, and quickly, the reason for her insulting response. She replies that the Sovereign will never really let him retire.

"That is a sweet offer, my Lord, but you are too valuable," she tells him cautiously. "And too dangerous. You know too much. The priesthood is your only shelter."

"A prison, not a shelter!" Frowk springs up from his bed and begins pacing the room. "It is my *right!*" he shouts. "The Sovereign has promised me, and I will have my due!"

She sits up and scoots to the edge of the bed, holding out her hand to her lord. Reluctantly, Frowk takes it. "Answer me just one question," she says carefully. "Will you please?"

"What is it."

"Who has ever retired from the priesthood of the Vivika Assassins?"

He drops her hand and gives her a hard look. "I am not like the others," he hisses. "I have served the full 10 years without a single fault."

"You are a living legend, my lord." She looks away, troubled.

"What. What's wrong?" he demands.

"You are... you are still *living.*"

"Meaning?"

"No one else has even served half as long. Not in all the centuries."

"I have been promised!"

"But it has been two years since the Sovereign has discussed this with you. He refuses to engage you on the subject."

He flairs in anger. "What are you implying?"

In her pride, she presses it defiantly. "Why can't you see this? There is only one way out for you. And it will never be an off-world paradise."

"I warn you..." he seethes.

"Remove your tracker," she says.

He cannot believe his ears. *"What did you say?"*

"Remove your tracker. I know someone who can do this. And apperate to some far corner of the galaxy where they will never find you!"

This unhinges Frowk.

"I am a priest!" He slaps her, hard. *"Not a coward!"*

And she runs from the room, heartsore and outraged.

Two days later Frowk got the call from the Sovereign that he had been hoping for.

ॐ

"My Lord, thy devotion is misplaced." Lady Aracelis was afraid of this. Her husband is so profoundly loyal and idealistic. And naïve... "If only I could prove to thee how wrong thou art, and how deeply in mortal danger. Prince Elecitas was murdered. I fear thou art next."

248

It is almost evening and the rose light of sunset luminates old Lord Aracelis' chambers. He knits his brow in consternation and rises from his chair. He paces the room in tight circles, his habit when troubled. "I concur with thee that Prince Elecitas' death is suspicious, but there is no evidence of foul play outside his realm."

"It is the assassin priests. I know this."

He stops and considers his wife. "My dearest, the assassin priests are but a fairytale to frighten children and the credulous. As head of the Senate my protection is second only to the Sovereign himself. It is thine own fears and the love thou hast for me that gives voice to the unbalanced imaginings of thine own devoted heart."

"But I know this!"

"And where is thine evidence?"

The Lady is seated in the middle of the chamber as the Senator resumes his circumambulation in agitation that he is trying to hide. Lady Aracelis cannot share her evidence because she does not trust her husband to act properly with it. If she reveals the beacon and tells her Lord of the plan, and if the beacon is disturbed, the Sovereign will know that they are onto the plan and worse is bound to follow. It is better, she thinks, that he knows nothing of this. Her Lord is awaiting her reply.

"I just... I just know," she sighs.

Lord Aracelis stops in front of her chair, leans down and embraces his mate. "Thou hast been my advisor lifelong. Many are the times when thou hast seen what I have not seen and thine actions have often been my surest, betimes my only, shield. But thou asketh me now to presume highest treason against my Sovereign and thou asketh me to presume such with no evidence to present. My dearest – I cannot acquiesce to thee." He stands and looks down at his wife, his aspect full of devotion. "It is I who moderate the untoward tendencies of my Sovereign and I have been successful. I will yet lead him to a more joyous and inclusive rule."

"Then allow me but a single favor, my Lord and Love."

"Ask me and it shall be thine."

The lady smiles up at her husband and will beg his favor. It's a small thing, really.

&

"bis Harsa," the seated Sovereign, addressing the standing man by his formal name, holds out a hand in greeting to the svelte, formally attired priest. Frowk takes the Sovereign's hand and bends to kiss it but the Sovereign will have none of it.

"No, no, my friend," the Sovereign says to the priest, thwarting the motion. "We have been through too much together for that gesture." He points to the chair beside him and bids him sit.

The Sovereign is a small man, middle-aged, with large eyes and sharp features. His hair is a helmet of premature grey, almost white. He is dressed in a simple black tunic without adornment. He looks like a monk.

"I've summoned you here to congratulate you on a career of unprecedented mastery." The Sovereign's voice is almost whisper-quiet, not a voice to ring an auditorium with stentorian authority, but the kind that stirs and resonates in the very soul of the auditor. "You have served the 10-year term, the first of your order to do this for many centuries. I... rather we, are grateful for your perfect service."

"I am grateful to have served, my liege."

"We shall discuss your future."

"I have hoped for this day."

"What would you like to do, Frowk — I'm sorry, may I address you by your familiar?"

"Of course."

"Now that your commission is about to expire?"

Frowk catches that phrasing and his spirit ebbs. *About to expire?* He struggles to recover his composure.

"My liege, I had hoped to marry and find a place not so close to the center of things. Perhaps a world with water. As a boy I had sailed with my grandfather on the seas of Aenope."

"Ah! I visited there as a student. A world of many wonders," the Sovereign enthuses. Then a silence ensues. A heavy silence that is growing most uneasy.

The Sovereign is blunt. "Most of my advisors want me to have you killed."

Frowk closes his eyes and drops his head, saying nothing, waiting in anguish while his Lord elaborates.

"You bear the most vital secrets of any living person. Not a single one of my advisors want you to leave Acherth. They bear you no malice, understand, it's just that changes are about to occur that will alter the face of the galaxies. The old Commonwealth has become brittle, decadent and corrupt, and a new order is imminent. I am suspected of wanting to destroy the Commonwealth, but it is about to fall of its own weight and accord, and soon! It has fallen to me to decide *how* the old order shall fall – into chaos or rise to a new and better order. Action must be taken. Impediments to a new beginning must be eliminated. In the face of such a transition, allowing you to…" The Sovereign searches for the right words.

"Setting me free, you mean. Upholding our sacred pact. You aren't going to do it." This is said with calm and deference. And no offense is taken.

"As a teacher, you will be invaluable."

"I will not teach," Frowk answers. The Sovereign had not even considered insulting Frowk bis Harsa, Master Vivika Priest Assassin, with offers of material gain, or even political power. Such would be an inexcusable affront.

The two sit for a long space, each deeply immersed in his own thoughts, and finally the Sovereign puts forth his verdict.

"I have no choice but to honor my agreement with you."

Frowk sighs with relief and thanks his Sovereign.

"But there must be a bending of our contract. If I simply release you to your own devices – which are so potent and so potentially dangerous – I will endanger not only my own position in the realm, but the fate of the realm itself at this delicate time. You understand that this contingency was never foreseen when our pact was originated."

Frowk sighs again and asks, "How long must I wait?"

"Until this crisis passes, and the new order is free to rise up. That means one more assignment. And then you shall be free. I give you my solemn word."

ॐ

The tiny beacon of the sort that the servant Myla had positioned on the desk of Lord Aracelis serves two purposes: it surveys the area for activity and changes in state, and it allows a Ting master to connect and apperate efficiently and in safety.

Acherth, the ruling center of the old Commonwealth, and Ebos, the administrative planet of the systems ruled by Lord Aracelis, are thousands of light-years apart. It is the mission of the Ting Masters of the Diplomatic Corps, the only fast-as-thought agency known to exist, to knit the far-flung worlds into a synchronized federation. In contrast, physical travel in infraspace via spacecraft takes months to get from one end of the Commonwealth to the other, and even messages through infraspace takes days to transmit through such a distance. The Ting Masters of the Diplomatic Corps reduce communication times to a matter of scant minutes, often seconds.

The beacons are tightly-controlled tools that all ruling families possess but there are no diplomatic missions scheduled in Ebos, and even if there were, a servant covertly scheming to conceal an unregistered device in the Lord's own chamber is all the evidence that Lady Aracelis needs to confirm her suspicions that the stories of the ancient order of mystical assassins are true.

The Senator is huffy about the idea of abandoning his bedchamber for an entire week, but a promise is a promise and he has become resigned. At 140 of our years-old, he is no spring chicken, not like the spry and lovely Lady who is still on the happy side of 70, not yet in her prime. He dodders a bit, much slackened in his dotage but still as alert and dangerous a politician as any. He is used to sleeping alone and has so done for the past five years. But he is a creature of habit and he hates the strange new bedding and mattress, the unfamiliar noises and nothing where it's supposed to be! And he cannot find his robe and cap! He sooths himself with the idea that it is only for two more nights, but he wishes he had pressed his dear wife harder to tell him why why *why!* this change is so necessary. But that, the wily Lady said, was not part of the deal.

And why has she cut her hair? All that beautiful hair. She looks like a boy. She never even asked his permission!

ༀ

Lady Aracelis misses her *own* bed. She has not slept well in five days, awake all night and catching snatches of naps during the day. She looks as haggard as she feels, and her own ladies are worried about her. They are also plaguing her with questions about the health of her bodyservant Myla, who is well-loved and whom they had not seen for days. They check one another daily for signs of blackpox and the Lady feigns concern for their health, knowing there is no threat.

There is a single recording device in Lord Aracelis' bedchamber. He would never have permitted it, but the Lady had concealed one in a subtle spot after Prince Elicitas' murder. It's how she caught her servant in the treasonous act. In the six days since she had evicted her cranky Lord of his bed, there has not been a single change in the room of contents nor position. She has made sure of it.

For a sixth night, she enters the anteroom of her husband's bedchamber and locks the door behind her. Still out of sight of the beacon, she opens a small cupboard and removes her Lord's robe and tugs it on. It's just a little big. Next the cap (the Senator is always chilly and is well-bundled for sleep), under which she hides her remaining hair so that none is visible. (Her Lord is nearly bald.) Barefoot (for that is how her husband sleeps), she pads slowly into the bedchamber from the anteroom. She is bent and slow, stopping at the side of the bed she pulls the bedding back and tumbles in gracelessly, taking care to grunt and groan loudly, coaxing forth the most unladylike sounds by the time she is finally settled in, her cover pulled up around her ears and only her eyes peeping out. She's pleased with her charade, but she worries that her performance has not been good enough, that she has been found out, and other measures to assassinate her Lord are in progress. In any case, *she has no idea what she is doing.*

Now, through half-closed eyes, fighting the urge to sleep, she waits... and waits... The clock is not visible from her position in the bed, so she can only guess at the time. Minutes pass like hours and the urge to sleep is becoming hard... to fight... very difficult... impossible...

She sleeps. And dreams.

బౖ

After four days of fasting, Master Frowk has just finished the colonics, making him at last ready to commence his final mission. He enters the apparition studio and the apprentices drape his naked form with the ceremonial robe. All bow and Frowk ascends to the altar dais while celebrants chant a blessing. When they are finished, Frowk crosses his ankles and drops gracefully to the floor, assuming now a full-lotus position. He is ready at once. He seeks, finds and visualizes his destination beacon in seconds. He smiles. They all smile. There is no one like Master bis Harsa.

"I have the beacon," he intones.

"Prepare thyself, Master," the celebrants respond.

Frowk scans the vision. There is nothing suspicious. All is as it has been for days and nights – the sparse room, the few elegant furnishings, the Lord's body bundled in his bed, and the beacon has registered not so much as a change of position of the sleeping body for hours.

"My terminus is secure," he chants.

"All blessings on your sacred mission," the celebrants respond.

Frowk fades from view and a glimmer of scarlet haze gleams where he had sat, quickly dissipating. All that is left behind is the cloak, a dust of dead offal from the master's body and scant trace of urine. The newest of the apprentices prepares the cleanup ritual, thankful that it was the fastidious Master bis Harsa; he has dealt with much worse.

&

They stroll together, arm in arm on the palace roof. The rich glow of sunset bathes their forms. Lady Aracelis has never looked nor felt so beautiful, and her Lord seem more youthful, tall and straight, with bright eyes and noble brow, smiling beside her. He notices that a sadness beclouds her face. They stop, and he turns to face her. She needs him desperately and he sees this.

"I should never have doubted thee, my Lady and my Love," he confesses. "In this last season of my life I shall have no repose, for I shall grieve every day that I did not attend to thee and thy greater wisdom and offer thee my thanks."

"But my dearest Lord, I do not know what to do! It is not enough that I have seen what thou hast not. Help me, my Lord. I trust thee that thou can lend me the counsel I so desperately need."

The old Senator takes her hand and smiles a last smile. "Nor shall my words fail thee, my Love. Attend to them." He raises her hand to his lips and kisses her fingers, then meets her frightened eyes and shouts, "WAKE UP!"

In a panic she pops up in the bed. She throws off the covers and stands, quaking with anticipation, her breath coming hard and fast as she scans the room frantically. And directly in front of her, between the bed and the desk, she notes a rosy glow, faint but it's there. Instinctively she flies at, and springs upon the gathering scarlet radiance, swinging and punching, flailing her fists into the now-dulling light in the heart of the gathering apparition, now kicking hard and punching into the jellying form until finally she is held fast by the nearly-solid figure and she cries out, falling into blackness.

ဆ

The next morning Lord Aracelis cannot enter his room. It is locked from within and he calls his sentry. In seconds the door has been splintered to pieces and the Senator rushes in with his guards.

They stand amazed. It takes them all a moment to comprehend what they are seeing: a misshapen blob of pink flesh, leaking gore and scarred with blooded cloth, with eight limbs and two heads and faces frozen in agony, centered in a foul puddle of blood and fluids. It finally dawns on them that one of the faces is of the Lady Aracelis, and it dawns now on the Senator that the ancient priest assassins are indeed not a fiction, and that he has been a fool.

Later that morning, after Lord Aracelis had calmed enough to face the wreck of his spirit, he summons the Captain of the Lady's Guard. The Captain tells the Senator of Myla's treason, shows him the beacon and together they listen to Myla's detailed confession. Lord Aracelis orders the Captain's arrest on grounds that he had known so much and kept it from his Lord. Before he is jailed, the Captain gives the Senator a sealed letter from Lady Aracelis, from which the Lord shares nothing, except her last request that no harm will come to her Captain and with this an eloquent testament to her Captain's honor and discretion. This last request Lord Aracelis feels bound to honor.

Lord Aracelis has fled with his court into space. He is eager to reveal to all The Known Worlds irrefutable evidence

256

of the existence of the fabled Vivika Assassins, and proof of the Commonwealth in mortal peril and the chaos that looms.

৪৩

Hey! I Needed the Books.

In the pages of these many stories is my hidden autobiography. Maybe it's like that for all story writers, I can only speak for myself. Although the sum of these stories offers a much more interesting read than an actual straight accounting of my life (and if not, then this is surely the most boring book ever published), a few of my experiences may be offered up in a frank and forthright way, with a minimum of elaboration, with hopefully satisfactory results. Surely we all have such tales to tell.

I think I was 18 when my parents fled the town of Dearborn, Michigan with my five younger siblings to seek a safer, saner place to grow their family. They both hailed from the hills of eastern Pennsylvania, from a small town near Scranton. My father, a trucking company middle-manager, was approved for a transfer from the Michigan facility to a branch in the Pocono Mountains, not far from where they grew up.

The oldest of the six kids and something of a problem child, I was an impractical artsy musician type of guy who fell in with a bad crowd. Check that. I was a founder and stellar member of that bad crowd. Lots of marijuana, alcohol, macho swagger, poetry and music, cool cars and motorcycles—teenagers who would live forever, large and in-charge, that was us.

I declined to follow my family back to my parents' roots because I hated Pennsylvania. I felt no connection to the 'family' out that way and dreaded the few visits I made as a youth. Rural PA? To me it was the most boring and un-cool place in the solar system. I convinced my dad and mom that I would be fine on my own. I pumped gas at a local Mobil station and was eking by very nicely, thank you. And where would I live? Umm… why, at my buddy Pat's house! (They were a large and beautiful Irish family who welcomed all comers.) So no worries. And soon I can get a small apartment.

They were skeptical, naturally, but their need to flee the decadence of the Detroit area and save the rest of the kids from turning out like me spurred them in their resolve and a few days after my high school graduation—they were gone.

I was in jail for possession of marijuana the very next day. The Irish gentleman referred to above was a distinguished attorney and sprung me from the hoosegow, guiding my case through the courts with little consequence.

The haven to which my family fled, a town in the Poconos, was in fact the vacation wonderland for the east coast mob. They ran everything there—the hotels and resorts, the restaurants, even the laundries, and had much influence in the trucking industry. There was massive drug addiction, alcoholism, prostitution—in short, everything my parents feared and fled from in Michigan. they were now steeped in up to their eyeballs. In their naivete, my mom and dad thought they could go home again. Well, you *can't*.

They missed me terribly, especially my dad, who would have a few beers and sing maudlin songs while my mother played piano on Friday nights, lamenting my absence.

In the meantime I was trying to settle into my new life. It was all over the map. I sometimes stayed at the old house, which hadn't yet been occupied and into which I broke and entered on several occasions, hosting many drug-infused parties. One night the cops were called. We turned out all the lights and climbed out on the roof. The cops combed the yard with flashlights, looking through windows and shrubbery for noisy burglars, and all the while we sat on the roof, tripping out of our minds, looking down on the cops who only had to look up to spy their quarry but never did.

I stayed at the homes of many friends, and eventually got a job at the local hospital as an orderly, then took some EMT classes and worked for a local ambulance company. The great thing about that arrangement is that I could sleep there when I wasn't on-duty. They would also let me use an ambulance as my private vehicle should I need to run errands or make friendly visitations.

And during all this time, instead of being in college like a good little pinhead, I studied music and was becoming a good pianist. I knew where all the unlocked grand pianos were in Dearborn, mostly in the churches. I also hit on their pipe organs. Oddly, no one ever asked me who I was or what the hell I was doing there. They let me be.

I decided to try Ann Arbor as my base. It was home to the University of Michigan, the famed Liberty Music record store (where I got a job), and the best unlocked Steinway grands in the state. I found a cheap room in the student ghetto. My music studies were taking all my time, and I needed access to the library at the School of Music. To my anger and dismay, mainly anger, they declined my request for library access. The bastards!

I was not to be daunted. I found a way to slip the desired scores, theory and biography books between the stairs and the bottom of the steel grates on the stairwell that prevented egress down the unlawful rear exit. One had to come and go through the main entrance only, heavily fortified with detectors and alarms to catch scofflaws such as myself from ~~stealing~~ re-allocating books. I just wanted to *read* them; they'd get them back. Eventually.

So I crammed the books in the cracks between the stair and grate where they fell crashing into the stairwell a floor below. I then exited the library lawfully, went to the back of the building and up the forbidden stairway till I found the piles of books scattered all over the place. Many were damaged this way, but I considered this to be 'job security' for the library's excellent Book Repair department.

I did this many times. I actually ended up reading and studying everything I wanted from the library this way. It took many months and several escapades, but it worked out well for me. Not conveniently, but well enough.

I hosted many lively gatherings in my Ann Arbor ghetto flat. One fateful eve I had gathered with my friends and we decided it would be fun to each take ten hits of LSD.

It wasn't.

I had a 'bad trip,' and my friends were so high as to be completely useless to me in my travails. It became clear to me, that jumping off my second floor balcony would be the solution to all my problems.

It almost was.

I landed on my ass and broke a bit of pelvis. To this day I cannot cross my right leg over my left. My body is literally 'bent' though it is detectable only in my lack of flexibility, not visually.

I had a hard time recovering from my bad trip. I was fearful and depressed for months. I had never visited my family in the Poconos, and I missed them terribly in my saddened state. I hitchhiked all the way, without incident.

When I arrived at their home, I noted a large black dog unleashed in their backyard. He looked up and bolted directly at me. I thought, *Oh, they have a dog! How nice.* The big hound ran to me, leapt up, and slurped me with wet dogkisses. *A fine welcome home!* thought I.

The dog (who was dubbed Diogi—D.O.G., get it?) and I headed to the front door and I knocked. My mom answered the door. She was delighted to see me, but shocked.

"My god!" she said. "Why aren't you *dead?*"

Geez. I liked the dog's welcome better. But she explained that Diogi was a problem dog and very violent and protective. She once jumped through a picture window to attack the mailman. The dog, not my mom. So Diogi recognized me as a family member! Wow. Dogs!

It was unspeakably great seeing my family again, I missed them so. But after a week or so, the boredom set in. The remedy was study. My parents had a piano, sort of, or a PSO as we call it in the trade—a *Piano-Shaped Object*. It was an old Baldwin console to be precise. It was also a terrible POS, and most of you will know what that means. There were no other instruments available to me in this mafia wonderland of glitz.

The closest college was in East Stroudsburg. The college was small, but the music department was good, and the library was wonderful and well-stocked. I found all my new interests therein. Sheet music galore and bios of new favorite composers like Xenakis, Feldman, Ligeti and Stockhausen. I gathered them all and placed them in a neat pile atop a table in a remote reach from the bustle of the big room.

I had to have them. But I had to *steal* them, as there was no other way. I would, as always, return them when I was finished with them (for even now I can think of nothing more useless than a book I have already read). Alas, my ingenuity would fail me, and humble me to a pitiful stature.

I stuffed the books into my pants, the inside of my greatcoat, every pocket in and out, even under my arms. I observed no anti-theft portal to negotiate at the front door, so I figured I would be home clear as I shuffled uncomfortably toward freedom. I miscalculated.

As I hobbled confidently toward the door, freedom just inches away, *the alarm went off* and I was so shocked at the sound that I stumbled, and most of the books hidden in the several recesses into which they were so cleverly squirrelled came tumbling out onto the floor, tripping me, followed by my large, graceless body.

The several students and staff who witnessed my witlessness were open-mouthed appalled. I struggled to my feet, as embarrassed as a person could be. How do you wiggle out of something like this?

"Umm… they aren't mine."

"Heh heh… how did *they* get in there?"

"Jeez… I guess I forgot to check these out!"

I didn't even try. I slowly picked up the nine or ten books and stood to the side as I spied a uniformed security guard jogging my way. He stopped right in front of me and appraised me. He was a big guy. He seemed to have little sympathy for my situation.

"You a student? You ain't a student, right?"

I admitted it.

"Gimme them books," he ordered.

I complied.

"Follow me," he ordered. In route to what I imagined was a grim interrogation chamber with a single bare lightbulb waiting to illuminate my soon-to-be bruised and black-eyed face, we encountered a well-dressed fellow who pulled the guard aside for a word. The guard handed the stack of books to the well-dressed guy and he examined them, shaking his head. The guard shot me a dirty look.

"You go with him," he gruffed.

The well-dressed guy was even bigger than the security guard (they grow 'em big in rural PA) and he seemed very angry. He was starting to make me miss the security guard!

It turns out that this grim and angry large man was the head librarian. He pointed me to a seat in his office, and I sat facing him at his desk.

"So what?" he asked. "You couldn't find the porn section, so you decided to steal some music books?"

"Ah... not exactly."

"*Well exactly what, then?*" He was yelling. "*Why did you do this?*"

"Well, you see-"

"Drug money? Right?" he interrupted. "You need booze? That it?"

"It's nothing like that," I said. I was getting a little heated myself.

"WELL?!"

"*I need the books!*" I yelled back.

He snorted with derision, picked a few volumes up and examined the titles. Then he gave me a look that just dripped with skepticism. He held up a selection and read the title aloud.

"*Formalized Music?*" he said. "What do you need that one for? Doorstop? Kindling?"

"It explains the mathematics and stochastic approach to music that Iannis Xenakis uses," I said. "I need to understand that better."

He took a closer look at the other titles and looked back at me with a scrutiny close and long. He slammed the book down hard onto the desk.

"Right!" he said. "You better have I.D. You got I.D.?"

I figured the jig was up and surrendered my Michigan driver license.

"Christ..." he said as he examined it. "You're not even from around here. Is this your usual M.O.?"

"I'm visiting my family in Canadensis," I explained.

He laughed. "Sure you are." He stood, gathered the evidence in his big arms and opened the office door. "Stay here!" he ordered. When he left the office I could hear him lock the door.

Oh god, I thought, *what now?*

It seemed like an hour waiting in that damn office for what grisly conclusion to all this I did not know but my mind reeled to all sorts of unpleasantness. At last I heard the door unlock and the big man reentered. He held out my license and a piece of paper and I took them.

"What's this?" I asked.

"Your library card," he said. And he *laughed!* He handed me the stack of books.

He stopped smiling and pointed a big threatening index finger.

"And they goddam better come back *undamaged* and *on time.*"

They did! They did!

∞

The Other Mary

ather Michael Byrne was a beautiful man. His features were almost feminine but for the squareness of his jaw, a faint five o'clock shadow, and his eyes, which were doubtless a man's eyes. In his sleekness and youth and glow of health he reminded one of the sort of young cleric one finds in the movies — a good, intelligent, honest priest tinged with just enough sex appeal and self-doubt to keep the plot spicy and the ladies engaged. And the ladies *were* engaged.

And Michael had visions. He would be visited by saints, he said, different ones, and they would talk together, and each would listen to the other, and after every episode Michael would visit the Bishop in a barely controlled tizzy and they would discuss what happened and what it all might mean.

The Bishop rather enjoyed these meetings (there was no priest in the diocese or in his memory remotely like Michael) and felt a little fatherly and protective toward the lad — the Bishop was 70 and Michael only 30. Michael had, since his ordination, been the brunt of sometimes unchristianly cruel jokes and cutting remarks from other priests in the diocese. And though Michael had ceased to share his experiences with just anyone, the cat was long out of the bag and he was branded. Some of his brothers in the Church maintained Michael was a fake; some claimed he was crazy, but his congregation loved him, and some of them inappropriately so.

The Bishop loved Michael too, but reserved judgment. It's not that the Bishop didn't believe Michael's claims; he believed *Michael* believed them, but as for himself, the Bishop, like most, never experienced anything like what Michael claimed, and he had seen and heard enough in his years to be skeptical. He wondered if he were *too* skeptical.

So, Father Michael rose this day as he always did at 4:30 a.m., showered and dressed, and then to the church to say Matins, the morning prayers. He liked to say his morning prayers in the locked church, have coffee in the cloakroom and enjoy a few minutes of peace before 6 o'clock Mass, which was his to say every weekday.

It was a January morning in Minnesota, cold and without stars, and dawn at least a couple hours away. Michael pulled the rectory door closed and started the short trudge to the church. He was tired from lack of sleep, and for some days now, for he could not clear his heart of the feelings he had following the resolution of the lawsuit against him. Though it had been weeks since he was exonerated fully in the eyes of the law, the Church, his congregation and all the locals, his heart was heavy still.

The gist of it was this: an unstable young married woman in the parish had quite fallen in love with Fr. Michael. This was not an uncommon occurrence. But the poor woman pressed her case to him, quite literally, one afternoon while visiting in the rectory. Michael gently rebuffed her. In the act of rebuffing her, they were observed by the church secretary, who was used to frequent visits by parish women of all ages who needed Fr. Michael's 'counseling,' for only he, it seemed, could help them. The secretary knew Michael never took advantage of these ladies – it just wasn't like him. But she thought him too gentle, and his rebuffs too sweetly done to really stick.

Caught in the act of pressing her affection, the young woman panicked and accused Michael, on the spot, of trying to seduce her. Fearful of what might ensue, she brought noisy suit against him. In short, his exoneration was swift and clean. No one on the jury believed the young lady for a minute (she had a reputation), nor did the many parish ladies who craved his attentions and were shorted by him. Sweetly.

The old Bishop responded as most middle-managers would — he was horrified by the field-day the local press was having, trying their usual best to make news where there was none, but even more so at the attention this was getting from the Bishop's authorities in the Church. He knew Michael was a magnet to the ladies, and that he was almost certainly blameless in these relationships, but he allowed doubt to enter, as there was so much at stake right now should he be wrong about Michael.

Michael ran through the details for the hundredth time as he unlocked the back entrance to the old church, entered, stamped his shoes snowless and relocked the church door. There was so much he couldn't help. He couldn't stop the visions, no matter how much ridicule was poured upon him by his priestly colleagues; and he couldn't help it that women flocked to him. As a new priest, he tried to use this attraction as an advantage, trying to bring these ladies closer to Christ, but as the years passed, he began to consider his charming gifts as curses with no upside.

"Maybe I should cut my nose off or something," he grumbled aloud as he spooned coffee into the filter. "Probably shoulda been a monk."

He put the coffee away, hit the brew button, and then to the switch box to turn on some lights in the sanctuary. He entered, genuflected to the tabernacle, found the lighter and fired up a couple of candles near his chair. He spied a wadded sheet of paper on the floor, picked it up and retreated to the cloakroom to trash it, re-entered the sanctuary, where his attention was caught by something bright in the pews.

Second pew, right on the aisle, a woman, naked, sitting calmly and smiling. Naked. A naked woman. Smiling at him.

It took Michael a few moments to comprehend what he was looking at. (Could there be a more unexpected sight in a church pew?)

"What—" he croaked softly, cleared his throat, and again, "What—" more words would not come.

The woman grinned sweetly.

"Who are you?!" he almost shouted. *"Who are you... What are you doing!?"*

She stood. Naked as a new baby. She stepped into the aisle, stood straight, hands at her sides, smiling that smile.

"How did you get in here? The church is locked," he asked, his teeth on edge.

"Oh!" she waved. "I don't need doors." Her voice was light and lyrical. She advanced. Michael, on the altar, retreated. She stopped at the altar railing. "Don't be *afraid* of me," she said in her smiling voice. "I'm not here to hurt you."

Finally, he allowed himself to look at her. An unexpected reaction overwhelmed him: *she was perfect*. There was nothing too tall short large or small about her. She glowed in the soft churchlight, her long black hair in wild tangles about shoulders that were pale and without blemish. He detected no makeup (he had gotten good at that), seeing pale red smiling lips, a perfect nose, and large eyes cornflower blue. His gaze dropped to her breasts and rosy nipples, her firm belly, and soft tangle of…

"*Whoa!*" Michael stepped back putting both hands in front of him as if to ward off what he was seeing. She took the step up past the railing, and another step toward Michael. "Stop right there." She did. "Who are you?"

"Don't you know?"

"How did you get in?"

"Like I said, I didn't need the door."

"What if someone sees you? Like this…" he pointed at her nakedness.

"I thought you said the church was locked? Besides, no one can see me but you. You brought me here."

Michael had recovered his sensibilities enough by now to be rational. He took a deep breath. He looked at her more closely. She was too perfect to be real.

"Just tell me, okay? Just tell me who you are."

"Woman," she answered.

"I can see you're a woman."

"No. Not 'a' woman." She reached out and touched Michael's cheek. He pulled back a bit out of reflex but let her make her touch. "Not 'a' woman, Michael. Woman."

"I don't get it."

"But you do 'get it' when saints visit you, right?" her smile was impish. She withdrew her hand from his cheek. They stood now, toe-to-toe. Big heavy damp wingtip to perfect naked little goddess toes. She was half a foot short of Michael's six feet. He took a step back and regarded her darkly.

"I'm all the women, Michael. Your mom, Janice? That's where you got your own beauty. She is a great mom, and she loves you. Remember Judy from 5th grade?"

He was jarred. "What?" *How does she know about Judy?*

"You were a nasty little boy, weren't you?" her laugh was like bells.

"How do you know about..."

"And your three sisters worshipped their big brother, and they still do. Especially Karen. You were there when she needed you most. When no one else was."

"Karen..." *How does she know Karen?*

"And prom night? Shelly was amazing, wasn't she?"

"I was 17 and drunk... wait, why am I telling—"

"And you never even talked to her again. That made her sad. She still thinks of it. And then Robin, and then the other Shelly." Then her tinkling silver laugh. "You must have really liked that name."

Michael stepped back another step, hit the chair with his heel, felt for the arms and slunk down into the seat. He looked down between his feet. He was dizzy.

"Goodness!" she whispered. "You don't act like this when the saints come calling!"

He looked up. "They're not really there. Well, they *are*, but not like *you* are. Not like this."

She held out her hand. "Give me your hand, Michael." He regarded her blankly and offered up his hand as if bewitched. She took it and placed it between her breasts. He did not resist.

"Can you feel my heart beating?" she smiled at him like his mom. "You need to let us back in, Michael. That's your true calling. And that's why I'm here. That's why you sent for me." She moved his hand from the cleft of her breasts full onto her right breast and cupped his hand close. The cold church made her nipple like a raisin in the middle of his palm.

He yanked his hand away hard. He pressed himself into the back of his chair.

"What kind of a… demon are you?" he hissed at her.

"That *would* be your easy answer!" she fairly hissed at him and recovered herself. "I promise you I'm no demon, Michael. I'm *Woman*. There's a *big* difference. Don't imagine for a moment that I'm more or less than that." She was indignant. She standing, he sitting, for a moment, silently. She softened while Michael retreated into himself, thrashing about in his mind for some guidance in this strange moment.

He looked up at her, his face full of entreaty. "Why?" he whispered to her.

She smiled. "I am created for you. You need to let women back in. This is a great gift from yourself to yourself. To stop all the loneliness. Every woman feels it in you when she's near you. All she has to do is look at you. How lonesome you are. How alone." She reached out with both arms and grabbed the top of the chair on either side of Michael's head, "You need to come back down to where you know you need to be. Not solitary. Not so lonely." She lowered herself to him until her nipple touched his trembling lip. He smelled her warmth.

He grabbed around her naked waist and pushed, straightened hard in his chair and pushed again. Holding her at arm's length he looked at his hands, pressing into her flesh, and in the middle her soft belly. He stood up hard pushing her away so forcefully that she almost stumbled. They stood and beheld one another from a few feet away, both of them upset.

"Go." Michael pointed to the door. "Whoever or whatever the hell you are, *just go."*

She smiled. "I don't need the door, remember?" Instead, she descended the three steps down the altar and took a seat in the front pew. She leaned back, bent her right leg and lifted a dainty foot up on the seat. This most intimate display wrestled Michael's attention, and for a moment, just a moment, he abandoned himself to her, and just as instantly pulled himself back in. He closed his eyes and took a breath.

"If you won't leave, then I've got to." In a daze, he stepped toward the door to the sacristy. He turned and pleaded. "Please. Go. And don't ever come back. *Please* don't ever come back." He searched her face for some affirmation in her eyes to his most urgent plea but found nothing there. She sat with her pale mocking smile, betraying nothing, rocking her bended leg open and closed in a slow flag. He turned and vanished through the doorway.

Michael was so unnerved by all this that when it was time to unlock the church to admit the few morning patrons, instead of going through the warm sanctuary, he walked out the back door, unlocked the front door from the outside (for it was indeed locked), without even looking in, and walked around back into the church through the back door. And when he emerged finally onto the altar 90 minutes later, still not nearly recovered from his wild ordeal, his desperate confrontation with the Adversary in the form of Woman, he noted gratefully that there were no naked women among the sparse congregation.

All the usual suspects were present, except for a young woman in the second row he had not seen before. With a fresh shot of anxiety he studied the lass. At first, she smiled and nodded her head in greeting to her priest, but as he kept staring her eyes widened and she looked away, and Michael realized that she was wilting quickly under his fierce and probing stare. He snapped out of it, smiled at the rest of the congregation, said good morning, then looked back at her briefly to confirm with a gush of relief that her nose was too big and her hair was brown.

Michael, of course, called the Bishop right after Mass.

"… but this time, it was flesh and blood. Not a vision. A real actual visitation!"

"Is that so?"

"Your Excellency, I swear to you. It started when I entered the sanctuary, you see…"

"Michael Michael Michael, calm down."

"Sorry. It's just that…"

273

"Come and see me. And come now. We need to talk. No, wait…" the Bishop muted his phone to mutter something and was back in a moment. "Michael? Come at noon."

The Bishop hung up and Michael was seized by new anxiety. *Of course, we need to talk. But what did he mean by that? He thinks I'm crazy. But I'm not crazy. This really happened. He'll understand,* he assured himself. *He knows me, and he loves me. Right?*

Michael arrived at the diocese campus exactly one hour later. He greeted the bishop's secretary, Julian, an old seminary acquaintance whose talent for ingratiation was bound to lead him to this sort of job. Michael never really cared for him very much, this short toady with his bushy blond hair. He especially disliked the way he walked, with his head tilted always to the right as if trying to avoid hitting his head on a basement pipe. Michael knew it was uncharitable, but he couldn't help it. Julian ushered Michael into the Bishop's office, empty of His Excellency, where Michael sat waiting an eternity (ten minutes) for his return.

When the Bishop entered it was an undignified scene. A great old bear of a fellow, he was in a white shirt and old trousers, munching on what appeared to be a very long hot dog, wrapped in a napkin that wasn't really doing its job.

The Bishop stopped, swallowed and smiled at Michael, who sprang up to greet him. "Hey, on Mondays they bring me Coney Islands from down the block. Nice bunch of fellas."

Michael tried for the Bishop's hand, but he waved him off and sat down behind his huge oak desk, put the Coney down, licked a streak of red sauce from his hand, and pushed his monitor out of the way for an unobstructed view at Michael in the chair across.

"So," the Bishop chirped, settling in. "What's all this now about your newest visitation?"

Michael had the feeling that he was being made sport of, and dropped his eyes. The Bishop got it.

"I'm not making fun of you, Mike. Lighten up. But actually, this is quite serious."

274

"Oh God," Michael groaned. "I know it's serious. But you have to understand. This was an actual…"

"An actual what, Mike?" The Bishop resumed his lunch, munching quietly and studying Michael closely.

Michael closed his eyes and considered carefully. The next words would probably be important.

"It was… a physical visitation. This thing, this creature, this woman, knew all about me. She had no way into the locked church. She just… appeared! She was… *perfect.*" Embarrassed, he hid his face with a turn to the wall.

"Start from the beginning, Mike. Give it all to me and spare me nothing." His Excellency serenely resumed his hot dog.

So, Michael turned back, got as comfortable as he could, and spun the tale in excruciating detail, leaving out not a thing. He stumbled a bit over the spicy parts, which amused the Bishop a good deal, but he remained stonefaced so as not to embarrass or distract young Michael. They sat for almost a whole minute in silence when Michael was done.

"So where did she come from?" the Bishop asked, giving his lips and chin a final wipedown and pitching the napkin into the trash.

"Like I said, Your Excellency — she wouldn't tell me."

The Bishop nodded and for a few seconds gave Michael a level stare. "Well… where do you *think* she came from?"

Michael threw up his hands in frustration. "I have no clue!"

"Guess." The Bishop pressed.

Michael considered for a stretch. "Maybe I created her from my own imagination," he said, then looked up and added urgently, "But I swear to you, Excellency, she was as real as you right now. I… I could *smell* her."

"So you couldn't smell St. Francis?" the Bishop quipped.

Ignoring this, Michael dropped his head and closed his eyes. "The things she knew… no one knows about that stuff." He looked up defiantly. "You think I'm insane, don't you?"

The Bishop laughed. "Oh no, son. Not at all." He gave Michael a tender look. "You see, Mike — I sent her."

Michael looked blankly. "I'm sorry. Say again?"

The Bishop only smiled.

It sank in. "You WHAT?!"

After Michael vanished through the altar door, Agnes Teazel heaved a sigh, stopped waving her leg back and forth provocatively on the pew and put her foot back down on the floor, clenching her thighs together and inhaling sharply through clenched teeth. She was cold. She crossed her hands in front of her breasts and shivered. *I am not dressed for this project!* she thought to herself and laughed. *Actually, I suppose I am!*

She rose and padded gingerly to the back of the church, to her backpack in the last pew, snatched it up, and was out the door into the vestibule. There she quickly donned panties, bluejeans, and a sweatshirt with a Red Wings logo. Then she sat on a folding chair and pulled on socks and her furry boots. She found her keys in the bag, also wallet, phone and the keys to the church, deposited all in various appropriate pockets, ran her fingers through her enwildened hair, and was out the door in a jiff, locking it behind her.

It was a short drive to the cathedral office, the heat in the new Audi blowing through only just as she hit the parking lot. She parked and sprinted coatless though a cutting wind, through the office door, breezing past reception, and to the Bishop's office, where the vigilant Julian stood *en garde* in front of the Bishop's door.

"Can I help you?" Julian inquired pointedly.

She screeched to a halt. "Yeah. He knows I'm coming."

"*His Excellency* knows you are coming?"

"Oh please. Just let him know I'm here, hey?" Agnes would share in none of the sanctimony.

Julian moved toward his desk. "He's on the phone right now, why don't you just have a seat—"

But Agnes merely smirked at the lackey and entered in a flash, unbidden, into the Bishop's lair. Julian moved to stop her but too late, for she had shut the door in his face and locked it. She turned to the Bishop and grinned like an imp.

"No, wait..." the Bishop muted his phone and looked over at Agnes. "That was fast. Just a moment." He clicked at the phone. "Michael? Come at noon." He hung up.

"That was him?" she inquired brashly.

The Bishop sighed. "Mary Agnes..."

"Yeah, okay. Sorry. None of my business." She plumped down across from the Bishop in the guest chair.

The Bishop regarded her for a moment. "So?"

She smiled gaily and perched herself on the edge of her chair. "I was *good.*"

"Oh dear." He was distressed. "Who did he think you were?"

"Yeah, he fell for it. He thought I was some supernatural thing or another. Just like you said he would."

"Yes..." His Excellency dropped his eyes and she could swear he looked ashamed. Without looking up, he asked, "And Michael? Did you seduce him?"

Out of pure mischief, she let some time pass in suspense, while the Bishop waited in agony for her answer. But he could wait no longer.

"Well, dammit! *Did you or not?*" he gruffed.

Agnes started at his bark and drew back in her chair. "Relax! Geez. No. I didn't succeed. And it wasn't for lack of trying. I mean, I was good, but... I don't think *anybody* could be good enough. Not for *that* duty."

The Bishop sighed deeply in relief as she went on. "I was naked as a jailbird," she sang, "and all over him. And I may as well have been... I dunno. Tell me he's gay or something."

"Michael?" the Bishop laughed. "Sorry. He's not gay. He's what we call, an actual priest."

She rolled her eyes, then considered this sadly. "I guess I failed you. You're still going to pay me though, right?"

The Bishop had never been able to tell when Mary Agnes was serious. "So, he believed that you were something other than a mere mortal woman, and as hard as you tried, you could not get him to participate in your playing? Is that a correct summary?"

"That's about it," she agreed with a sad face.

His Excellency opened his desk drawer, fiddled about inside for his personal checkbook and took it out along with an old fountain pen. He uncapped it and looked at Agnes. "We agreed on $500?"

"Yep," she said, no longer sad. "A personal check, huh? Not diocese business?" she smiled.

The Bishop scribbled away. "Your promise of confidentiality goes along with this check, as you agreed."

"I keep my word. You needn't remind me."

"I know." He tore the check loose and gave it to Agnes, who placed it snug in her wallet's fold.

The Bishop considered her sadly. "Come back to the Church, Mary."

She stood, put her wallet in her jean's pocket, and regarded the Bishop. "Well, I was going to come back, see? But an evil Bishop made me do this horrible sex thing with a priest, and now I'm so *traumatized* that I could never—"

"Yes yes yes, very funny, Mary."

"And stop calling me Mary. My name is Agnes."

"I've called you Mary all your life. It's your *name*."

"I get to say what my name is."

"Agnes," the Bishop said quietly, "ironically, was your *confirmation* name."

"I like it. It's why I *picked* it." She regarded him for a long moment. He met her stare. "Why did you pick me to do this? You'll go to hell for this you know." The bishop looked away and sighed.

Mary Agnes went on. "Let me tell you why you picked me," she said as she resumed her seat and leaned forward. "First of all because I'm beautiful. You couldn't have done this with just any girl."

"True. You are most beautiful, Mary."

"Thank you. And secondly, because you know I'll never change. I'll always be what I am. I make a living with my charm and with my body. Like my mother did. *And* with my brains, which my mother did *not."*

"But she was part of my Church."

She ignored that. "And I'm very good at it. And I have no patience with your ideas of God or salvation or sin or hell, which you invented to control people or any of that cult nonsense that weakened and tortured my mother to *death.* Invented by men out of shame and cowardice and lust and *guilt."* She grew hotter. "When she lay there dying of the overdose, I tried to calm her down while we waited for the ambulance. She thrashed and mumbled about her sin and her guilt, remember that? You were there. But it was like I *wasn't* there. She died there and never so much as noticed me holding on to her."

"I had hoped that would have kept you off her path. You were only, what, 12 then? We offered you a place with us at The Home."

"Oh puhleeeze," she sat back and groaned. "The Home."

"But you'd have nothing to do with us. Not even for a meal when you were hungry. There was always a place for you here. But you went your own way and broke our hearts. And you always have, and you still do. And I fear you always will."

Did she hear a quiver in his voice? "And that's why I was a safe pick for this," she said quietly.

There was a pall of silence between them, long, but not really uncomfortable as they each considered the other. "You don't have to be a repeat of your mother, Mary."

She looked appalled. *"You still don't get it,"* she said. "I am my mother *perfected.* I enjoy everything good and beautiful and loving that I remember about her and none of the guilt and weakness. I'm *proud* to be who I am. I don't drink or smoke or use drugs, I have a lot of money, a nice car, a lovely home, good investments, friends that are good people — I have everything mom struggled for and failed to get for herself." She pointed a finger at him, "And I support your charities."

He nodded in acknowledgment. "Do you hate me for what I asked you to do?"

"No." She shook her head slowly. "I could never hate you, Bobby. You won't tell me what's going on with this… this incredible movie star priest of yours – *my god is he hot* – but I know you needed to test him for some reason. And it must be important. You would never have done this otherwise," she said, standing up and adding quietly, "and I was kidding about you going to hell."

The Bishop looked up at her. "No. You were right. Though I like to think it's less about individual events and more about overall choices and the effects of a lifetime." He considered. "I did what I thought should be done."

She rose up and stood beside his chair, placed a fond hand on his old shoulder. "Don't worry, Bobby." She said. "There's no hell."

He smiled up at her, rose from his chair and embraced her tightly. "Oh yes there is, my dear, but thank you just the same."

She hugged him harder. "You can use me anytime, you know."

He held her at arm's length. "Only once and never again, Mary. I'm retiring. This is it for me. I'm done." He smiled at her fondly. "Goodbye now. I love you and I pray to God for you."

"Let me know when you go and where, okay?" She made him promise. Mary Agnes kissed his cheek and headed for the door. She stopped and turned to him, reached to her waist and pulled up her sweatshirt to uncover her fine white breasts. "Can you *believe* he didn't want to play with these?" she said with a mock-serious look.

His Excellency sighed and put his face in his hands, mumbling through them, "Goodbye Mary."

She laughed gaily, pulling down her Red Wings top and, turning, yanked on the door. It was locked. Remembering, she laughed again, unlocked it and stepped into the hall, turning toward the secretary and waved with wiggling fingers.

"Bye, Your Toadiness!" she chirped and headed for the exit.

Julian rushed to the Bishop's door. "Everything all right, Excellency?" he said, breathless. "I couldn't stop her."

"No." the Bishop said. "None of us can, evidently." He sighed heavily. "What's for lunch?"

Julian smiled. "It's Mondaaaaayyyyyy!"

The Bishop regarded Julian as if he were a lunatic. "I *know* it's Monday. I didn't ask what *day* it is, you—"

Julian just smiled, and the grumpy Bishop came around with a start. "Oh, Right! Monday! Good!"

"What do you *mean, you* sent her?!" Michael's eyes fairly bulged from his eye-holes.

"Her name is Mary Agnes Teazel," the Bishop recited dryly. "She's the daughter of Jane Teazel, one of my parishioners from St. Thomas when I was pastor there. No one knows who her father is. Jane died of a heroin overdose when Mary was 12. I've kept track of her ever since. And I've tried to bring her to Christ every time I've encountered her. She resents us and she hates the Church." He sighed. "And she always will."

"But… but how could you do that to her? Make her do such a thing?" Michael began to pace the Bishop's office. "I can't believe this."

"We tried to get custody of her," the Bishop looked at the wall. "Put her in The Home. She refused. Evaded the law. Never went to school. Lived on the streets and never took a thing, a dollar or a piece of bread, from us. When she was 17 she took the GED test and passed. She went to State – how she got the tuition money I don't even *want* to know – and got a degree in Business. She's a professional escort and… and prostitute. Not a madam; she has no girls and won't go for that. She has an office in town, with a *secretary*, if you can believe that, and her client list takes her all over the country; maybe the world by now. She's wealthy. And she's managed her money so well that when her… her charms fade, she can live with no worries."

Michael collapsed into the chair, looking beaten. He closed his eyes and dropped his head. The Bishop's heart ached, for what he did to Michael, and for both what he did, and what he could never do, for Mary.

"So, you gave her a key to the church?" Michael asked without looking up.

"Yes."

"And all that stuff she knew about me? You... briefed her?"

"Carefully. Her memory is amazing," he said. "I supplemented what I know of you from our years together with notes from your Jesuit interviews, and various other records."

"That's so... *out of line!* I'm amazed at how dispassionately you're just laying all this out to me," he looked up at the Bishop. "I mean, after what you've done."

"Well, that's between me and God, Mike."

"No. I mean yes, but, it's also between me and you." Michael had calmed down and would have his answers. He made a pleading gesture. "So why? Why did you do this to me? And to her?"

"Why I did this to *her* you have to leave between her and me," he answered. "She and I are square on that account."

"Did you pay her? How much?" Michael asked sharply.

The Bishop stiffened. "Father Byrne, I remind you to keep a civil tongue with me. There is much you don't know that's at work here."

A long moment passed, and Michael apologized. He sat up in his chair, took a deep breath and awaited his due explanation.

"Mike." The Bishop leaned forward and paused to considered his words. "You have visions, and you're a magnet to women. You're learnéd and wise beyond your years. You worry that the priests make fun of you, tease you... but they respect you and their attitudes hide their awe of you. Their ridicule makes them more comfortable with themselves and one another. Understand? They're just men. Christ! We're just men.

"See, if 'fitting in' is what you hope for — forget it. It'll never happen. You're too different and too uncompromising to *ever* fit in." The Bishop's brow darkened, and he said with some bitterness, "And to hell with fitting in."

Michael sighed. "Okay. So?"

"I was obliged to test you."

Michael gave the old Bishop a cold, narrow stare. "Test me for what?"

"Look. The outcome of my project with Mary Teazel could have gone one of four ways." He counted on his fingers. "Number one: you would know that, no matter what she said or how hard she tried, that she was merely a woman trying to dupe you, you would be suspicious of her Salome routine and throw her out on her ear. Number two: you would believe she was just a woman in your church, and you would simply succumb to her charms. Number three: she would succeed in making you believe she was a vision, or something conjured up from within you, and you would fall into her seduction."

"This was about tricking me into *sex?*" Michael was angry again. "You're still not convinced that I am not that kind of priest? After all that—"

"*Listen to me!*" The Bishop was just as heated. "Number four: you would be convinced that she was a vision of some kind but would refuse her offers." He paused for things to settle. "So. Which of the four was it, Mike?"

Michael looked ashamed. "I already told you it was number four," he said. "You and she fooled me pretty good, but she didn't seduce me." He looked at the floor and there was an agony of confusion on his face.

"What." the Bishop asked.

"There was a moment. She was away from me, not touching. But the way she looked, and what she was doing… with her leg… I, in my mind, I abandoned myself to her for just a second, and…"

"Mike Mike Mike!" the Bishop touched his arm. "We aren't sweatin' the small stuff here, okay? I think you'll agree that you could not have been tested more thoroughly by any other woman." The Bishop leaned back in his chair. "No one I ever met, anyway."

Mike looked at the Bishop with a bit of wonder in his eyes. "She was so amazing. She was perfect." He looked back down to the floor.

And so sat the two priests, silently in praise and wonder at the overwhelming beauty of this singular woman.

"So, do you see what this tells me, Michael? And what it ought to be telling you?"

"That I'm a chaste idiot?"

"Your chastity was never in real doubt, Mike, but I had to be more than sure, and I'll tell you why in a moment. But your visions…"

"Yeah… those visions."

"I don't doubt that you have them, but you can't be *fooled* like this," the Bishop said. "I mean, as beautiful as she is, and as good as the setup was, and as good as she was at her deception – she was still just a woman. You've got to be more *careful*, more… skeptical."

"I will be," Michael sighed, disgusted at himself. "So, this one little test covered all the bases." He gave the Bishop a steady look. "That was pretty clever."

"It's why I get the big bucks," the Bishop explained, without a smile.

"Well, then I suppose I should be grateful, Excellency, for your concern and your lesson."

"In private, call me Bob," the Bishop said, ignoring the hint of sarcasm.

Michael perked up. "What?"

The Bishop laughed. "Things are about to change."

"Like what? What things?"

"Everything. I'm retiring, you're about to become a Monsignor, and I'm sending you to Rome."

Michael looked blankly and blinked. He looked away, assimilating.

"That's the reason behind all this nonsense," the Bishop explained. "You see, Mike, I needed to *know*. I needed to know that you could tell the difference between a vision and a fake, *and you can't*. I'm here to tell you *that's not good*. And I needed to make sure that the most charming woman I ever met could not seduce you, the unofficial chick-magnet of the diocese. What did she call you? The 'movie-star priest.' And... she couldn't."

Michael tried to follow all this.

"You see, Mike, where you're going... the visions thing, it might be difficult, but I think it's real, and if you're careful it can even become a blessing on your path in Rome. But the sex thing... I needed to be sure. Roman women, Mike. See, if there's any real scandal, it's *my* ass they'll be coming for, not yours. The way things are now? I had to be more than just sure."

"Okay," Michael said, resigned. "I just wish you didn't have to drag her into it all. I'm ashamed at that."

"Ashamed for *me*," the Bishop said. Michael made quick to correct but the Bishop stopped him with his hand. "I understand. Don't equivocate. In your position I would feel the same way. But I'm a lot older than you, Mike. Grant me the benefit of the doubt that I may understand some things better than you do in my age and position and experience. Please. This is about me, and on me. Not you."

"I *hate* her," Michael said, unexpectedly.

The Bishop was startled and alarmed by this. "Why, Mike?"

"I don't know."

"Meditate on this. You *need* to know."

"The kind of fool that she made of me... I could never have imagined," he whispered.

"That's your ego. Stop it! Hate the deed then, if you have to. But learn from it. And be gentle with her in your mind. She'll never be one of us, but in her way she's a good and honorable woman. We are not allowed to judge her."

"Yes, Your Excellency."

The Bishop raised his eyebrows and stared, waiting.

"I mean… I mean, Bob." They laughed. "But why Rome? I mean, I'm not complaining. I just don't know what to think."

"I don't see you as a parish priest. Your gifts are too unusual. You're… special. You'll bloom with others who are deemed likewise." The bishop threw his hands in the air. "That's the plan, anyway."

"But what will I do? I mean…"

"I don't know the details yet. You'll be interviewed until your ass falls off, I know that much. Be up front. Your future depends on it. And I'll tell you a little secret here: Go after what your heart wants, not what you think God wants for you or any of that other bullshit. Well… not bullshit, but you know what I mean. And Mike, *you need to know what it is that you want.* And in Rome, your charisma will be a plus, not a minus like it is here, if you don't mind me sayin'. You can do a lot of good with it. The Cardinal likes the idea. He likes *you.* So, you're in. You have a month to get your things in order."

The newly-minted Monsignor Michael Byrne, neither glad nor sad, floated home as on a cloud. When he arrived at the rectory, he canceled his few appointments and spent the day staring into space. Not so much meditating as just staring, his mind oddly blank. He supposed he was assimilating things in a way that was not yet conscious to him. He prayed the Hours and went to bed early.

When he rose Tuesday morn, he was still fuzzy, but deliberately locked himself into the old routine. Gradually, he was feeling himself again, and excitement and anguish began to mix as he thought about a new life in Rome.

Bye mom, he thought. *Bye everybody.*

In church for his morning prayers the next day he made his coffee in the cloakroom and turned on the lights in the sanctuary. He stepped out onto the altar, and there was the hated thing itself in the front pew.

He had to look closer to be sure. For on this occasion she was dressed in a grey business suit, her hair was up, and she wore glasses. She looked like she worked in a bank. But it was her. She smiled. She took off her glasses and put them in her purse.

Michael felt rage in himself of a kind that he had never felt before, and to this day knows not whence it came. He clenched his fists. "Get out of here," he hissed, and added, "I think if you were a man, I would hit you."

She laughed her music laugh. "Well, Michael, if I were a *man*..."

"You profaned this place," he said. "you're profaning it now, and you made me a fool."

Her smile vanished. "That takes two." She rose up and walked toward him just as she did the day before, without fear or hesitation.

Michael stood firm. "Get out or I'll throw you out," he warned.

"I came to apologize, actually," she said, and stopped within a foot of him, noting that Michael's face was red, and his teeth were clenched tight. "If I had to do it over," she offered, "I would decline."

The rage Michael was holding so dear was knocked down a notch. He tried hard to maintain it but could not.

"Well that's just swell," he said sarcastically. "So now that that's out of the way why don't you run along."

"We're not done, actually," she said.

"Why? What do you want now? Some way you forgot to humiliate me? Are you getting paid for this, too?"

She took it; brushed it aside. "I got $500 for yesterday. But I sent it back this morning with a nice note to the Bishop. Besides, I failed." She smiled weakly.

Michael nodded. "So what do you want? Forgiveness?"

"That's it," she admitted.

He snorted. "So, for the deed that's filled you with guilt and misgiving, I should forgive you?"

She looked surprised then genuinely baffled. "What? Oh no. I don't care about *that.* You need to forgive me for *your* sake. Not *mine.*" She laughed. "That other thought never entered my head."

Michael was bewildered. "What?"

"Well, I mean, that's what priests need to do, right? If you can't forgive me for *your* sake, then there's something terribly wrong with your soul. Or something. Right? Like, you're in mortal danger or something? And you a priest. I don't want that. If you don't forgive me, *for you own sake,* this hatred will fester in your heart like a disease."

This hit him hard, right between the eyes. He turned away from her and looked at the altar. He held his breath, looked around at the church, the statues and stainedglass, as if he had never been here before. He turned back to Mary Agnes. He looked down and his eyes filled. He started to say something but choked it back and swallowed. Nearly a minute would pass before his calm returned.

"I forgive you," he finally whispered. "I forgive you for your sake," he took a deep breath, "and I forgive you for mine."

"Okay. I'll go now," she whispered back.

"Wait." Michael stepped back, and with the sign of the cross he blessed her in a quiet voice, "I bless you in the Name of the Father, and of the Son, and of the Holy Spirit."

"Amen," she said, without irony. And smiled. "That was nice of you. Thank you." He nodded. She tilted her head, considered a moment, and approached him.

"I can only bless you back as a woman," she said, putting her hands upon his shoulders. "But those are important blessings, too." And she pressed her soft lips to one cheek and then the other, and then sweetly upon his forehead, and then looked into Michael's eyes as she cradled his head in her soft hands.

And Michael saw in her perfect face his mother, and he saw all his sisters, and his playmate and his first love and his fiancée, and he saw them all at once and he saw them all distinctly and separately, and then he had to close his wet eyes tight because he couldn't look there anymore and finally this woman released him of her sorcery, and all alone, and in his darkness, he listened as she walked down the long aisle and at last left the church.

Monsignor Michael stood thus for a moment, lifted his head, finally opened his eyes and wiped his face of his tears. And with sadness he stepped up onto the altar, lit his candles as he always did, sat, and began his morning prayers.

But his mind kept slipping from his prayers that morning, insidiously diverting him into a lifelong game of discerning the subtle but vital differences between the ideas of lonely, solitary, lonesome, and alone.

ಬಂಡ

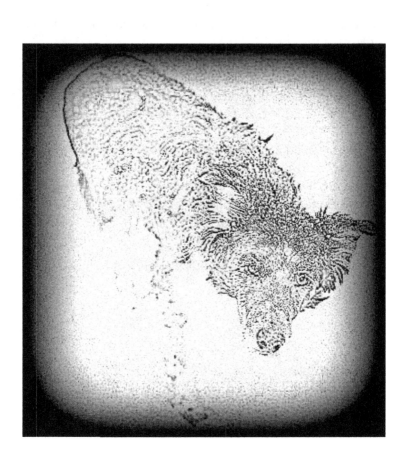

Christmas Story

Dustin has a new truck. It's an F-150 stuffed to the gills with every conceivable option. It's a Christmas gift to himself. In the back is another gift—a Wilson Combat AR-15. That set him back two grand and the scope another $1500. But for the first time in his life Dustin has money and lots of it. His daddy died and his ship came in to the tune of four million and change. A new house is next, and he wonders *build or buy? ...*

It's Christmas in three days, and Dustin thought he'd head to the Upper Peninsula and do a little hunting—the third gift to himself this holiday season. Thus the new truck; thus the rifle. He hasn't hunted in what, 10 years? The AR is vastly different from his old bolt-action Savage—a hand-me-down from his grampa. The AR is semi-automatic, light, black and 'scary-looking' as his sister noted the day he bought it. He's only shot it on one occasion and that was to sight it in at the range.

He's 32 come January. He lives alone, no woman, no kids, no pets. He's lonely and though women like him for his slim good looks and kind manner he just hasn't found that special someone. He has fond hopes but he's getting tired of the singles' scene. Dustin teaches English to middle-school kids but that was before his newly acquired riches, and he's been re-assessing his future. He likes kids and would like to have a family someday. *Tick tock, tick tock,* he thinks to himself and laughs. He'll finish out the schoolyear but is considering, at the very least, a sabbatical. A long vacation. Maybe in the Caribbean. "Why the hell not?" he says aloud. He understands that his new millionaire status will dramatically increase the number of interested females, but he sees the trap there and he finds it worrisome.

He crossed the bridge about 90 minutes ago and it's snowing. There's about a half-foot on the ground (very light for this time of year up here) and he's actually hoping for more. He's anxious to test the new truck in harsh conditions— something the U.P. is happy to offer, especially this time of year. His uncle has a cabin south of Munising not too far from Perch Lake. He was there a few times as a teenager and Dustin has always had an open invite to hunt up that way but never took his uncle up on the offer.

He just spotted the logging trail that tells him he's only a mile or so out. It's been a long drive and it's almost dark. That happens early up here in late December.

Dustin found the cabin with no trouble, unloaded, turned on the baseboard heat and started a fire (his uncle had a put a cord of wood under a tarp outside the rear door). The fridge contents, courtesy of Uncle Jake, was filled with beer, lunch-meat and assorted frozen delights that will pair deliciously with the microwave on the counter. Dustin nuked up a frozen pizza. He matched it with three beers and fell asleep in front of the fire listening to classical music from Interlochen on the radio.

He slept like a log and rose at 7 a.m. It was still black as night. There was no moon, no stars. It was cloudy and still snowing, maybe another half-foot on the ground since last night. He made breakfast and watched the sky gradually brighten and the clouds thin out, and by sunrise at 8:30 the snow had stopped, and golden morning rays flooded the small kitchen of the cabin.

Dustin grabbed his gear and dressed in his all-new hunting clothing. It seemed to him more like a costume. He copped a look in the bedroom mirror as he was on his way out the door and had to admit that he looked more like a model in a hunting gear fashion show than an actual hunter. He took comfort in the notion that running into a single other human being in this remote wild was unlikely.

He strapped on his daypack with some sandwiches, water, map, compass, skinning knife (the only thing that wasn't new; his granddad gave him the knife when Dustin was just a boy) flashlight, rope and such. The magazine that came with the gun holds 30 rounds of .223, but in Michigan you're not allowed in the field with that much firepower. He had to use a small 5-round hunting magazine. So he had to carry some spare ammo in that pack, too. Up here his phone was useless. No signal. But he put it in the pack, admitting to himself that he felt naked without it.

He opened the cabin door and stepped outside to a glorious, if chilly, Michigan morning, and slung the rifle over his shoulder. He had parlayed with his uncle by phone and email about how best to proceed to maximize his chances at a successful hunt. The terrain was splayed out exactly as his uncle had described and Dustin trudged northwest through a foot of snow toward Perch Lake, through a landscape of young pines, the area logged out about ten years previously. It was good habitat for game. Dustin was optimistic.

Dustin was 'still-hunting,' which is the opposite of what it might seem. One doesn't stay still, rather, one sneakey-petes about the woods in a glacially slow and stealthy manner. It took Dustin about a half-hour to move through about 200 yards of trees and brush before he saw the movement. He stopped and slowly brought the rifle up, peering through the scope which was giving him nine times more magnification than his naked eye, and he saw the snout of the beast the same moment that it broke through the brush and sprinted toward Dustin.

He lowered his weapon as the skinny mutt came to a dead stop in front of him and started to sniff his boots. Disappointed, but he had to laugh. What was not so funny was the fact that unleashed dogs, or even fenced or leashed dogs outside the home are anathema to a decent hunt. Sometimes the dogs will chase the deer, and the mere barking of a dog that gets wind of a deer in the vicinity will alert the deer to avoid the area.

Dustin squatted down and petted the poor dog. He... check that... *she* was emaciated to an almost skeletal state. She shivered in the cold. Dustin took off his daypack, unbound it and fished inside for one of the two ham sandwiches he had packed, unbagged it, and tossed it near the poor mutt who fell upon it, gorging and whimpering in, what, joy? Relief?

He considered the dog as she fed. It was medium size and of mixed breed. Dustin thought he could discern Golden Retriever and maybe German Shepard in the mix. No collar or tags, nothing to identify the animal. She bolted her meal in short order and turned to her savior, hoping for more food. It dawned on Dustin that he was about to be faced with a tough decision.

The poor stray would not last long, likely not survive the *night*, as a cold front was on its way that would pull the mercury down to a predicted -20F. The dog whimpered and its shivering had not stopped. After a tortured few minutes, Dustin decided that the humane thing to do was to put the tormented dog down. *Could I even do this?* he wondered. He reconsidered.

Finally resolved, he bent to his pack and unwrapped the other sandwich, tore off a third of it, and tossed it a few feet from the dog, who sprung upon it. Dustin raised his rife, snicked off the safety, and fired a single, instantly mortal shot.

He stood there like a mannequin for what seemed like minutes. The ordeal had quite completely taken the ginger out of him. He wanted to go back to the cabin. Call it a day. No joy for this right now. *What am I doing here?* he thought. At length he reasoned that he had committed a defensible act of mercy, so he reconsidered his reticence to go on with his day as planned. He concluded finally that he would continue his still-hunt to the shores of the lake and head back the same way, determined now to at least try to enjoy the hunt as intended.

But he saw nothing in the way of big game, in fact, not so much as a squirrel or rabbit all the way to the shores of Perch Lake. He slogged back along his trail for a couple hundred yards and sat inside a gaggle of young pines. It made a good blind. He drank water and finished his sandwich, all the while looking sharp for a whitetail he might claim as his own.

Securing his pack and rifle to his body he stepped outside his blind to resume the hunt and saw another hunter through the pines about 50 yards away moving toward him, waving. The fellow was average height and build, with well-worn field clothes and a pair of binoculars hanging from a strap about his neck. He had a bolt-action rifle, also slung onto his back so there was no feel of a threat to his advance. The stranger stopped right outside Dustin's comfort zone. The man looked a little frantic.

He nodded at Dustin. "Hey, buddy," he said. "I'm Wayne. I live nearby."

Dustin offered his gloved hand. "I'm Dustin. Staying at a cabin nearby."

"I wonder if you can give me a hand?" Wayne said.

"You look upset," Dustin said. "How can I help you?" He noted the man had tears in his eyes.

"Have you seen my dog?"

There was not another sentence that could have been uttered by anyone on the planet that could have shaken Dustin more deeply to his core. It took him a moment to come back to himself and when he did, he realized that he had could not have possibly concealed his reaction very well. He closed his eyes for a moment and opened them again, giving Wayne a level look.

"No," he said flatly. "No dogs. Actually, no nothing. Not a rabbit or a squirrel. Nothing."

"Oh, Jesus," Wayne looked like he was about to cry. "Well... will you help me look for Rocket?"

"Rocket?"

"The dog used to be a real ball of energy. No more, though. Only five years old and looks ten. Sick for a year now, but I don't have the $600 to fix Rocket. The kids love that dog, I tell you what! I gotta find Rocket. Please... let's just walk and keep an eye out. We can head back the way you came so you won't be put out none."

"Well... sure." Dustin knew the danger of backtracking toward the carcass of Wayne's dog, but he wasn't about to tell him no. "Maybe we ought to split up."

Wayne considered this briefly. "Nah. I'll look to the right, and you look to the left and I'll call out for her."

They walked for about 20 minutes, looking out while calling out to Rocket that she might come running through the brush or that they might hear a familiar bark. As the pair approached the scene of the crime Dustin's anxiety naturally increased and his mind raced for a way out.

Dustin stopped and pointed 45-degrees right from the line they were walking. "Why don't we try it my way? You head off that way," he pointed left, "and I'll try our luck in that direction and we'll meet at the cabin for some coffee."

Wayne gave Dustin a look of suspicion that sent a chill down Dustin's spine. "Why do that?" Wayne asked. "I can see the smoke from your chimney. We're almost there."

And with that Wayne gave Dustin a curious look and continued along the line to the cabin. Dustin began to panic. He was yards away from the man whose dog he killed, that man was anxious and unstable, and he had a rife strapped to his back.

Wayne spied something about 20 yards away near the trail and broke into a run. He came upon the dog, fell to his knees and cried out. Dustin's blood froze at the sound. Wayne bent over the corpse of the dog and wept loudly. Dustin's mind raced for a way out of this predicament that hadn't even begun to resolve. All the unpleasantness was ahead, and Dustin had not a clue.

Suddenly Wayne ceased his crying, stood and trudge over to a small bush wherein something gleamed a golden glint. He reached into the snow and picked up the item to examine. He held it out to Dustin to see.

"This is a brass cartridge case ejected from a .223 rifle," Wayne said with a ghostly calm. "This is *yours*. No one around here hunts with one of those things. Underpowered for one thing."

Dustin was always a terrible liar, but even the best of dissemblers would realize that the jig was up. He bowed his head and spoke.

"I thought it was a stray. It was emaciated, sick, shivering… no collar, no tags. I gave her a last meal and put her down in a happy moment. I am as sorry and ashamed as a person can be."

"She wasn't neglected, she was *sick!*" Wayne cried. "We try to take care of her but she's just too *sick*. The kids worship that little bitch. My youngest let the door open and Rocket got out. That was yesterday. We knew she didn't have long but we wanted to take the best care of her that we could until she passed."

"I never would have…" Dustin tongue was slow. "I took no pleasure…"

"Yah know, buddy…" Wayne was not placated. "The holidays are hard enough without…" Wayne closed his eyes and just stood there in the sunshine, looking as miserable as a man could be. Nothing happened for a full minute as each man wallowed in his own torment.

"I know it's a lame thing to do," Wayne said at last, "and please don't be insulted, but I would like to compensate the only way I can."

Wayne opened his eyes. "How's that?"

Dustin took off his gloves and tossed them in the snow. He unzipped a hip pocket and removed his wallet, unfolding it and removing nine $100 bills. (He keeps $1000 of cash on him. A new habit.) He held the bills out to Wayne, who studied the proffered wad of money for a moment before he took it from Dustin's hand.

"There's $900 there. I know it can't make up for your loss but it's all I can do. That's most all the cash I brought with me."

Wayne put the folded bills in the pocket of his jeans and looked at Dustin. "Well…" he began, "I guess-"

At that moment Wayne was interrupted by a lumbering fellow approaching them from where back where they had tread, calling out, "Hey, Doug!"

"Shit!" Wayne hissed.

The man walked up to 'Wayne' and punched him playfully in the shoulder. "Yo Doug. What up, brother?" The fellow looked down at the corpse of the dog. "You finally shoot that old stray? I almost took him out yesterday myself. Poor things was goin' fast." He looked up at Dustin. "Who are you?"

"I'm Dustin."

"I'm Eddy. You a friend of Doug?"

Dustin shook his head slowly as the reality of the situation began to dawn on him. "Not exactly."

In a fluid move, Doug, AKA Wayne, slipped the rifle from his back with a jerk of his shoulder, held it ready, snicked off the safety and raised the barrel to point at Dustin's chest. Dustin stepped back.

Big Eddy's brow darkened. He looked at Doug. "What the fuck's goin' on?"

Dustin studied Doug. "Well, you already robbed me. Now you want to shoot me?"

"I didn't rob you; you *gave* me that money."

"You know what I'm saying." Dustin narrowed his eyes at Doug. "How did you even know?"

Without taking his eyes off Dustin or moving the barrel of his gun from covering Dustin's chest, Doug gestured with his head to his left and somewhat behind him.

"See that ridge where you can't see the lake anymore? That little rise?" Dustin nodded. "It ain't high but it's high enough. I was up there and heard a shot. These binoculars gave me a good view of you and the dead dog."

Dustin nodded. "I get it. Pretend it was yours and hope for sympathy in the form of a payoff."

Doug chuckled. "It worked."

"But that's not right," Dustin said simplistically. He felt oddly fearless. "How could a man... I want you to give me my money back."

298

"Alright, let me explain something to you. You come up here in a new truck, with some goofy-ass small-calibre urban battle rifle, and the new designer clothes make you like the spokesman for Gay Hunters Unlimited, and you pull $900 out of your wallet like it wasn't nothin'."

"That doesn't mean-"

"I ain't finished. I'm out of work. I got a wife and two kids and will lose the house if something doesn't click for me soon. But I'll tell you something, buddy." He takes his hand off the rifle stock and pats his jean pocket. "My family is going to have an actual goddamn *Christmas* this year. There'll be a tree, and presents, and good booze, and a dinner fit for the Green Bay goddamn Packers on the table. And you—*you can afford it! You see where I'm comin' from?*"

Dustin studied Doug for a moment then, carefully and slowly, reached out his hand with index finger pointed and raised it to touch the side of the barrel of Doug's rifle, and gently pushed the barrel away from the point of Dustin's chest. Doug got the message and somewhat reluctantly dropped the barrel to point safely at the ground at his side. He snicked the safety on.

Doug repeated, with more calm now, "You see where I'm comin' from?"

Dustin reached up to his zippered coat pocket, too suddenly, and immediately the barrel of the gun came up again, pointed at Dustin's chest.

"Whoa!" Doug demanded. "What are you doin'?"

Dustin held the palms of both hands out, then slowly unzipped the pocket and took out his wallet. He opened it and removed the remaining $100 bill, closed the wallet, put it back into his pocket and zipped it shut. He held the bill out to Doug, who studied the gesture for a moment then held out his rifle for big Eddy to hold onto. Eddy took the gun. Doug reached out and took the bill from Dustin.

"What's this for?" he asked.

"I'm sorry for your bad luck. I want you and your family to have a good Christmas. And I hope things turn around for you this year." Dustin nodded at both men. "Merry Christmas," he said, picked up his gloves and started to trudge back to the cabin.

Doug watched him walk away and after a few seconds mumbled "No."

"You say somethin'?" Eddy asked.

Doug looked at Eddy. "I said 'no.'" He called out to Dustin. "Hey! Wait up a minute!"

They stood now face-to-face. Doug reached into his jean's pocket and shoved the ten $100 bills at Dustin.

Dustin looked at the bills, then at Doug. "No. I don't want it back," he said. "I want you and your family to have a good Christmas." He laughed to himself. "You were right: I can afford it. Plus... all my new stuff. It's a bit much. I'm not much of a hunter. I don't know what I'm doing up here, really. It isn't me. Know what I mean?"

This seemed to make Doug feel even worse. He shook his head, and his eyes were glazed with wetness. "I don't... I ain't got no kids. I got no family. I got an all-right job. I work with Eddy at the foundry." He stood looking down at the ground as if unable to meet Dustin's eyes. "I can't take the money, mister. I was wrong. About this whole thing." He looked up. "And I'm sorry. But please... please take the money back."

Dustin took the wad of bills and stuffed it into his pants pocket. "I understand. No hard feelings." Dustin took off his glove and offered his hand to Doug. "Merry Christmas, Doug."

Doug embraced Dustin's proffered hand and held it for a moment. "Merry Christmas, Dustin."

Dustin turned and trod back in the direction of the cabin. Eddy moved to join Doug, who frantically wiped at his eyes and cheeks to hide evidence of his humanity before another guy showed up.

"I can't believe you gave all that cash back," Eddy said. "You got that by your own wits, dude. Shoulda kept it. That sucker was a godsend."

Doug's laugh was alloyed by a little bitterness. "You don't get it do you, Ed?"

"Guess not," Eddy said. "But I am gettin' *thirsty*. How 'bout you?"

Doug looked at his watch and sighed. "I guess it's noon somewhere." He laughed. The bitterness gone. "Let's do it."

Christmas Day, 2021

Stumblebum

So anyway, here's why they called him Stumblebum. He was a music professor at the University and his real name was Stanley Bumbrey. He had peripheral neuropathy in his feet, and he had it bad. He said it felt like he was walking on electrified gravel. It was painful and gave him balance problems, so he stumbled a lot. And he dressed like a bum because he never cared what he looked like. So they called him Stumblebum behind his back but rarely to his face. His friends and colleagues called him SB. Ess-Bee. He said only his mom, dead for years, ever called him Stanley. I always called him Stumblebum.

Bran Englander was a composer. He's famous now in music circles, even more so since his untimely death at age 38, but that's how the arts work. Die and get more famous. For a while. But back in the day he was just another college-age kid who wasn't in college.

He didn't go the Music School at the University, but he loved hanging out on the campus and he particularly enjoyed playing and practicing on one of the many Steinway grands available inside. That was forbidden to non-students, but he was a good pianist and had an air about him that you would naturally just let him go about his business. Bran's parents wanted him to go to school and would pay the full ride, even housing for the lad, but something held him back.

Bran drove up to North Campus that day for a fateful stroll around the fountain and some meditation on his future. But his mind was a blank and the strolling was an annoyance. He sat on a bench near the fountain and decided to look at girls. That often jarred his brain in a fruitful direction. But instead of a lovely co-ed, his eyes alighted on the opposite—a bum who was walking funny and heading right toward him. At length Bran recognized him as Stanley Bumbrey, the famed recording artist who used to teach here. Bumbrey walked right up to where Bran sat, and Bran stood to acknowledge him.

"Mr. Bumbrey," Bran extended his hand. "It's an honor, sir. I have all your Liszt records."

"Call me SB."

"Yes, sir, SB."

"Did you steal them?"

Bran was confused, then anxious. "Steal? Umm... you mean the Liszt stuff?"

"Yeah. Did you buy it or steal it? Don't lie to me."

Busted. "Yeah I... I got them online. At a file sharing site." *Embarrassing much?*

The bum laughed. "Yeah, I figured. You kids never buy music do you?"

Bran was too embarrassed to reply to this.

"Relax," Bumbry said. "I was just bustin' your balls." He bid Bran to sit and he sat next to Bran on the bench. "You look forlorn, kid. What's the matter?

It seemed like a sincere question, so Bran answered sincerely. "Well, sir, I mean SD, I have a chance to go to the U but I'm not sure it's for me." Poor Bran thought they were going to have a nice light chat.

"Huh," SD gruffed. They sat for a space in silence. "You a composer? You look like a composer."

"Yeah, mainly. I play piano, too."

"Good as I was?"

Bran laughed. "Hell no. Not nearly."

"Then forget the piano. You're not thinking of trying to be a pro pianist are you? Because you don't have it in you." He waited. "Do you?"

Bran looked at SB and studied his face for the first time. He shook his head. "No. I'll never be that good."

"Are you even a composer?"

At this young Bran took offense. "You're goddam right I am!" he almost yelled. "And I'll spit in the eye of any son of a bitch that says I'm not!" It was a reflex action that surprised him more than the old man.

SB smiled a big smile. "That's more like it."

Bran settled down and immediately regretted his outburst. "Sorry... I didn't mean-"

"Sure you did," SB said. "What do you expect to get out of going here?"

"To be honest-"

"The minute you're not, I'm gone."

Bran considered his words carefully, then decided on just one. "Connections," he said. "For the connections."

"So, what, you think there's nothing that a seasoned composition teacher or theory teacher can teach you?"

Bran's honesty controlled his tongue. "Correct. I don't need teaching. I know what I want to do, and I can do it."

SB nodded and considered. "So you want connections. Do you know what you have to do to get connected?"

Bran was quick. "Sell my soul?"

"You catch on quick." SB laughed. "Listen Bran, there are two kinds of composition students. The first is someone who needs to be taught. These people are useless because anyone who is any good already knows these things because most of it is inborn and the rest he's already taught himself. The second type is the one who wants connections. And he's useless because once he's sold his soul he has nothing worthwhile to say."

Bran felt like he was having a religious experience. He wanted to tell this man everything.

"I'm writing a symphony."

"Huh," SB gruffed, unimpressed. "You sure? The form is pretty worn out by now."

"It might be the last one of an era that's about to vanish," Bran said.

SB smiled and nodded. "You have some understanding."

Bran rose from the bench and took SB's hand with tears in his eyes. "Thank you, sir." Bran touched SB's shoulder with his other hand. "Thank you."

Bran turned away and went home. Decision made. Sorry mom and dad.

That was the sort of thing that Stumblebum did. He always seemed to know whom to target, and he never stopped teaching. But he had transcended the teaching of mere music; he showed artists how to find themselves and blossom.

Stanley Bumbrey, aka SB, aka Stumblebum had made a good living as a professor, but he made even more money with his recordings of the *Complete Piano Music of Franz Liszt*. He recorded all of it. 121 hours of piano music. 99 CDs. Some of the hardest stuff ever written. That's what made him in the music world. Professors are a dime a dozen like anybody else, but Stumblebum, he was amazing.

He would also play recitals. All over the world even though he hated travelling. Not just Liszt, he could play anybody. Never needed the score. Did it all from memory. And all solo recitals, never with orchestras and no chamber music. He was a solo piano guy and it made him rich and famous. Well, in classical music circles he was famous.

The tragedy was that his peripheral neuropathy started to show up in his hands. He managed to complete the Liszt project and was contemplating recording Bach's *Well-Tempered Clavier*, but he couldn't do it. His fingers were slowly but surely turning into electrified sausages. He gave up playing and he gave up teaching. But still he haunted the North Campus area like a crazy old monk, talking and giving advice to music and art students who would dare engage him. His walking got even worse and he no longer cared what he looked like. Or smelled like.

So. There it is. Stumblebum.

Andre Floyd worked in glass. He was in his third year at the School of Art & Architecture. His father had offered him a job in the insurance firm he owned back in Chicago. Andre was insulted. Why couldn't his father understand that he wanted to be an artist!?

SB spotted him sitting on the nearby hill staring at the play of waters of the big fountain. As SB made his way to Andre the lad thought the old fellow reminded him of a character in a Samuel Beckett novel he read, dressed like a panhandler from downtown whose feet splayed in different directions when he walked. He stifled a laugh as the man got close.

SB presumed to just sit down right next to Andre. SB looked him over and asked, "So what are you so down about?"

Andre was too startled by SB not to answer. "Just... just thinking about the future, I guess."

"You an artist? You look like a... wait..." SB gave him another good look. "A sculptor?"

"Close," the kid smiled. "I work in glass."

"You any good?"

Now, Andre never thought about this quite so starkly and no one had ever asked him. "I dunno... I guess."

"You guess, eh?" SB looked away from the kid, stared at the fountain for a space. "So what's your big dilemma?"

"I'm sick of being poor, for one thing."

"Being poor sucks plenty. What else?"

"My dad offered me a job at his firm." Andre looked hard at SD and wondered why in the world he was spilling his guts to this old bird. "But I want to be an artist."

"But you aren't an artist."

This took a moment to sink in. "I'm sorry. What did you say to me?"

"You're afraid of poverty, you don't know if you're any good or not, and you're seriously considering selling insurance."

"Well... no one wants to be poor and doesn't everybody have doubts about themselves?" He was a little indignant.

"And you didn't even defend yourself against me saying you aren't an artist. You even admitted that you weren't one, but you wanted to become one."

"Yeah, but..." Andre was angry. "Who the hell are you to be telling me this stuff?"

"Well," SB laughed, "it's true—your teachers should be the ones letting you know this, but if they all did their jobs properly there would hardly be anyone in the classroom."

"That's cynical," Andre said lamely.

"You don't want your dad to think you failed."

Andre couldn't even answer this. He looked away from SB and stared at the grass between his shoes.

"So it's a pride thing. Sounds like you're lucky to have a dad that wants the best for you. Seems to me he gave you a chance at this, this hobby of yours, and you don't even know if you're any good at it. I wish

to hell I had a dad like you have. At least I would have known he cared."

SB stood and winced at the pain in his legs. "Don't let pride ruin your life, kid. Leave the art to the poor bastards who don't know where their bed is from night to night or what they're going to eat but have no choice about any of that because they're on fire. The ones who know they're already artists and have never doubted it for a minute. Let those poor bastards do the art. Don't force a path that's not yours. Misery waits there."

SB walked away and never even noticed that the kid was in tears. Cleansing tears.

So Stumblebum not only showed the few artists he encountered how to live and blossom, he was also brilliant at culling from the garden the many weeds who had no claim in it.

Stumblebum's neuropathy wasn't really the biggest tragedy of his life. Meeting me, that's what really did him in. He did quite a number on me, too.

I had problems of my own at the time. Back in my high-school years my psychological issues were really starting to become, well, *vivid*, let's say. My dad raised me, and he was a monster prick. He abused me bad. Not sex, never with sex, but with just about every cruelty imaginable and he regularly beat the shit out of me. I ran away when I was 15, after I beat the shit out of *him*, then went to live with older friends and parents of friends.

I managed to finish high school. It was all I had as an escape and I was a good student. Mainly, I was a good artist. I drew and painted but mostly drew because to paint you need stuff and a place to do it and drawing you can do anywhere. I took three years off before I started college. Here at the U I get to paint—you wouldn't believe how awesomely the studios there are outfitted. Anything in the world you could want.

Jail got me a few times. So I had a record. Assault. Aggravated Assault. Vandalism. No biggies. Some jail, no prison. But man could I draw. I got into the University on a scholarship. They thought I was a friggin' genius. They even started to convince *me*, but then... well... then I met Stumblebum.

I was walking down the steps of the art school and I bashed right into him. I wasn't paying no attention. I was listening to music on my goddam iPhone and I blanked out. Stupid thing to do, not being aware of what's going down around you but that was me. Nearly knocked him on his ass. He was always pretty unsteady. I was carrying my portfolio, such as it was, and it fell and blew all over the steps.

We both rushed to collect the papers—drawings and oils I remember they were. This old guy, he picked up a few and stopped. Just stood there looking at the stuff. I gathered everything finally and approached him for the things he captured. He looked at me.

"Who are you?" he ordered.

"Who are *you?*" I answered. I was pissed that he would ask me that, but then I looked and saw who it was. "Wait," I said. "You're that professor and piano guy. The one they called Stumblebum." I like music and I knew he was somebody big.

That annoyed him but he recovered quickly. I admired that. "Yeah, some call me that. And I guess I am. But I asked you what your goddam name is, and I expect an answer."

Now, nobody talks to me that way. Not without some very unpleasant follow-up. But he was old, and he was the real deal. So I didn't fuck him up.

"I'm Darrell Lane," I said. "And you're the guy that did all that crazy Liszt shit."

"Not a fan?"

"Too much glitz. Shallow."

SB nodded. "Some of it. It was a different age."

"You taught here for years. Stanley... Bumbrey, right?"

SB offered his hand. "Pleased to meet you," he said. I shook it. I should have just walked away, I think, sometimes. But at that moment we entered each other's world.

"Can I have my stuff back, please?" I was being polite.

"How about I look at the rest of it?" he said. "Let's sit near the fountain."

"Maybe I got stuff to do."

"Maybe you don't," he laughed. "C'mon."

"What the fuck *is* it with you, man?"

"Here." And he shoved my bundle of stuff at me. "So what's the problem? You ashamed of this stuff? Or what?"

I swear I nearly smacked him for that, but instead I just laughed and shook my head. "Man you got some balls to be sayin' that shit to me. Or maybe you're just crazy."

He thought about that. "Maybe a little of both." He reached into his pocket and brought forth a small bottle of spring water. "Here," he said, "you look thirsty."

I *was* thirsty. I took the water and unscrewed the cap and drained half of it right there. I considered the situation. It was weird. So I went along. I had nowhere to go and nothing planned.

"All right," I said. "Let's sit for a minute and you can look at this stuff if you want."

So we did. He looked at all of it, about 20 drawings and five or six oils. It was nice out. Leaves falling. Cool. Breezy. Hot chicks walking by. I was just chillin'. I might have fallen asleep if he hadn't asked me so many questions about the work. *Good* questions. He was smart. Like I said—the real deal.

His last question was a real kick in the nuts though.

"Darrell," he fixed me with that look he had. "What are doing here? At the art school."

"*What?!* What do you mean?" I snatched my portfolio back. "You don't like this stuff? This is good work! God *damn* good work!"

"Yeah, calm down. That's what I mean."

"Oh… well then… I guess I'm here to learn stuff," I said, defensively.

He laughed. At *me*. He said, "No you're not." I clenched my fist and he noticed that, and then he laughed some more.

310

I was so mad that I started wondering what I was going to do with this guy to straighten him out on a few things. But he kept talking.

"You're not here to learn anything, and you probably haven't, other than how to use tools you never had access to before. But you know how to use those tools now. I know why you're here and so do you: You need a good studio, and you can't afford one. So, you use the scholarship for access to tools and space. You're here on a scholarship, right?"

Those were, literally, stunning observations. "You are one clever-ass Stumblebum." He hit all the nails on the head and that, for some reason, annoyed me tremendously. I stood. "But when I want your advice, I'll ask for it."

He looked up and smiled. "I never gave you any advice," he said. "But if you want some, be here tomorrow about the same time."

"Hold your breath, Stumblebum."

And I was out of there.

SB watched Darrell as he left in a huff, envying his youthful grace as he ascended the hill near the fountain and lost sight of him as he disappeared down the other side. He looked at his watch and decided to go home and make some dinner.

He was always quite a sight on his walks home from North Campus. It was almost a mile walk to and from his condominium, but he did it every day except Sunday, when he rested for most of the day. By the time he arrived home it was almost 5 p.m. and he was particularly stiff and sore. He opened his front door and threw himself with a groan of relief onto his big couch. He wondered, briefly, what to make for dinner but promptly fell asleep before he could decide.

When he awoke it was after seven and getting dark. He felt lousy, as he always did when a nap was too long, or too short. He stumbled to the kitchen and poured himself a Scotch, shot back half and put the glass on a table near his La-Z-Boy. He shuffled through a stack of old LPs, found Busch Quartet Plays Late Beethoven, *and queued up the Opus 130 on the turntable. The record sounded staticky and like it needed cleaning, but SB was not terribly fastidious about this sort of thing, not when he was impatient to hear something.*

He was the only one he knew who played LP records, so ancient was the technology. For what he paid for his stereo gear one could have bought a nice house in Detroit. Maybe two. This was unusual for a musician. Most can't afford a great stereo or don't care enough to own one. But he wasn't a musician anymore, was he? The 9-foot Steinway D in the middle of the living room was out of tune and hadn't been touched in years. He just couldn't sell it. It was a piece of his heart.

He turned the music down and called Clarence, his old secretary when he used to need a secretary. Now he was simply SB's oldest and only true friend. Clarence idolized SB and they were devoted to one another. They talked for nearly an hour, as they usually did once a week or so when they couldn't otherwise get together in person. SB told Clarence of his new discovery, the wayward and brilliant Darrell. SB had a plan and wanted to bounce it off of Clarence. He wanted to protect the kid, open doors for him and take care of him with his greater wisdom, worldly savvy, and of course, money.

After the call concluded he sipped at his Scotch and decided to look in the refrigerator for food; it was too late to cook a decent meal. There were leftover spareribs and for that he was most grateful. He nuked them up, refilled his glass with booze and sat, listening and eating, and thinking about what he was going to do with this one-in-a-million talent, this Darrell boy. This could be an interesting hobby!

The next day was a Saturday and there were no classes. And it was raining. So I figured fuck even thinking about seeing that stumbling bum Stumblebum. I mean, who the hell does he think he is? I guess he was right about how come I'm at the art school, but he is one rude mother. I ought to have bitch-slapped him. Prick.

What advice could he have for me, anyway? I thought, maybe he's an old queer trying to get at me. Never did get married. Except to the piano. Then I figured, nah. He doesn't seem gay.

So then I thought I'd put a raincoat on and grab an umbrella and drive to campus. I mean, if he was crazy enough to

312

be sitting there in the rain then maybe… maybe I oughta hear him out.

So I drove to campus and figured I could see if he was near the fountain from the C Lot. So I tooled over there and sure enough, there was the crazy bastard sitting on the bench in the rain. Same clothes he always wore. No coat, hat, umbrella—nothing. I looked at the raincoat and umbrella in my back seat. Shit. I'd feel stupid with all that stuff on. If Stumblebum can take it, so can I. So I get out of the car, it's raining medium-hard, and I was soaked to the bone by the time I got to his bench.

"Welcome to my office. Come on in." And he patted the empty side of the bench and I sat my ass down on a cold puddle. Marvelous. I didn't say a word. I just stared at him. Gave him my best stare. I truly hoped I wasn't there just to get a case of swamp-ass.

My menacing glare seemed to have bothered him not at all. "How do you get by, Darrell? What do you do for money?"

That was a reasonable question, so I answered. "I got that full scholarship, so I don't need much. I do some commercial drawing. The school has contacts with different companies, and they hit on us for one-shot deals or various projects. So I get by. Barely, but I do. Plus I sell weed sometimes." Fuck him if he didn't like it.

"Live in a dorm?"

"Apartment with three other guys."

"Friends?"

I shook my head thinking about them. "Not really."

Stumblebum sat there looking thoughtful. The rain was just a mist now.

"Let's go for a ride."

"What? Where? *Now?*"

SB stood and grimaced in pain. "Yep. I wanna show you something."

I rose and shook my head at the old man. "I don't know why I'm curious. But I am." And we walked together, slowly, back to my car. Soaking wet, we squished into the seats of the old Toyota Corolla and were off. The rain stopped and the sun was out.

We drove about 15 minutes to a small building on a rural road in good shape, brick and lots of windows, and pulled into the small asphalt lot which badly needed resurfacing. We got out, SB fumbled out a set of keys and opened the front door. The place was completely empty. I mean totally. No chairs, tables, appliances, nothing. Nothing except—glorious sunlight.

"Whaddaya think," Stumblebum asked me. I didn't dare let on.

"About what?"

He looked at me like I was a dumbass. "About *this*. As a studio. And you can live here. Look around." I did. There was another room, also a small kitchenette like an office might have, and a good bathroom with a shower. But the sunlight! What a place to work. My mind was racing.

I walked back to the big room. "How much?"

SB snorted. "You can't afford it. But I can."

"Be clear," I said.

"You move in here, I'll help you furnish it, bring your stuff, we'll order the tools you need. You draw and paint here and give me the works to sell."

"What? *Sell?* To who?"

"I know people. Chicago. New York. I'll take a cut. 20 percent I think."

I laughed. "Too high. That ain't happenin'."

He smiled. "Don't play games with me, Darrell. This isn't a drug deal. Take it or leave it."

I felt like smacking him again. The way he said some of the things he said. I pretended to think about it, but I was really trying to get my bearings back after being so effectively dissed by this old fucker. I had no choice. I was being offered a life.

I met his eye. "I'll take it… thanks."

We shook on it.

It took me less than a week to get settled. I went on the shopping spree of a lifetime. Bought everything locally, no mail order, and got everything I needed. SB never came with, just said to get what I needed for the studio with his credit card. Okay, I admit it. I was tempted to pick up a few non-related items, but the only thing outside the lines was a bong. I always wanted one and you would think with my history I must have had a few, but nope—it was my first and set me, well, Stumblebum, back about $30. This was a drop in the bucket compared to what I spent on that studio and it went unremarked upon.

SB took care of furnishing the living quarters with a big bed frame and new mattress, a good couch and a comfortable chair. It didn't recline but it was good. Also a small fridge, a microwave, a toaster, and all the doodads and dishes and whatnot. He put up window coverings that rolled up from the bottom. He brought over some of his old stereo stuff and about a hundred CDs, which he says he doesn't listen to anymore. Then he sent me to the grocery store to stock up. Even that was huge fun.

I was all set and full of ideas. I still bristled at the 20 percent commission he was screwing me on, but I understood what I was getting in return. I started on my work immediately.

It turned out old Stumblebum wasn't interested in everything I drew and painted. He was very selective, and, in truth, he had a madly good eye for art. I pretended to be insulted by his interest in less than a third of what I was putting out there for him, but he knew, that I knew—that he was right.

I had done 12 items that first week, eight drawings and four paintings, when he came to visit and assess my progress. They were small but intricate. Nothing bigger than 12x12.

"Are they all oils? These paintings? That one. That's not oil, is it?"

"No," I said. "That's acrylic. When I go thick I like acrylic." He moved to the drawings.

"Ever do watercolors?"

"When I was a kid. I might do them again."

He examined the drawings carefully. Funny—when I look back I can never remember him saying he liked or didn't like something. He just used the keen eye to separate the "wheat from the chaff," as he put it. Which also pissed me off. "Chaff." Huh.

"The ones I saw at the college. They were abstract. But all these have a figurative element in them." And SB lifted his bushy eyebrows at me, waiting for comment.

"Abstract is like 12-tone music. It's easy, but it's synthetic. This is a direction I'm gonna explore for a while." Note that I didn't ask his permission.

He nodded his head. "I suppose it's a fair analogy. With the music." He stared at me for a moment and smiled. "Let's see where this goes for you."

That first week he took one painting, the acrylic, and three drawings. He bundled them up and moved toward the door.

"What are you going to do with those?" I asked him.

He stopped and turned. "Photograph them. Store them properly while I try to sell them." He waited for me to comment, but it sounded pretty reasonable, so I just nodded. "Let me know if you need anything," he said. He held up the bundle. "This is a good start. But you might want to think bigger. You know. Larger canvasses. More painting. Fewer drawings." And then he left.

That felt good. *Real* good. I looked around for the so-far unused bong and whipped out my phone. It was time to *party*.

It took five weeks before I saw some money that wasn't his. He popped by early on a Monday morning. Not my best time.

"Jesus, you look like my feet feel," he greeted me. Nasty, right? Okay, I was hungover something tremendous, but it was *my business*.

"Always nice to see you, too, Cary Grant," I croaked, and waved him inside.

He stepped in and observed the unaddressed post-party shambles. "Good God, man, you could not *possibly* have done this mess by yourself." He didn't say it in a nice way.

But I laughed. "Right, I had help. Couple friends and a couple chicks. We had *fun*, Stumblebum. Remember *fun?*" I thought that would piss him off, but he just laughed.

"You got me there, I suppose. Yeah. I remember fun. I hope it was worth it."

"Yeah, well it *was.*"

He reached into his pocket and brought forth an envelope. He handed it to me.

"Open it," he ordered.

I ripped it open. Inside there were five crisp hundred dollar bills, new from the bank. I grinned.

"What's this?"

"It's yours. I sold two drawings for a little over 600 dollars."

I was flabbergasted. *"No shit!"*

"Congratulations."

"Thanks, SB. This might work out after all!"

"I'll stay in touch," he said and turned toward the door and left with a wave.

"This is the best lobster bisque I ever tasted," Clarence said, sipping next at the glass of cold golden Sancerre.

"We haven't been here in years. I thought it was worth the drive," SB said.

Clarence opened the breadbasket and carefully selected a warm buttery roll from within, examined it lovingly and took a bite. "How's your boy Darrell?"

"Well... let's see," SB thought for a space. "It's been almost three months and I sold..." he ruminated a bit, "almost ten grand of paintings and drawings."

"Jesus! Really? The kid can live on that. What do you take? Twenty percent? Still..."

Clarence ate so enthusiastically he didn't notice the silence. When he finally did he looked up at SB sitting motionless staring at his salad. "What's wrong?"

SB met his eyes and shook his head looking weary. "It's not going to last."

Clarence put his spoon down. "How come?"

"He's too... unstable. He's gonna blow it. I can feel it."

"What makes you think?"

SB let out a big sigh. "Experience. The more he makes the more he drinks, the more drugs, the wilder the parties..."

"He has parties?"

SB laughed. "Does he have parties? Saturday night about 11:30 I drove out to his studio. I could hear it before I could see it. Cars on the lawn, dozens of people. I just sat and watched. Through the windows I could see many ladies in various states of undress!"

"Really? Wow." Clarence's mind reeled. "Naked ladies, eh?"

"And he looks terrible," SB said. "But the work keeps coming. And it's good, saleable stuff. But it's not gonna last. I know his type. I'm starting to feel sorry I ever took up with him."

"Sorry to hear." We sat in silence and finished our appetizers.

"We need to talk back at my house. See... I don't blame the kid. I blame me. I should have seen this. This is all my fault."

"That's debatable."

"So if things go sideways... I mean really sideways... then we need a plan. See... I made this monster. And he's my responsibility."

"Why does the son-of-a-bitch insist on coming over on a goddam Monday morning?" I remember wondering aloud on that fateful day. I probably looked like I felt, which was not good.

Let me tell you about a severe cocaine hangover if you've never had the pleasure. That morning when SB woke me from a restless sleep I was dizzy and sweating like a pig. I had a headache and the morning light hurt my eyes.

I opened the front door, turned back, and went to the big chair and sat without greeting. SB walked in, looked me over without comment, which was wise, and sat across from me on the couch. I stood suddenly, unsteadily, and bolted from the room.

Have you ever vomited and shit your guts out at the same time? It hard to engineer depending upon the layout of your bathroom. Let's just say that the architect was not considering that scenario when he designed mine. I started to clean up the mess but figured to hell with it, washed my face and went back out to confront the most unwelcome Stumblebum.

I sat. "What." I said. He just sat, looking at me. "You got some money for me?" I asked him.

SB slowly reached into his inside coat pocket and took out the usual envelope. He tossed it to me. I badly wanted to see how much was there. (I lost a bet on the Lions and I couldn't cover it.) Instead I just looked over at Stumblebum and waited.

"Darrell. I've known dozens of great artistic people in my life," he began quietly, "but a lot of them didn't make it."

"What do mean they didn't make it?" Where was this going?

"They lost focus. They let their bad habits run away with them. They became-"

"When the fuck will you lighten up on me, man? That's none of your business. You're my fucking agent. Not my goddam dad!"

"I can get you a different agent. No problem. At this point they'll beat your door down if they find out I'm out."

I don't want no other-"

"But I feel responsible for you, see?" He shouted that.

I didn't know what to make of this. I should have heard the love in it and instead I was just pissed off.

"I ain't in the mood for this," I said. The fan in the bathroom wasn't keeping up with the stench and I was getting angry and embarrassed. I wanted SB the fuck *out!*

I stood up. Still unsteady. "Come on. Time to go. We ain't doing this today."

SB stood. "We need to talk, Darrell. I can see where you're going *and it's a catastrophe that you can prevent!"*

I grabbed him and turned him around and shoved him to the door, reached in front of him and yanked it open. I pushed him.

I pushed him.

Not hard. Just enough to get him the fuck out of my house but his stumblybum feet got confused and he fell.

He fucking fell.

He hit his head on one of the flagstones on the path and lay still. I ran to him and tried to bring him 'round but nothing happened. His eyes were open but there was no light behind them. I slapped him and screamed at him. I begged him. I prayed to a god I never talked to before and guess what? Nothing! I ran in and got my phone and called 911. I never even thought about the drugs.

I didn't lie.

Not to the police or my court-appointed lawyer. They found the drugs. I didn't lie in court. They wouldn't kick the drug charges, but a witness was brought in from the University to testify to my "excellence in studies," as she put it. That probably helped, for they let me paint in prison.

I was convicted of Criminally Negligent Manslaughter and Possession of Cocaine and sentenced to no more than 17 years in the Ionia Correctional Facility. It could have been a lot worse.

There are two different facilities in that prison, Levels 2 and 5. Level 5 is for bad motherfuckers. Level 2 is where you go if your antisocial tendencies aren't too out-of-control.

Early release was always my goal. I was a good prisoner, and for a full 14 years, prison life was pretty uneventful. I drew and painted and taught other inmates, and the prison sent my stuff to an address that SB's estate provided and I okay'd it. I was up for parole in a couple of months. I was on track for early release.

Except there was this one guy. A new guy.

His name was Malconi and he had no business in a Level 2 prison. I figure he must have had a great lawyer. He was a wealthy surgeon before he got here, also on a manslaughter charge. Something about another guy and Malconi's wife. Anyway, he didn't like me. He was a big mean mother and a bully. And a queer. And no way was I going to be his or anybody else's bitch. We had a few run-ins, mainly fists and feet. I'd like to say I held my own with him, but I didn't. I got tired of the weekly ass-beatings and my attitude toward him had become next door to murderous.

I had a shiv. See, there's shivs and shanks. Shivs have a blade of some kind, any kind. Shanks are pointy; they're for stabbing. It was good to have one or the other. I used the bottom part of a metal tray cart that was easily broken off and sharpened. I was stupidly proud of my shiv. Kept it razor-sharp and ready to go. I was at my wit's end with this Malconi bastard, and I had a little surprise for him that Tuesday morning in the laundry where he worked.

The problem was, Malconi had a *knife*. Remember—he was a surgeon, and he knew how to use that knife as if it was a scalpel. He advanced on me, the way he usually did, and I pulled out my shiv. He pulled out this scary-ass knife and gave me a big grin, like he was waiting for this to happen all along. The fight lasted about five seconds. He only gave me a single cut, in my arm near my armpit.

He completely severed the artery causing massive bleeding, and the doctor said that the artery retracted a bit into my arm, which meant emergency surgery. That same idiot tried to fix it by bridging the gap with a graft but botched it. There was more bleeding, then infection, and eventually *necessitating the amputation of my right arm.*

Life over. Right there. Life over.

Malconi was moved to a different prison. But by the time I got out of the hospital two weeks after the fight I didn't even care. Life was over, and I still had three years to serve. They had threatened to tack on more because I drew my shiv first and therefore I "had initiated the confrontation." They never did add on time, but there was no early release for me.

I was on suicide watch for almost a year, then they made me see a counselor. She tried to convince me that I could paint with my left hand. Jackass. I always painted with *both* hands, the brush or knife in my right, and I worked simultaneously with the fingers of my left hand *right on the canvas*. It was what gave me my style. *It was the way I painted.* Her stupid idea was a non-starter. I was mean to her and I regretted it later but wasn't allowed to communicate with her.

So that's the story of me and prison. I was 22 when I went in, poised to become the golden boy of figurative abstraction; I was almost 40 when I got out, a one-armed unemployed ex-con.

It was an early fall afternoon when I got released, me and a bag with my stuff in it. I had nowhere to go. I stood at the prison gate and just stared at the little clump of trees beyond the parking lot. Sugar maples. They were blazing red in their autumn splendor. In a week they'd be as dead and grey as me. I was frozen in place. My legs wouldn't move. I didn't have any smokes on me (I started smoking the first year I was in prison) and I wanted one desperately.

An old Cadillac sedan started up in the lot and headed right toward me, stopped in front of me and an old man got out. Tall skinny nimble guy with white hair. He closed the car door and looked over at me.

"Are you Darrell Lane?" I never saw this guy before in my life.

"Who are you?"

"My name is Clarence."

"Clarence what."

"Clarence Noneofyourbusiness. Are you or are you not Darrell Lane?" He sounded impatient.

I had nothing to lose by playing along. I remember thinking that I really didn't care if he took out a gun and killed me right there. Doing the job *for* me.

"Yeah," I said. "That's me."

He pointed at the car and said, "Get in."

I grabbed the handle and got in. Clarence did the same. The car was magnificent. Then it clicked. This was Stumblebum's old ride. It was like new. Beautifully maintained. Rode like a pillow on a cloud and was quiet as a tomb.

"So," I looked over at my driver, "where we headed there, Clarence?"

He looked at me with frank disgust, turned his eyes back to the road and did not respond. He said not a word the entire hour we were in the car. I was enjoying the drive and didn't mind his silence. I hadn't seen anything different in 17 years. I-96 East, then US-23 South and I knew we were headed back to my old college town of Ann Arbor.

Once in town we drove to a subdivision with really nice condos, and Clarence halted in front of one of the biggest. He hit a button, the garage opened and he pulled in, shut the car off and the garage door automagically closed.

"Get out."

Okay. I got out. We entered the condo and walked to the kitchen. I rubbernecked as best I could on the way and noted that the place was furnished beautifully and tastefully from the little I could see. Then I saw something that froze me in my tracks. It was a large oil painting in the livingroom, one of mine, one of the last ones I did before prison. *I was in Stumblebum's old home.*

"Figure it out yet, Sparky?" Clarence said. "Get in the kitchen and take a chair at the little table." I obeyed like a child. He added, "All the drawings and paintings you did in prison are in one of the rooms upstairs. There are more than 2000 drawings and almost as many paintings."

Hey. I had nothing else to do.

There were documents and binders on the table. I sat. Clarence sat across from me. He just glared at me. Most annoying.

"So!" I said. "This is Stumblebum's old house."

Clarence stood and his face got red. "Yes." He said calmly. "He was a *stumbler*, wasn't he?" I realized what a stupid thing I just said and was about to apologize but Clarence interrupted me. "If I ever hear you use that word again I'll strike you."

My temper flared reflexively upon being threatened. "I don't think you'd have a chance even with my one arm," I said.

Clarence smiled. "So, do you want to kill me, too?"

I looked away, ashamed. I wished I was dead. It had become my default feeling, but it was really flaring sitting there.

Still standing, he went on. "I'll come to the point. SB thought you were his fault, so he insisted on providing for you after he was dead, if his death were to predate yours, which it did, because you murdered him. I tried to talk him out of it, but he made me promise. Still... I don't believe he took into account that his death would be at your hands. That you would eventually pay back his kindness by *killing* him might have made him reconsider! But I gave him my word. Which I deeply regret."

I never saw a man that angry who didn't erupt in a violent outburst, but Clarence was wrapped pretty tight. He took a moment to calm himself then continued.

"This place is yours. The car is yours. Your bills will be paid automatically. In addition, you may draw upon the account provided for you in the documentation on the table there to a limit of four thousand dollars per month for discretionary spending. You will purchase your own phone, food, drink, gas and clothing and whatever else you require, from your discretionary monies. There is three thousand dollars there in cash to bide you over until you are settled in with the paperwork."

It was all so bewildering! I looked at the pile of stuff on the table and pointed to it. "I got no experience of all this legal and finance stuff so-"

"Not my problem. There are business cards in that top folder so you may direct your queries to the indicated accountant and lawyer. Nor will I give you a tour of this home nor spend another minute with you than is required." He dug in his pockets. "Here are all of the keys." He lobbed the keyring onto the tabletop. "You'll need to renew your driver's license, which reminds me—you are responsible for your own tickets and any legal entanglements. Lawyer fees are not part of SB's generosity. You'll be on your own with any legal entanglements."

He turned and headed out of the kitchen, stopped, and turned back to me. He pointed his finger at me like it was a gun.

"If you dare to abuse this home as you abused your own *I will abuse you.* I'm not an artist or a man of any note, but I loved SB and he loved and appreciated me. I have few talents, but he prized me for one in particular—I am *resourceful.* You'll test that at your peril."

I stood and faced him, my righteous accuser who had brought me lower than I thought I could yet go. "There is nothing left of me to abuse," I said, my voice quivering.

Clarence dropped his arm and grinned. *"Good!"*

And he was gone, and I never saw him again.

That whole next week I considered my newfound good fortune, but it really availed me nothing. I didn't bother buying food, I ate out. I wore the same clothes I walked out of prison in. I bought good wine and drank to sickness every night that week. I wished I was back in the joint. I was used to that. I wasn't used to this. It felt like a more sadistic type of prison. I left the pile of documents on the table without a glance and stuffed the cash in my pockets.

I kept telling myself: *I was given such a gift!* I would never have to work again. All my needs taken care of. I could have anything I wanted but the curse was that I wanted nothing except oblivion. *I could not paint.* I had no friends nor family. By the end of the week I knew that there was nothing more for me in this life and that I was postponing the inevitable. I had no reason to live, and I began to plan how I would die by my own hand.

How would you do it?

Shoot myself? I had no gun. Overdose? I had no pills. I could step in front of a train, as we had plenty of those in town. Or else drive my big shiny car into a bridge.

At last I decided on a more classical approach: I would open my veins in a warm bath. Like Cicero! And I would do it tomorrow night. I would spend one more night, and part of the next day among the living. Then I'd do it after dinner. A real nice dinner at a good restaurant tomorrow night. I would go 'home,' then get drunk as a lord on a thousand dollar bottle of wine and then be off to the fateful bath and all of this horror, this torture of two decades would finally be at an end.

I slept well the night of my decision and when I rose it was a lovely fall morn, warm and colorful. I had lunch, then decided to take a last drive to the important places in my life.

I drove by my childhood home and I forgave my recently-dead father. I sat outside the house in a township outside of Ann Arbor and meditated on the old homestead and cried like a girl. I said a prayer, though I am not a prayerful man, to my long-dead mother. I drove by my old schoolyard, the school long since demolished but the lot abides. What memories there!

Finally, I visited the fateful studio house that SB had got for me. A small family lived there now. The mother, pretty and stout, was raking the front yard and two little kids were playing in a big pile of leaves. I sat in my car a few yards down the road and watched this happy scene until I dozed off and when I woke an hour later it had turned chilly and they had gone inside.

Before I headed off to downtown and a last dinner I decided to end my reveries at North Campus and take a stroll by the Art School. I parked in Lot C. The last time I was there I saw Stumb- I mean, SB, sitting in a cold rain on the fountain bench, and I joined him. The place looked much the same. I got out of the car and headed toward the Art School. I sat on the steps and observed the students with their earbuds, staring into smartphones messaging wildly, most completely un-aware of anything around them. I remembered those days.

I saw a former professor of mine come down the steps, Professor... Hurley. Yeah. That was it. I stood to make certain, and he saw me. He gave me a curious look, smiled big and came toward me. We shook hands. Left hands.

"Jesus, look who it is! Darrell Lane in the flesh."

"Professor Hurley." I smiled. My first smile in a long time. Most of my teachers were vapid nobodies on a power trip but Hurley was all right. "Nice to see you."

He frowned. "I'm sorry about your misfortune. We all read about it. You had an amazing career in front of you." He gestured toward the gaggles of students moving to class. "The sort of thing these kids dream about."

"Do they? How did you know about what happened to me?"

"It was in the papers. Plus we saw pictures of the art you made in prison. It was more than impressive. Were you recently released?"

"About a week ago." I wondered how he got pictures.

"What's your plan?"

I decided not to tell him that I was going to kill myself after dinner. "I have no plan. I... I can't paint." I was holding back tears like a little pussy.

He knotted his brow and considered me.

"You can lecture."

"What? *Me?*"

"History. Theory. You were a pain in the ass in class, but you knew it better than most professors."

I laughed. "I'm an *ex-con!* They'll never hire me to talk to kids."

"I might have some say in the matter."

"You're a professor."

He smiled. "I'm the *Dean.*"

Whoa! Big move-up. Good for Hurley. But I couldn't see it happening. Not even close. I didn't tell him that. Instead, I told him he could look at the prison stuff back at 'home' and to call and we'll set up a time. I didn't tell him I'd be too dead to answer the phone. I just gave him a fake number because I didn't have a phone. He was so excited when we parted. Too bad but I knew it was for the best.

It was near five o'clock and I decided that it was time to spend four figures on dinner and wine. Like a last meal on Death Row except a hundred times more expensive.

Before leaving I decided to sit and watch the fountain for a while, sit right where me and SB used to, so I wandered over, stretched to pop out the kinks and sat, just looking. I was so calm. I don't think I was ever that calm.

Finally it was time to go. I rose up and was walking by the fountain back to the car when I heard a splash and turned to see a kid who, apparently, was pushed into the fountain by a really big guy, who was screaming crude and colorful insults at the kid he just pushed in. The kid in the water stood up and he was a skinny little runt of a boy. The big guy kept pushing at the kid, not letting him come out from the water, smacking him in the head and face when he got near. Normally (ask any con) you mind your own business over a thing like this, but this big bastard was a bully, and he was acting like a sadistic prick to the little guy.

I ran over and grabbed the big kid by the collar of his jacket and pulled him away hard from the edge of the fountain. He was off guard and fell flat on his ass. The little kid saw his opening and climbed out from the wet. The big guy got up and turned his malice toward me.

"That was a mistake, asshole!"

"Really," I smiled. "How come?"

He looked me over. "Because I could kick your ass."

"Well… I only have one arm, you're bigger and younger than me, and I'm right here. Your move."

He wisely thought better of it all, flipped me the bird and walked away mumbling to himself.

"Thanks, mister."

I looked behind me, and down, and there was this kid. Soaked to the gills. He looked like a drowned rat.

I smiled. "You okay?"

"I'm all right."

"What the hell was that all about?"

"I told him if he can't draw he shouldn't be going here."

I considered this. "Really? That's *it?*"

"Well... I may have told him he was a worthless poser who wasn't worth the canvas he was shitting on."

I had to laugh. "Well, that's different."

He got blustery, the little guy. "It's all true!"

"You look cold."

"I'm fucking *freezing!*"

I took off my jacket and gave it to him. "Keep it. I got a million of them," I lied.

I got curious. "Tell me more about the big guy."

"He thinks he's an abstract painter, but like most of those clowns *he can't draw!* He admits it!" They sat together on the bench. "He thinks it's an unnecessary skill for an abstract painter. It's like a guy who bangs a few songs out on a piano and then bragging because he can't read music. Thinks it's a virtue that he can't do something completely fundamental. What the fuck?"

"Let me guess—you like to draw."

"And goddam well, too. But I ain't finished about that big fat clown."

"Okaaaaaay..."

"Our craft has fundamentals. Total mastery has a number of steps. That slob throws paint willy-nilly on a canvas, takes him two minutes, and then he comes up with some stupid pretentious name like he's got one called, what was it... Oh! *Athena in a Boxing Ring with the Lord of Hyenas.* I'm not making this shit up!"

"Easy, kid. You'll lose your blob."

"I don't paint yet," he said, "but I'm about to."

"What are you, a freshman? 18?"

"Yeah, so?"

"Draw me."

"What?"

"Right now. Speed draw me. One minute. Got a pencil? Notebook?"

"Over there by the fountain," he said. "You think I can't?"

"I double-dog dare you." (This was fun.)

The kid bolted to his backpack and back, whipped out a notebook and pencil and sat down looking at me. He hovered the pencil and waited.

"Set your phone for 60 seconds." I told him. He did. "Ready? Go."

His eyes flashed to me and the paper and his hand never stopped. A minute goes by quick, but when the phone beeped, he was done.

He showed me. It was brilliant, in spite of his subject. Every stroke was necessary and evoked my ugly mug in a good honest rendering. I smiled at him.

"I see you can draw."

"Thanks. You want it?" He ripped the page free and I took it.

"No thanks," I said. "Besides," I traced one of his lines that formed my neck, "I want to talk about this line, here."

"Yeah," he drooped. "It's weak."

"What do you like to draw?"

"Nudes. Male nudes actually. I'm not gay or nothin', but I'm fascinated by the musculature of the body and it's easy to see on men."

"You and Michelangelo."

"He's the best."

"Yes, for drawing men, but his women are mostly a failure. They're men with boobs."

He laughed.

"Michelangelo could say everything he wanted to say with the male nude," I said. "He wasn't distracted by anything else—not landscapes, not still lifes, not female nudes."

"But how does he get the muscles like that? There's something not natural about it but at the same time it seems like the most natural thing in the world."

"Excellent question. It's because his figures are always *exerting* themselves," I explained. "They're usually striving for something but are restrained. Bound. And all the muscles are tensed simultaneously, *which is anatomically impossible*—that's what you find so odd yet so compelling. It's impossible, but it's deeply poetic. Michelangelo made a landscape of the human body. And do you know why?"

"Because... because he was a sculptor?"

"Correct." This kid! This kid was something else.

The young man sat for a space in deep thought. "I wish you could see some of my stuff. I don't show it usually, but I'd like you to tell me what you think."

I started tearing up like a little pussy again, which made me mad. I wiped my eyes and glanced away from the kid, focusing on the fountain. A pretty woman, a teacher? well-dressed with a confident walk was strolling by. She stopped and caught my glance and gave me the sweetest smile. She was so beautiful. We exchanged a little wave, and I turned back to the kid.

"You all right?" he asked me. Which embarrassed the hell out of me.

"Yeah... umm... I'll be here tomorrow," I said, "about noon. That work?"

"Hell yes." He held out his left hand. "I'm Andrew."

I shook it. "Darrell."

"See you then!" and he ran off with that grace and fervor that starts to get lost about his age. I watched him till he was out of sight and turned back to the fountain.

I was hungry.

I decided to go shopping.

And then... I would go home.

ॐ

331

The Murderous Hounds of Satan

"Pagan babies my arse," Billy mumbles to himself as he chews the last of the banana bread. He swallows and wipes his mouth on his filthy sleeve. "It's Billy-boy needs that money."

Billy has a plan. The banana bread is gone; the milk is gone and just as well as it's gone sour what with no refrigeration. No power. No money to pay.

William Sumner, a.k.a. Billy-boy, has spent an immodest portion of his 22 years in one jail or another, in North-East England and now Michigan, avoiding prison due to the petty nature of those violations at which he had actually been caught. This was simple thieving, mainly of the petty sort. For the larger robberies though, he had never been pinched. Now those paid off! Back in dreary old homesicky Newcastle he had scored plenty and often with his mates, and weren't they finally living high until the fateful night that compelled the nearly-nicked Billy to leave England altogether and bust his way to The States all by his lonesome. And lonesome he has remained here in rural Michigan for the past four years. With the money from the festival, he can return to Newcastle and start over. That's the dream, the plan. *The pagan-baby festival,* he thinks to himself, *it's a god-send, really.* And he laughs.

Of course, it isn't called the pagan-baby festival. Properly it's *St. Martha's Charity Festival,* an annual celebration that is the largest of its type in the county and beyond, now that half the parishes have closed up shop with their flocks consolidated into the few remaining. There will be fun and games, all sorts of stuff for the kids, rides and music. Oh yes, also beer and liquor and gambling – poker, roulette, 21, and of course, bingo. In a good year we're talking four- or five-thousand dollars profit after expenses are sorted. Of the final

333

booty, half goes to the church and school, and half to whatever charity or cause chosen to share in that year's bounty.

This year it's *Money for the Missions*, hence – the *pagan-baby festival* as it's dubbed by the local wags.

Billy is a thief, but he isn't godless. *Hell* no. Priests and nuns had him by the shorthairs in Newcastle from tender youth to full-blown juvenile delinquent and it took, surface-wise, at any rate. He still goes to mass every Sunday, even the odd confession when he can manage his story properly, gallantly sparing the priest the worst of it. Other parishioners have even developed a wary acceptance of Billy. Though moms and dads instinctively keep their daughters away best they can, this is unnecessary, as Billy is very shy with the girls and a bit homely in a pug-ugly way. But Billy counts a few of their sons as good mates to have, for he's as brassy with the lads as he is reticent with the lasses. His influence is naturally corruptive – reefer, booze, coarseness of expression mainly – but all this pretty much under the radar. He's careful. He socializes within the parish, but he thieves alone.

Billy-boy has walked a narrow path these four years, living by his wits, winning the few big scores while losing a few trivial ventures that ended in the local lock-up. But he's feeling the pinch and he wants to go home. Never the brightest of boys, but it doesn't take a genius to know he's been living on luck and it can't go on like this much longer.

His plan is coming together, enough at least to set the ball rolling, Billy changes his shirt for a less fragrant one and heads outside and down the stairs of his little apartment building. Skinny and lank, he takes the steps two-at-a-time whistling as he descends. It's a lovely fall day, sunny and breezy. Billy climbs into the passenger side of his old Buick (the driver-side door badly dented and up-openable) and scoots behind the wheel. The Buick starts right up. Old and rusty but it never fails. He's on his way to the church rectory to talk with old Father Mike. If he's still alive.

"I'm here to inquire after Father Mike, and if he's not too poorly, perhaps we can have a word." Billy stands looking into the cubicle of the church secretary and she looks him over.

"You're… William… umm…"

He waits for her to guess but it's just not coming. "William Sumner, ma'am. Call me Billy."

She snaps her fingers. "That's right. I remember now." She a short, big woman, dressed nice. She stands and walks up to Billy. Her expression darkens. "Oh… yes, I *do* remember now. Billy Sumner." She crosses her arms and gives him a stern look. "And what do you want with Father Mike?"

"To talk about the festival," Billy says. "I want to help."

"To help how?" She looks him up and down, arms still crossed. She's the gatekeeper all right. "Father's very ill."

"I understand, ma'am," he notes the plastic name card on the cubicle wall, "umm… Barbara. I know that, Barbara. Me and Father Mike are… we're mates." He smiles, all sincerity.

"Father's always been there for you and tried to help you when you needed him," she says.

"That's why I need to-"

"But he's so ill… in bed now for a week. I don't know if it's good for him to see you now."

"Ask him," Billy pleads. "If he says no, I'm on my way. No bother."

Barbara gives Billy another long and thoughtful look and returns to her cubicle chair. She pokes a button. "Father?"

No answer. "He might be asleep, and I don't want to-"

"WHAT," the machine barks.

"Oh, Father. You're awake."

"Yes. I had to wake up to answer the intercom," he snaps.

"I'm sorry, Father."

"No bother. What is it?"

"I have Billy Sumner here."

"Lucky you."

"He wants a minute," and here she shoots Billy a stern look, "and *just* a minute of your time. Will you see him? Or I can send him home."

A big sigh over the speaker, and then a long pause. Finally, "Send him up."

She nods and looks up at Billy. "Take the stairs and it's-"

"I know where he is," Billy chirps on his way to the stairs. "And thank you, Barbara," he remembers to say.

Dash up one flight and a brisk stroll to the padre's chamber door, Billy knocks. He's bid come in and opens the door to Father Mike's big study room, and through another open doorway then to the priest's bedroom. There lies skinny old Father Mike, his best days, all of his good days, obviously behind him now.

"Billy, for god's sake don't you own a clean shirt?" the old priest grumbles.

"Laundry day, Father." He tries to be funny.

It works. Father Mike laughs in spite of himself but recovers quickly. He sounds a little annoyed. "And to what do I owe the pleasure of your *unscheduled* visit?"

"It's about the festival, Father."

"What about it?"

"I want to help out."

"So, help out."

"Mrs. DeSantis says she don't need me. I think maybe she don't like me much."

"Really!" pipes Father Mike. "You think maybe Mrs. DeSantis might not be keen on having you hot-dogging around her four teenage daughters?"

"Maybe that's it, sure, but she'd say okay if you said it was alright."

The priest fixes Billy with a sidelong glance. Billy can feel the suspicion streaming out from the rheumy old eyeballs. But the old man chuckles to himself. "And what are you offering for our use from your diverse skill set?"

Billy notes the sarcasm and wisely lets it pass. "Gopher. Runner. I'll watch over things. Help keep order. I got a good eye, Father. You know that. And I know how to move in a crowd. They use them walkie-talkies. I'll be at the service of all the vendors, and all the gamers. Keep an eye on the kids, too. All that sort of thing."

"Why do you want to help?"

Billy goes blank. "Dunno…"

"I need to know."

"Well… you've been good to me, Father. Helped me get settled." Billy is on uncertain ground here; he is actually speaking honest thoughts about his relationship with another. "You overlooked some things… didn't judge me."

"Oh, I've judged you, Billy. Plenty. And you've come up wanting in my view many a time, but I always had hope for you."

Billy nods. "I guess that's what I mean."

"And now you want to help out, and why is this do you think?"

"Maybe a little payback? Maybe that's what it is?" He's lying now and is more comfortable.

The priest sits up a little in his bed and fixes his eyes for a moment above the crucifix on the opposite wall, thinking it through. Billy waits for the verdict, all respectful with bowed head, eyes closed and pursed lips.

"I'll talk to Agatha. Mrs. DeSantis. She'll ask you what you want to do, and you tell her what you told me. It's a useful idea."

"Ah, thanks Father."

"People will be watching you, Billy. It's important that you deport yourself in a way that will do you proud and make me proud of you."

"I want that to be so, Father."

"All right then. Off you go. And God bless you."

"And you, Father. And I hope you're better soon."

Father Mike grunts, and Billy gives a little bow, spins on his feet and heads for the door.

Father Mike calls him back.

"Yes, Father."

"Help me up."

"Father? But you-"

"Do what I say."

It takes the better part of a minute to get the old priest on his feet, very unsteady, and the old man holds fast to the headboard of the bed or he'll fall for sure. He stands facing Billy in his t-shirt and boxers, skinny to the point of emaciated, and a look comes over him as he struggles to stay upright. His face is red with exertion and he's bared his teeth, breathing hard with the effort of standing, and his eyes have bugged out and they're yellow with the jaundice. Billy is transfixed with a core discomfort. He takes a step back, and the priest speaks.

"William Sumner. Listen to me," he seethes. "Are you listening to me, Billy-boy?"

"Yes. Father! What's... Jesus... Yes. I'm listening!"

The priest raises his arm and points at Billy, accusingly.

"If you steal a penny of that festival money, *I swear to Christ that the Devil's own mastiffs will feast on your bowels!*"

"Mastiffs? What are-"

The priest lowers his arm, leans forward and shrieks, *"SATAN'S HOUNDS WILL EAT YOUR GUTS, BOY! DO YOU HEAR?!"*

Billy is too astonished to move his mouth.

"DO YOU!?"

Billy has retreated step by step in terror and now his back is against the wall and he rips through his mind to find words.

"I hear! Christ almighty, Father, I heard! But why did-"

"Get out! GET OUT!!" and the old priest slips and tumbles face down onto the bed. Billy takes a step forward to lend aid but the old priest yells again, "Get. *OUT!*"

And Billy, horrified, flees the room.

Billy drinks plenty this evening. Due to some recent shenanigans that played out well, he still has a good store of American whisky on hand, which he hates, all but for the active ingredient, which is dear as life itself. His sleep this night is rocky and full of dreams, all stupid drunkard dreams, save one.

In this one, *Billy finds himself in a strange forest and he hears odd noises all about him. Then come the growls, and rattling trees and rumbling bushes and finally they show themselves, one by one. Seven, they are, and as tall as horses. But they aren't horses, they're… they're dogs! Red-orange, the color of fire and they have flames for eyes, and all together they raise their giant heads and howl, all of them at once in a wail so beastly loud and overwhelming that Billy's legs turn to jelly and he collapses to his knees in terror. The lead beast leaps and holds Billy by the throat, knocking him flat and he thrashes and flails about, trying to scream but his throat is held closed by the hideous devil dog. The others dive in now, competing to rip Billy's belly open and tugging at his insides and now he can feel his bowels stretch and pop loose. Several keep digging in to feed but two have broken loose, playing tug-o'-war over what looks like a long grey hose, but Billy knows what it is. The beast at his throat is feeling left out and releases Billy's bloody neck to share in the bounty that is Billy's own guts. Billy screams in the throes of his final agony,* and this is how he wakes.

Hot and sweaty he stares at the ceiling trying to catch his breath and calm himself. Minutes pass like this. His phone rings and he looks at the clock. It's a little after nine in the morning. He fumbles for the phone.

"Hello."

"William?"

"Uh, yes?"

"This is Agnes DeSantis."

"Oh! Mrs. DeSantis" Billy sits up and pats flat his wild hair, as if this matters.

"Call me Aggie, William. May I call you Bill?"

"Billy, ma'am. Call me Billy."

"Well, I have news for you, Billy, in case you don't know, Father Mike passed last night. Just before sunrise. Father Adrian and Barbara were at his side. It was all very peaceful."

"Oh jeez, I didn't know…" *What a way to start the day,* he thinks. *How does this affect the festival?*

"Well, it was hardly unexpected. He long outlived what the doctors predicted, you know?" Aggie pauses and heaves a great sigh. "He was a good man," she said.

"Yes," he mumbles. "We were... we were mates."

"But I have something else to tell you. This won't affect the festival. Father Mike was very insistent on that. And last evening Father Mike called me and asked if I would include you in the staff for the weekend. And I said of course. He told me what you proposed, and it sounds like a very useful idea. So, if you can meet us at the fairgrounds Friday at about noon, we'll get you outfitted and introduce you to the other staff. How does that sound, Billy?"

"That sounds just grand, Aggie. I'll be there. See you then."

Billy presses END and lays back down. He closes his eyes, sighs and smiles, devil dogs be damned. Visions of Newcastle dance in his head – football at St. James, tooling down Grey Street with a nice buzz, dancing at Flares, fish & chips at Whitley Bay – all things close to a real Geordie's heart. He falls back asleep.

Billy arrives early for the Friday meeting. It's a schoolday, and Billy has a hunch. He jogs across the fairgrounds and opens the door to St. Martha's Elementary School. The school frowns upon adult male visitors and when Billy knocks on the open doorjamb of the administration office, he gets a frightened look from the secretary, the only person in the room.

She's young and pretty, so Billy is instantly flustered.

"Oh, don't be afraid," Billy says, his palms outstretched. "I'm with the festival staff. I'm Billy."

She thaws instantly. "I'm Janice," she says with a sweet smile. "How do you do."

"Very well, thank you. Umm... Is the staff meeting here in the school?" Billy inquires as his eyes roam the room, finding rest on the stout steel cabinet with the three hefty padlocks on the door. A wave of relief washes over him that there is no safe in the room. He was never very good at safes. *This*, he says to himself, *this looks like the place.*

He mumbles his goodbyes to the pretty girl and joins the festival staff at the fairgrounds, right on time. He gets his walkie-talkie (a fantasy device from his youth). He meets the other vendors, gamesmen and a few roughnecks that do most of the setup. That sort of thing is way too much like work to interest Billy-boy, so he spends most of his time getting the lay of things and gossiping with the other lads. He is most interested in how the proceeds will flow, from vendors and the various gambling tents and tables, and where it will all accumulate at the end of the night on Saturday and closing on Sunday. Of course, he never asks about it, just observes with a keen eye and ear. He feels he was born for just this sort of caper and he is pleased to be alive.

The staff of the festival were pleased by Billy's performance on Saturday. Even Father Mike would have been proud. Seems Billy-boy was the glue that held it all together, and by day's end they wondered how they ever used to manage without someone doing the jobs that Billy did.

The walkie-talkie crackled all day.

"Billy, can you help me with…"

"Say, Billy, I really need…"

"We got a little problem here, Billy…"

And Billy took care of everything. If there was a sudden call for manual labor, Billy played the foreman, having recruited some young helpmates to do the heavy lifting. They were Billy's lieutenants and they took pride in their station. He even stopped a few fights before anyone got hurt. The worst of these, oddly, between two former Bingo-buddies in their 80s. Slaps were administered, and objects hurled, but both ladies (yup, ladies) lived to play another day.

But now it's Sunday and Billy still has no certainty about where the money will end up when the smoke clears. All he knows for sure is that all the vendors and gamers congregated at closing time Saturday with their bags and drawers full of loot, retiring to parley in a room somewhere in the school. Billy was not invited therein.

He stayed up half the night pondering how to proceed. Thinking, thinking, thinking, then all of a sudden – Bingo! Billy had a plan.

Mrs. Kirby, old and infirm, runs that Bingo operation. She's played since she was girl, attending weekly with her grandma right here at St. Martha's. She's been a patron of the game here for 70 years and has run it every week for the past 30, and nobody is going to wrangle that away from her as long as she has a breath in her body.

Billy noted that at the end of the day on Saturday, old Mrs. Kirby had a hard time getting her bag of goodies to the school. Her Bingo helpmates were no less infirm than she, and it took a lot out of her to lug her booty, a football field away, to the schoolroom. It would be Billy's last helpful act at the fair: to play beast of burden for the old missus, sack of money in one hand and Mrs. Kirby's bony pale arm in the other, guiding her over the bumps and through the puddles on way to the school to assure her healthy passage and the Bingo cash safe with all the rest of the day's take.

"Billy dear, thanks for helping. I thought they were going to murder one another!" Mrs. Kirby tries to hide her mirth at the memory of the two Bingo gladiators the day before. The festivities have ended, and the pair are sweeping the floor of the Bingo tent before the men break things down.

"Ah, you gotta watch out for you older folks," Billy says. "That one lady packed one heck of a swing!"

"I went to school here with the other one," she recalls. "She was a royal bitch even back then!" She covers her mouth, mock-shamed at her language. Billy laughs. He has taken a shine to her.

Mrs. Kirby has taken a shine to Billy, too. They finish their task and the old woman finds her coat, and underneath a large canvas bag. Billy nearly salivates at the sight. She bends down slowly for the coat and Billy is instantly at hand to help her inside it, one arm then the next. She turns and gives him a big smile as she does up her buttons. She thinks it's cold out. Billy is in a tee-shirt. He smiles back.

When she bends back down for the money bag, Billy stops her mid-bend with a touch to the shoulder. She straightens.

"Billy dear. What is it?"

"Mrs. Kirby, I confess I saw you struggle with your load to the school last night. I saw you stumble and almost fall. We can't have that, now. I'd feel bad. And you'd feel worse if you took a spill. Let me take the load and you walk with me. Nice and slow."

"Not too slow, they're expecting me," she frets. Billy hoists the bag with a single flourish and takes the old missus by the arm.

"Let's be off then!" And off they go.

About halfway there Billy notes with a few sidelong glances that Mrs. Kirby's brow is furrowed and she's working her lips like she's anxious, as if she's having second thoughts about this little stroll. He wonders, *what does she know about me?* Among some of the parishioners, especially the oldsters, Billy's rep is even worse than the facts would have it, gossip being what it is, and gossipers what they are. Strangely enough, this would sadden Billy if she thought poorly of him.

"Mrs. Kirby," he ventures, "is everything all right? You look like… like something's not sitting so well."

She stops, turns and looks up at Billy, studying his face, then smiles, reaches up and pats his ruddy cheek. "No dear," she says. "I'm just old." And they resume their walk.

When they arrive at the school Billy senses that Mrs. Kirby is trying to part company at the door. Billy ignores her dally there and with a big smile nudges the door open and guides her through. She pulls her arm free and is about to speak but Billy pre-empts her.

"Almost there!" he chirps, his free hand now at the small of her back, setting the pace as they stroll down the hallway.

"Well, I can take it from-"

"Oh, it's no bother a'tall," Billy says, adjusting the bag on his shoulder. "Lord, this bag is getting heavy! Bigger than yesterday's! Now, which room is it?"

In another moment they have arrived. Unsurprisingly, it's the administrative office they're gathered in. At the threshold Billy gallantly bows and bids Mrs. Kirby enter the room before him. The others, ten or twelve, give her a little cheer as she enters, but the cheering stops when Billy appears with the big canvas bag on his shoulder. He feels the very picture of a young thug with a bag of stolen loot.

This is an uncomfortable moment, until one of the men, Sully, the concessions manager, pipes up and says, "Billy, you've been a great help to all of us this year. Thanks." This surprises Billy. Sully was very short with Billy, almost rude, with the few interactions they had the past two days.

Billy feels the appreciation, an odd feeling indeed, and he blushes. Everyone relaxes and murmurs their own thanks aloud to bashful Billy. He smiles and nods and gives everyone a wave. "I know you all have work to do and I'll be off," he says to all. "And we'll do it again next year if you'll have me!" They bid him a cherry goodbye, Mrs. Kirby blowing him a kiss.

Billy leaves the office, but he doesn't leave the school. He scampers down to the auditorium, opens the big door and slips inside. He takes out his phone and dials up the flashlight, now carefully making his way down the aisle and backstage. Billy finds a corner with an old velvet curtain rolled up on the floor, sets an alarm on his phone, kills the light and settles in all snug for a few hours of sleep.

At 2:30 am his phone gives Billy the chimes. He actually slept, but now he's instantly alert, rises and turns the flashlight on his phone. Billy negotiates the backstage mess, out to the stage, down the steps, down the aisle and out the door. He takes a bathroom break and washes his face. He heads for Room 109. It's a classroom, outside the window of which Billy has stashed a pair of bolt-cutters (a caper of the night before) and a large canvas bag, cylinder-shaped, with a long strap from end to middle so it can be slung over the shoulder. All this is hidden by the shrubbery.

Billy unlocks the window and pulls the lever, opening it just enough to slip the items into the room. Securing the window, he heads for the office. It's locked, natch. He digs in his pocket for another familiar tool of his trade, the lock-pick, with which Billy is quite facile. There is no rush. Maybe that's why he pops the lock in record time.

And there it is: the stout steel cabinet with three stalwart padlocks. It's quite dark, the little ambient light available shines in from the security lights on high poles in the parking lot. But this is crude work. Brute force. The bolt-cutters have always served Billy-boy well and tonight is no exception. In 90-seconds the locks are locks no longer.

The moment is upon him. He realizes that this is all guesswork, the location of the sanctuary holding the festival money was never clearly revealed to him. It could be a safe somewhere else in the building; someone could have taken it all home with him or her; it could be locked in a car for all that he knew. He has only his instincts to follow. And if he's wrong they will discern who the vandal is, and Billy will have to leave town without a dollar to his name. It's the gamble of a lifetime.

Billy discards the locks into the wastebasket. He pulls the lever on the cabinet door and hears it release. He takes a deep breath and holds it, closes his eyes and yanks open the steel door. He opens his eyes, and even in the dim light he knows he has scored. Billy takes a little penlight from his shirt pocket and shines it inside the cabinet. Zillions of bills still unsorted but banded together in thick stacks. Dozens of them! Cash, beautiful cash.

Billy gets busy stuffing the bills into the bag and it becomes evident that he hasn't room for it all. He'll have to abandon some of the bundles. He tries to estimate as he packs the goods, and almost weeps when it becomes clear that his new fortune may be well north of $10,000. He realizes that some of the festival bills haven't yet been paid, and this would account for the stash being much larger than anticipated. Billy bitterly regrets leaving so much money behind, thousands more, but there is nothing to be done about that. He also leaves behind the bolt-cutters. He knows he will be suspected of this heist and doesn't bother to tidy up the scene.

They'll notice the robbery about 7:30 – four short hours from now. They'll call the cops, go to his house, send out an alert. The few material items Billy cares about are in the trunk of the Buick, which is parked behind the woods a quarter-mile from the schoolyard. He'll head there now, steal a car within the hour, transfer his load and be off. He'll worry about the rest later.

Billy heads back to Room 109. He opens the window and dumps the bag through. He can't exit through any of the doors because of the alarms. It's a tight squeeze but the skinny lad finally makes it through the window, tumbling into the shrubs. He stands, looks about, brushes off, pulls the bag from the bushes, hoists it up and adjust the straps on his shoulder. Now a brisk, comfortable stroll through the woods to the car, Billy heads out of the bushes and toward the sidewalk.

Not so fast. Between the shrubs and the sidewalk stands Sully, the concessions manager who praised him to the others. He's holding a large chrome crescent wrench about a foot-and-a-half long in one hand, gently beating with it on the palm of his other hand. Sully is tall and stout, standing spread-leg in the half-light. A grim apparition.

"Ah, Billy…" Sully says. "I had my doubts about you. Then I saw your car parked over on Polk Street on the other side of the woods and I figured maybe I'd just watch over the school tonight." He takes a couple steps forward and stops. "Why, Billy? How can you do this to us? To the church and the school, the kids?"

"Cops comin' I suppose?" Billy is tasting defeat.

346

"I thought about it," Sully says. "But then I thought, no, I want to handle this myself. I'll call the cops when I'm *done* with you. You've slipped through the cracks too many times, Billy. Tonight, you go down." Sully holds up the big wrench. "By my hand. That'll be justice. Finally. Jesus, it's hard to believe a man can sink as low as you."

"You want to kill me."

"Just stop you. But I know you won't come quietly. You can't. You're finished. You have to try to get by me, but your loot is weighing you down."

Billy almost thanks Sully for laying it all out so terribly clearly. He drops the bag from his shoulder and sprints at Sully, who takes a step back and fakes like he is going to swing the wrench at Billy but instead jabs it into Billy's gut. Billy falls, rolls and pops back to his feet. Sully is big and strong but in his 50s and no match for Billy's wiry speed. Sully comes at Billy with a swing of the wrench, but Billy closes on him with lightning speed and delivers a punch to Sully's soft gut. The wrench never finds its mark and Sully drops to his knees. Billy pounds at Sully's head and neck with a dozen quick blows and Sully falls forward onto his face in the grass. Billy snatches up the wrench and whacks Sully once in back of the head.

Sully lies still. Billy wonders *did I kill him?* But there's no time! He must get to his car. He finds the bag, straps it on and starts walking. Only now does he notice the pain in his gut. He stops to assess. There's blood all over the front lower half of his ripped tee-shirt and on his pants. He lifts the tee and can see in the dim light the gouge in his flesh, right below his navel. It's bleeding steadily and though it's only a couple inches long, it's quite deep. He curses and continues to walk, unseen, across the street and into the woods.

It's too dark to walk. Sharp branches brush his face and his footing is unsure. He stops to unclip the penlight in his pocket, pokes it on and resumes his walk. The lighting is barely satisfactory and it's slow going. The walking has become extremely painful and the bleeding is not stopping. He continues his robotic slog through the dark thickets.

Five minutes and almost halfway through now without incident, Billy hears a rustle behind him. He turns and flushes with terror at the sight of... *is that Sully plowing through the brush?* and he has a very big and bright flashlight.

His pursuer's voice confirms it. "Billy, you son-of-a-bitch!" Sully rasps loudly. "There you are! I will fucking kill you!"

If Billy runs, he leaves the loot and it'll be prison or worse. But even in Sully's badly wounded state, Billy knows that, at this rate, Sully will catch him. Sully's fierceness makes Billy think twice about confronting him in his own injured state. Sully is moaning and groaning like a madman, now falling and getting up slowly. Billy tries to make headway as best he can, hoping for a miracle. Sully sprints forward, stumbles and falls again.

Maybe 30 yards separate the two by now and Billy clutches his loot-bag tightly in front of his face to protect from the branches and keeps moving. The beam of Sully's light pans wildly right then left, then smack on Billy, then Sully falls again. Billy stops and looks behind him. Sully's flashlight is in the grass and Billy hears Sully's pathetic moans. Billy turns with new hope in his heart and thinks he can spy the end of the treeline, when he senses Sully's flashlight beam holding steady on him.

And then a shot rings out. Just one, but it finds its mark at the base of Billy's spine. He drops like a stone.

Billy knows he's been shot but he feels no pain. But neither can he feel nor move his legs. He's trying to calm himself. He thinks he knows what happened, but he isn't sure. He lies in the dark and can hear Sully yards away, mumbling, "I got you, you little bastard... I got you... I fucking got you..." And then, no more moans and groans, no more anything. It's as quiet as a tomb. Billy moves a hand to his back and feels the wetness there. He feels the hole.

And he can't move his legs.

The black curtain of failure falls over his soul. He can't feel his legs! He knows, this very instant he realizes – *he's finished*. He is accepting it. Billy is giving up. His thinking has become oddly clear, and he is calm. Billy doesn't want to die, and he's trying to sort out his options, few and awful as they may be. As they surely are.

Billy closes his eyes and drifts. There's no hurry now, though he's lost a lot of blood and he's losing more by the minute. He has drifted into a twilight, but there is comfort here and he dallies in that coziness for a space.

He's coming back now. He's... he's being tickled? Yes. He is. Billy opens his eyes and looks down. He spies a little dog, a small spaniel. He's seen it before roaming about the neighborhood. The pooch is licking at Billy's wound. He chuckles and gently swats the little dog away. The dog hops onto Billy's chest and starts to lick his face. Billy laughs. In his near-delirium he feels like a boy again and swats the pooch away, laughing. The little dog barks playfully.

In a moment he's joined by a couple more little doggie buddies. Medium-sized mutts. He's seen them before. Might have shared a bagel with them on his stoop back home. The little spaniel hops again onto Billy's chest and starts licking playfully, but the two stray mutts are much more interested in Billy's belly wound. At first a few tickling licks, all playful, Billy swats them away. Then a bite. Billy cries out and the dogs retreat a few feet. They're growling now, and they can sense Billy's distress.

Billy sits up and the three dogs no longer seems so friendly. The largest of the three goes for Billy's belly again but Billy strikes out with his fist and connects with the shoulder of the dog, who bares his teeth and springs at Billy, jetting through his guard and biting at his face, Billy pulls at the dog who regains his poise and strikes out at Billy's neck. The other two curs are back on the belly, and the medium dog gets a purchase on Billy's belly-skin and tears a long strip open. Billy squirms and cries out from the pain, but the dogs weigh him down at the waist and Billy's hands are now a bloody mess from fending off the worst of the bigger hound's bites to his face and neck.

The smaller mutts have burrowed inside Billy's belly! He can feel them! They're ripping! He drops his guard on the big dog to try to clear his belly and then the big dog strikes at Billy's throat and there is a gout of fresh blood spouting from his neck. Billy is so weak! He falls back to the dirt and tries to scream but he doesn't have the energy. The big dog turns his attention to Billy's belly and the three of them are now ripping at him freely. The big one asserts her dominance, burrowing deep while the medium one tears at the skin, and the little guy is resigned to licking at the bloody mess the two larger dogs are creating.

The big one tugs, tugs, and rips hard and Billy feels something pop. Paralyzed with weakness all he can do is lie there inertly and feel the pain. The Pain. Only the big dog is at his belly now, excavating deeply. Billy turns his head to see the two little ones right next to him, playing tug-o'-war over what looks like a long grey hose. But Billy knows what it is.

(The story of the outlaw Billy-boy has since become a local fable and a cautionary tale to all the children of the parish. Mr. Sully has become a saint and martyr to the people of St. Martha's, and every fresh festival a commemoration of his courage and sacrifice.)

After the three mutts had had their fill, a family of foxes and a small murder of crows enjoyed an exotic breakfast, but only until three turkey vultures staked their claim after the sun came up. They were quite indignant when the cops shooed them away.

That next morning it didn't take long to find Billy's corpse and the bag of money. A few minutes later they found the body of Sully, his flashlight and his pistol, an army .45. The investigation was short and sweet, as these things go. The case was cut-and-dried, with no loose ends.

Unlike Billy-boy, who had plenty.

The Twilight of Iggy Flynn

to my brother
Terry
who likes this sort of thing

The blond man, sleek and nattily dressed, sauntered in through the back door of the tavern, stepped toward the chair at a little table across from the bar and sat opposite the giant. The giant, carefully observing the newcomer, was working his jaws on a bite of a sandwich. He stopped chewing when the blond man sat. Swallowing, the giant tilted his head and asked, "Do I know you?"

"Well, you see," the blond man said, leaning forward with a squint at the giant sitting across from him, "I have a *stone* in my *shoe*," he whispered grandly.

The big man furrowed his brow and, quizzically, met the blond man's stare. "You *what?*"

"I said," with a little pause here, "that I have a *stone* in my shoe."

The giant considered the remark. "Well, take your shoe off and get the stone out."

"What?"

"What the hell are you talking about, 'I got a stone in my shoe,' what the hell does that even *mean?*" He gestured at his half-sandwich. "I'm havin' my lunch here. Or tryin' to."

The bartender closed the west-facing window curtain with a swoosh. The blond man called, "Thanks, buddy." and the bartender nodded. "Sun was in my eyes," Blondie said.

"Yeah, well it ain't anymore. Who are you and what do you want?"

Blondie got all whispery. "I know who you are, Iggy."

"That's 'Mr. Flynn' to you, pal." Mr. Flynn's voice had an edge. He took another bite of his ham sandwich.

"Okay. Mr. Flynn. I know who you are and what you do."

"Not likely. Who are you?" Iggy gruffed.

"Sorry. Alan Picola." He reached his hand across the table for Iggy to shake, but Iggy just stared at his hand till Alan coughed and pulled it away.

"What's this 'stone in my shoe' horseshit and what's it to me?"

"It's a euphemism."

"It's a *what?*"

"A euphemism."

Iggy looked blankly at Alan.

"That means-"

"I know. Stop. Start speaking plainly, right now, or get the fuck away from me."

The bartender called from behind the bar, "Hey pal! Iggy, everything okay?"

"Yeah, Manny. Probably," Iggy called back.

Alan said, "Okay, I'm sorry about meeting like this, but I know who you are and what you do."

"Yeah? How do you know that?"

"I can't tell you."

Iggy scratched his beard and looked at Alan as if he were a very puzzling and poorly-rendered painting. "You obviously have conflated me with someone else."

"Allow me to speak plainly."

"Please."

Alan looked away and took a deep breath. He looked back at Iggy, drew closer, and whispered. "I want someone killed. He's a local, name of Jonnie Greer, and I have fifty thousand dollars, right here with me, cash, if you take the job."

Iggy stared at Alan with a small smile, nodding. He gave a little laugh, and said, "Alan, I'm not the guy you think I am. And you need to be more careful." Iggy put the last of his sandwich in his maw and mumbled, "you just asked a total stranger to murder somebody. Do you see what I'm sayin' here?"

Alan leaned back with a disgusted sigh. "Yeah. Sure. I get it."

354

"Just out of curiosity. This guy – I already forget his name," Iggy held up his hand, "and I don't want you to repeat it – what did he do to you?"

Alan frowned. "I thought you weren't supposed to ask that sort of thing."

"You just asked a guy you never met before to kill another guy, and you think it's *odd* that he asked you why?"

"I thought you never asked questions."

"Well, obviously you thought wrong." Iggy sipped his Scotch. "Anyway, you got me curious. So why you want him dead?"

Alan brightened perceptively. As if he saw a glimmer of hope. He gathered his resolve with all the dignity he could master and let the words fly.

Alan leaned forward conspiratorially, intoning solemnly: "He fucked my wife."

Iggy was incredulous. "He fucked your wife?"

"That's right."

"So?" Iggy was amused. "That's it?"

Alan was baffled. "What do you mean, 'so?'"

"So he fucked your wife. You wanna have a guy *murdered* for fucking your wife?"

"Well… there's more to it."

But Iggy had had his fill. "Alan, I'm gonna do you a big favor."

Alan brightened. "Oh jeez, thanks, Ig… I mean, Mr. Flynn. I knew you'd-"

"No no no no. You don't get it. Now listen to me."

Alan listened, baffled.

"I'm gonna forget you ever came in here, and rudely interrupted my lunch, and confused me with some murder-for-hire goon and bothering me with all this horseshit. Now. While you can," Iggy shot down the last of his Scotch. "Did you get that? I said, 'while you can,' get up and get the fuck out of the bar. Now."

Manny at the bar was aggravated. *"Hey, pal!"* he barked.

Alan, now many shades paler, stood up and, like a wind-up soldier, did exactly as instructed without so much as a look back.

Manny walked over to the table. "You good, Iggy?"

"Yeah, Manny, I'm good. Another Scotch."

"You got it, pal."

Iggy waited, and mused.

I gotta stop doin' this. A lifetime of this is too long. What am I at the point now I gotta contend with monkeys comin' in here off the street tryin' to get me to kill? Jesus, what next. And how the fuck did he-

"Here ya go, buddy. Jack Daniels. Double."

"That's not Scotch, Manny," Iggy observed. "And a *double?*"

Manny shrugged. "I figured you'd want a double Jack-Black instead."

Iggy laughed silently. "Thanks, Manny. Seen Brian?"

"Speak of the devil. Right there."

And through the door comes Brian, right on time. He's the only guy Iggy ever knew that looked more formal in jeans and a tee-shirt than most guys, including Iggy, *especially* Iggy, looked in a 3-piece suit. So perfectly groomed that some made the mistake of thinking him a gay blade, and tactlessly bringing this to his attention. That never, ever went well.

The three shook hands and did the smalltalk for a minute, then Brian sat across from Iggy while Manny discreetly went back to work.

"You got somethin' for me?" Iggy asked.

"I got *three* things for you," Brian said, laying a large yellow envelope in front of Iggy. Iggy didn't even look.

"I know what this is. What else you got."

Handsome Brian hoisted his trimmed eyebrows and gave Iggy a big, cartoony grin.

"Stop that," Iggy laughed.

"What I got you, is a date, for the Anniversary party." Brian sat back to let that sink in real good.

"Great. Who is it? Some tranny from downtown?"

"Fuck you, Iggy. And no. A *beautiful* woman. You know me. She's a smart one, too. *Your* type."

"Really."

"Her name is Twannette."

"Nobody's name is Twannette," said skeptical Iggy. "What's her last name?"

"What's her last name? What's her last name? Who cares what's her last name, you're not *investigating* her. I told her about you – you know, up to a point – and she said she'd like to meet you."

"So, you don't know her actual name, right?"

"Yeah. I do. Iggy. Her name is Antoinette Oliver, and her friends call her Twannette. And get this: she's a *cosmologist.*"

"A cosmologist?"

"Right."

"A *working* cosmologist?"

"Yeah! She's a pro. It's what she does full-time. She got a nice place near the university."

Iggy smiled. "Brian, do you know what a cosmologist is?"

Brian tried to look offended. "Of course I know."

"Well… I dunno how to put this exactly…"

"Yeah, yeah, I'm sure you're having trouble *choosing* your *words.*"

"But what the hell would a cosmologist be hanging around with you for?"

Brian was annoyed that he had to explain the obvious. "Because I'm young, handsome and charming, unlike *some people.* Women of all types are oddly attracted to me. Even the brainiacs need some premium lovin' now and again. Listen. And you're stalling. I'm going to tell her that you're looking forward to seeing her on Saturday. You're welcome. I'll give you her address." Brian pointed with a perfectly manicured index finger. "Actually, it's in that envelope with the other stuff."

"Got a photo in there?"

"My friend, you will be *most* pleasantly surprised."

"Alright. What's the third thing?"

357

"What third thing?

"You said you had three things to tell me."

Brian looked blank. "Oh, that! Didn't want to forget that. Our friend would like you to drop by The Castle before six o'clock."

Iggy considered this with a furrowed brow. "That's pretty weird."

"But that's what he said. Get Iggy here before six."

"Thanks, Brian. Gotta run then." In a blink, the whiskey was gone. "Need a ride?"

"Can I sit in the back?"

Iggy chuckled and shook his head. "Nice try."

"I got the Harley, anyway."

And they shook hands and went their separate ways.

2

Iggy drove a factory Lincoln limousine from the late-'60s. Think total elegance, not prom-night glitz. It was stretched about two-feet. It had a bar, a TV, computer, nice stereo, he even had the original crystal glasses and decanter. Only thing was, this was a car to be *driven in*, not so much to drive. So whenever he arrived at his destination, instead of having his man open the rear door for him to emerge, tycoon-like, from the wood and velour cavern within, he simply clambered out of the driver side door, looking way too much like a chauffeur/bodyguard without a client. All he needed was the little hat.

But what care saucy Iggy? He liked what he liked and knew who he was, and if one were moved to make sport of how Iggy looked or acted or talked or take issue with one of his two hobbies, at six-feet seven-inches and 350 pounds, with a turbulent disposition, one had better be one of Iggy's few friends.

Iggy had a long, if stylish, drive from his Ann Arbor turf to the Orchard Lake home of Redmond Quinn and was full of disturbing thoughts on the way. Quinn was Iggy's em-

358

ployer, and had been since Iggy left the army 25 years ago. They were both 55 now. They had come up through the Irish ranks together since childhood, but Quinn was royalty, whereas Iggy was simply brilliant at his work.

In the army, Iggy learned what would become the fundamentals of his civilian trade. He was a gunnery sergeant and taught martial arts to Army Rangers. Anyone who knew Iggy had never known a more formidable individual. Nor would they ever have a better friend. He was passionate about his friends.

But he dreaded meeting with Quinn at The Castle. All their business was necessarily done by proxy, and other than the odd social gathering, such as the Anniversary party Quinn would host on Saturday, visits to Quinn's imposing mansion were clandestine and very rare. And despite their long and close association, Quinn had not really been a friend since Iggy returned from the service. The closest anyone ever got to Quinn was arms-length, physically and spiritually. So, there was something unusual going on, and this made Iggy uncomfortable.

Before Iggy hit the freeway, he yanked the big Lincoln to the curb, put it in park and regarded the yellow envelope next to him. He opened it and withdrew neat bundles of $100 bills that would add up to $30,000. He didn't bother to count it. And there was a rolodex card with the contact information for one Antoinette 'Twannette' Oliver, cosmologist. He had to admit that she sounded interesting. Iggy was well-educated and well-read, kept up on the arts and sciences, much to the amusement of his friends and colleagues, who did not share these interests.

It would be nice to meet a smart woman, he mused. *It would be nice to have conversations that weren't always about work, or sports, or pussy.* He laughed as he reassembled the contents of the envelope, then headed on toward US-23 and out of town.

3

It wasn't called The Castle for nothing, but then again, they were all castles up this way.

Iggy had the good sense to stop by a snooty booze vendor for a $400 bottle of Scotch as a gift to Quinn. He would not expect this and would be pleased with the gesture. There was a gate, natch, and Iggy pressed the button.

"Whom should I say is calling?" squawked the box.

"Iggy."

And the gate automagically opened with all due majesty. Iggy knew the drill and wheeled the big limo toward the back of the manor. He never knew if he was instructed to use the back entrance to keep out-of-sight, or because he was part of the family or just one of the help. On the way to the rear Iggy saw Quinn's wife, Brigid, in a second-floor window. She waved. His heart jumped.

Seeing Brigid always made Iggy all at once very happy and very sad. On the one hand, they grew up together as kids, had a thing once, they were very close, lovers briefly, and his heart always sang when he saw her; on the other hand, she was Quinn's queen, swept away by loneliness and the trappings of immense wealth and status while Iggy was in the army. He could have taken leave to attend their wedding, but he did not.

Quinn met Iggy at the entrance. They embraced, and Quinn ushered him into his study, all wood and leather and old art on the walls. Quinn's *visage* was unmemorable, average in all respects, but this afternoon he was dressed like an ambassador instead of the casual togs he always wore at home.

"Why so dolled up?"

"This evening I dine with Luchesi. Can't put it off any longer," Quinn said.

Iggy gruffed. "That sounds uncomfortable. Shall I tag along?"

Quinn smiled and shook his head. "Ignatius, you have your job, and my guards have theirs. But I appreciate the offer. I'll be okay." Growing up, it was always "Iggy" and

"Red." Now it's "Ignatius" and "Redmond." Protocol insists upon it.

Redmond Quinn embodied a fourth generation in a dynasty of Irish wealth and influence that these days has not the glamour of the Italians nor the notoriety of the Mexicans but works under the surface and in the seams of society with amazing efficiency, a reach across continents, and a long-practiced tenacity. Quinn sat in his power seat behind a truly enormous desk, and Iggy sat beside him in overstuffed leather comfort. He presented the Scotch.

"Jesus, what's this?" Quinn examined the bottle. "I didn't know Bowmore made a 25-year old. This'll be amazing, Ignatius, thank you. Completely unnecessary of you." He read the label, enchanted. "I'm going to take a dram. Will you join me?"

"With pleasure."

And Quinn poured the elixir into two crystal goblets from the old school of bulbous bouquet-trapping tasting glasses. Quinn spun the red amber liquid and put his nose as deep into the glass as the glass would permit. "Mmm… smoke, peat…"

Quinn's palate was legendary. It was part of his breeding, but it was genuine, a real talent, and he liked to show off. He filled his mouth, closed his eyes and spun the medicine around his mouth, and finally, reluctantly, swallowed. He looked at Iggy. "Ripe lemon zest, a touch of pecan and hazelnut…" He was still working it, closing his eyes again. "Jesus. Now cocoa and orange… still isn't over! What a finish! Sherry infused chocolate crème brûlée with a last stream of… peaty smoke. *Wow.*" He opened his eyes. "Jesus, Ignatius. Come over more often."

"I come when you call, Redmond," Iggy said, sipping unceremoniously at his drink. "Brigid home? Haven't seen her in a while."

"No, ah… she's out with her mom I think," Quinn said, and instantly changed the subject. "Tell me, was your latest compensation delivered today?

"It was."

"And all is satisfactory?"

"All is well."

"Good." Quinn nodded and looked out his window, across the pool and tennis courts, the grove with the hated old treehouse, and out over the lake. It was as if he were thinking about how to phrase his next words.

"I have another commission for you, and I know it's very soon after the last, but it's unusual, and it's... personal. That's why I called you here."

"No agent in the middle."

"Just me and you."

Iggy nodded and waited. *Here it comes.*

"There is a man, lives near you, and I know you don't like that, and most of the commissions you get from me involve plane tickets and hundreds of miles, but it can't be helped, and you'll be compensated for this facet of the situation."

"Okay. What else?"

"His name is Jonnie Greer. Ever heard of him?"

Iggy thought to say, *not until this afternoon,* but thought better of it. "Doesn't ring a bell," he lied.

"He's blackmailing me."

Lots of red flags, Iggy thought. But he knew he could not refuse this job. It was masked in the form of a friendly, heartfelt appeal to old friendship, but Iggy knew what this was. It was an emergency; it was an order. He tried to stay unreadable, but his sigh betrayed him.

"I know. This is a tough one. And I know you've never asked for details, and I like to think that the main reason for that is that you know in your heart I would never send you to execute a good man. And I never have, Ignatius. All your commissions have involved people in our business who, *with full knowledge of the consequences,* have somehow betrayed us, or who, for their own gain, became a threat to our world and the people we love."

"I've always understood that, Redmond. As the foundation of our work together."

362

"But because of the enormity of my request, I feel that I must give you details."

"Well. Okay. There's some comfort in that."

Quinn got up and began to pace the room. "You see, Ignatius, I had sex with a woman who is not my wife."

"Steppin' out on Brigid. Does she know?" *The rat the rat the fucking rat.*

"She has no idea."

"And you're being blackmailed with, what, photos?"

"Photos."

"May I see them?"

Quinn pointed to the envelope on his desk. Iggy opened it and removed three 5x7 prints, made on a home printer, no store markings. *Yep, that's Redmond; nope, that definitely ain't the missus.* "May I ask who is the lady?"

"That I won't say."

"I understand." Iggy put the pictures back and placed the envelope where he found it. "What's the proposed arrangement?"

"$15,000 per quarter."

"End date?"

"None."

"Ballsy or stupid."

"I'm counting on stupid."

"Pay him anything yet?"

"No."

"How was the demand delivered?"

"By mail with the photos. Copy of the letter is in with them."

"You got all that for me?"

Quinn removed a large envelope from a file drawer and placed it in Iggy's hands. "More than you'll need."

"Anything else I need to know?"

"Yeah. There's $50,000 in there."

"All at once?"

"And a match of that when we meet again."

Iggy stood and shook Quinn's outstretched hand. "Generous. Thank you."

"I hope, as I'm sure you do, never to ask anything of you like this again."

That was it. Meeting adjourned.

Quinn walked Iggy to his car. They embraced. Quinn shook his head and said, "Jesus, this thing you drive around."

"Hey! Don't hate the Lincoln."

"It's so *conspicuous*. That doesn't bother you?"

"Hey, Tom Selleck drove a Ferrari in *Magnum, P.I.* and it worked okay for him."

"That was a TV show. You're coming Saturday?"

"Of course."

"Alone?"

"Hell no."

"You have a date?"

"Of course."

"Human female?"

Iggy shook his head in mock disgust. "See you then."

As he left the compound he mused about his day and was deeply troubled by two aspects of this visit. *That rat bastard fuck doesn't deserve Brigid. I could kill him for this. He's plowin' some whoor while he's got Brigid at home.*

Then the second issue muscled into his head. *It's too much money. A hundred grand for a hit on a stupid amateur greedy blackmailer? That's too much money.*

But he had to acknowledge the silver lining. *Eighty grand. In one day. I guess things could be worse.*

Things would get worse.

4

On the turn into his secluded driveway, Iggy noted his skinny 18-year old neighbor lugging out his family's trash from next door. Iggy stopped the car and zipped down his window. "Tommy!" he called to the kid.

Tom stopped lugging the can and smiled. "Hey Iggy, what's happening?"

"What are you doin' Saturday night?"

"Partying with my friends. Usual stuff probably."

"How about driving me and my date to a party? You can use the car for a few hours, then come back and get me when I call you."

Tom scratched the back of his neck. "Gee, Iggy, I don't know. I was looking forward to hangin'."

"Ah, horseshit. I know your game. I'll give you 300 dollars."

"How about 400?"

"How about I tell your mom and dad you're a pothead?"

Tom looked down and thought it over. "Okay. 350."

Iggy laughed. "I'll give you your four. But be here by six. And look good. You have to open the door for a beautiful woman, and I don't want you scarin' her."

"She's going out with you, so she can't scare too easy."

Iggy had a good comeback for that but reconsidered. "Just don't be late. And I'm making bread next Sunday. So be here at ten for that."

Tom brightened. "I'm there, Iggy!"

Iggy fancied that, if he were not already a master in his unusual occupation, he would have been a baker. In his basement, he had pro equipment, including a beautiful oven in which he made some of the best bread in town. He and Tom gave away to anyone who would eat it or claimed they would eat it. He fancied Tommy as his apprentice, though in his heart he knew Tommy had the touch, and Iggy's bread was always best the more he gave Tommy the reins and stayed out of the process himself. But Iggy loved his hobby and did not resent his boyish colleague's magic touch.

He aimed the big Lincoln down the bumpy dirt drive to the oversize garage attached to his modest ranch home about 50 yards through the trees, drove in, pressed the door-closer, grabbed the two envelopes and entered his home. Once inside he poured himself another Scotch, and though it wasn't a $400 bottle, it tasted like home.

Iggy deposited $80,000 in $100 bills into his safe and logged the transaction in his book. He looked at the figures. *It helps to have no hobbies. Well. Except the bread and that don't count. Or the car.* In 25 years, he had spent almost nothing of his earnings. In the safe, he had amassed well north of two million dollars. He would never have to work again, if such could be arranged.

But such could never be arranged. It was the life he chose and the nature of his business. Iggy always figured he was different, and things would work out okay somehow, but he could see the clouds gathering. He could sense a reckoning was upon him.

The only way this can work out is if I check my mark out and find that he is indeed a stupid amateur greedy blackmailer. Iggy fulfills his commission and that's that. *So, I may as well stay optimistic. But I gotta see this guy before Saturday.*

Iggy put some Chopin Nocturnes on the stereo, then clicked it off after a few seconds. He wasn't in the mood. He sat and examined with care the contents of the big envelope, now minus the cash. He found a photo of Mr. Greer, and all the contact information he could want. Greer was not married. Never had been. The photo showed a good-looking man in his late-30s, casually but carefully dressed. His brow was clear, he had that open look of naïve kindness about him. Benign. He was on the skinny side and wore a nice easy smile, not for the camera, like, this is how he really is.

The older I get the less I find that looks are deceiving. This guy doesn't look any more like a stupid amateur greedy blackmailer than Shirley Temple.

He examined the blackmail letter. Well-formatted, no misspellings, and all very businessey.

The address put the mark in Barton Hills, a closed and wealthy enclave in north Ann Arbor across the Huron River. People live there with a high expectation of safety and privacy. Lots of cameras up there. More red flags. He couldn't hit him at home.

Lots to work out.

5

But work it out he did, because he was Ignatius Flynn, and this was his job.

It wasn't hard to find out that Greer worked near the sleepy town of Chelsea as a software engineer. It was easy to tail him to work, not in the limo, but in a 2000 Mercury Sable, which Iggy loathed but the car had one indispensable asset: it blended in so well you could stare at it for ten minutes and still not recognize it in a parking lot an hour later.

Iggy had a whole stack of out-of-state license plates and decided for this job he would be from Ohio. *(Birthplace of Aviation)* It was a cinch to stake the place out to follow Greer homeward when he finally left work. Iggy was pleased that Greer was more of a nine-to-nine guy than a nine-to-fiver. Even though the wait was a grind, it was almost dark when Greer at last left the office. Darkness had always been Iggy's ally.

Greer wound his way out of Dexter in a new BMW sedan, Iggy well behind. The half-way point through woods and fields was a little area called North Lake, and Iggy knew well the little tavern about a mile down the road. He knew for a fact that the bar had no outside cameras. (He knew all about all his bars.) It was one of the reasons he liked the place.

Iggy stepped on the gas. Coming up behind Greer, Iggy moved to pass, politely, no faster than was required, signals and all. When Iggy was safely in front of Greer's car, he continued a few hundred feet, then slammed on the brakes. Greer's BMW hit the Sable's rear, not a catastrophe, but enough that both drivers knew they had to get out and check damage. They pulled up into the tavern parking lot, way in the back, and both emerged from their dented sedans.

The first thing Iggy noted when Greer got out was that he was calm and smiling the same smile he wore in the photo. No macho indignation, nothing close to it. In fact, the first thing Greer said when he approached Iggy was a sincere, "Are you okay?"

"Yeah, a little shook up, I guess, but, yeah, fine. You?"

"I'm good."

Iggy noted that Greer was a full foot shorter than he was and had not even half of Iggy's mass. "Airbag?"

"No... no. It never deployed."

Iggy gave himself a little invisible pat on the back. He needed Greer to hit hard enough for damage but not hard enough to deploy the airbag. Messy, that.

"Did you see the deer?" Iggy asked. "I almost hit a fawn, but I think it's okay."

"Really? Jeez, I didn't see it. They're all over the place, aren't they?" The pair stood between the rear of the Sable and the front of the BMW. "The Mercury has quite a ding there."

"Ditto for your Beemer. Sorry about all this."

"Well, they're both drivable. I guess we just call the sheriff and make a report, eh?"

Iggy's brow darkened, and he shook his head with pursed lips. "Actually, Mr. Greer, I was lying about the deer."

"What do you mean?... Did you just call me 'Mister Greer?'"

"It's your name, is it not?"

"Well... yes. I'm afraid you have me at a bit of a disadvantage."

"You have no idea." Iggy pulled his hands from his pocket, revealing that both hands were covered in tight latex gloves. He pulled a pistol, a short-barreled Ruger .22 with a silencer attached, from his coat. Greer stiffened, a look of panic spreading across his features. "Mr. Greer, if you try to run, I will shoot you. *Listen to me.* Are you listening to me?"

"Y-y-yes."

"I don't *want* to shoot you."

"My wallet is in my coat!"

"I don't want to *rob* you. I want to *discuss* something with you." Iggy spoke with measure and calm.

"D-discuss... something?"

"Yes. But you must not panic. If you run or do *anything stupid*, even innocently, out of panic, I *will* shoot you. I can put ten little holes in your head with this and no one will even hear it. Understand? Your *only hope* here is to stay composed."

"Yes." Iggy sensed it was working. Greer was slightly decompressing.

"Do you have any idea what this might be about?"

Greer stared at Iggy. After a few seconds, "Yes."

"Honesty. Good. Now, if you try to flee or attack me or call for others, I will take that as an admission of guilt for what I am here to investigate, and I will kill you on the spot. But listen now, here's the thing: I suspect that there is more to all this than I have been told. And that doesn't sit well with me. So you see now how we *must* discuss this? For *your* own benefit."

"Yes."

"Good. Give me your phone. I'll give it back when we've concluded our business."

He dug and gave Iggy his iPhone. Iggy turned it off and put it in his coat pocket. "We'll talk in my car." And he opened the front passenger door for Greer, who sat obediently. Iggy slammed it shut, walked around the car and entered the driver-side door. He shut it and pressed the lock button. "You'll note that you do not have a door handle. Also your window and lock won't work. You're sealed in here, and now we're going to chat."

"I'm frightened." His voice quaked.

Iggy held up a palm. "Mr. Greer, if I were here simply to kill you, you would be dead by now. You would never have gotten out of your car. Relax. I need you to relax. *You* need to relax. Now breathe."

They sat in silence for a full minute, and Greer at last grew calm enough to converse.

"Now," Iggy began quietly, "what I-"

"I have good reasons for doing what-"

"Whoa *whoa* WHOA!" Iggy interrupted, and Greer was silent, holding his breath.

"Mr. Greer. Two things. First of all, breathe." Greer exhaled and slumped back in his seat. "Secondly, we're going to do this simply and systematically. Understand?"

"Yes."

"I talk, and when I'm done, I'll let you know, then it's your turn."

"Got it."

"Good. Now. Here are the facts as I have been given to understand them. You have taken photos of at least one man, possibly two, possibly more, having sex with a woman, or women, who are not their wives. With these photos, you are accused of blackmailing at least one of these men for fifteen-thousand dollars surrendered to you every three months."

"WHAT!?"

"Quiet now. You're doing very well, and I'm almost done. Now. You are also accused of having sex with one, possibly both, of the wives of these two or more men. I'm going to ask you three yes-or-no questions. You'll be allowed to elaborate when I'm finished, but to these questions *I do not want to hear anything out of you but yes or no.* If I hear more, I'll take it poorly of you, Mr. Greer. Understand?"

"Yes."

"Question one: Did you ever have sex with either of the wives of these two men?"

Greer sighed. "Yes."

"Both?"

"Yes."

Iggy was starting to feel some reprieve. *Maybe I can just kill this guy after all and everything will be well. Life will be normal.* "Did you take photos of either or both of these men having sex with women who were not their wives?

"Yes."

Oh, this is a relief. "Either or both?"

"Both."

"Last question. For now. Are you blackmailing either or both of these men for large amounts of money on the threat that you will release the photos in a manner that will do these men harm?"

Iggy had a clear draw ready for his pistol. It would be over in less than one second.

"No."

Iggy blinked. "No?"

"No."

Son of a BITCH! Iggy shouted inside his head.

"Okay, Mr. Greer," Iggy sighed. "Now it's your turn. Explain to me what I need to know. And listen, Mr. Greer? I've been doing this sort of thing a long time. If I even *suspect* you're lying to me I'll kill you where you sit. And then I'll go inside and have a beer. Got it?"

"Got it."

"And, if by some infinitesimal chance you *do* deceive me, I *will* find out, and the consequences will be swift and inescapable."

"I *get* it."

"I'm all ears."

Greer sat for a long time, obviously working to tell his tale in a cogent way as simply as possible. He was having trouble.

Iggy, though, was patient. "Mr. Greer, why don't you just start at the beginning."

Greer brightened and nodded. "Okay... okay..." He swallowed and began. "It started in a sex club. A swingers club."

"Where at?"

"Private home. I can give you the address."

"And you will. Go on."

"You see... I'm, I'm not married. And I don't date much. Mainly I work. But I've got needs... like anybody else. So, an old neighbor of mine, used to be my friend, I *thought* he was my friend-"

"What neighbor?"

"Man named Alan Picola, I used to live near him."

Bingo.

"Anyway, he invited me to this sex club. In this house. Pretty sophisticated. Maybe four, five couples. Older. Everybody there is wealthy. Bentleys, Ferraris… all men with their wives. A few single girls sometimes. No unattached men. Except me. I was a guest. When I saw what went on, well… I liked it. I went back a few more times – they meet once a month – but from then on I had to have a woman with me. So I could 'join in,' you might say."

"Same woman each time?"

"No. Always different. At first."

"How come?"

"They never wanted to go back. They all seemed enthusiastic, this sort of thing is a lot more common than people think, but it was always too much for them."

"What. The sharing that went on?"

Greer nodded and looked out the window. "Yeah. Plus, when it got rough. They weren't really into that. Except one of the girls. She *really* got into it. I think that's why they kept inviting me back."

"I'll need her name when we're done here."

"All right."

"How long this been going on?"

Greer thought. "Maybe a year."

"So, go on."

"So, after the fourth or fifth time with Sherri, that's her name, I was asked to stay late. By that time the parties had grown to eight or nine couples. Turns out that the two men you're talking about had… an idea… to spice things up a little. That's how they put it."

Greer stopped here. He had a hard time going on.

"You're embarrassed, ashamed, at the rest?" Iggy surmised.

Greer met his eyes. "Yeah. I am. And that's how come we're here."

"Continue."

"Well, about midnight it would be just us three couples. And then these two guys would arrive. A black man and a white man. They were a team. Big guys, great shape. And they had... well, they were very well-endowed. Christ. I can't believe I'm talking about this."

"You're doin' good. Don't stop."

"So these two guys, they would sort of, take over. Anyway, Sherri liked it. The two wives, not so much. They were being forced. After a few meetings, all this got out of hand. These two guys were hurting the girls, in all sorts of ways, if you know what I mean. They put up a fight, they cried, it didn't matter. One night as a diversion, they decided it would be amusing if the women were spanked. Well, they were spanked so hard that Sherri bled. Even she had a problem with that. And all the while this team of sex bruisers had their way, the two husbands... and me, at first, before it got more about pain than sex... would... join in, or else watch and... Okay? *Do I have to go on?*"

"No. But I need to know about the pictures."

"The last night Sherri and I were there I took the pictures of the two men having sex with the other's wife, along with other photos of some of the other rituals going on there with the sex twins. The husbands didn't know, of course. But I was afraid for the women. By this time the bruises they were getting hadn't healed by the next party! They were losing weight. Jesus... Every month the sex got weirder and more violent."

Jesus, that's why Brigid is gettin' skinny. "So, you..."

"So, I stopped going, and sent the two husbands photos of everything, and said I would spread them around if they didn't stop. But I never – *got that? Never!* – asked for money. *I don't need money! I have more money than I'll need in ten lifetimes!*"

"Okay, okay, calm down." The confession was hard for Greer. He was crying now, and almost bent double in his seat. "That's it?" Iggy asked.

"Yeah... that's everything."

"No, it isn't. And Mr. Greer, you have one more chance to come clean here or you'll never make it home."

Greer slowly straightened and looked upon Iggy with an expression of awe mixed with terror, as if it were dawning upon him that he was in the presence of a mind-reading super-sleuth and avenging angel. In truth, Iggy had no idea whatever if Greer were holding anything back, but he knew that by now he had Greer by the short hairs, and his challenge would empty him of every last scrap of pertinent information. Iggy waited for the punch line.

"The two wives... they've come to me for protection. I love them both, and I want to take care of them. Both of the husbands... they know."

"They know you're having an affair with their wives?"

"Not an *affair*. Not about *sex*. We all fooled around together at these parties, sure, but... I was always gentle with them. Never wanted to hurt them. Never wanted to see them hurt." Greer smiled and smeared tears away from his eyes. "I loved their *company* more than anything. When things turned weird, the women got scared and came to me. Finally, I had to act. So I took the photos and sent them to the husbands. The men know... they know that in their hearts, their wives have left them. For me. Even if we hardly see one another. And they're desperate for me to help them out of the situation they're in. They love me... and I love them."

Iggy sat quietly, staring into the vacant lot behind the bar. A minute passed; then two. Greer said, "So. Am I a dead man?"

Iggy twitched awake as if from a trance. "What? No. No, you're not a dead man, Mr. Greer. You're just stupid. *I'm* a dead man."

"What should I do? What's going to happen?"

Iggy thought. "Don't do anything different. When is the next party?"

"Not this Friday but next."

"Good."

"What's going to happen? To me?"

"I need the address of the sex house, Sherri's full name and contact information. Also, the two sex guys who do the brutality stuff. You know who they are?"

"Yeah. They actually were soliciting business there. It's not like they wanted to be anonymous. They gave us their business cards. I got it at home."

"Listen carefully," Iggy said. "Put all that info, including copies of *all* the photos you took, in an envelope and drop it off at Kelly's Bar in Ann Arbor. Say it's for Mr. Kowalski. Understand?"

"Yes."

"Say it."

"Kelly's in Ann Arbor; Mr. Kowalski."

"Do it tomorrow, before noon, and include everything I asked for, or you'll see me the next day, and I'll kill you."

"Jesus Christ! *You don't let up!*"

"*We want the same things here, dumb ass!* The difference is that I can take care of the situation, while you're so far over your ignorant pussy-drunk head you nearly got it chopped off tonight! You have *no idea*, who you're fucking with here. No idea! Now, I'm gonna let you out and you're gonna drive home in your newly fucked-up Eurotrash-mobile and you're going to do as instructed. When you deliver that envelope, you will be free of me forever. You will *never* have to see me again. How does that sound?"

Greer closed his eyes and nodded. "Good."

Iggy thought a moment. "You might want to take a vacation. Couple of months. Let things settle down."

"But the women..."

"That's in *my* hands. Listen. You can take my advice or not. I really don't give a shit. The only reason you're alive is that you tried to protect those women. Now I'm trying to protect *you*. If you stay here while things are hot, you'll be murdered. And not by me. Okay? *That get through to you?*"

Iggy got out and opened Greer's door. Iggy had Greer's iPhone in his gloved hand. He proffered it to Greer.

"If I see a camera flash before I'm clear of this place, I'll come back and shoot you."

And they both went opposite ways home.

6

The next morning, Iggy called an associate of his whom he had met in New York. Iggy decided to buy a painting. It is the *Venus y cupidillos*, painted in 1925 by Salvador Dali. A small painting, about nine inches square, and his cost was almost two million dollars. It would have been about $1.8 million, but the purchase was complicated by the fact that Iggy had to make the purchase with almost twenty thousand $100 bills. The fine art market had become one of the only 'safe' ways to launder money, so a hefty handling premium was tacked on to the purchase price to assure discretion and smiles from all involved. Iggy would take delivery Sunday morning.

Iggy knew it was a wise purchase. Dali was not as popular these days as he was a few decades ago, but the smart buyer knew that would change. Iggy knew it didn't matter, but he wished he liked the painting more than he did.

That afternoon, Iggy also decided to try to buy a certain bakery just outside of Ypsilanti. A popular baguette-maker named Morgan made the only bread in town that Iggy thought was as good as his own. Okay, so he thought that it was *better* than his own. But Mr. Morgan was 85, and sometimes weeks would go by before patrons all over the county could get their fix, religiously visiting the few grocery and party stores that carried Morgan Loaves, only to leave with empty hands or inferior bread. He had no apprentices, only a young woman who made deliveries.

Iggy stopped by and, auspiciously, spied through the window Mr. Morgan sitting alone in his office doing the dreaded paperwork. Iggy knocked, Morgan looked up from his desk and sighed.

"Flynn, I already told you everything about the goddam bread I can tell you!" he grumbled. "The magic is in the magician. Deal with it."

"Always nice to see you, too," Iggy said as he walked in and sat across from Morgan, who put down his pen. "Place smells good," Iggy noted.

"Wanna drink?" Morgan asked.

"Yes." Iggy nodded. "Yes, I do."

Morgan opened a desk drawer and extracted a bottle of rye and two shot glasses. He poured to the brim. They each picked up their glass, nodded wordlessly to the other, and shot it back.

Morgan gave a little shudder, then asked, "So, what do you want, Flynn?"

"I want to buy your building, the property, and your business name."

Morgan stared without expression at Iggy. Then a slow smile spread across his old face. Then he laughed. "Get the fuck outta here, Flynn."

"I'm serious…"

Morgan poured himself another shot (none for Iggy) and let it sit. "Listen to me, you overgrown potato-head mick – I buy YOU, you don't buy me. I work my nuts off for 40 years bakin' the best goddam bread in the fucking state, bread on its *worst* day that's better than anything you'll ever make on your *best*, even with that kid you got, and you come in here and want to *buy me out*? It would be a fucking *sacrilege* to sell this place to the likes of you. Like taking everything I've ever been proud of and throwing it in the fucking garbage! Are you *trying* to make me throw you out of here!? *And don't think I can't do it, goddam it!*" screeched little skinny Morgan.

Iggy slid a check across the table. Morgan spat on it. Big gob of spit. And then looked daggers at Iggy.

"Oh, for Christ's sake just read it," Iggy said.

Morgan kept his hateful stare into Iggy and after a few seconds leaned forward and dropped his gaze to the check. Morgan slammed his palm hard onto the desktop.

"SOLD!" he cried.

7

It was late on Thursday morning, and Iggy had been following Brigid's car for about ten miles now. No one behind him. Lovely sunny summer day, Brigid in a lovely sunny summer dress (or so he hoped) – it was time to make his move. He pulled beside her at a light on Woodward and zipped his window down.

She looked surprised, even through the big sunglasses, and waved, then zipped her own window down. "Hi, Iggy!" They always cheered one another. "What are you up to?"

"Brigid, darlin'. What a coincidence! Hey, pull into the chop house lot and I'll buy you lunch!"

She looked sad. "Oh, Iggy, I can't."

"Coffee then."

She considered. She looked troubled all of a sudden.

"Brigid, please, honey. I got something to tell you. It's important. Won't take but a few minutes."

She gave a sad smile. "Okay. Just coffee."

"Just a coffee."

And together they pulled into the lot, and as Iggy preferred, far in the back of the place and out of sight of the road. Iggy got out in a hurry and rushed over to Brigid's car. When she got out he gave her a hug and a kiss, and then another hug, a real embrace. She could feel a special gush of his heart toward her, sucking her own heart into him, and for a moment they basked in it. Iggy broke it first.

"We don't need coffee. Let's just talk in my car," Iggy said, and she was all right with that. Iggy opened the back door of the limo and Brigid took her seat while Iggy dashed around the car and muscled into the seat next to her.

Iggy touched her hand. "I haven't seen you in a while, Brigid. How have you been?"

She nodded and smiled. "I've been good, good. You?"

"Not bad. Why don't you take those sunglasses off so I can see those beautiful blues."

"Oh, it's just so bright today, Iggy."

Iggy looked out the window and squinted dramatically. "Jeez, it really is, ain't it?" He pointed to the side of his nose. "But you got a... I dunno what the hell that is, on the side of your nose there."

Her vanity was mortified. "Oh, God. Where?" and started to smear about at the indicated area while Iggy chuckled playfully.

"Nope, nope..." he laughed. "Here. Stop that. I'll get it." She put her face forward and Iggy reached carefully and snatched the glasses off her head.

"IGGY!" she shrieked.

He made a fist and bit it. Before she could turn her head, he saw the black eye, and a little butterfly bandage under the eyebrow. And Iggy started to cry. He covered his downcast face with his hands and his shoulders shook. Reflexively, Brigid hugged him and held him, finally rocking him gently like she would an enormous child, trying as best she could to quell her own tears.

"I can't lie to you, Iggy. *Please* don't ask me about this."

Iggy brusqued her away and sat straight. He mopped at his cheeks with his palms and looked at Brigid. "Did this happen at the sex house?"

Her jaw fell. "Oh, my *gawd!*" She turned her head away again and looked out the window. "Do you know *everything?!*"

"Brigid, you need to answer if this happened at the sex house." He was calm now and getting into interrogation mode.

"No," she answered, still dizzy from Iggy's discovery. "No. It didn't. How do you know?... about...?"

"Greer spilled the beans. *All* the beans," he answered.

She blanched. "Did you hurt him? Is he-"

"He's fine. I'll try to protect him. I dunno where the smart money is on that, though."

"Oh, my God. What must you think of me?" she whispered as if to herself.

"So, the eye. Red hit you?"

"Yes. Never before did he do anything like that to me. One punch."

"You threaten to leave him? That why?"

She sighed. It was all out there now. "Yes, Iggy. That's why." She added hastily. "He was drunk. He apologized. He begged me to forgive him."

"And did you? Turn around and look at me. Did you forgive him? Do you?"

She turned and met his eyes. "No. I can't. Ever." *She said that with poison,* Iggy noted. *She hates him.* "The punch, Iggy…," she hissed, "the punch is the least of it."

For a minute they did not speak. Iggy sensed she needed to explain.

"At first, I did it for Red, because I thought he was losing interest in me. And I surprised myself, 'cause at first it was a real unexpected… erotic adventure. To be completely worshipped by five or six men. I never even *thought* about such a thing before. Everyone was nice, and clean, and respectful and gentle. No meant no. Everybody got that."

She leaned over and buried her face in her hands with disgrace. "Oh, Iggy, I'm so ashamed to tell you this stuff." She straightened and looked at Iggy with pleading eyes. "I never felt good about it afterwards but I put up with it for Red's sake, and always dreaded the next month's gathering, and tried to wiggle out of it with every excuse imaginable. But for Red it was like a *drug*. It completely changed him! Him and this other guy, this Alan. *Ugh."*

She opened her purse, took out a tissue and wiped at her nose. "And then one night they stayed late and invited this pair of, I dunno, porn stars, I guess. And they would 'perform' with me and Birdy. That's Alan's wife, and with that crazy slut Jonnie had with him. And that was *horrible.* Everything changed then. It gradually got sick and violent, and Red loved every minute of it. Like I said, it *completely* changed him. And every month it got worse and weirder, and I never wanted to go back there, and he said they wouldn't do those things this time, but he would force me, with the most awful threats. And finally I threatened to leave him no matter what he did to me, no matter what would happen to me because nothing was worse than what was happening to me. And then he hit me."

"Where were you goin' just now? To see Greer?"

"Yes."

"You love him?"

She smiled. "No. But he was my lifeline through this horror."

"Not me?"

"Iggy..."

"You never thought of telling *me?*" His voice quivered.

"Oh, Iggy – if I had told *you*, you'd be *dead!*" She began to cry again. "But now you *know!* You have to go away! *You can't do what you're thinking!*" She fell into Iggy's bulk, pressing her head hard into his chest, and let the tears flow. He stroked her hair and kissed the top of her head. *The smell of her thick black hair.*

"Are you being tailed? Anybody follow you? Today or on your other trips?" he asked softly.

"I don't think so." Iggy didn't note a tail on her on the drive here, but he could have been spotted. *Should have taken the Sable.*

"We can't take the chance. You need to go home. Call Greer and tell him... tell him you'll see him next week. He needs to go away for a few months. Convince him. Keep our encounter to yourself. Nobody must know about this, understand? Not even Greer."

She lifted her head, her face close to Iggy's. She kissed him as sweetly as she could, and he felt every drop of it, but the taste of the kiss was alloyed with sour worry. "Iggy," she whispered. "My dearest Iggy. What are you going to do?"

He forced a smile. "Trust me," he said. "And lay low. Don't leave him until after the party. That's important. Trust me to do the right thing. Everything will be okay."

She was shaking her head. "No... No, Iggy. I *know* you'll do the right thing. And that's why I'm so upset. Please. I beg you, my love. For once in your life. Consider. For *me*. Consider *not* doing the right thing. Do the *smart* thing."

Iggy was puzzled. "What's the smart thing?"

Brigid put her glasses back on and opened her door. "You're Ignatius Flynn. You'll figure it out. *Please,* Iggy." She kissed his cheek and was out the door.

And as Brigid walked away in her sweet summer dress, Iggy watched her lovely bottom sway and for a moment his troubles vanished and the bird in his heart sang. This was followed by the most heartbreaking thought of his life, for once and at last as clear as a bell:

She was the one.

Sometimes there is no right thing.

Sometimes there is no smart thing.

Sometimes, there's just The Thing.

8

When Iggy got home, he called Alan Picola. He decided to accept his $50,000 commission. He then found the contact card for the *Hercules Twins*, the black and white fellows with the big sex appeal, to secure their service for a cozy party he wanted to throw. He invited all three of them over the next morning, which was a Friday, to meet with Iggy at his home.

But the day was young. He took a cab to an Avis dealer and rented a car with phony credentials. When he returned, he screwed a New Mexico plate to the rear *(Land of Enchantment)* and headed to the address of the sex house in a toney section of Ferndale, a suburb of Detroit. He was playing a role and he looked the part.

The door was answered by a disheveled man in his forties, bald, skinny, still in a bathrobe at 2 p.m. Iggy, in a cheap grey suit, opened a leather wallet and straight-armed his identification for the benefit of a Mr. Archie Collins.

"Archie Collins?"

"Yeah?"

"I'm Special Agent Marshall Potter of the F.B.I. May I come in?"

"What's this about?"

"It's about a matter concerning your next door neighbor, a Mr. Darrin Fields."

"Yeah. I know Darrin." He looked down and gave it all a few seconds of thought. "Okay. Come on in. Always glad to help the law." Iggy stepped into the middle of the room, turned and smiled reassuringly. Collins shut the door and turned. "Darrin in some kind a trouble?"

"No." Iggy had pulled the silenced .22 pistol from his coat and put three shots in Collins' forehead before he fell.

Then Iggy cased the house. He knew Collins was unmarried, but he needed to make sure the home was empty. When he came upon what was obviously the 'party room' he became upset. Iggy never allowed himself the luxury of feeling anything when he was working, so he shook it off and concluded his survey of the house as quickly as he could. It was indeed empty, and so he set about the project of burning it to the ground.

The ride home was uneventful. The fire headlined on all the local TV 'news' shows that night. A "murder-arson" it was billed. He knew he was being messy, but he also knew, at this point it really didn't matter.

No other homes were damaged, and the house was a total loss.

The start of the most mournful mission in Iggy's career had a most auspicious beginning.

9

Friday morning and Alan Picola was right on time.

Iggy welcomed him inside, and they sat in his studio office over coffee, Iggy in the middle of his long couch and Alan on a leather chair a few feet in front of him. Alan was pleased that Iggy had come to his senses.

"I was hoping you would call me back, Mr. Flynn." he sipped at his hot drink.

"Ah, hell," Iggy said, "call me Iggy. May I call you Alan?"

"Of course!"

"So… Alan… business first. I believe fifty-thousand dollars was your offer?"

Alan patted at the bulge in his coat pocket. "And I've got it right here."

"May I see it? You don't have to give me the money, you doubtless have questions and concerns here, but I would like you to simply demonstrate that you have the cash."

Alan considered this a moment. "Well, your reputation is sterling, Iggy. I got no problem with this." And Alan extracted the envelope from his coat and put the money on display for Iggy's benefit. Iggy eyeballed it quickly, nodded and Alan put the envelope back in his coat.

"Thank you, Alan. I'm wondering… aren't you a little curious as to what changed my mind about all this?" Iggy asked earnestly. "Why I'm eager now to get that stone out of your shoe?"

"Well… I suppose I am. You *were* rather dismissive, if not downright *rude* to me at the tavern." Picola sniffed and sat back, getting cozy now in his role as boss-employer of handyman Iggy.

"I'll tell you what really did it for me," Iggy leaned forward and confided, looking thoughtful. "I would have to say that, when I found out that you and my employer, Redmond Quinn, you know, the guy who recommended me to you, were sexually abusing the only woman I ever truly loved in my life – who happens to be Quinn's wife, well… I guess that's when I decided to call you here, beat you to death and then take your money."

The color left Alan's face and he instinctively looked about the room for doors and windows, anything to get away and quell the instant panic visited upon him. He made a dash for the door and twisted wildly at the knob. Iggy just sat and watched.

"It's locked. And you'll note that there are no windows."

Alan turned, wild-eyed, with his back to the door. *"I'll give you anything you want!"*

Iggy shook his head. "At this point, Alan, all I *want*, is to kill you with my hands." Iggy rose and became oddly introspective, talking now not so much to Alan as to himself. "You see, in my entire career as a professional, I must have killed a hundred men. At least that. But I never killed with passion. Never! I always considered that to be vulgar, unprofessional. A *sin* even. I enjoyed my work, see? But I never *reveled* in the act of killing another man."

Alan was not hearing any of this. "Just tell me what you want! I can arrange it! I'm rich! *Just for god's sake tell me!*"

And Iggy, for his part, was not hearing Alan. Iggy's own voice sounded faraway and hollow to him, as if someone else were saying these things. He began to walk toward the door, easy one step at a time.

"But I must admit, *and it shames me to do so,* but I would be dishonest and untrue to myself if I even tried to *pretend* that I will not wallow in the pure joy, and savor the bliss, and… and *ecstasy*, of beating you to death using only my hands as my tools."

Alan was about to make some feeble attempt at a fight, as flight was out-of-the-question, but suddenly he bared his teeth and looked like a feral dog. *"Those women asked for it! They weren't innocent! Those bitches enjoyed every minute of it!"* he hissed.

Iggy stopped at arms' length from his prey, fascinated. "What an odd tactic. To say such a thing to me."

Alan sprung at Iggy with a shout, but in a single second he was face-up on the floor with Iggy sitting on his pelvis, his knees on Alan's arms.

Iggy hit him in the face. "BRIGID!" Iggy screamed.

He hit him again, bringing his fist down like a hammer onto Alan temple. "BRIGID!" he screamed again.

And another punch, and another scream of the beloved's name, and Alan was out at the fourth punch, but Iggy hit again and again and again, alternating his huge fists as if they were hammers pounding at the glowing metal on an anvil, and after each stroke he bellowed his beloved's name until at long last there was nothing recognizable as a man's head attached to Alan's corpse.

Iggy stopped when he was too exhausted to go on and rolled off Alan's cadaver onto his back and stared at the ceiling. And he wept like the abandoned child he was for many minutes, and when that finally ceased, he stared vacantly at the ceiling…

Eventually, his eyes drifted to the clock on the wall and he came rushing back to himself, realizing that the *Hercules Twins* would arrive within the hour, and there was still much to do.

Showered and changed, jittery and hollow, Iggy waited for the twins, who were late. Iggy hated that in a man. When they finally arrived, Iggy greeted them cordially, discovering thereby that he had all but lost his voice. He coughed and tried to clear his throat and apologized to the young men for his indisposition. They were cool with that, dude! Iggy usher the pair into Iggy's old TV room, empty now, a large rectangle with an open floor space.

Iggy, all but drained, had no more drama in him, no more speeches, no more desire to explain to another, nor to himself, about The Thing which confronted him, and the hows and whys of it all. He was weary, and his hands were swollen and sore. The twins noted that the floor was covered in a plastic tarp. (After surveying the damage to the carpet in his office, Iggy decided that, even though he would likely never see the place again after tomorrow night, a totally fouled floor was just unacceptable.)

"Oh, that! yeah," Iggy croaked. "I got to do some painting in here. You know. White carpet and all."

"I get it, dude," White Twin said. "No paint on the floor."

"Exactly," Iggy croaked. He set up two kitchen chairs for the twins to sit. "Have a seat. Can I get you guys a beer?"

"Beer sounds awesome," Black Twin piped as the pair took their seats.

Iggy left the room, opened the closet door and took out his 12-gauge semi-auto shotgun. A nice Browning, a gift from

Redmond a lifetime ago. He re-entered the room, and before the twins could get the picture, Iggy swiftly snugged the barrel of the gun into White Twin's crotch and pulled the trigger twice. As he fell to the floor, the astonished Black Twin rose up and shouted, *"What the fu-"* and Iggy shot him in the crotch, too, twice, before he finished his sentence.

Now the Hercules Twins were on the floor writhing and moaning and babbling and crying and vomiting in their agony, and Iggy sat, waiting for as long as it would take, and noting with exhausted serenity how glad he was that he had put some plastic down!

10

Young neighbor Tom, now in the role of chauffeur, stopped at the red light and turned to eye Iggy. "You don't seem too thrilled to meet your date," he observed.

Iggy nodded his head in acknowledgment, removed the crystal decanter from its holder and poured himself a stiff one. He swallowed half. "Something happened that's taken the fun out of it," Iggy said, and about this he said no more.

On the drive to Twannette's condominium, Iggy gave Tom his instructions for the evening, and Tom questioned the oddness of Iggy's directives. But a stern look from Iggy set him straight.

"Not very chatty tonight. All right. I get it, boss-man," Tom said.

"Thank you. Be a good boy and there might be a tip in it for you."

"Golly! Thanks, Mister Flynn!"

Iggy laughed in spite of the sarcasm. "Shut up and drive. And drive nice, not like you're stealing it."

"Got it," the boy said. "Don't drive like Iggy."

When the big Lincoln pulled in front of Twannette's condo, Tom got out and opened the back door for Iggy to emerge, tycoon-like, from the dark velour and wood cabin. He liked the feeling. He had on his tuxedo, as ordered, and he looked monumental in it.

"Dude, if you had a monocle, you'd look like a huge version of Monopoly Man," Tom observed as he closed the door.

"Stand here, and while you're waiting, develop some impeccable manners, okay?"

"As you wish, Mr. Flynn."

Iggy snapped his fingers and pointed. "Yeah. Like that," he said and sauntered away in the direction of Twannette's porch.

He rang the bell and Twannette appeared, and she was pretty magnificent. Short brown hair, brown eyes that were almost oriental, angel face. And she had the formal thing down! When they walked to the car together, Iggy noted that she walked in heels like she was wearing sandals. She just drifted. The dress was tight, but not vulgar, and there was no tugging or adjusting or any of that behavior one notes in girls on prom night. Twannette was a natural. *All this and a brain? What a package,* Iggy mused.

Tom opened her door with a nod and a smile, and Twannette scooted over for big Iggy to fall in after her.

She looked around. "My gosh! I've never been in a more gorgeous back seat! You hired this old thing, right?" Her voice had sugar in it.

"Nope. It's all mine," Iggy said as the limo pulled away. "Kind of a hobby." He opened the little cupboard and removed a crystal glass. "May I pour you some cognac?"

She was dazzled. *I still got it!* Iggy joked with himself as he poured her a small portion. She took the glass with slim, perfectly groomed hands. Nails polished but not colored. No rings to detract from the hands. Jade bracelet to match the dress and necklace. Classy stuff all around.

They smalltalked the way there. Tom drove like an angel, none of the usual jackrabbit stops and starts to purposely annoy Iggy.

"Some quiet music, Twannette? We got a long ride." Iggy thought hard that afternoon about what a lady cosmologist might like to listen to. "Bach okay?"

"Bach? Umm… suuuuuuure."

She sounded definitely *un*-sure, but Iggy turned the knob and there it was. Just a quiet background, Bach on the piano, for their conversing.

Maybe some shop talk. Get he into her own thing, Iggy thought.

"I like Bach 'cause he didn't regard himself as an artist but as a scientist," Iggy said. "a *cosmologist* of music. Like Newton worked out the laws of planetary motion, well, Bach discovered the laws of the musical universe."

Twanette looked at Iggy with a look of complete blankness. "Wow. You must really like Bach. Honestly, he's a little far up there for me," she said.

Ah, shit. I blew that one. Iggy switch the music off.

"Oh, no," she objected. "You don't have to turn it off!"

"It's okay, it's okay. I got all sorts of stuff here. What do you like?"

"Well… at the salon, we play a lot of Garth Brooks. And the black cutters they're always fighting for more of that urban stuff. They *hate* Garth," she confided.

Iggy wore a befuddled look. "The salon?"

"Oh, yeah. Didn't Brian tell you? That's where I met Brian. He's a sweet guy. I'm a cosmetologist!" she revealed.

"Cos-*met?*-ologist?"

"Yep! I got a whole line of cosmetics with my name that they carry there at Wendy's downtown Royal Oak," she said proudly.

"You know, come to think of it, Brian did say something about that," Iggy said with a smile.

So, it was back to smalltalk for the remainder of the drive (he had no Garth Brooks), and there was *lots* of smalltalk, but blessedly one-sided. She would not shut up. *At least she's comfortable with me.* Finally, Iggy began to tune out. *Ah, hell, maybe it's a good thing. Makes it easier to concentrate on the night.*

11

No drive-around-to-the-back horseshit tonight, Iggy thought, as the stately Lincoln came to rest at the festooned entrance to the Quinn estate. Tom never left the driver seat, as Quinn had a doorman for the evening who graciously helped discharge splendid Iggy and gorgeous Twannette from the limo. What a pair.

Inside there were a couple dozen revelers, Iggy knew most of them, all from the upper ranks of his colleagues and associates over the decades, and almost all locals with some national ringers thrown in for appearances. Iggy noted that he was the only one there who represented the enforcer side of the business nationwide. Well, Brian was there, but he didn't really count. Yet. Coming up through the ranks the kid is an eager beaver, good military background and showing some promise but he has a ways to go.

The real reason Iggy was invited was likely due to the fact that Quinn and he were lifetime pals and the closest thing that Quinn still had left as a friend. But the events of the past few days suggested to Iggy a far more treacherous motive. Iggy knew he would be assassinated tonight.

Iggy and his consort were, in fact, two of the chosen to dine at the King's table, along with Brigid, her pain-in-the-ass brother and his wife (Sean and Angela), and a visiting dignitary from the old country who was dispatched to show his respect for Quinn's happy occasion. Quinn had long confided in Iggy that he disliked the man immensely, as he was, officially, a notch above Quinn in the hierarchy of things and was capable, though to-date never inclined, to make life difficult for Quinn should he be inclined to do so. His name is Devin Greene, about 70 years-old, accompanied by his perky wife Alice, nowhere close to half his age. Those were the eight diners at the King's table.

There was lots of milling about and happy conversation, also a live band, and Iggy enjoyed slow-dancing. Twannette was as good a dancer as she looked, and both of them enjoyed many slow numbers together – she was willing to boogie, but Iggy, not so much – breaking for the up-tempo tunes to drink champagne, of which they drank a lot. Iggy was, well, Iggy, but Twannette unwisely tried to keep up and was very much out of her league.

Iggy in a tux was a sight to behold and all the ladies loved it. Lots of the women wanted to dance with Iggy, the tallest and largest person in the room (in every room, pretty much always), and, as most knew him as his shabby and lovable self, they were all stunned to see how well he 'cleaned up.' He was amused to note that, with each new glass of champagne, Twannette got more and more intolerant of the attentions Iggy was getting from other ladies. She danced with other guys, but her eyes were always glued to Iggy at the expense of her partner. When he returned to dance with her, he observed that she snuggled closer and closer as the eve wore on, pressing herself against him in most delicate but increasingly obvious gestures of wanton lust.

Finally, dinner was being served. Across from Iggy and Twannette were Sean and Angela, Devin Greene and Alice to his left, Quinn and Brigid to his right, closest to the wall. Quinn always sat with his back to a wall. In their line of work it was the prime place to be. There were four other tables-for-eight in Quinn's ballroom and everyone was settling down.

Quinn had retired the band, which was replaced for dining by a string quartet. After a few bars from the first piece, Twannette whispered loudly to Iggy, "Is this Bach?"

He was charmed. "No, uh… this sounds like Haydn."

"Hi-den?"

"Yep. Think so."

"Can I have some more champagne?" Which Iggy gleefully supplied.

It was a marvelous banquet. There was a lobster bisque, Cesar Salad, prime rib with an array of vegetables and (Iggy thought, natch) inferior bread. Presently, dessert, a 24-layer chocolate cake, was now just arriving.

As the meal progressed Twannette got increasingly drunk and Iggy, too, kept pounding down the champagne. He was by now slurring his speech and seemed to have difficulty focusing his eyes. He was also dominating the conversation with progressively booming tones and the odd vulgarity – something no one had ever heard Iggy do before. Quinn was getting annoyed by all this, for Iggy was starting to embarrass him in front of his Irish better.

The tipping point came in the middle of desert.

Brigid, who's bruised eye was hardly noticed thanks to the makeup she expertly applied, ended a lull in the conversation with the subject of Iggy bringing Redmond that amazing bottle of Scotch the previous day. "He said he rarely had a Scotch with so many amazing flavors. He really appreciated it," Brigid said.

Iggy pointed at Quinn. "That guy! He's amazing!"

Old Devin took note. "Really, now? How so?"

"Oh, man, *nobody* has a palate like this guy! He a *genius* at it. He could work in the goddam circus!"

Quinn was getting uncomfortable. "Well, I suppose you could say that I-"

"He reminds me my brother, Patrick!" Iggy cut him off. "My brother Patrick works as the sound guy at Comerica Park for the Tigers. Great musician. Has his own studio. Lemme tell you, *that guy can hear a frog fart in a hurricane!*" Iggy said with emphasis.

Tipsy Twannette just cracked up at that one. So did Brigid's sister Angela, but that was it. The others were trying to pretend that Iggy never told that one, and Quinn was obviously deep in thought about what to do about his unruly underling. He was growing livid at Iggy's increasing incivility and trying not to show it.

"Sean!" Iggy hailed Brigid's brother-in-law across the table. "I been talkin' too much. What's with you these days? Get any good tax-payer grants lately for your... what the hell is it? Anthropology? That's what powers your machine there at the college, right? Them grants? Am I right?"

"Yeah, pretty much, I suppose…" Sean said meekly but was quick to warm to the subject. "Actually, we're working on a big commission."

Iggy waited. No follow-up from Sean. "A commission for *what*, Sean?"

"Oh! Umm… to try to ascertain, what Jesus, umm… actually *looked* like, in person."

Iggy chewed on that for a few seconds. He crinkled up his face. "What?"

"Yes. Umm… there is a particular foundation who thinks it would be a most interesting thing to resolve. And we, have been, umm… chosen for the project."

"Huh." Iggy huffed. "Did you see the new *Salvator Mundi?*"

Sean was jarred by Iggy's familiarity with the painting. "The new Leonardo painting just authenticated? Yes. Yes. I've only seen pictures."

"That's because the lousy Russian son-of-a-bitch that bought it for 130 million dollars won't let anybody see it!"

"Yes, I know. That's a tragedy. The painting is amazing."

"It's more than amazing. You know why?" Iggy asked.

"Ahh… well… why?"

"Because every other Jesus work of art I ever saw, real or pictures, makes him look like a woman, or else queer. Or else like a pussy wimp."

Then he shouted, *"I fucking HATE paintings of Jesus!"* This silenced the entire hall, except Twannette, who burst out laughing.

"Ignatius! Calm down!" Quinn ordered. Iggy brushed him off without eye contact and leaned forward.

"That's the first painting of Jesus Christ I ever saw in my life that *scared* me," Iggy whispered. He leaned back. "Next time you see it ask yourself: 'Do I wanna fuck with this guy?' Look at his eyes. *That's* what Jesus looks like, to me!"

Sean coughed, and said, "Yes, but… that's what he looks like to *you*. But what did he *really* look like? I mean, objectively speaking."

Iggy looked at Sean as if he were a three-headed poodle. "Do you even know what you're asking? Do you have *any* idea what you're doing? You got a grant, to study what Jesus Christ looked like, and you're too goddam dumb to see the answer smacking you right in the gob."

"Now, Iggy," Sean's wife said.

"And it's *free*. You don't need a grant." Iggy chuckled. "Hey, maybe that's why you can't see it!"

Twannette thought that was just hilarious, and she and Iggy clinked champagne glasses and drained them, but no one else joined in. All were focused on how Sean would react, except Brigid, who was looking down at her untouched dessert with her hands to her temples.

"So, what answer am I too dumb, umm... evidently, to see?" Sean asked, his usual pale, bony cheeks rosy red.

Iggy leaned forward and enunciated the way drunks do when they try to speak perfectly.

"Jesus Christ always looked, *exactly*, like whoever saw Him *needed* Him to look. That's why he's Christ. You think he's a *guy*? You think... just some *guy* who had a certain *look*? Really? You're that fucking *dumb*?" Iggy drained more booze.

Quinn had reached his limit. "Ignatius, we need to have a talk."

"Yes. Sure. I gotta talk to you about that thing. It's all taken care of."

"Now, please," and Quinn moved to stand.

As Iggy pushed his chair away from the table and stood, Twannette grabbed him around his thigh and looked up. "You're gonna get lucky tonight, baby," she cooed.

Iggy kissed the top of her head. "When I get back, we'll take off, okay?" She nodded gooey assent as Iggy followed Quinn to his office, stumbling drunkenly on his way.

Before Iggy was out of earshot of the ballroom, Sean appeared at the end of the hall. "Iggy!" he called.

Iggy stopped and turned.

Sean said, "I never thought about those things. Those things you said. I will, though. Thanks."

Iggy smiled and waved goodbye.

Quinn unlocked his office suite and they entered, Quinn first and Iggy stumbling behind, Iggy turned and closed the office door as Quinn approached his desk.

"I'm on to you, Ignatius," he said, still with his back to Iggy. "I have an idea what you've been up to these last couple of days. And in your shameful condition you're making all this very easy."

Quinn opened his desk drawer and removed a large .45 pistol with silencer attached. He turned and leveled the gun at Iggy's chest. Iggy was trying to focus his eyes and swayed back and forth precariously.

Iggy belched. "Whazzat? A *gun*?"

"I'm sorry it's come to this, Ignatius," Quinn said flatly. "I gave you a clear assignment, with extravagant compensation, and you went off the rails. You are now an organizational liability." And he pulled the trigger.

And nothing happened. Again. And again.

Iggy reached into his coat for his own silenced .45 and leveled it at Quinn. "Put the gun down, Red."

Quinn stopped fiddling with his gun, straightened, and regarded Iggy. "You're not drunk!"

"Of course I'm not drunk, you idiot. See, I'm on to you, too. Not for as long as I *should* have been, but…"

"My gun," Quinn was quizzical. "It was loaded."

"Well," Iggy admitted, "you know when I went to the bathroom? I didn't really go to the bathroom."

"That door was *locked*!"

"Well, oddly enough, Red, that's never much of an impediment, considering."

Quinn tossed the heavy gun onto his desk with a loud clatter. "What are you going to do? Shoot me?"

Iggy shrugged. "That's up to you. If you resist *anything* I tell you to do I'll kill you where you stand."

"And if I comply?" Quinn asked. "What then?"

"Then I swear on the head of the only woman I ever loved that I will *not* shoot you."

Quinn thought a space and smiled. "I suppose you may think by now you have nothing to lose. It's not true. But I'm the only one who can help you out of this."

Iggy returned the phony smile. "I realized I had nothing to lose when I heard Greer's story, and confirmed it."

"Yes. Noble Ignatius. Did you get to Picola? He's missing. Did you kill him?"

"Picola's dead. Sex house guy is dead. I burned the funhouse down. The big dick brothers are dead."

"And if you kill me, *you're* dead," Quinn said flatly.

"Blank sheet of paper and a pen," Iggy ordered. *"Now!"*

Quinn moved slowly, but he complied, the gears of his brain turning carefully.

"Now what."

"Write: 'Be back Monday,' and then sign it 'Redmond.'"

Quinn made a quizzical face. "Where are we going?"

"Do it!" Iggy barked, and Quinn wrote as instructed.

"Now what?" Quinn asked.

Iggy holstered his gun. He stood relaxed with his hands at his side and studied Quinn. "You hurt Brigid, and you deceived me. You dishonored me. And... oh yeah, you just tried to *kill* me. I trusted you and now I have doubts about everything I've ever done. 'Organizational liability' my ass. I'm a *personal* liability. How many of your messes have I cleaned up?"

Quinn closed his eyes and sighed, relieved at Iggy without a gun. "I made a mistake. Just this once."

"I know what that means coming from a man like you," Iggy said. "It means you think your mistake is that you got caught."

In a wink, Iggy sprang upon him and wrestled his huge and still swollen hands around Quinn's throat, and a shocked Quinn tried to thrash away. After a few seconds, Iggy had the grip he wanted, and he squeezed, while forcing Quinn to his desk, now lying upon it, his legs dangling from the edge. Iggy witnessed the popping eyes and the flesh turn from pale to red, red to purple, the swelling and cresting of Quinn's savage animal resistance and the gradual ebbing of his strength. The physical magnitude and martial mastery of Iggy made a trivial thing of Quinn's struggle. Soon Quinn was still, but Iggy kept his grip until there was no doubt that Quinn's soul was on his way, Iggy fervently hoped, to hell.

Iggy dragged Quinn's carcass off the desk by his ankles, taking no care in shielding Quinn's head from the floor bounce. He then cleared the desk chair from his path and shoved the body under the desk. For maximum concealment, Iggy needed to get on the floor with the corpse and position it properly under the Texas-sized desk, and when he was underneath, he had a flash from childhood, vivid and sad, remembering when they used to build forts under the desk (then used by Redmond's father) to fight Indians and aliens together, and sometimes they would allow little neighbor Brigid to share in the big-kid games.

Snapping from that lucid reverie, he rose up, slid the desk chair fully back in its slot, tidied up the office and positioned prominently the piece of paper on which Quinn advised that he would return on Monday. Iggy straightened his tux, opened the door and peeked down the hallway. Finding it clear, he scuttled to the rear stairway and out the back entrance, nodding at the familiar guards stationed there. Iggy whipped out his phone and alerted Tommy that he would soon be at the appointed pick-up spot a block away.

Tommy was there (good man, Tommy!), and Iggy heaved his bulk into the rear seat of the limo. He zipped down his window as they sped off and chucked his phone into passing bushes, zipped the window up, spread his legs wide, took a deep sigh, and smiled at Tommy's questioning face in his rearview mirror.

"So, kid. How was *your* night?"

12

Iggy had prepared the bakery he purchased the day before with a few furniture items brought from home – chairs and a couple of army cots. Mr. Morgan already had a refrigerator (which Iggy stocked with goodies) and even cable TV, which would help while away some of the upcoming hours. Tommy had already alerted his parents, as instructed, that he would not be home for a couple of days.

So, it was to the bakery they drove after the party, where they settled down for an attempt at a good night sleep and a busy Sunday.

At dawn Iggy made coffee, and as he savored the brew, he watched young Tommy sleep. *He reminds me nothing of myself,* Iggy pondered. *He's a good kid, good parents, good education. College boy. But he has no idea what he's doing. He hates school. Like so many his age, he's lost. I remember the night he was born. He's gonna be all right, though. I'll be goddamned if he isn't going to be all right.*

At 10 a.m. a car pulled into the bakery drive. A man got out with a briefcase, and once inside the bakery, he opened it in private for Iggy to examine. There was a painting inside, and two pieces of paper. He gave it to Iggy and Iggy gave the man two duffle bags in exchange, the contents of which the man examined. It was all very clinical and brief, and Iggy was relieved when it was over.

Iggy rented a car for the day. A little Chevy that no one would suspect would even *contain* Iggy, let alone interest him. He had many ends to tie up, and a little project that would take most of the day. He instructed Tommy to stay inside, call no one, and go nowhere. Tommy realized that he was in the middle of something very big and possibly quite dangerous, but to his credit, he did what Iggy asked and did not plague him with questions.

Iggy returned late in the evening with a pizza and a bottle of Scotch, looking sad and worn out. They were in bed by 10 p.m. It was raining.

13

Monday morning was gloriously sunny and mild, and a check of the forecast assured that inclement weather would not be a factor in the day's events. At about 8 a.m. the pair took a drive to a nearby diner and enjoyed a breakfast far better than the façade and décor had hinted they would get. Then it was back to the bakery to start the day.

Iggy told Tommy that today would not be as boring as yesterday. Tommy was pleased, but Iggy thought, *Kid, sometimes boring is good.* He instructed the lad to stay inside as Iggy stepped into the alley in back of the bakery to make a phone call with his new cheap flip-phone, a 'burner' they call it in the drug trade. It rang and rang, and Iggy dreaded the sound of the phone-mail picking up. But it was finally answered.

"Hello?"

"Brigid? It's me."

"Oh, gawd! Iggy! *Where are you?*"

"You alone? Can you talk freely?"

"Yes and yes. Iggy, is Redmond there with you?"

"I'll answer all your questions, Bridg, but you need to listen, okay?"

There was a pause in which Iggy could sense Brigid composing herself. Then a big sigh. "All right. Tell me."

"First of all, what's going on at the house?"

"Nobody knows where Redmond is! And everyone's going crazy."

"That old Irish fuck. Is he in charge?"

"Yes, the guy from the party. He's still here. Him and his stupid wife. This is a big thing, you know."

"Red is under his desk in his office." No response. He could sense her confusion. "He's dead, honey," Iggy said. "I killed him."

Brigid was incredulous. "He's been under his *desk* this whole time? But that note! It's Red's handwriting. He said he'd be back today."

"I made him write it, then I killed him. It took some of the heat off."

"Well, Iggy – it's pretty damn hot around here right now!"

"Have they been to my house?"

"Of course they have. They found three bodies, but nobody knows who they are yet. Well, they know *who* they are, they just don't know why they're there."

"One of them is Picola. The other two are the porn star guys." No response. Just breathing. "I also killed the sex house owner and burned his fucking house down."

She was now all calm and whispery. "I saw that on TV. I wondered if that was your handiwork."

"Did you enjoy…" Iggy's voice had cracked. "Did you enjoy watching it burn?"

Her answer surprised him.

"No," she said.

"No? Really?"

"Because I knew right then that they would be coming for you." And then, much to Iggy's anguish, she began to cry. *"And they will never, ever stop."*

Iggy let her waterworks flow for a spell as he tried to collect his thoughts.

"Listen… Bridg."

Sniffle. Noseblow. "What."

"Will you come see me?"

"When."

"Now."

"Where are you?"

"In Ypsilanti."

Brigid made her calculations. "It'll take me a half-hour to dress, then an hour to drive, but I'll stop to pick up a latte. So. Two hours, max."

"Perfect. Write this down." And Iggy gave her the address of the bakery, along with instructions not to reveal the location of Quinn's corpse. He figured it wouldn't start stinking up the joint for another day or so, but he kept that bit to himself.

"Tommy. I got one more thing I'll ask you to do. Then we'll be done with all this crazy shit."

Iggy leaned back in the only comfortable chair in the building, an old La-Z-Boy from the last owner, and lit a cigar, a Cuban he had been saving for a special occasion. This qualified.

Tommy took a deep breath through his nose. "Wow. That smells good. Strong. But good."

"At a hundred bucks a pop it oughta."

"Anyway, so what do you want me to do?"

Iggy blew a series of perfect smoke rings and smiled. "I want you to take the rental car and drive home. To *your* house. Stay away from mine. Under the mat, at your back door, there's a flash drive. There's a movie I made on it. I want you to go to your room and watch it on your computer. Alone."

"Oh… you mean I can't share a movie with my parents that my much older and unusual friend Uncle Iggy made?" Tommy cackled gleefully.

Iggy laughed, too. "Not even with your *cat*. Understand?"

Tommy stood. "Yeah, I understand." He looked puzzled. "But all this stuff is pretty crazy lately."

"No more crazy," Iggy said. "This is it."

Tommy grabbed the keys and headed for the door. "Suuuuuure it is."

When Tommy left, Iggy donned a shoulder holster. He took a Browning 9mm pistol from his bag, screwed a silencer to it, racked a cartridge into the chamber, snicked on the safety and inserted the gun into the holster. Concealment was not an issue, so no coat.

He sat and waited, looking out the window and listening to the birds and the sound of the nearby highway, considering for the umpteenth time if he had made the right moves in the last few days. Iggy had many a reverie while he smoked, having to relight several times after these little trances, thinking about things he hadn't thought about in years, decades. Things so vivid it was like reliving them. He checked the clock. He figured maybe another half-hour. He relit the stogie.

14

"Where were you, hon?" Tommy's mom called from her desk in a nearby room as Tommy entered through the back porch.

"Helping Iggy with some stuff."

"Your Uncle Iggy is an odd duck," mom said. "But the bread he made us last week was the best ever. All them walnuts or whatever. Did he have some work for you?"

"I made it, actually. *With* Iggy. Yeah. Lots of work. Good money." He stopped at her office door.

"Good money doing *what* I wonder."

"Nothin' bad," Tommy said. "Drive him places. That sort of thing."

"All right. Listen, your dad wants to talk to you about school next fall when he comes home tonight. You're going to need some student aid money next year, I'm afraid."

Ah shit, Tommy thought. "Okay, mom." He stepped down the hall to his room, shut his door and booted up the PC. As he waited, he sat and brooded. *They can't afford to send me to a place I don't want to go. What's wrong with that picture?*

He inserted the flash drive into the USB slot and sat back. After a moment up popped Iggy on-screen, walking back to a chair to take a seat in front of the camera. Tommy made the picture go full-screen and tweaked the volume, so no one might overhear. Iggy looked tired on camera. Tired and sad. He looked into the camera and smiled.

Hey Tommy.

TV Iggy looked down at the floor and wrinkled his brow as he considered how to proceed.

I know it's been an odd few days. He looked back into the camera, then back down to the floor and scratched the back of his neck. *I guess I should have thought about this more… made an outline or something.*

"Jeez, just say it, Iggy," Tommy whispered to himself.

Listen, Tommy… you won't be seein' me for a while, see? And you've been good. You know… a good kid. Helped me out with stuff. I could always trust you. And you could always trust me. That's kinda rare, see? It's been fun, too. So, I figured I'd try to make it up to you. So I did some things. And I hope they help you out. I'm just gonna tell you what they are, and then, I'm gonna give you a few instructions that might be helpful, okay? So here goes.

"What the fuck, Iggy," Tommy whispered. "You don't owe me. I owe *you!*"

Well, for starters — just a minute. Iggy disappeared stage right to grab a bottle of water, sat back down, opened and drained it. He tossed the plastic bottle across the floor. *That's better. Anyway... the bakery we're stayin' at. That's yours now. I bought it clear. Building, land, and all the equipment. It's all in your name, but I also bought Morgan's bakery name. So you got instant recognition, but the bread better be good, eh? You're a good baker, kid! You make better bread than I do. You got the magic. If you like that sort of thing, well, it might be an alternative to college. I know you don't like that university routine. So you can sell it off, or you can start a business there. Now, how you go about the bakery stuff, if you decide to roll that way, the team you need to do it, all that stuff — that's up to you to figure out. But you got a leg up if you want to chance it. And if it don't work out, what the hell, you can always sell the place.*

Also, Iggy was on a roll now, *take a look in your closet. There's a briefcase in there. Inside there's this little tiny-ass painting. Nine by nine. It's by a guy named Dali. It's called 'Venus and Little Cupids.' Now listen close here. It's worth about two million dollars.*

"What the hell!"

I had to do something with all my cash, see? And buying art is a good way to solve the problem.

"You're a millionaire?! How the fuck did you get into my closet?!"

Anyway, it's yours. There's an authenticity certificate in there with it, and the transfer papers. Now, you can keep it and let it appreciate in value, and it will. Or you can sell it. But whatever you do, what do you want to be very, very careful that you don't do? What do you not want to be in this situation, Tommy?

"Oh, come on, Iggy."

Come on now. Say it.

"A Goddamn Idiot."

That's right, Tommy. You don't want to be a Goddamn Idiot. So, if you lose it, or get it stolen, or let some cat shit on it or some other thing, then you will be an official Goddamn Idiot and you deserve to lose two million dollars, I'm not gonna worry about it. Understand? You're a man now. With responsibility. Don't fuck it up.

Tommy was feeling lightheaded.

Tommy, do you understand?

"Yes, yes. I understand! All right?"

Also, in the closet is a duffel bag with two hundred grand in it in hundreds. That's for you. Do NOT try to deposit it in a bank. What else... Oh, yeah. I want so bad to give you the Lincoln, but I can't. They're gonna come for it and take it. They're gonna come and take everything, but they can't take the cash and painting you got, and the bakery is yours with no encumbrances. Which reminds me, you need to stay away from my house and the cars. Don't even look at my house for a week or so. Understand?

"Yes," Tommy muttered automatically.

"*Oh, and Jesus I almost forgot the most important stuff. In with the painting, there's an envelope. Inside are two business cards. My lawyer, and my accountant. You take the money in the duffle to my accountant. You'll have your bank account the next day. He knows all about the painting, too. They are both expecting to hear from you within two weeks. This is crucial, or else kiss all this other shit goodbye. What will you be if you do not call these men within the next two weeks?*

"Iggy..."

Saaaaaayyyyy it.

"A Goddamn Idiot."

That's right again, lad. Now... Iggy looked away, thinking hard to make sure that was all. *Let's see... Oh, your parents need some decent security on their house. Or at least some. And umm... I guess just... Just stay away from the bakery today. Okay?*

And it finally began to dawn on Tommy.

You need to not go there. I'll umm... I'll get back to you when you can go back there.

"Iggy!" Tommy bolted from the room.

"Tom, what's wrong?" mom yelled. "What happened?"

"Iggy's in trouble!" he yelled back as he ran to the car and zipped out of the driveway, his mom staring after him from the back door.

So anyway, I guess that's about it. For now, you know. Umm... One other thing I need to tell you, and it might sound a little strange, but I just need to say it so, cut me a little slack here, kid. Iggy looked down and wiped at his cheeks, then forced a final look into the camera. *I love you, kid. I love you, Tommy. I just... want you to know that if you didn't already.*

TV Iggy stood and stepped to the camera, reached behind it, and it all went black.

15

Brigid had arrived in her little Lexus. She asked if the car was okay here in front of the bakery and Iggy said it didn't matter. They just stood there and looked at one another until Iggy stepped forward and took her in his arms. He kissed her a nice kiss, not messy or lusty but nicer than any time he had kissed her since he got out of the Army. Then they hugged and stayed with the embrace for a full minute in silence and tenderness.

"Were you followed?"

"No. I was careful to look. Nobody."

So it might be Brian. He's excellent at that sort of thing and Brigid would never have seen him.

Iggy led her down the walk and in through the front door of the bakery.

"Let's sit in the office here," he said loudly to Brigid as he pushed her inside the office door with one hand and with the other slipped the pistol from his holster, then he made a 'shush' gesture with his index finger at her and scooted toward the back door and turned with his back to the wall next to the door entrance.

In sneaks Brian, takes two steps and he feels Iggy's pistol barrel pressing into his back. He stops and raises both hands.

Iggy breathed a sigh of relief. "Brian. Thank God it's you."

"Iggy. Think."

"Squat down and put the gun on the floor next to you. C'mon. You know the drill. I taught it to you."

Brian complied. Iggy ordered him into the office to join Brigid, and on the way, Iggy stooped and picked up the gun.

"She knew nothing about this," Brian said, looking at Brigid.

"I know. Sit down. You did a good job with the tail." Iggy was actually proud of Brian here.

Brigid stammered, "He's right, Iggy! I had no idea!"

"I know, Bridg, I know." He looked at Brian. "Why'd they send *you?*"

Iggy stood in the middle of the room a pistol in each hand. Brian and Brigid sat six feet away against the wall with a coffee table between them.

"I know the territory, and I know you. And they think I'm a real go-getter. Where's Redmond?" he asked Iggy.

"He's under his office desk at home. I killed him at the party."

Brian was appalled. "All this time? Right under everybody's nose?"

"Well," Iggy quipped, "He'll be very much *in* everybody's nose by tomorrow."

"Jesus," Brian said.

"It's a big desk," Iggy said.

"Wow. And you made him write that note." Brian was impressed. "Nice job!"

"Thanks."

"But now I gotta bring you back with me," Brian said.

"I know."

"So, let's go."

"Nah." Iggy shook his head.

"Why did you kill Quinn?" Brian asked. "This makes no sense to me."

"He wasn't the man you thought he was. He was beating and torturing Brigid. He was being blackmailed by someone who tried to make him stop. Quinn wanted me to kill that guy and he lied to me about it all. I investigated. Quinn hurt Brigid. He needed to die."

Brian, shocked, looked at Brigid. She nodded. "Iggy's right, Brian. He was a pig."

"Brigid," Brian said. "If I knew Quinn was hurting you, I would have stopped him."

Brigid smiled a tender smile. "I know, Brian. It was all a big secret. Plus, *you'd* be dead!" she whispered.

Brian looked at Iggy. "I'm fucked anyway."

"No, you're not," Iggy said.

"The Kings won't care that Quinn was a sick-fuck. He kept the trains running on-time. He was good at his job. So how am I not fucked?" He asked. "How are *you* not fucked?"

"Oh! *I'm* fucked, all right," Iggy said. "No matter what happens here, they'll never stop looking for me. I'm finished." Then he added, "you're not."

"How's that?" Brian asked.

"If they had sent anyone but you, I'd have killed them. But then they would send five more. Then ten. I know how this works. I helped craft the strategies and the policies. I could never use a phone or a credit card. I could never see an old friend or go to any of the places I like. All my life would be devoted to not making that one little misstep. Relax for one minute and I'd be gone the next. No."

"No?" Brian said. "What do you mean, 'no.'"

"It ends here. I'm ready."

Brigid got hot. "What do you *mean*, you're ready?! What do you *mean?!*" She looked pleadingly at Brian. "What does he *mean?!*"

Brian knew what that meant. Brigid didn't want to know.

"Don't you want to go down swinging? Die in the saddle?" Brian asked.

Iggy shook his head. "Nah. I'm done with all that."

Brigid would not see it and was starting to panic. "What do you mean, you're *done?!*"

Iggy ignored her. "If you don't bring back my scalp, they'll kill you, too, Brian."

"Yeah, Iggy. *I know.*"

Iggy turned to Brigid. "I need to talk to Brian alone. We'll be right outside the back door. I'll even leave it open. You stay here."

"Iggy…"

"*Stay here!*" he barked. Then recovered himself, now soothing. "This is very important, and you can't become part of the problem now. *You have to listen to me!*"

She looked down at the floor. "Hurry back."

Out in the alley now, Iggy threw his gun onto the grass, then put on a latex glove. He checked the chamber of Brian's pistol. Locked and loaded.

"I'm using your gun. Remember. This was not a suicide. You were sent to do a job and you did it. You see how it has to be like this? Explain this to Brigid. She'll keep the secret. Also, you're taking my body away, right? The kid who owns this bakery… I like him, *and you mustn't involve him in any of this.*"

Brian was not prepared for this after all. "Iggy… Jesus… Don't do this. We gotta think this *through!*"

"*Brian – did you understand my instructions?*"

"I did. Yes. I'll do all them things. But Iggy…"

Iggy looked away, and his brow darkened. "What we do… It's a good life. I hope my kills were righteous. See… I'm not so sure anymore. Red was a bad man. I just never knew *how* bad." He looked into Brian, almost pleading. "I didn't know!"

"Just put the gun down, Iggy, and let's talk for just *five minutes!*"

Iggy smiled wanly. "Tell her I loved her. No… Tell her I *love* her."

He snicked off the safety, pressed the barrel of the gun to his temple, closed his eyes, braced himself and squeezed the trigger, and through the open back door flies Tommy and he slams against Iggy at the same moment as the muffled pop issues from the pistol.

The wound was therefore not instantaneously mortal, but slightly off target. Brigid screamed and ran outside, where

Brian was holding Iggy's bleeding head in his hands and Tommy had his head on Iggy's chest, hugging his bulk, crying and confused. Brigid collapsed to her knees next to her wounded Iggy.

It's a good fort. They had the cushions in there. Red's daddy has the biggest desk anybody ever saw. Probably the biggest in the world. And the tablecloth makes a door. And Brigid is here! Yay! The fort is so good, and Brigid likes it but Red always wants to go outside to his stupid treehouse and sometimes he drags Brigid out and makes her go play there. But today Brigid is playing with me and Red is mad and threw a truck at Brigid and it hit me instead. And now Brigid is crying and I don't know how come and Red whispers at her and she says what, and Red whispers again in her ear and she says okay and goes outside with him. But we were playing! And Red pulls her arm to the stupid treehouse.

Brigid!

Brigid come back here!

The boy ran to the window and saw them running to the treehouse.

Brigid!

The boy had an idea. He remembered the chocolate ice cream in the freezer when the maid opened the door.

Brigid! He yelled through the closed window. I know where's ice cream! Come back! I know where's ice cream, Brigid!

Then he started to cry. And the fort looked stupid.

And then his head hurt. And he rubbed it and had to sit down and O how it hurt.

"O Brigid."

"He's awake. He's alive," Brian said.

Brigid gasped and bent to kiss his cheek. "Oh, Iggy, I'm here, my love. I'm here."

She took his hand and Iggy opened his eyes. And he smiled the biggest, brightest smile. She left the treehouse to play with *him!*

O Brigid! I know where's ice cream.

"What was that?" Brian asked.

"Something about ice cream?" Tommy whispered.

And a wretched Brigid pressed her lips into his big bright smile, as contented Iggy closed his eyes and drifted away in bliss.

ഇ൮ഌ

Blochyface Grampa

My name is Gretchen Buchanan. I'm a pediatric nurse with a husband and two grown kids. I'm about to retire, and my husband Dale and I are preparing to move from this old house, our home for 44 years, to a small condo downtown. No more lawn-cutting, snow-shoveling, trudging up stairs – all the usual reasons folks like us make this kind of move at this time in our lives.

The packing experience was miserable. So much stuff! But there was a hidden gem, long forgotten, that had made this chore-of-chores all worthwhile. I found my daughter Allison's diary from when she was 11 years-old. I hadn't seen it since Allison and I read through it together when she was 18 before packing her off to college. We laughed so hard at the daily accounts with her unique spelling and clumsy handwriting (which she still has) and it brought back so many memories. Most of them good; one of them hard. But a lesson was learned there that shaped my daughter's life and it brought back so vividly the recollection of my father-in-law, Allison's Grampa, who passed not long ago. For he was a main character in Ally's big little drama which caused so much anguish for us at the time.

> *Thursday*
> *We're going to play a trick on Blochyface Sammy tomorrow at lunch. He is so ugly he deserves it I guess. Debbie thought of it but everybody said I should do it because why? I don't know but I said OK. So it goes like this. I ask ~~Sammy~~ I mean Blochyface to come over here and he'll do it because he is so shy and we go to the trees behind the playground. Then I say do you want to kiss me? And of corse he'll say yes and I say "close your eyes Sammy and he will because I know he will and then everybody when his eyes are*

shut will come from where they hid and when Sammy
opens his eyes it will be SO FUNNY.! Everybody
will laugh!!!!

None of us had a heads-up on the little scheme, of course, because no one read Ally's diary but her. She told us weekly, in no uncertain terms that year (the only year she kept her little journal), that she would run away if anyone ever read her private book, and no matter how sneaky someone thought they could be, just forget it, because she would know!

Well, the little villains actually did it. The entire episode was observed by a teacher's aide, which was something the conspirators hadn't counted on. This was reported up the chain of command, verified by a principal-office interrogation of my daughter, and eventually it all got to my attention with a polite-but-firm call from Mr. Hastings himself. I got all the gory details, but what stood out most was Allison's lack of regret. She just didn't see the problem here. Wasn't it a good joke? Why is everyone so serious about it? Didn't everyone laugh? Well... almost everyone?

I was furious and heartbroken that Ally could be part of this awful prank. I could accept that she did a stupid childish thing – as a child, who hasn't? But her lack of empathy and any awareness of wrong-doing seemed downright pathological to me.

She was home from school when I got the call and I could tell that she sensed that something was on my mind, but I just tried to ignore her presence in the house. I hadn't seen my husband all day and would have to wait until he got home from the movies with his Dad. We were all having dinner together that night, all but my oldest boy, Mike, who was at a friend's. For hours I mulled over various ways to break this to Dale. I decided that we would at least try to have a nice dinner and then I would spill the beans to Dale after he took Dad home. It didn't work out that way.

We had all finished our soup and I was contemplating the dry overcooked chicken warming in the oven (I was too upset to remember how to cook a chicken) and got up to fetch and serve it. I stopped midway, turned and sat back down. I glared at my daughter.

"Allison," I said. She knew by my tone and that I had not called her Ally that she should be on her guard. Clever darling.

"What?" she answered, all wide-eyed innocent.

"I got a call from Mr. Hastings today. Can you guess what it was about?"

She dropped her head and mumbled, "Blotchyface Sammy."

"What?" her Grampa piped.

Ally looked at her Grampa and repeated flatly, "I said Blotchyface Sammy."

"Would you like to tell us all what you and your friends did to Sam on the playground today?" I pressed.

"I don't care..." she mumbled. "If you want."

"We want." Dale was already angry.

Defensively, "We just played a trick on him. It's okay!"

"I'll decide if it's okay!" Dale almost shouted.

Seconds of silence ticking by. Ally was squirming.

"Well... we were-"

"Wait a minute, honey," Grampa interrupted. "Explain 'Blotchyface Sammy' to me, will you?"

Ally tried to summon some defiance here, but it wasn't working for her.

"Sammy is a boy in my class and his face is all blotchy-" she began.

"Rosacea," I interjected. "It's rare in kids, but Sammy's had it for a year now. They're worried about his eyes. It's no joke."

Grampa looked over at Ally, who would not meet his eyes.

"Go on, honey," he said. "Tell what happened."

So she did, and she spared us nothing, as if there were nothing to be truly ashamed of. She told how she asked Sammy to talk and that he was very shy, and she beckoned him to the trees behind the playground. There she asked Sam if he wanted to kiss her. He said yes and closed his eyes as instructed. Then she quickly backed away to join the gaggle of kids formerly hidden in the bushes now standing in a line a few yards from poor Sam, lips all puckered up and ready for his first kiss. At last Ally piped, "Open your eyes, Sammy!" and he did. And they all laughed. All but Sam.

Dale listened patiently with eyes closed. When Ally was finished, he breathed, "I can't believe this…"

"So, you must be a very popular girl now, huh, Ally?" I was seething.

"What? What do you mean?"

Tensions were at the breaking point all around when Ally noticed something.

"Grampa? Why are you crying?"

And so he was, head down and sobbing.

"Why is Grampa crying?" Ally asked, a little frantic. *"Grampa what's wrong?!"*

Dad lifted his head, cheeks wet and eyes rheumy with tears, and he said:

"Ally… I'm Blotchyface Sammy."

Ally was stunned. "What?"

"I," and her Grampa sniffed loudly and pointed to his chest, *"I* am Blotchyface Sammy."

As if in a trance, Ally said, "No you're not. You're my Grampa."

And Dad put his face in his hands and started to weep again, ever harder than before.

"Grampa, stop! What's wrong with Grampa? Why is he doing this!? *Why did he say that? Grampa please stop!"* she pleaded.

But he wouldn't stop. Not for another minute or so as we all sat silent and bewildered. Most uncomfortable minute of my life? Maybe. When he finally calmed down, he got up from the table slowly and said in a shaky voice, "I'm really not very hungry tonight. Dale, would you mind driving me back?"

"No… no problem, Dad," Dale got up and pointed a stern finger at his daughter. "Allison – you're grounded. All weekend."

"But-"

"Quiet!"

I had never in my life, before or since, seen Dale so angry. Ally shriveled up into a little ball and kept very quiet indeed and was in bed by the time her Dad returned.

> *Friday*
> *So we did the thing and*
> *My Grampa said hes Blochyface Sammy. But he's*
> *not. OF COURSE.*
> *Nevermind this is stupid*
> *Is grampa still crying*

There is no diary entry for Saturday, Sunday nor the fateful Monday. It took many years before Ally would unburden herself of the specifics of that day. What follows is what I recall before and after school, and what Allison finally confided so many years later.

That Monday morning, after our wordless breakfast and before she and her brother left the house for school, I broke the silence.

"Ally, make sure you-"

"I know, I know, make sure I apologize to Sammy and my teachers," she interrupted. Ally looked sleepy, and very gloomy.

"No," I clarified, "that's not what I was going to say. Actually, your grandfather asked us *not* to order you to do that." A quizzical look passed Ally's face. "I was just going to remind you to take home the two sweaters you've left in your locker, along with the one you're wearing now."

She made a deep sigh and nodded her head. "Okay. I won't forget."

"Yeah you will," brother Mike taunted.

"Shut up, jerk," Ally said as she pushed by out the door.

It was almost time for recess to the playground on that sunny autumn Monday in Michigan. Ally's teachers were getting a bit antsy, as there were still no apologies forthcoming and the day half-over. The bell rang, and the noisy knot of grade-school boys and girls burst onto the playground, instantly disentangling into assorted clots of cliques and loners forced outdoors to get some sun and exercise.

Ally had her own friends but played the loner that noontime. Eventually, she spied little Sam with his ever-solitary self at the edge of the playground, reading at one of the little tables placed about the play area. She stared at Sammy for an entire minute, gathering her spirit, and finally, as if 'walking the plank,' she made her way to him.

Sam looked up from his book with a little shocked gasp at the unexpected sight of his tormentor so close once again. He looked back at his book.

"What!" he barked, defiantly.

Ally closed her eyes. This was so much harder than she even thought it would be. She opened her eyes and said, "Sammy, can we talk?"

Sam glowered up at Allison, cramming into his glare all the hate and anger he could summon, which, being Sammy, wasn't much. "Why?" he asked in a loud voice.

"Please, Sammy. I just need to talk to you. Just me and you."

At that, they both looked about the playground and saw that just about everybody was looking at them, then suddenly pretending that they weren't. Grudgingly, Sam laid aside his book and stood, and Ally began walking toward the bushes and trees, into the very scene-of-the-crime of Friday last. Reluctantly, suspiciously, Sammy followed.

When they got to the spot, into the very heart of darkness that they had stood three days before, Ally took Sammy by the hand and said, "Sammy... I'm sorry," and she began to cry. "I'm so sorry for what I did." And she tried to say more

418

but her crying would not let her speak. Sammy put his free hand on Ally's, which made her cry even harder. After a space Ally had calmed enough to lean forward (he tried to pull back at first) and gently planted a kiss on Sammy's unprepared lips. She stepped back, now wiping at her cheeks and nose and all the while keeping eye-contact with the still-anxious boy.

Suddenly, she burst out crying again and hugged Sammy violently to herself. He hung like a terrified ragdoll in her embrace, and then she lifted her head just enough to find the reddest, most florid patch of rash on Sammy's cheek and kissed it with passion. Then she resumed her bearhug and whispered into Sam's ear, "I love you, Grampa."

Sammy yanked his head back. "What?"

But Ally did not respond, resting wordless in her embrace of Sammy, recovering her composure, till the boy twisted his head for a better view and said, "Oh-oh. Look."

Ally released Sam and they both turned to see about a dozen kids lined up in a row, just as they were last time. As if on cue, half of them broke out in that forced laughter of children. But half didn't. Defiantly, Allison took Sammy by the hand and headed for the middle of the line of tormentors a few yards away, a few making space for the pair to pass through.

Debbie stopped her fake laugh long enough to singsong, "I wouldn't want to do what you just did!"

Ally stopped and met Debbie's phony grin with a very authentic glare of contempt. "I wouldn't want to be as stupid and rude as you are."

And the laughing stopped, and everybody looked at Debbie, who had no snappy comeback but stared blankly at the odd couple as they passed, heading back toward the school, hand-in-hand.

Allison never did get around to apologizing to her teachers, but word traveled fast, and they never pursued the issue.

Naturally, Ally forgot the sweaters, even the one she wore that day. I forgave her for obvious reasons. She had volleyball practice after school, so her Dad picked her up and got her home right about dinner-time. Ally was silent in the car all the way home. Dad didn't press it.

Her Grampa had joined us for an odd Monday-night dinner visit when she and Dale arrived home. Allison was surprised. As soon as she entered and took off her shoes, she noticed her Grampa seated at the table and stopped dead in her tracks. Her eyes got big and she started to tear up, but I noticed her Grampa smiled and shook his head no, beckoning her to him. Ally nipped her tears in the bud and padded up to her Grampa and gave him the usual kiss hello.

She smiled shyly and said, "Grampa, at school today I-"

But he shushed her with his finger to her lips, and with a gentle smile said, "I know, sweetheart. I know." They embraced. He released her, and she stepped back, her Grampa giving her an appraising look. "You handled that well. I'm so proud of you." And she beamed him the most precious smile.

None of the rest of us had the slightest idea what her Grampa meant for we had heard nothing about her day and how she handled her situation. But we never pressed him on the subject, though now, with him gone, I wished we had. He seemed so certain of what it took the rest of us a couple of days (and for some of the details, many years) to find out.

The entire incident, which seemed so urgent and appalling when it arose was resolved in a blink and never spoken of after that week.

But still I wonder – how real were those tears of his? I know it doesn't really matter. What matters is the love. That's all. Just part of the toolbox, I suppose, of the Grampa who loved her.

৪৩৪৪

Grampa's Terrible Teeth

I've been out here a half-hour now so it must be almost time. Fifty degrees in January. In Michigan. I don't even need the heater on. Why is the car even on? Hell with that. Gas ain't *that* cheap. I can even crack the window.

All this brings back the memories, all right. Goddam dentists. First visit to a dentist and he pulls every tooth out of my mouth. How old was I? Five? Six? They all turned black and had to be pulled. So first the needles. All over my mouth. Then the waiting and then the pulling. Why needles and not gas? Why not knock me out? Why torture a child? Why all at once? Why not two or three visits? He was such a benign-looking old German fella, but he was a goddam monster. I think he enjoyed it. I could never let a child I love go through this if there were any possible way...

My dad's teeth, they were perfect. Grew up an orphan and I don't think he even owned a toothbrush till he was in the army. But perfect teeth. Not a single cavity in his entire life.

My mom's were tragic. She had tragic teeth and she gave them to me. Thanks, mom. Worry who's gonna get my teeth. My genes. Mom had dentures and most of mine are fake, too. I got seven left. I call them my Seven Jewels, I take such good care of them.

O Jesus. O that hurts. Like a sonofabitch. Ohh... Needles. Again with the needles. Shake it off. Shake it. God DAMN... shake it off... This is good, though. Maybe it's working.

Take your mind off it. Think about something else. Something nice. Not teeth. God, remember when the neglect couldn't go on? That truly sucked. I hadn't seen a dentist in so many years that when I got a toothache I had to find a dentist and he said root canal, or else pull it. No money, no insurance, so pull the goddam thing. He convinced me to-

Jesus Christ! What now! O the fucking pain. Maybe it's working. Maybe this will work. How else to explain... O god

my whole jaw! Jesus. Just breathe. Just take nice deep... O...
man...

Where was I? Oh yeah, he convinced me to try to save my
teeth and so come back in a week to get a cleaning. Never
had one. In 30 years. When I did it was with this new-
OUCH! FUCK! Ohh...

...it was with this new girl and I was one of her first patients and she kept making faces and was having such a hard
time and I asked her what's wrong and she starts crying!
Crying! She's a goddam dental technician and she's having a
breakdown. 'I just can't do this!' she cried. 'Your disease is
just so bad!' I'm thinking 'what disease?' The plaque buildup
was-

O FUCK! O JESUS! OH... OH... OH... oh... oh...
oh... godamn sonofabitch... Breathe. It can't go on much
longer... whew! Take a big deep breath and just... just
relax... It's gotta be working. There's no other explanation
for this than that it's working. It'll be worth it.

So anyway... where... O yeah. The plaque was so thick
that she couldn't break it off with the tools she had, and she
left the room in tears and the dentist came in a few minutes
later and apologized and then he chiseled away the plaque
and did the scraping and such. So guess what, I never went
back! Big surprise, right?

O! What the fuck NOW?! Breathe and stay calm breathe
and stay calm breathe and stay calm... O Jesus it was never
this bad. Was it? O I hope this is working I hope it's what I
think it is. How much can you love? How deep can you love?
O... just... just rest a minute... Distract. Distract yourself,
idiot. You don't have to think about teeth. Think about nice
things. Music. Pussy! That... what's her name. O man I
couldn't get it up right now at gunpoint. Jesus!

Maybe after this I'll go see Steve. He doesn't even call himself a chiropractor anymore. What the hell is he? He's pretty
amazing. His hands. You can go there with a complaint and
he'll pretend he's listening to you but he's just feeling your
body and hearing it through these hands of his. And he

424

pushes here and cracks there and touches gently here—and you leave refreshed. He's got the gift. I went there once all cramped up and stiff and told him that my sister has colitis real bad and I was worried, and that I had bad pains in my lower bowel ever since I found out. He yelled at me 'Stop it! It won't help her and you're making yourself a wreck!' He was right I guess, but I've always been that way and I might be on to something. Maybe it helps. I hope I hope.

O god, remember when it got so bad that I had to go back and the infections-

AAAAARGGH! WHAT the hell was THAT! O fuck. I am not prepared for... O Jesus... breathe real deep. Blow it out... whew... no more, please... breathe it in... blow it out... whew...

What was I... Oh yeah, so it got so bad that I started having all these gum infections. That was the end of the line and I had to get an upper denture. Fuck me. That meant all the top teeth that hadn't fallen out had to go. Again: ALL AT ONCE. All 12 of them or however the hell many. And remember the surgeon's name? FEAR! Doctor FEAR. DOCTOR FUCKING FEAR. First the needles. I couldn't believe it even while it was happening to me. Seven injection sites. Bang bang bang bang bang bang bang. Done. Didn't take ten seconds. Even slumped into near unconsciousness by the agony of the ordeal I had to admire his skill. Then the pliers. Yeah. They're fucking PLIERS. And he ripped them all out of my mouth in a bloody gush.

O Christ this pain has got to stop! PLEASE! Jesus please somebody stop this! I'll join what ever goddam religion of any god that stops this horrible fucking PAIN!... Better... okay... just sittin' and breathin'. Whew! Just sittin' and breathin' deep... It's working though... I think it's really happening...

Doctor Fear. Remember the insurance lady? A month later my insurance lady asked who was my dental surgeon and I couldn't remember. How could I not remember that? I fucking repressed it, that's how not! So I thought and thought and then I had it! 'Doctor Pain,' I said. She tried not to laugh but failed. 'You mean, Doctor Fear?' she said, so I guess he was well-known. I gotta laugh at that even though the fucking pain is coming back... It hurts to laugh...

So my bottom teeth all except my Seven Jewels had to come out the next month but a week after Doctor Fear raped my mouth I had one of the lower teeth act up and it was so painful I had to go to an emergency dentist. He took my blood pressure and said, 'No, I'm not doing it. It's 210/100. I don't want you dying of a stroke in my chair.' That's how badly dentists have traumatized me over a half-century. I can't even sit in the chair without it nearly killing me. So my physician had to write him a note saying go ahead and pull it, he'll be okay, he's just a little freaked out by dentists.

O shit. What time is it? Almost an hour. At least I can finally relax a little. Much better... And think straight. Man, that sucked. I got drool all over my shirt. I'm surprised it ain't blood. Feels all puffy in there.

Hey. They're back!

"Hey! How did it go?"

My daughter-in-law is fixing the seatbelt on my grandson in the backseat. He's five. "It went great!"

"It *did?*"

"It was pretty amazing," she said, buckling herself in next to her boy with a big happy smile on her sweet face. "He never once-"

"I didn't cry, grampa! Plus look!" And he holds up a wrapped deck of Pokémon cards.

"Wow, pretty nice. All I ever got as a kid was a stupid lollypop."

"Yeah," his mom said, "That guy's got the kids' number, all right. He had all sorts of stuff for him to pick from." She looks concerned. "Thanks so much for driving us this morning. Why are you mumbling, though? And you're drooling."

"O. I am?" And I wipe the drool with my sleeve and cough. "I'm fine. Really. Jesus—it worked."

"What? What worked? Anyway, he was great. All our fears were for nothing. And all the crying last night. No reason for that, was there, honey?"

"Grampa! Even the needle didn't hurt me. And then I couldn't feel anything and I'm still nunned. Look!" And he poked his little finger at his jaw a few times and grinned.

"Numb, honey," mom corrected. She looked at me as I started the car and pulled away. "Are you crying? What's wrong?"

"No! No. I'm fine. Just relieved, okay? I was worried. Crying? Why would I be... I ain't *crying*. What the *hell?*"

ೞೞ

Ambrosia

or,
WRITE WHAT YOU KNOW

"When life hands you lemons, make lemonade."
goes the tired old saying.
I didn't just make lemonade. I made Ambrosia.

"Write what you know," my old buddy Miles advised me the other day. He's a fellow writer, a successful one, who is not fond of my stories.

His idea of a good story is, though I must admit, shared by most of the West's intellectualoids these days. The salient factors appear to be these: there should be much naval-gazing because introspection is just so terribly fascinating, the more unfathomable and wordier the better; nothing should actually *happen*, because that's kind of crude, not to mention... well, I'll just come right out and say it – *jejune*. (After all, we're all adults here, *n'est-ce pas?*); and the story should either not *have* an ending, or else the end should be ambiguous, so as not to be too chauvinistically assertive in one way or another.

After all, Miles would contend, what do I know about being an opera singer or a star-fleet officer, a mom, a priest or young Indian boy or an Irish assassin? Yet I have presumed to spill ink from all these perspectives. He calls my tales "pulp." I looked it up: *popular or sensational writing that is generally regarded as being of poor quality*.

Well, if what's come before and what follows here is good or bad, Pulp or a Legitimate Story, this is not mine to decide. And although my personal life rarely inspires me with story fodder, there is that awful thing that happened with... I have to change the names, right? I'd better. Even mine. I'll call him Alex, and I'll name her Katherine.

429

So how much of it is true? Enough. Too much.

The troubles began in earnest when my peers and I were all in our early 50's. I had known Alex for about 30 years and had been good friends with him for most of that time. We have both of us spent most of our lives in the music business: I as a composer, pianist, recording artist, publisher, journalist and a few other positions right down to piano-mover. Alex, easily the most knowledgeable person about art music I have ever known, was the manager, then owner, of one of the nation's great record stores, back in the day when such hallowed temples to art dotted the land. He was also, at a later date, the most highly paid writer about classical music in the world, pulling down six-figures a year for his opinions on the recordings of art music. I'm familiar with his income because I was the one paying him from my director job at the world's largest music media company where I reigned for six years, till I was fired for fighting with the new president, who was a corrupt jackass. (That's the story of the music industry. The corrupt jackasses rule.)

Oddly, as good friends as Alex and I were, on a certain level we never really got along. On the surface, it was political. Alex is a Democrat party member; I am so libertarian that the Libertarian party literally wouldn't have me. But the roots of our mutual distemper go far deeper. Politics is only a surface feature, emblematic of deeper stuff.

Alex lives in a world where he clings to this most dangerous of delusions: that he is the *Objective Man*, not realizing that it is precisely the ways in which we *lack* objectivity that furnish us with our personalities as human beings. I would tease him about this foible, so obvious to all but himself, and he would get mad.

"Let's see," I would tweak him, pretending to think hard, and counting on my fingers. "There's the Gautama Buddha... there's Jesus Christ... and... there's *you!*"

He would get so angry with me about not acknowledging his impartial, unbiased awesomeness that he loudly threatened to leave a party one night, crying out, "I don't have to stay here and be insulted!" My crime? I denied that he was objective.

Alex is a passionate ideologue with a narrative to defend. That narrative can be characterized, in his case, as party-line Marxist-Progressive. Whatever he was 'supposed' to think about a topic, that's what he thought. Or what he *thought* he thought. When his opinions were confronted to the contrary by history, evidence or logic, Alex protected his narrative by reflexively rejecting these noisome factors, which he did without consideration, analysis or frank discussion. He would not discuss opposing interpretations. He simply believed that such infidels are too stupid to grok his Objective Wisdom, and if they cannot be silenced, they must perforce be snubbed.

For years I have ignored all this as best I could, but Alex's feral defense against challenges to his narrative over the past couple of years had grown progressively shrill, vile and uncivil. Alex is not here to defend himself, but I have been defending him in my mind and to others for decades and I had simply been worn down by it all. It's possible, I suppose, that I could have shrugged it off if it weren't for his wife… what am I calling her? Oh, yeah. Katherine.

Alex went bar-hopping one fateful day a couple years after his divorce and met a lovely woman sitting by herself enjoying a drink. Soon after, they wed. At their wedding, presided over by, natch, a secular female official, Alex wore a toy holster outfitted with two toy pistols. This lent a farcical, foreshadowing aspect to the proceedings that Katherine ought to have questioned, or at least picked up on, but because she is a very submissive woman, she did nothing.

Katherine has had four or five husbands in her time, most of them abusive bastards that I would have loved to have killed had I the knowledge and opportunity. Add to the murder list a few incestuous family members, and bosses who liked to abuse her at work, and if the opportunity had presented itself, my writerly buddy Miles would see that I have more of the Irish assassin in me than he suspects.

Katherine has not had men in her life that want the best for her. They use her. She is a magnet for this treatment, and I don't believe she knows there is any other kind of man. She has used sex as her currency all of her life and cannot imagine that a man would value her otherwise. That is the germ of the catastrophe that ended or changed so many relationships in a long-standing peer-group of many members.

Katherine has a Ph.D. in Anthropology. She is *Doctor* Katherine, at a celebrated university. An often-single mom in her early days, she raised two children in very stressful circumstances but never lost sight of her goals. Her achievement is amazing. She has made very good money at the university and pretty much supported Alex who, after losing his writing job soon after I was fired, makes little money himself. One of Katherine's greatest fears was that she would lose her job and Alex would leave her. That she felt this way always made me feel angry and sad. It got so bad that her health was adversely affected.

Katherine has a daughter in Vermont, Jane, married and childless. She and her man were trying, desperately, to remedy this. One option they were considering was artificial insemination, after a long study which proved that hubby just wasn't putting out much viable sperm. AI is very expensive. This fact, plus the idea that the baby's father would not be the same as his dad was causing the couple much stress and grief should they decide to go the AI route. They were getting desperate and the clock was ticking. There seemed to be no solution.

Katherine also has a son, Bob, with whom she is very close, but, like Jane, lives in Vermont. He is also married, and childless.

Katherine's greatest joys were her daughter and son, and her greatest tragedy is that they live so far away, and she sees them so rarely. She is never truly herself unless she is with one or both of them, then she opens like a flower, her cares far away. I used to love watching Katherine when her children were with her. When they go she pines for them. They are her happiness and she wants so *dearly* to have a grandchild. It's the beacon of hope in Katherine's life.

A farmgirl at heart, Katherine hates her house in the 'burbs (Alex loves it), and she hates her job at the university (Alex loves that she can support his lifestyle). She is a world-class quilt-maker, and in their large home she is allotted a tiny room crammed to the gills wherein she is permitted to pursue her art. (Alex has, as his essentially un-productive office/studio, an entire floor and basement, his lair replete with awesome stereo and fine piano.) Katherine uses a laptop she gets from work (Alex has a nice PC with a 50-inch TV/monitor).

Alex told me one night that he did not really *like* women. This was obvious, but his admission was interesting. Katherine is dissatisfied with the structure of her life and Alex has never indicated that this is much of a concern.

So, I need to talk about *me* for just a minute. I am married to Gail. Happily. I have sired upon her two now-grown men who are princes of the earth and I rejoice in six grandchildren between them, from daughters-in-law that are so dear that the law has nothing to do with it. They are as my daughters.

I love women, but not enough to wreck myself and loved ones on their famously rocky shores. From the first week I met Katherine, I loved her, too. Never denied it. Told her I loved her often, and she often said to me that she loved me back. (I think now, was she lying?)

I never had sex with her, never caressed her, never kissed her, never even once *hinted* at such activity between us. But Katherine is a woman who could not believe that she was worthy of being loved by a man for reasons other than her sexuality. It was my fatal error to think that she would understand and appreciate another way of being cherished. I would literally not have had sex with her for a million dollars. It would destroy my marriage, her marriage, my friends would detest me, and I wouldn't be able to look my own family in the eye. Sex is fun, but nothing is *that* much fun.

What I liked about her so much was her temperament, which is the opposite of my own. She despises confrontation and will do anything to avoid it. Her self-confidence is not high. She is placid and soft-spoken to the point where, if she is interrupted in conversation, she never raises her voice to get the floor back. She just fades back and lets others take over. This used to bug the hell out of me to the extent that I would tell others that they were interrupting, and Katherine would (often reluctantly) regain the floor.

With me gone, no one will ever do that for her again. Certainly not Alex.

Anyway – the temperament thing. One of the pleasures of the opposite sex that one may enjoy is to *open them*. To break through the shield, pierce the armor. I could, and would, do that with Katherine and she was always appreciative. I was always gentle and patient with her.

She thinks she is a feminist, her opinions provided for her courtesy of the faculty lounge, but she is far closer to a *burqa* than she is to feminism. There are many ways to abuse a woman and the physical way is only one, and not necessarily the worst. Katherine would deny that she was being abused; she doesn't know better. She never had a man who put her needs above his own and loved her for who and what she really was, or, as I suspect, even cared enough to find out! No one ever worked hard to make her flower. But when we don't value ourselves, how can we expect others to value us any higher?

I never wanted anything from Katherine. And that was the secret to the ease I had with her. My terrible mistake was to let her know that I loved her the way I did, a way she did not know could even exist.

At first, I thought I was just imagining that Alex was showing signs of resentment at my attentions to Katherine, which were of the hugs and friend-kiss type, at the most. Perhaps it was our conversations with one another which she actually enjoyed. She certainly never objected to my attentions (if she had, I would have been mortified, crawled up my own butthole, and never come near her again out of shame), but Alex would get all antsy when I was around her.

The last year or so before his violent rejection of me, Alex would go out of his way to show affection for Katherine in the silliest ways. If we were sitting and talking outside together, Alex would come out and start smothering Katherine with kisses, insisting that "sometimes ya' just gotta show them how much ya' love 'em!" (My wife, Gail, a professional expert on the subject, told me that this sort of bizarre public 'affection' is a prime sign of an abusive spouse.)

I noticed at the same time that Katherine would sometimes be a little stand-offish toward me. This troubled me a great deal. A few weeks before the big blow-up, I was at a gathering at Alex's. Katherine went out of her way *not* to wish me a proper goodbye. I wondered if it was something I had done, some stupid over-display of affection that she found presumptuous and insulting? I had no clue because I remembered no such act, and in my entire acquaintance with Katherine, she had never acted *for even a moment* that my attention to her was unwanted or making her uncomfortable. I was disheartened.

The following week was one of Alex's monthly music parties, at which he would lecture on the program he picked for the month, where six of us 'music monks' would smoke, drink scotch, and listen to Alex bloviate, and then to a program of the seminal recordings of a single (usually rock) artist for a couple of hours. I enjoyed these sessions immensely, learned so much, and miss them terribly. Only males were invited, and, tellingly – out of dozens of these gatherings, there was never a single woman featured as artist, either as songwriter or performer.

On the way out of Alex's house that night, I encountered Katherine upstairs. I grabbed my fedora, and, still stung from my last encounter (or more properly, lack of encounter) with

Katherine, simply turned to her and said "Goodnight." She turned and walked away. She just wordlessly walked away from me into her kitchen. I was so ashamed that I had done something to offend her, I turned without another word and headed toward the front door.

"Wait," I heard her say. I turned and saw her walking back from the kitchen. "I was just putting my drink down."

And she walked up to me and put her arms around me, and I had the sweetest embrace of her that I will ever remember. The embrace spoke eloquently about things we can never put into words. And we stood like that for a moment until at last, reluctantly, and a little confused, I released her, kissed her on the cheek and wished her goodnight. She followed close behind me.

She started to talk about this and that, doing her best to draw me into conversation on my way out of her home. (She had never done that before.) Once outside we chatted a bit, she on her porch and I on the walk in front. I don't think either of us was actually caring about what we said, as long as we dallied a little bit. It was as if she were trying to tell me that the estrangement I sensed from her was not of my fault, and she was trying to make it right.

Just then, the most vulgar thing I had ever witnessed unfolded before me. Alex opened the door, and without even a glance of acknowledgment my way, looked at Katherine and gruffed, *"Hey, baby, get in here. You know what I want."* And then he vanished from the doorway.

Katherine was so shocked, so embarrassed. She looked at Alex as he said those crude words, and then, when he vanished, turned to look back at me, but there was a moment, a tenth of a second as she swung her head back to look at me, that I felt a burst come from her of pure hate and humiliation, for a few milliseconds there it was, raw and bare and sincere, but by the time her head had turned back and her eyes had met mine again, it was all gone, and Katherine was once again the tightly-wrapped practiced submissive trying to be nice. We blew one another a kiss and I was off.

I have never shaken that uncouth and loutish scene, never purged it from my mind's eye. It was emblematic of what I now saw as the entire shared pathology of the pair of them. The little sympathy I had by then for Alex and his ways was finally blasted to hell. By now, I knew the only reason I would accept invites to their home, or have them to mine, or see them at a gathering, was to stay in touch with Katherine.

As it happened there was only one more encounter that we would ever share as married couples socializing in a setting of peer group bliss. It was at a large gathering shortly after the last reported at Alex and Katherine's. It was their Summer Solstice Party.

Near the end of the party, Katherine and I sat outside together in a couple of lawn chairs. Katherine had been losing weight, and her aura had a brittle character which was never so pronounced. Her job was in jeopardy, and this was weighing heavily on her. As a measure of how far down the dark path the woman had travelled, Katherine told her girlfriends that she was terrified of losing her job because if she was not bringing home the bacon, *then Alex might leave her.* As low as my opinion of Alex had become, this I do not, and did not, believe. Instead, this demonstrated the wayward gearing of Katherine's mind. She was acting as if she were in danger, as if something awful were about to happen to her.

I wanted to reassure her that if she felt in danger for any reason, that I would always be there for her and she would never want for anything. That was the root of my undoing. "I'll never let anything bad happen to you," were my words to her. This un-nerved her, but I knew it not.

The next day I sent her an email "clarifying" my response to her, which actually had the *opposite* effect, brilliant writer that I am. "Nothing bad will ever happen to you that I can prevent," I explained. "No danger, no state of want." To reassure her that I was not "after her," I added. "...know that you'll never be put upon by me, not even by any more emails." Oh yeah – Katherine hates email conversations. I thought I laid it all out pretty well there and signed it with love.

Evidently, despite my painstaking phraseology, Katherine was convinced that I wanted her as my, what? Mistress? She was terrified and confused and made the abused wife mistake of dutifully confiding in her master. Did she eagerly forward it to him? Was she forced by the terrible aspect of her master to do his will when she told him I sent her a personal email? Yes. That's exactly what happened.

Katherine misread me disastrously. Because I knew her as well as I did, I knew that Katherine needed another fuck like she needs another hole in her head, and it would take a much crueler heart than mine to have pressed such a thing on her. I believe there is only one answer to this, and you've heard it before: *Katherine could not believe that a man could possibly have a loving interest in her unless he was playing for sex.* I realized this too late.

But I believe my email stirred something dark and unthinkable in her. As if, buried down among the repressed portions of her personality, she actually understood what it was, *who* it was, I was willing to protect her from. In these thoughts, I believe she found terror she could not face. It was easier for her to play the innocent, the victim, of the scheming man who was not her husband that was trying to get into her pants. So? So she threw me under the bus.

It was the coward's 'solution' but Katherine's pathology had turned her into a coward. And I think this hurt her so much that I feared for her health and sanity, and I was more concerned with the wound she would have to endure even more than the wound she had put upon me. How would she bury *this*? What more fiction would she have to invent to keep herself afloat? Or was she so damaged that this would all flow clear of her soul like water off a duck's back?

Alex's email to me in response to all this was pure outrage, but to explain *him* is easy – I made him jealous to the point of irrationality, though he could detect no evidence of actual shenanigans on my part. (You can't find what isn't there.) He hated her ease with me, that I presumed to embrace her, dance with her, and give her the friendly kiss, that I showed deference to her in public. But mainly – that there was something between Katherine and me *that did not include him, or with his permission.* Such was his stranglehold on her.

As large peer-groups dynamics go, the break was catastrophic. I was happy to see that few whom I cared about believed Alex's slanders against me, but this caused hidden but unrelated grudges and grievances to appear among the numbers. One peer canceled his monthly *salons* after many years because attendance suffered so badly, what with X refusing to go if Y were going to be there. It got so bad that Alex and Katherine canceled their Winter Solstice party, citing all manner of excuses that fooled no one.

And that's how things sat, for a long time. I suffered for more than a year about all this, thinking about it every day.

Then I had an idea.

There was only one thing I knew that might open a change in Katherine's life that could save her from what was happening to her and the direction she was heading. But I had to wonder: was this just one more example of me not understanding her enough to know that I should just *leave it alone?*

Well, I didn't. It took some work, but I found out where Katherine's daughter, Jane, and her husband lived, way up Vermont way. After I roughed-out my plan, I had to wait a month until my wife Gail was out-of-town on a two-week visit to a friend in California. I did not consult her on this. For the first time in my life, I undertook an urgent project in secrecy. No one knew.

This idea of mine – it was pretty crazy, and the odds of it working were not very high. Also, I was afraid that my plan would get back to Alex and Katherine, though I could think of nothing actually *illegal* in my plot. But potentially embarrassing? *Oh, yeah.* If Gail found out I would have *lots* of 'splainin' to do. But if it worked it might make many people very happy and change lives for the better.

I flew into Burlington International Airport, rented a terrible tiny car, and drove the 50-odd miles to Hardwick. I was going to have trouble hiding the expense of all this, and I did not call ahead to make sure Jane was even home. I needed to see her in person, and I had already guessed that Katherine had confided to Jane all my terrible misdeeds and shameful intentions. So I had to, as the salesmen say, "cold call" her.

Hardwick, Vermont is a little burg containing about 3,000 souls. It's in the central part of the state, a little north. It's quaint, and lovely, and surrounded by lush hills. It was September, school was starting, and the leaves were turning. It was getting dark when I arrived in town. I found Hill Street and, in a few minutes, pulled into the Village Hotel, old-fashioned but nice enough. The bed was good. I slept like a baby.

At 8 o'clock that morning, without benefit of rude alarm, I sprung awake, did my thing, and went to breakfast, of which I ate plenty because of no real dinner the night before. It was sunny as could be, a rarity this time of year (so the locals had given me to understand) and it was going to be 'warm,' whatever that would mean in this neck of the woods. After breakfast I dressed, achieving a *visage* that was, for me, pretty darn presentable. No tie or coat, as these things do not suit me, but new pants and shirt, and good boots, and, natch, my trusty fedora, which goes perfectly with anything, though some still dispute this.

The drive to Jane's home was straightforward thanks to the car's map app, and when I identified her modest home in the middle of her modest neighborhood, I kept driving around the block, then back again, parking in front of the house before Jane's. I kept the car on and the heater humming because the alleged 'warm' air had not yet arrived. I could see two heads in her dining room window, hers and hubby's. I didn't know what to do, so I waited.

About fifteen minutes passed and I was getting frustrated, patience not being one of my few virtues. But presently they stirred from the table and then from the room, and in a few minutes the front door opened, and Jane emerged solo, hopped into her sensible older-model Camry, and sped away. I followed discreetly.

Like first-world women everywhere, her first morning destination was a café. It was a Starbucks, half-empty. I parked in the lot and moseyed inside. I stood off to her flank as she ordered some fancy lady's drink with much whipped cream and headed to a table for two, sat, opened her purse and took out an e-reader, flipped it on, and (after a tongue-flick at the whipped cream) settled into a nice morning read. This was obviously her routine.

I had a black coffee in my hand as I stood looking at her. She looked good. I could see lots of her mom in her. Unlike the nervously thin Katherine, Jane was kind of a big girl, but very attractive, and, like her mom, she cared for her appearance. That was a relief, for if she were unappealing then my plan would be harder to bring about. I immediately felt guilty and low for such a thought but brushed it aside. Well, it was now or never. (Actually, it was now or *later*, but now seemed right.)

I simply walked up to her table and said, "Hi Jane. Remember me?"

She looked up from her reader and pulled her head back in surprise. "Bran?"

"Yep. It's me. May I join you?"

"What in the world are you doing here?"

"Well..." I fished around in my brain. "I have some business here."

"Here?" She was clearly incredulous. "In Hardwick?"

"Jane," I said, "may I sit for a moment?"

She looked confused, but she agreed to share the table. "You know, I talked to my mom yesterday." She paused and studied my face. "Are you and her okay?"

"No." I closed my eyes. "It's one of the reasons I'm here."

"What are the other reasons," the clever girl asked. "Mom never mentioned you coming here."

"Will you *listen* to the reasons?"

She stared over my head for a few seconds, trying to sort the unsortable. "Well, I suppose I'm curious about what the hell is going on," she said.

I sipped at my plasma-hot coffee and sat across from her. "I'm trying to help your mom. I have an idea."

"I wasn't aware mom needed help," she said.

"This idea of mine," I plowed ahead, "will help a lot of people, if it works out."

"So? Tell me."

My mind was a blank; I had forgotten my prepared speech. I plowed ahead.

"You and I have always gotten along, right? I mean, when you visited, we had nice conversations, you seemed as happy to see me as I was to see you. No?"

She nodded (reluctantly, I thought). "Yes."

"So, you know I'm not crazy or anything, right?"

"Well," she laughed, "I never thought so *before*."

"Well, I'm *not* crazy. And I think your mom needs help. I'm worried about her," I looked about us, "and I'm not comfortable discussing this *here*."

"Well, where should we discuss it? And what's wrong with mom? You're scaring me." I tried to calm her but it didn't take. "I need to know what you're doing here and what you want!"

I held my palms out to her. "Okay, okay." She waited. "You mom's in no immediate danger, but I sense she could be."

"Why? Is Alex making her crazy?"

A wave of relief washed over me at those telling words. "I want to stop that from happening before it can't be undone. If it's not already too late."

I thought I might have overstepped the limit with that. Jane clammed up tight and sat there staring at her drink.

After a long silence she spoke. "Can my husband be present when you tell your idea?" she asked.

"Absolutely not and under no circumstances. You'll understand why when I present my idea to you. I need to meet you – somewhere else, not a café – where we can sit and talk. Dinner, maybe. You name the place, a quiet place, out-of-the-way, you name the time, but please, if you tell your husband about this, *everything* will be a waste of time, and a waste of an opportunity to help not just your mom."

"Well, I can see I'm not going to get anything out of you here," she observed. "Tonight…" she paused, thinking, tapping her finger on the table. "Tonight, my husband won't be home till after 11."

"Okay."

"Do you know Mackville?"

"That little blotch on the map south of here?"

"Right. There's a nice Italian place there. Romano's. I'll make reservations and meet you there at 6 o'clock tonight."

"I can drive."

She wagged a finger. "Oh no. I said I didn't *think* you were crazy. So, if you *are*, I'll have my own car, thank you very much."

We both had to laugh at that. I stood, put my hat on, and took leave of the lady.

"Till tonight," I said.

I had a little lunch at the local diner. When I returned to my room I realized that I didn't feel like going out and I read a novel until I felt sleepy, then napped, then woke up and watched news shows on TV. With plenty of time on the clock, I gathered my wallet, keys, and hat, then struggled to wedge my bulk into the stupid ugly cramped buzzy craptastic sub-compact car I rented out of guilt, and headed to Mackville, feeling every bump in the wretched road, and arriving with a sore ass.

She was late.

"Sorry," Jane said as she plopped down across from me out of nowhere, smiling and offering no explanation. I was just glad she showed at all.

I poured her some Chianti, not the house plonk served in green bottles with fake straw, but a nice one I ordered from the list. I raised my glass, she raised hers, we nodded and drank. She put her glass down and looked at me expectantly.

I cleared my throat. "First of all, I want you to know that there is much more to the story about your mom and me than you probably know."

"Did you ever have sex with her?"

"What?!"

"Mom says you never did but did you?"

"Listen, and please get this straight. I appreciate you coming to meet with me, but you need to understand something – I would not now, or ever, have had sex with your mother for a *million dollars*. I love her, and I was her *friend*." My stage-whisper was getting louder. "She finds little value in herself, so she can't believe when another finds it in her. Maybe you can understand what your mother cannot: *It's actually possible to love someone and care for them without wanting to fuck them!*"

Okay, that was too loud. The bartender gave me a dirty look. Folks don't speak that way up here, but the nerve Jane touched was still very, very raw. As for her, she sat there, poker-faced.

"Mom always said you were a passionate guy," she said and drank some wine. "So, what else?"

"What else is that she is a slave to Alex, and it's hurting her. She hates her job, her house, the neighborhood, her tiny-ass room where she's *allowed* to make quilts, she hates being minimized while her husband maximizes himself on her efforts and on her dime. But she'll never admit it. She spends most of her mental energy convincing herself that her life is just swell. Does that sound familiar?"

At that, Jane burst out crying. Might have laid it on a little thick there. The waiter came by, gave me a dirty look and asked if "senora is all right." He was about as Italian as a leprechaun. She assured him that she was fine, and he asked if we were ready to order. We were not. He buggered off, but not before giving me another dirty (and tip-reducing) look over his shoulder.

I continued. "You know what she loves? More than anything in the world? What brings her to herself and gives her the strength to shrug off her troubles?"

She wiped at her eyes and gave a little smile. "Yes," she said.

"Of course, you know. It's you and your brother."

She sniffed and looked sad. "What does *that* have to do with things?"

"Your mom needs to live out here. Around you and Bob. Her life would change. Everything she loves is here."

"I would love that. Bob too. Is that why you're here? *You* think *you* can make something like that happen?" Skeptical doesn't begin to capture the way she delivered that line.

"I do. I have an idea."

"Finally. I better brace myself," she said, which was my cue to address her empty glass. She downed half of it at a gulp. A basket of bread was placed before us, and the way she was putting the wine away made me happy that she grabbed for a piece and started in on it.

"I know this is personal. Beyond personal. But I need to ask you something, you know, *very* personal."

She stopped chewing and regarded me with puzzlement. "Well," she observed, "what have you been doing so far?"

"I've been mild. Compared to what I need to discuss."

She tossed her long brown hair and said, "Fire away. I've come this far."

"What Katherine wants most in the world... well, I don't have to tell you what that is. She wants a grandchild."

She nodded sadly. "Yes."

"That would bring her here. She couldn't stay away. It's a drive so strong that it would break Alex's hold on her. *It's the only thing that could.*"

Another nod. "It probably would. You know her pretty well. Bob thinks the same. We've talked about this."

"So, may I respectfully ask – any luck with that? Katherine always told us you were 'trying.'"

"Gee, thanks, mom."

"It's huge to her. She couldn't help mentioning it from time to time."

"Well… for whatever reason you need to know, my husband's sperm is not terribly… what's the word?"

"Viable."

"Viable. Right. So, we're investigating other possibilities."

"Fertility clinic?"

"Yes." She leaned forward. "You need to tell me what's going on, now, okay? I've been very cooperative here, but I'm losing patience."

I would not be perturbed. "That's very expensive. How about artificial insemination?"

"Is *that* what this is about?"

"No. I'm almost done with the preliminaries here. Please. Just… just tell me."

"Well," she laughed, "you think fertility specialists are expensive. The AI option is… pretty unaffordable. Neither of us has insurance for the 'turkey baster' solution, anyway."

"But that's not all, is it?"

"No. My husband doesn't want to know that our baby is someone else's. Or half of it is."

"He doesn't want to *know*. Right?"

"That's what I said. Will you *pleeeeeeze* get to the point of all this." The waiter stopped by again to take our order, took one look at my scowl, turned and went away.

"Use *me*."

Jane looked at me and blinked. Then stared at me, and after the longest time, I finally saw cognition flood her face. And then – she started to laugh.

"You have *got* to be-"

"My sperm is viable," I remembered my script and was counting on my fingers. "If we succeed your mother will likely break her slave bonds to the jackass she's married to, and live around here near-"

446

"with."

"*with*, you; you will have a baby; your husband will not know it's not his unless you *tell* him; instead of a stranger, the father would be *me*, someone who loves your mother so much that he's committing a dangerous act of love for her; your family, your brother and his wife, and your mom will be near one another in her later years; she'll be surrounded by the natural setting she loves and misses till the end of her days."

Jane stood abruptly and put her hand on her purse. I could not decipher the expression on her face. She stayed this way for a half-minute, just standing there staring at me. I held my breath. Then – she sat back down. I exhaled. I poured her more wine and she drank.

"The only thing I like about your idea..." she was actually considering this. She snapped out of her reverie. "And for you?"

"Katherine would be happy."

"Revenge?"

I shook my head. "No. On whom? Alex? Alex was my dear friend for decades, but Alex has issues. Somewhere inside him there is a good man, but not for Katherine. They enable the worst in each other. If I didn't think an emergency was on the horizon I wouldn't be doing this. I'm married and happy. Never had an affair. I'll break that perfect record for your mom. If we do it right, everybody is happy."

"Except Alex."

"He won't come with her. He'll never leave his house and his life to live up here in East Bumfuck Egypt."

"Hey!"

"Sorry. But you know what I mean. That's how he sees it. They'll split. It isn't a healthy love that keeps them together. He doesn't deserve her."

She sat and considered. I got the vexing waiter's attention and pointed to the bottle of wine, now empty. He got the message.

"I don't think I could have sex with you." She wore a fierce look all of a sudden. Now that she thought about it, she was insulted at the impropriety.

"Well... it's not exactly *recreational*, is it?" I said. "Just because you're young and attractive, that doesn't make this easy for me. Not with *my* past. I'm a good boy. It will be strange for me to do such a thing. As strange as it is for you."

Jane looked away and considered. The fierceness faded as she thought things over. The wine came. No we are not ready to order. Bring more bread.

"There is a 'window' for this to work, you know," she said.

"I know. When are the best days."

"Oddly, today and tomorrow." She drank more wine. "That's an interesting coincidence, I suppose."

I smiled. "Very interesting. Almost an omen. If your mind goes that way."

"I'm doing this for my mom."

Oh, the relief. I tried to hide it. "Yes. So am I. Remember that, please."

The bread appeared. "Do you want to order?" I asked Jane.

She shook her head with resolve. "No. We should go."

The waiter corked our bottle. I left a big tip.

Once settled in my car, Jane turned to me and asked, "Where are we going? We *cannot* go back to the hotel in town."

I pointed to the small travel inn right across the street. "If you'll forgive my presumption, we already have a reservation for the evening right there."

Again, a hint of outrage tinted her features. "You were so sure of yourself and this crazy plan, that you *knew* I would..." she struggled for the words.

"I had desperately *hoped* you would. It's just a reservation."

"Maybe I should be having some *reservations* myself," she huffed. Then looked over at me and said, "Well?"

"Okay. Let's just leave the cars here and walk over."

448

"*You* walk over and get the room. Come back and tell me which one it is. Give me a key. I'll meet you in there. You know. Like some whore." I waited in case there was more. She was impatient. "Well? *Go on!* Let's get this over with."

I hopped out and aimed for the Inn. I was not looking forward to this, but it made me feel better to tell myself that this was an appropriate response. I regretted the adultery, which, no matter how I spun it, or how much I would not enjoy all this, is exactly what it was. I was also party to the corruption of a young woman who did seem like a formerly 'nice girl.' I could hardly imagine a more awkward situation. I, literally, hoped I was up to it.

The desk clerk had my reservation and keyed me to an upstairs room. "How many nights, sir?" the little guy asked. He seemed too young to be working. A kid. Family, probably.

"Two. I hope."

We settled up in advance, and I took the two plastic cards he offered and made way back to the car. Jane rolled the window down.

"208," I said, breathless, not from the walk but from nerves. "I'll see you there." I handed her the card and I turned back to the Inn, wondering if I would indeed see her there.

Once in the faux-rustic but well-appointed room, I noted the king-sized bed. Images flooded me, unsettling me even more as I pulled the covers back. I sat on the desk chair and waited. And waited a good 20 minutes before I decided she wasn't coming. I strode to the window, looking for her car. If it was gone, then so would I be. When I reached the window I heard a card in the door, and there she was. She looked different. Militant.

"It took me awhile to commit to this," she said, closing the door and pulling the safeties. "I can't do something half-way. I have to commit." She nodded. "I have."

I approached her, smiling. She held out both palms forcefully. *"No hugging or kissing. I swear to god if you do that, I will be out of here so fast your head'll spin. And I'll tell my mom."*

"Agreed," I gulped at her fierceness.

"And another thing. *I want you in, and out. Fully clothed. I don't even want your shoes off! And the only way you are to touch me is to find a grip that works. Is that clear?*"

I must have looked like a scared rabbit. Wide-eyed, I nodded consent.

"And look away from me. *Don't look at me while you're...*"

"I'll do exactly as you say, Jane. This isn't a sex vacation for me, you know." I said, with more of an edge than I intended, but I was done walking on eggshells. "And, if you already didn't figure this out, my reputation, the nature of my marriage, and even legal entanglements await me if you make what we do here public. I am *completely* at your mercy here. That's how important your mom is to me. I would risk all that."

Those were the right words, and she thawed instantly. She took her shoes off (I didn't mention the double-standard here), went into the bathroom and shut the door. I thought of stripping naked and provocatively posing on the bed, and that made me laugh and helped to settle me. I sat back in the desk chair and waited. Shoes on.

Jane eventually emerged looking exactly the same as when she entered. She looked at the bed and pulled all the covers back *up!* Then gave me a little dirty look and shook her head in, what I hoped was, *mock* disgust. Jane positioned herself in the middle of the bed, laid herself down, legs flat together and smoothed her skirt, then grabbed a pillow and rammed it under her head.

Then she glared at me. "Well?"

Was I expected to 'perform' in these circumstances? I knew I couldn't. "Things would go a lot smoother, and quicker, if you would stop being so hostile to me. Don't you think?"

She huffed and looked away. "All right." She looked back at me, but not at my face. "You're really not ready for this, are you?"

450

That was annoying. "Are you?" I replied. "I can't imagine, the way you're acting, that you're all rarin' to go down there, either!"

She considered this. "Turn around," she ordered. I did and heard her gentle rustlings. This went on for about a minute. "Alright," she announced, clinically. "I'm ready." I turned. Skirt down and smoothed and legs together. She looked at me. "But you're not."

"You could help, you know. Without violating your rules."

"By doing what?"

"Well... let me at least see where I'm headed. That will be enough, probably. I haven't... done this... in a week. I wanted to build up a good head of steam for us, and-"

She giggled. "'Head of steam for the project?" I made her laugh. That had to be good, right?

"Please. Just give me a peek... and I'll be okay. And we'll be done."

Expressionless, Jane lifted her skirt to her waist, laid her feet flat on the mattress with her knees bent and spread her legs, staring at me crossly. I immediately felt guilty for how much I was enjoying that sight. But the desired effect was in progress. I approached the bed, unzipped, freed my expanding wiener and lay on top of her as gently as I could, pressing against her entrance. Finally, we were one in this tender effort, and I pushed in. I remember that the tightness was a shock. Her body shuddered. I thrust once, twice.

"Do it! Don't hold back. Do it *now!*" she hissed the orders.

With my week of abstinence, her wish was granted at the fifth stroke, and I pumped hard to empty myself. When she judged I was spent, Jane took my shoulders and pushed me to her side, where I lay, panting. She resumed her position: legs together, skirt down and smoothed, arms at her side, looking at the ceiling.

"Again?" she said.

"Well... *Jesus, Jane!* – maybe in a few minutes!"

She was silent and immobile, but patient, and when about ten minutes in complete, unbreakable silence had passed (nearly nodded off there) I finally told her we could give it another try. "But you need to give me another peek."

She sighed, disgustedly, and hiked her skirt, resuming the old position. I knelt between her legs. We both noted I was not 'there yet.'

"I'm not doing *anything* else for you," she stated flatly.

"I have an idea," I told her. I positioned myself for intercourse and in a few moments, in that warm wetness, I felt myself stiffen. I entered her a second time, but this was going to take longer than she was hoping.

As I was stroking away, I detected a change in her breathing. "What's wrong!" she hissed. "Get this over with, *please*! And stop looking at me!" It was like with the shoes; apparently, it was okay for *her* to look at *me*.

As her breathing increased, she began to move her hips against my thrusts. That was all I needed, and it was soon over. Again, she pushed me off, adjusted herself, and we lay side-by-side, both of us panting softly.

"I want you to go now," she said.

"And you? What about you?"

"I need to lie here for a while to increase the odds of conception. I'll meet you back here at about 12:15 tomorrow. It will be my lunch hour. And try not to take so long doing it next time."

That was the first time in my life I had ever been accused of 'taking too long.'

So that was it. I stood, zipped, grabbed my hat, tipped it goodbye, and left the room, closing the door. I stood outside the door and listened, saddened by what I knew I would hear. She was crying.

With mixed feelings, I headed back to Hardwick.

I had a dream that night.

I was at a school play, a pageant on stage in a school gym. The Queen of the pageant was a little girl in a long dress made of fabric flowers, with

452

a glittery crown and a wand with a purple star at the end of it. Queenly music was blaring from the loudspeakers. She stood on a prop hill in the middle of the stage and she was magically blessing all of her subjects, who were bowing before her.

Suddenly the music petered-out mid-phrase, and the Queen looked out into the audience, and right at me. All the little kids on stage perked up and wondered what was wrong, and the little Queen left her hilltop and climbed down from the stage. She deftly made her way back in among the sea of folding chairs to my aisle, and turned in, walking directly up to me.

She looked at me and smiled, this perfect little-girl Queen, raised her wand and brought it down, not to my head but to the middle of my chest, and proclaimed in a clear regal voice:

"Don't be afraid! I forgive you!"

And then I woke up.

I believed Jane, even though I knew how she suffered with this, that she was willing to see it through and would meet me one more time. I had breakfast at the town diner, which was really good, and putzed about the little town of Hardwick, ending up at the used bookstore. That ate up the time, and I left early to head back to the even littler town of Mackville, in case I had a flat, got in an accident – anything that might delay a fellow from his appointed rounds. Finally, I was back in the room, looked at my watch and realized I had a whole hour to burn. Cable TV to the rescue.

At exactly 12:15 Jane's card unlocked the door and she entered, closing and securing us inside. I switched off the tube. Without acknowledging my existence, she took off her coat (it was nippy out there today) and shoes, nodded to me curtly, went into the bathroom and closed the door. When she emerged, she repeated yesterday's routine. In a flash, there she was in the middle of the bed, legs together, skirt smoothed, pillow under head. I approached the foot of the bed.

"Do you need your 'view?'" she asked with a ton of sarcasm.

Boy did I ever. I felt almost entirely response-less, largely due to the utter lack of the slightest hint of eroticism in the room, but also because of my sexual gymnastics (for me, anyway) the day before. I felt... spent.

"Jane. Yesterday... it took a lot out of me."

"What do you mean?"

"I haven't done it twice in a row since I was a teenager. And that was always with *myself* as a partner."

"*Eeeeuuuu.* TMI," she said, with a face. "So, what does that all mean?"

I gave a gesture of surrender. "I dunno," I sighed. "Let's try The View."

Robotically, she lifted her dress, opened and spread her legs.

I unzipped to assess the status quo. Nothing. I tried to make light of it. "I'm afraid Mr. Friendly isn't getting the message," I said.

She actually laughed. "'Mr. Friendly?' I never heard that one before."

"We have hundreds," I confided suavely.

She pulled her skirt back down. A change had come over her. "I won't touch you," she repeated her vow. "Is there some other..." she couldn't find the words.

I had an idea. "Would you mind changing the view?"

"Oh god. What does that even *mean?*"

"Turn over and get on your elbows and knees?" I asked, sheepishly.

She considered, she narrowed her eyes and glared at me for a space, then sighed, and flipped over, deftly assuming the position.

"Good. Now," I said, "leave the rest to me and we should be done pretty quickly."

It was a wild boast. I knelt behind her. Almost there. "Would you please put your knees farther apart?" She complied without any wilting comment, which I did not need at the moment.

I lifted the hem of her skirt and pushed the material on to her back. Yes, this could work. Yes, this was working. With a little handy familiar help, I was ready to go in moments.

We were soon joined, and I was working hard, but I knew this was going to take more than a few seconds. Jane's breathing was changing and, in a minute or so she had started to participate in the movements. Still no luck from my end.

"Oh my god," she said. *"You have to come now."*

"Almost there," I breathed.

"Quickly!" she said, and her breathing became louder. After another minute or so she was well beyond objections, and suddenly grabbed at both of her breasts and exploded into obvious orgasm, bucking like a little bronco. I held on like the cowboy I was not, and my work consummated easily after that. After a few moments to recover I, *unthinkingly*, leaned over and kissed her bare back as I bent to exit her.

"No!!" she cried, reached back and pulled her skirt down and flipped onto her back in one flash of motion. There she lay, ruddy-faced and panting, with a murderous look in her eyes.

"I'm sorry!" I whispered hoarsely. *"I wasn't thinking!"*

Then the anger melted, and she became the saddest little girl and burst out crying. I put my hand on her arm and she shook it loose. She covered her face with her palms and wept. After a while, she whimpered, "That never happened before."

"What never happened?" I asked gently.

She would not answer and just sobbed. When she finally calmed down, she looked over at me and said. "The orgasm."

Well, I didn't see that one coming. She lay there calmly for a while, looking at the ceiling, and at length went back into the bathroom where she stayed for a few minutes. I tidied up and collected her key, ready to walk out the door when she emerged, a wilted flower.

She walked over to me, hesitated, then put her arms around my neck and we embraced. The act rocketed me back in time to my final embrace of her mother, and I felt that part of her in my arms.

Jane released me and looked up at me. "I don't ever want to see, or hear from you, again." She said that with a sad little smile, and I knew there were no hard feelings, but that all this was very nearly impossible for her to assimilate. "Say you'll never see me again."

"I'll…"

"Say it, Bran."

"I'll never see you again, Jane."

"Promise?"

I nodded. "I promise."

She was out and down the stairs before I could even grab my hat.

That evening, on the plane ride back to Detroit, I felt awash in total exhaustion. I felt beaten-up, but proud that I did what I set out to do, the way that a man oughta feel when he succeeds at a great undertaking! I smiled at my silliness.

Mainly, I thought about Jane, about the effect all this might be having on her. That stern and grim attitude was her armor, and while she effectively braced one part of her castle, another side was left undefended and collapsed quite spectacularly. The only thing she did not want to show was vulnerability. I tried, along with her, to be as business-like as possible during our brief and clinical association, but it was just too difficult. I violated the rules and betrayed myself with a thoughtless kiss; she with her responses, and her tears.

I wanted to sleep here on the plane, even though I slept well the night before and it was only a little after 9 p.m. Entering my aisle appeared a young woman, college girl was my guess. She took her middle seat (I at the window, as always) without so much as a nod in greeting to me. She didn't seem shy, just rude in that young person way that I find more annoying with each passing year.

I could not settle into slumber, but the young lady was asleep before we even took off. As the minutes of flight elapsed she slunk further and further onto my shoulder. I thought about shaking her off, waking her and obliging her to behave more mannerly. Finally, I was about to make my move when she slumped further till the top of her head was touching my jaw, and she wiggled and snuggled into comfort. I could not relax like this, but the smell of her hair was nice, and I wasn't really that tired, and the longer we sat this way the more I felt that to awaken her would be something her cruel step-dad would probably do. But not me. *No* sir.

When I think back on this, I realize I had simply been bewitched.

Sucker.

Back at home, I had a couple of days to pass before Gail returned from her trip. The day she returned I was so glad to see her I courted her like we were youngsters. A little gift, nice dinner, flowers, much affection. I knew why I was doing it but it helped me get back into the routine, and she did not complain, though I sensed she felt it all a bit odd. It was all very heartfelt. I really do love her that much and more, and, yes, it helped with the guilt. I could rationalize it all day long, but I still had it, and still do.

The month passed, then October, then it was winter. Whenever we were with our few remaining friends at a dinner or small gathering, I would always inquire about Alex and Katherine. Katherine's job had become part-time and even Alex's meager earnings were drying up. Katherine scored some inheritance money, and it seemed that this is what they were living on.

Finally, in mid-December, we were out to Japanese food with our other good friends Evan and Lila. At length, I asked how Alex and Katherine were getting on.

"They seem good," Evan said.

Lila looked at him like he had grown another head. "Aren't you forgetting something?" she asked.

Evan looked wonderingly. Then, "Oh yeah! I forgot."

Lila smirked and shook her head, then brightened. "Katherine's daughter Jane is pregnant!"

"Oh my god," Gail said. "Jane must be thrilled!"

"Not just Jane," Lila said. "After all that trying, they have to be the happiest couple in Vermont."

"When's the baby due?" Gail asked.

"June," Lila said. "A June baby."

Staring into space, I realized I had said: "It worked!"

"What worked?" Evan mumbled through a mouthful of seaweed.

"What?"

He swallowed. "You said 'it worked.' *What* worked?"

I was caught between speechless shock that the plan worked and speechless witlessness at being called to account for what I just said out loud. I tried to form words with my mouth, but the effect was apparently so comic that the three burst into laughter and my outburst was forgotten without elaboration as the ladies' desserts arrived.

Jane had her baby. A girl. They called her Ambrosia. *A fragrant drink, a divine exhalation of the earth, conveying immortality upon those who receive it.* Actually, Ambrosia is her name, but they call her Amby. For every day of the next seven years, I was so eager for news of… *of my daughter,* that I skirted obvious obsession at every outing with anyone who might provide any news about my little Ambrosia.

I felt stupid that I never figured my own feelings into my plan. This, I now realize, is a pain I will never be free of, and there is nothing I can do about it. It is the greatest burden that I have ever been obliged to bear and sometimes, when alone, I *cannot* bear it. At these times I believe that, if I had a chance to do things over again, I would never have done it. When I recover, I curse my cowardliness, tell myself it is for the best, pick up my cross and move on.

Katherine had left to visit Jane when she still had three months before birthtime, then she "overstayed." She was at the birth and remained with Jane for a month post-partum.

When she returned, she and Alex had quite the dustup, so the gossip went. Within a month Katherine had quit the university and took her car and loaded U-Haul to her new home with her daughter, granddaughter, and son-in-law in the hills of Vermont, in easy visiting range of her son and his wife an hour's drive away. There was a large party for Katherine's farewell with all her friends in attendance. Alex did not attend, and Gail and I were not invited.

For seven years I lived under this pall. I dared not write nor call Jane. That, I knew, would be *the* violation. I felt I had already violated enough.

Then one day in September Gail allowed how she missed her bestie from school, the one from out west whom she visited when I put my fateful plan into effect. Gail spoke with her recently and asked if I would mind if she spent ten days or so with her again – it had been so long. Of course, this brought my anguish to a head and made me consider what till then was out of the question: *Was I planning to die without even setting eyes on my daughter?* Without ever seeing Jane, or having any resolution with Katherine? Even social media was denied me for the odd photo, as neither woman, I was certain, would ever accept me as part of their circle. I told Gail that she had my blessing for her trip.

In the meantime, I had to root around plenty for the information I needed, but my resolve spurred my success. Katherine worked at Ambrosia's school, I discovered from friendly gossip. I learned it was a public school and, considering Amby's tender age, I found the only school that it could have been on the map. It was too far to walk, so that meant (I hoped) that mom picked up Amby, or Amby and grandma, at the end of the day. Or, Katherine drove Amby. That would make things harder for me.

No way I would get a second chance at this, so I had to nail it. I had to be patient, and I had to be smart. I had doubts about actually being either of those things, but the consequences of never attempting to breach the barrier finally overwhelmed my oaths and the torture of the status quo. I had committed to my new plan. I made my reservations for the plane, the car, and that fateful little Inn in Mackville – close enough to Hardwick without a chance of being spotted until I was ready.

I rented a huge SUV for an unconscionable amount of money. Should have done that the first time. I actually *enjoyed* the drive from the airport to little Mackville. I insisted upon the same room at the Inn, a demand easily accommodated since I was the only guest. The now fully-grown little boy from my last visit almost eight years prior was still holding down the fort, and we did business. I climbed the stairs to my room, entered, closed the door and secured it, put down my bag, turned and stared at the bed. I pretty much tranced-out. What a fateful time that was and I relived it all. When I snapped out of it, I took a shower, and then a nap.

At noon I woke, dressed, and went to the bakery, which doubled as a gift shop, and tripled as a café. When I achieved appropriate caffeine levels I repaired to the room and read until about 2 p.m. Then I was off to the magnificent metropolis of Hardwick to spy on my... I was about to type 'my family' but that isn't quite right, is it?

When I hit town, I headed toward the school and realized I might be in for an extended stakeout, so I visited yet another café for a tall drink to accompany my vigil. It was one of those mom-and-pop joints, not a chain, and there was only one other car in the lot.

When I opened the café door I saw a dark-haired little girl sitting at a table by herself, and she looked familiar. In the line were two women, one youngish, one mature. They turned and looked at me and I realized that it was Katherine and Jane. I froze. It took a moment for the women to finally recognize who it was standing agog at them, and Jane's face was the first to react.

"Bran." A statement, not a question, quietly said.

Katherine put her palms to her cheeks and breathed, *"O my god."*

Jane's look asked the question 'what the hell are you doing here,' without benefit of voice.

I started to cry. I never cry. "I didn't plan to meet you here!" I blubbered.

"Mamma?" asked the little girl, now standing next to her chair.

Jane held out her hand, "Come here, honey." Ambrosia ran to her mom and took her hand.

Katherine said, "Bran, what is going on?"

My burst of tears stopped as abruptly as it came, and I tried to get my bearings while I wiped at my eyes. I did the only thing I could do on such short notice: I told the truth.

"I was going to go to the school and hoped that I might see the three of you together and ask you to see me for a few minutes, then I would leave. That's all."

Jane was recovered enough now to show full outrage. "Come on, honey." She looked at Katherine. "Let's go, mom," she said and walked with her daughter toward the door.

"I'll be with you in a minute, Jane," Katherine said.

Jane stopped and turned and gave Katherine an open-mouth 'you're kidding, right?' look, but Katherine waved her on. I moved out of the way and the pair brisked past and exited without a look in my direction.

I approached Katherine and when I was in reach she stepped toward me and we embraced. And the tears returned and they were upon her also. When I finally released her, I looked into her eyes, blinking tears away.

"I'm sorry," I said.

"It's not your fault," she whispered. "It's mine and I have regretted it for so long and I am so, so sorry."

"I only ever wanted to be your friend and protect you."

"And I couldn't see that."

I smiled. "You have a granddaughter."

461

"I do I do I do!" she said with a little laugh. The only laugh she has.

"No school today?"

"They're doing a *pageant!*" she said. "They rehearsed after lunch and let some of the kids go home early."

"A pageant." I nodded and smiled.

"She's a fairy princess, naturally. Costume, crown, the whole bit."

"And a wand."

"Yes! Yes, and a magic wand! She carries it around the house blessing everyone, or trying to make someone disappear!"

I pointed toward the car in the lot, lights on, engine running, pissed-off lady in the driver seat. "May I meet her?"

Katherine darkened. "Better not," she said. "Jane is furious at you."

"I see..." I said. "Should she be?" I asked.

Katherine raised her eyebrows and gave me an enigmatic look. "*Shouldn't* she be?" She touched my cheek. "I have to go. I'm so glad you came." She looked like she wanted to say more but could not. "I have no words..."

We held one another close again, for the last time. She pulled back and, smiling, turned to leave but stopped before the door. She turned. "And Bran," she said.

"Yes."

She closed her eyes and breathed the words warmly and fervently, almost desperately. "Thank you."

I smiled. "For what?"

In reply, she just smiled back at me, and we were locked in this happy realm for a precious space, the forlorn embattlements of love vanquished in these blissful seconds. Finally she turned, broke the spell, and was off to join her family in the car. Then they drove off and I suppose I will never see them again.

O *my only daughter...*

I have a lively correspondence with Katherine now, and I get tons of pictures that only a father could love from her on social media that she has shared with me. But Katherine is under strict orders that I shall have no direct contact with her or Ambrosia. I see the logic there, but I hate it. I console myself with the knowledge that Katherine will help me to watch my daughter grow up in a virtual way, but sometimes I wonder if the movies and pictures are actually making my longing worse, almost like a punishment for my actions dressed up as a technological advantage.

But every now and then, when I am most in need, my little Ambrosia will come to me in my dream and touch my heart with her purple wand.

ঙেওঙ

On Not Playing Chess

I don't play chess. But I love chess.

I go to YouTube to watch famous games. But I do not play because I do not engage in disciplines at which I have no natural ability, which includes almost all forms of human endeavor.

Much to my delight, my six grandchildren love chess. Every one of them. They are all on chess.com, which is one of the few indispensable websites for we poor Earthlings. They play games online with people who are approximately matched to their level of skill, opponents from all over the world, who are also registered at chess.com. And natch, they play one another, too. Their great aspiration is to beat my wife (grandma) or my two sons (dads) one day.

So I started to think about chess as a human endeavor, what it *means*, that sort of thing, since I love it but am so completely inept at it.

I think of chess as a deadly battle. So, is there no negotiation? But each game is a bloodbath!

So I started to wonder—what if, as in a duel, there could be some negotiation beforehand. I mean -- hey, *let's talk this over! There's too much at stake here!*

So I tried to imagine what such a negotiation might look like, and I came up with this:

Let me explain.

Of course, it's an impossible position. Opposite Kings and Queens in such combustible proximity.

But this is a negotiation! They are meeting face-to-face, being royal and civil, and eschewing their natural tendency to annihilate one another. It's all for show while others do the work. (Right… politics!)

The real negotiations are being carried out by the Bishops. True clerical ambassadors of Peace and Goodwill. Yeah, sure. A look at history will quickly dispel that myth. But that's the strategy, anyway. And talk about precarious positions! Look at them! It's a tinderbox and the slightest spark will set off a series of exchanges that will annihilate everything, and all goodwill and hopes for the future will be dashed!

The Knights and the Rooks are casually positioned for double-team protection on the four royals. Any shenanigans will be instantly neutralized, and the shit will hit the fan most explosively.

It's all a carefully balanced scenario of trust and readiness.

The pawns? They are out of the way, drunk and fighting. What else can one expect? I mean… they're *pawns!*

But, as always, negotiations will fail, and white and black will go to war in short order. But that's what they always wanted anyway, I suppose.

And I will watch.

∞∞∞

Castle Queenside

Currently there are 109 Grandmasters of Chess in the United States. Two of them, from Michigan, attended the same high school near Detroit, and for many years called one another best friends. Growing up, they shared three passions: chess, muscle cars (this was in the early '70s), and Celeste. She was the one passion neither young man wished to share, and it all ended badly.

Truman Babb and Lane Whitman, two lads about as different as boys can be, got close in grade school, and by the time they got their driver's licenses at 16, they already knew how to drive. It was the era of the muscle car and they called the Motor City their home. Chess was their main obsession but racing their cars on Telegraph Rd. was their relaxation. Truman had a hot '68 Camaro. Lane had a '67 Mustang. Both cars underwent heavy modifications, carried out by Truman and Lane personally.

Celeste was Truman's girl. Had been all through high school. Now all three were 19, and as hard as Lane tried, he could not get Celeste out of his head. The last thing he wanted to do was to hurt his friend, but she was so beautiful! And of course, at 19 and full of beans, the truth would not be stoppered up. After a night of pizza and many beers Lane made a clumsy attempt at stealing a kiss while Truman went to the bathroom. Celeste pushed him away. She was shocked. Briefly. Then she looked thoughtful for a moment, grabbed the back of Lane's head, and kissed him like he had never been kissed before or since. They lost awareness, and never even heard the toilet flush and Truman re-entering the livingroom.

Truman slapped Lane, hard. Lane popped up from the couch.

"You hit me, you son-of-a-bitch!"

"You kissed Celeste! How long have you been…" and then the Great Horror occurred to him. *"Have you been fucking my Celeste?!"*

"First and only kiss ever," Lane admitted. "Swear to God."

"You fucking liar!"

Celeste was staying out of it, trying to make herself invisible while the two men raged.

"You hit me and now you call me a liar?"

"That's right, bitch!"

And Lane hauled off and backhanded a splendid slap in return. "I demand satisfaction!" Lane hollered. (They recently came off of a TV marathon of sword-fighting and chivalry movies.)

Truman smiled. His lip was bloody. It was a creepy look. Enraged but tightly-wrapped, he uttered two words.

"Woodward Special."

Lane blinked. This was *beyond* serious. *But so was the insult!*

"For titles."

Truman wiped at his lip with his sleeve. "Agreed. Tomorrow night?"

"Ten o'clock. You know where."

Lane turned on his heel, or would have if he weren't so pickled, more like he pivoted drunkenly on his heel, and left Truman's apartment.

Truman looked down at Celeste who had apparently not succeeded in making herself invisible. "You go, too!" he yelled, retired to his bedroom, and slammed the door.

Celeste left the apartment, in tears.

The next morning each woke with that special kind of hangover that's not just about drinking too much but alloyed with the assurance that one did something incredibly stupid the night before.

Lane was sorry he kissed Celeste for the hurt it caused his friend, but excited by Celeste's enthusiastic response. Truman now hated the both of them. Celeste was sorry she hurt Truman, but she always bristled at the feeling that he thought he 'owned' her. Actually, she was hoping to see Lane again as soon as possible and do more kissing. But both men regretted the Woodward Special that was nevertheless a matter of honor and set to transpire that very evening.

Here is a translation for the uninitiated, and that would include anyone who is not from Detroit during the '60s and '70s and heavily into stock car modification and street racing: *They were to meet certain acquaintances near Woodward and Maple street in the heart of Detroit at 10 p.m., and there it would be arranged that later in the night the two young men would drag race for a quarter mile down Woodward Avenue. They were racing 'for titles,' which means that the loser signed the title of his car over to the victor, effectively losing his car in a bet.*

As they lay in bed that morning with their augmented hangovers both men bitterly regretted ever having made this a point of honor between them. But there was no going back, and this event marked the start of their lifelong enmity on a battlefield that would move in time from the city streets to the chessboards of the world's capitals.

But first the race. (Celeste had the grace not to attend.) It was not until about 1 a.m. that the two were officially lined up and ready to rumble.

It wasn't even close.

Truman and his hopped-up Camaro won by three car-lengths, a bitter embarrassment for Lane. They pulled off the street into the vacant lot designated for post-race pow-wows. Truman burst from his cockpit, the cocky victor, and jogged over to Lane's Mustang. Lane rolled his window down. He had the title to the Mustang on his lap and was scribbling his signature on the appropriate line. He had been crying. (Lane cried a *lot*. His friends made fun of him about this for so many years that it didn't even bother him anymore.)

Truman gloated. "The Camaro is supreme, bitch!"

"Lay it on," Lane said, too angry now to cry, "I can't help it." He thrust the paper title at Truman. Truman did not take it.

"Take it, god damn it!"

He just stood there.

Lane was steaming mad. "Take this fucking title. The car is yours. I'll drive it back to your place, put the key under the mat and walk home. That work?"

"I ain't taking your car," Truman said.

"It's yours, fucker. You won it fair and square."

"You took my girlfriend."

"Wait... *what?*"

"But I ain't taking your car. You think this'll square things? My girl for your car? Well... I don't want it. I ain't like you. I was a good friend. Keep your fucking car. Just know I beat you."

And at that Truman got back into his Camaro and headed on home.

This hit Lane like a ton of bricks. He had lost his best and oldest friend, actually, his *only* friend. His tears returned and he wept bitterly. *He wished Truman had taken his car, which he loved beyond reason.* For upon Lane's loss of face that night, Truman had heaped more shame and sorrow than he had ever felt in his life. Truman had also soured what Lane had hoped was to be his True Love. He never reconnected with Celeste and would reflect for half a century if his life-long bachelorhood could be traced back to that terrible night.

It would be two years before the two men confronted one another again.

They were both 21 now and had each achieved amazing mastery in chess, the discipline that would shape their lives. Literally, they were of master rank in the World Chess Federation, each with a score slightly above 2200. They weren't just good, they were brilliant.

Truman had stayed in Detroit, breezing through pre-med studies at Wayne State. He was quite the dandy—he always wore a suit, well-barbered and manicured, and a social success by any standard. The ladies loved him.

Lane was becoming more and more introverted and antisocial, having moved to rural central Michigan where he lived modestly, making a good living investing in the stock and money markets, putting his analytical and pattern-recognition skills to work in a most practical way. In his downtime, which was most of the day, he studied chess. He dressed like a bum, drank too much, and suffered poor hygiene. And the ladies? What ladies?

Both played tournament chess as their only true passion and had noted the presence of one another at several matches over the past year but had never faced the other as an opponent. That changed in '73, when as a consequence of drifting to the top of the pack they faced off in a sanctioned match in the final game of a large midwestern tournament. It was a brilliant game. Truman resigned after 51 moves, knocking over his King and storming from the room. Throughout, they never spoke a single word to one another.

This pattern repeated often throughout the decades, and they were almost even in their share of triumphs in total and against one another. By 1989, they had both attained grandmaster status and played in contests all over the world. By then, Truman was a noted neurologist with a modest practice in the toney suburbs north of Detroit. Lane had amassed a fortune and was contemplating a move to a home he hoped to build north of Marquette in Michigan's Upper Peninsula, a move that would make him, if possible, even more of a social isolate than he had become.

They were darlings of the chess world, never in serious contention for the very top spot but colorful characters known for their stylish play and intense, bitter rivalry. But by the time they had entered their late sixties each had begun to wind down. The fatigue of the road, the amazing new younger competition and some health issues all combined to compel each into a graceful retirement from the grueling life of the chess virtuoso.

It was in 2035, both men now in their eighties, that some wag from the Michigan Chess League had the idea of bringing the two local legends together to play a final game against one another. Grady Ryan was the fellow's name. He was a chess buff, a budding journalist and a video blogger. The League agreed to pick up the tab should Grady manage to engineer such an unlikely confrontation between the two rival grandmasters, but Grady had an idea.

He knew that both men would refuse right off the bat when confronted with the idea of a 'final battle' and he was correct—Truman politely declined, while Lane swore into his phone and hung up on the kid.

But the canny lad also suspected, that if he could convince each that the other believed he was too much a coward, and too out-of-shape to accept the challenge 'like a man,' that he might get their unwilling cooperation. It was too easy. They *wanted* to believe the propaganda. They both agreed instantly.

The match would take place halfway between Detroit and Marquette, and in early autumn, a spectacular time to be in upper Michigan—Traverse City to be precise—where the new Grand Traverse Concourse Hotel would host the event.

That was the plan, but Lane torpedoed it. He would only play in the Jellico Lounge, a frankly rundown saloon in Traverse City but his favorite haunt in that region, *and no spectators!* So they lost their sponsorship, but Grady Ryan was not to be derailed so easily. He wanted the video.

Lane finally agreed to the presence of a skeleton staff in the bar and an exemption for Grady and an assistant who promised to record the event unobtrusively. Lane didn't like that last rider, but the deal was off unless he acquiesced. Happily, there is an upper floor to the lounge where the video crew would be out of sight, and the four cameras are undetectably small.

Truman was looking forward to a big society occasion and was most disappointed that they would be playing in a seedy bar. But he was spurred to cooperate by his sheer need to put that son-of-a-bitch in his place, once and for all, and finally. *We'll see who's the 'out-of-shape coward'!*

Grady Ryan is good as his word. The setup for the video is all but invisible, and so are Grady and the crew. They are upstairs surrounded by video monitors and headphones, all set to monitor the event in complete seclusion to the live action below them.

It is Sunday about 2 p.m. and the game is set to begin at 2:30. At present there is no one in the bar except for a fellow by himself finishing a pastrami sandwich and putting on an early Sunday buzz. There is Leo the owner who is tending bar, and Bobby, a server/bouncer who was asked by Leo to join him for the afternoon. Grady asked that the bar be closed from 2:30 till 5:00, and Leo held out for a $300 check to cover 'lost business' during the closed time. As if.

At 2:15 an old man enters and hails Leo, who calls back, "Lane! Good to see you. They got things set up right in the middle there. Have a seat!"

Lane has on an old pair of jeans with sandals and an army-green tee shirt. He's skinny to the point of emaciation and hobbles to the table with the aid of a cane. He sits.

"What'll it be, buddy?" Leo calls out.

"Vodka martini." Lane growls. "Where's Mary?"

"She quit."

"Huh. Imagine. Nice place like this."

"Smartass." They laugh.

Lane takes out a cigar, snips the end, tests it, and fires it up.

"Excuse me, sir?" says the guy with the pastrami sandwich. "There's no smoking in here."

Lane glances over. "Who the fuck are you?"

Leo motions to big Bobby. Bobby paces over to the guy. He's a 'fudgie' (a tourist from downstate) not a regular, so no special considerations will be forthcoming.

"Time to go, pal."

"I ain't finished!"

"We're closed. Come on." And he takes the fellow by the elbow. He stands.

"I haven't paid for my stuff!"

"Happy Birthday. Meal's on us. Now get moving."

The fellow exits with no more drama. Bobby places a CLOSED sign in the little port window.

Lane leans back and exhales a lovely set of smoke rings from his big Cuban cigar.

There is a full-sized chessboard in the middle of the table, a chess clock, an ashtray, and salt & pepper shakers. Lane picks up the white King nearest him, notes the fine detail and heft of the nicely-weighted piece and puts His Majesty back in his square.

The door opens and a dapper old guy in a three-piece suit tools in. Like Lane, he looks almost frail. But this is not a good look for Truman, who unlike Lane, had always radiated a robust and vital vibe.

"Hey. Welcome." Leo calls from behind the bar. "You must be-"

"Call me Truman."

"I'm Leo. What'll you have, Truman? Your money's no good here today."

"Got champagne?" he asks. "I'll be doing some celebrating." He moves to the chess table.

"Like fucking hell you will," Lane says, looking up at his nemesis. "Unless you celebrate having your ass kicked."

Truman shakes his head. "Same old bile." He sits. "I'm going to enjoy this."

"No champagne," Leo says. "But I got a cold bottle of Asti. That do?"

"It'll do fine, Leo."

Truman picks up the black Queen near him and examines it. "Nice weighty pieces. Nice board, too!"

At that Lane leans forward and sweeps the board from the table, sending it crashing into the wall, pieces scattering noisily all over the place.

For about ten seconds you can hear a pin drop.

"Jesus Christ, Lane." Leo moans.

"You know…" Truman whispered, still holding the black Queen, "if you're too frightened to play me you could have just said so."

Upstairs, Grady was freaking out. *That was my best board and my best pieces! Goddam that crazy bastard!*" he whispered.

Ron, his assistant was choking back laughter.

"What's so goddam funny?"

Ron pointed at one of the monitors. "This… this is gonna be *awesome* today."

"It fucking *better* be."

Truman tosses the black Queen over by the now-broken board and stands. He is about to say something but Lane cuts him off.

"e4"

Truman looks puzzled. "Before? Before what?"

"No, you putz; EEEEEEE-FOUR!"

"Oh…" Truman resumes his seat. He gets it now. "c5. No. *Wait a minute!* Why do you get white?"

"Leo!" Lane yells. "Flip a coin."

Leo comes tableside, flips a quarter and Truman calls out "Heads!" The coin clangs onto the tabletop. Heads it is.

"Hah! You jackass. Okay, e4."

"c5"

"Knight to f3."

"g6"

"c4"

"Bishop to g7."

The lads upstairs are freaking out.

"Jesus!" Grady whispered. "They're playing without a board!"

"Yeah," Ron mumbles penciling down the moves as they are spoken. "No shit. Pretty awesome for a couple octogenarians."

Grady grabs his backpack and whips out a tiny magnetic board and hurriedly assembles the pieces upon it as the players continue calling out moves. He looks at Ron's scribbles and at last matches what the grandmasters see in their minds' eye.

"Bishop to e3," Truman says.

"Bishop to g4," Lane responds.

"dc5"

"dc5. I want my car back," Lane says out of the blue.

"I never took your goddam car."

"But you could've. It never felt like mine ever again. I want a chance to win it back."

"How?"

"If you win, you take my car."

"What do you drive?"

"Big-ass new Toyota Land Cruiser."

"I drive a new S-class Mercedes coupe."

"Yeah. You would, you and Hitler. You fucking Nazi."

"Ah. Here we go with your Poor Jew shit!"

"Besides. I don't want your car. If I win, we're square on the car stuff. Agreed?"

Truman considers. Why not? "Okay. If you win, I keep my car. But I get your car when I win. Just like I could have taken your car when you lost last time."

"Yeah? Well I took your girl!"

At that Truman shoves the table into Lane's chest, knocking him and his martini from his chair. Sprawling on the tiles, he looked daggers at Truman and hurls his martini glass at the man. It hits him on his forehead and shatters.

Leo runs from behind the bar with a clean bar towel. He yells at Lane, still on the floor.

"You know, you are a crazy son of a bitch, Lane," Leo is steaming. "No more of that or I'll put a stop to this. *Understand?"*

Truman lets Leo examine his face.

"You need stitches in your forehead."

"The fucker knocked me out of my chair!" Lane cried. "Help me up, goddam it!"

"You wanna go to the clinic, Truman?"

"No!" he yells. "Sorry, Leo. I mean... no thanks. I want to sink this shitbird where he sits."

"Well. Just keep pressure on it. It's clean." And Leo starts back to the bar. Lane, still on the floor, grabs Leo's foot.

"You wanna give me a hand here?"

Leo stares down at him. "Not really." But he does anyway and slams the frail Lane back into his chair.

"Jesus Christ!" Lane objects to the rough handling.

"No more shit outta you today, Lane. Got it?"

Lane ignores Leo.

"Queen takes Queen."

"Rook takes Queen."

"Bishop takes pawn."

"Bishop takes Knight. Can I get another martini, please?"

"Which one, you crazy asshole!"

"Oh yeah. The one on c3."

They're slowing down now, into the mid-game and both men are lost in concentration. There is no more nonsense now, just two grandmasters completely absorbed in their game. The first 42 moves have taken a little more than an hour.

On the 43rd move Truman calls out, "Rook to a5."

Lane closes his eyes and rubs his temples as if he has a headache. He gulps his warm martini, neglected since his refill.

"Mate in 8," Truman says, still pressing the towel to his forehead. "I know you see it."

Lane reaches over to the pepper shaker, puts his finger on the top of it, and tips it over on its side. He bursts out crying. *"I am so fucking old!"* he sobs, forehead on the table.

Truman looks uncomfortable. So do Leo and Bobby. It's a sad sight.

"It was a good game, Lane," Truman says over sobbing noises.

Lane picks up his head, sits up straight, takes a deep breath and wipes his eyes with his palms.

"It's just the sort of game I would have won… back in the day."

"Maybe…" Truman offers Lane the handkerchief in his suit pocket. Lane accepts it and wipes his face, offers to give it back and Truman declines.

"Thanks," Lane says quietly, and he blows his nose. He laughs. "Well, if it wasn't mine before it's mine now!"

Everyone laughs at that.

Truman stands. "Listen… I'll take your car if you *want* me to, but… but for Christ's sake Lane, what the fuck am I gonna do with that big Jap pile o' shit? I would appreciate it, as the winner, if you didn't make me take it!"

Lane considers this and nods. "All right. I'll do you a favor. But it's getting to be a habit and I don't like it!" The two men laugh. "Next time I will insist!"

"Won't be a next time, Lane."

"Pussy."

"It ain't that." Truman points to his gut. "Pancreas cancer. Stage four. That was our last game."

"O!" Lane starts crying again. "I'm sorry, Truman."

The two grandmasters regard one another in melancholy silence.

"I was never really your enemy, you know," Lane said. Blows his nose again. "Everything just got all… fucked up."

"Yeah… I wish we had a do-over." They smile at one another. "You were a worthy adversary." He holds out his hand to Lane. "It was an honor."

Lane takes his hand. They don't shake, they just hold on to one another, and finally let go.

Truman steps toward the door and turns, still holding the bar towel to his still-bleeding head.

"Thanks for your hospitality, Leo," he calls.

"It was my pleasure, Truman."

And he's gone.

Lane takes a deep breath. "May I have some more booze, please?" And at that he leans forward and puts his forehead on the table between his stretched-out arms. "I am so fucking *old!*" and recommences the waterworks. Loudly.

This goes on for a couple of minutes, then he stops. Is he asleep?

Leo puts another martini on the table. "Here. Be careful."

In the silence that ensues a figure descends the stairway. It's not one of the lads. They want every frame of video they can squeeze out of this situation. The figure is now standing next to the sleeping (?) Lane.

"Hey handsome, buy a girl a drink?"

All the muscles in his gaunt body stiffen. That voice! He lifts his head from his arms and beholds a silver-haired woman, about his age, slim and elegant. It's the eyes. The eyes give her away. There's no doubt about it.

"Celeste! I... I know it's you!" It's been half a century. Longer.

Lane struggles to get to his feet but she reaches over and touches his shoulder.

"No, Lane. Don't get up. But..." she points to the recently abandoned chair, "may I sit?"

"Please do! How... how could you possibly be here?"

"Facebook," she said.

"Facebook. Really?" Lane made a face. "I hate that social media crap."

"I never would have guessed," she smiles.

Leo materializes next to the table. "What can I get you, Celeste?"

"I'll have an old-fashioned, please."

"Comin' right up," and Leo is off.

"Who put it on Facebook?"

"Westbrook High! Class of 1970," she says. "They were all about it!"

"It?"

"The big game! You two are the only famous people from the entire class. We were a pretty dull bunch."

"Well… you missed the victor. He's the one you ought to be-"

Celeste put her hand on Lane's "I came here to see *you*." She gives him a big smile. "You're not going to cry, are you?"

"I don't think so."

"So I drove up from my home in Royal Oak and worked it out with dear Leo over there to sit upstairs until the match was over."

"Huh."

Leo serves Celeste her drink. "Yeah. It was supposed to be a surprise," Leo says. "Are you surprised?"

"Hell yes."

"Good." Leo heads back to the bar.

"Where you staying?" Lane asks.

"I have no idea!" Playing the Southern belle, she bats her eyes. "I'm a lost lamb in a strange city all by my lonesome!"

"Leave it to me," Lane says. Then, "I'm hungry."

"Me, too!"

"I know a place."

"Betcha do!"

Lane struggles to stand and Celeste moves to help him up. She hands him his cane. Lane turns to Leo.

"Hey, Leo. Let's do this again real soon."

"Let's *not!*" Leo calls back.

Lane offers Celeste his arm and she takes it. "He don't mean it."

As soon as the door closes there are whoops of joy from upstairs, and the two lads come rushing down.

"You guys get what you wanted?" Leo asks.

"Hell, yes!" Grady hollers. "It was better than a Hollywood movie!"

"And we got it all," Ron adds.

The two are collecting the four wireless cameras and putting them in their cases.

"We'll pack up the monitors and crap and be out of your hair in ten minutes," Grady assures Leo.

And again, true to his word, the pair are all set in minutes, their equipment stacked on a table and ready to be toted out to the car.

But before they make their exit, the door opens and in walk Lane and Celeste.

"Hey!" Leo calls. "Forget something?"

"Actually, yeah," Lane says. "I did." Lane looks at Grady. "Tell me, kid. How much did you pay for that data recorder?"

He points. "This Tascam? Umm… about six grand I think." Grady is getting a little creeped out. "Why?"

"I'll give you twenty thousand dollars, plus an extra ten thousand for a new recorder."

"But… but I don't want to sell the recorder."

Lane laughs. It's an unkind sound. "Grady? Is that right? Grady?"

"Yeah…"

"Grady, you are not leaving this bar with that recording."

"What? You gonna stop me?"

"No," comes a voice from behind the bar. "But I will." It's Bobby. He's in serious scary bouncer mode. He always did have Lane's back.

"I'll make the transfer to your account right now," Lane says. "Sit here and give me the numbers. You'll have the money before we leave the bar."

A little more drama, a few more threats, a little pleading… Anyhoo, in five minutes the deal is done, and Lane has the Tascam data recorder in his hand.

"Did you store any of this data online?" Lane wisely inquires.

Grady looks away, mute.

"Let me explain something to you, Grady," Lane says calmly. "If any of this video sees the light of day…" Lane considers. "Let me put it this way. You understand I am a millionaire many, many times over. Right? If this gets out, I will spend every nickel I have if that's what it will take to ruin your life, in painful and assorted ways. Do you understand, Grady?"

Grady looks at Lane and nods in the affirmative.

He thanks the lads, now completely disheartened and oddly insensitive to the fact that they are $30,000 richer, and Lane and his lady are out the door.

They walk a few steps down Washington Street, slowly, to the nearby restaurant that Lane is hot for. They walk in silence for a minute, then Celeste asks, "Why did you buy that recorder? That was quite a dear project to those boys."

Lane stops and faces Celeste. He rests his hands on her shoulders with affection.

"I hurt Truman. *We* hurt Truman."

"He thought he owned me!" she says, defensively. "And I waited until he left!"

"If he ever saw this video his heart would die. Do you see? I just made it impossible for him to watch... to watch you come to me again, and that gives me some... some *redemption.* See? I did... I did a good thing for him just now and he'll never even know it."

Celeste bows her head and sobs quietly. "You're right. Oh... I feel like such a heartless bitch now."

Truman presses her head against his chest, then holds her in a tight embrace.

"It's okay, dear," Lane whispers in her ear. "We got this."

And arm-in-arm, they resume their slow stroll to dinner.

ೞ�చ

Intensive Care

"What does it say?" Madeline asks.

The nurse examines the thermometer. "It's still high."

"What does it *say? How high?*" Madeline is Norm's wife. She's tired and testy.

"Still 105," the nurse whispers.

"mmnnwater…" Norm mumbles.

Madeline takes up the plastic cup from the nightstand and puts the straw to Norm's parched lips. "Sip slow, honey."

Norm raises his head but seems to have forgotten why he just did this, ignoring the straw at his lips and dropping his head back into the pillow, damp with his sweat.

Norm's son Blake sits nearby, trying not to appear upset for his mother's sake, but obviously coping poorly. "Should we call Father Owen? I mean… just in case?"

Blake, like Mom, is a Catholic, and serious about it all. Dad is not. So Mom doesn't know what to think about this.

"Your Dad wouldn't want it," Madeline says, dabbing Norm's wrinkled lips with a wet washcloth and giving Blake a pleading look. "Let's just not go there right now, okay?"

If the fever will break soon Norm will live; if not, and he cannot bear much more of this, he will die. That's what the doctors said. One of them strolls in. He listens to Norm's heart and lungs with his stethoscope. His brow wrinkles. He unplugs the thing from his ears and starts out of the room.

"Doctor," Madeline calls. He stops and turns. "Any change?"

The physician is really young. Looks mid-eastern. He smiles. "His tachycardia… his heart… it's beating very fast. We've done what we can to slow it down, but we can safely do no more. We have to wait." And with that the young fellow turns and leaves the room.

"God, what is he, 12?" Blake says.

His Mom smiles. "They've been good. All very conscientious."

Blake returns his Mom's soft look. "I guess…"

Norm opens his eyes and begins to babble incomprehensibly. His delirium came in spurts throughout the day, and they had had some hopeful respite throughout the evening, but now, in these most critical wee hours, the fever rages, and the delirium is back.

It seems Norm has had enough of this. He struggles from the bed and tries to stand. His son and wife rush to his side and he grips them tightly for balance, one hand holding on to the I.V. pole. He totters, unsteady, and then pulls the I.V. free from his arm. He shakes off his wife and son.

"Let me be!" he rasps, and they retreat. He lurches to his closet and finds a polo shirt and jeans hanging there, the ones he wore upon admittance. He pulls off his gown, ignoring the immodesty of the gesture and begins to dress. His son advances upon him and Norm sets himself against him.

"Stay back!" he says to his son, pointing menacingly. "I know what I'm doing!"

Poor Blake hangs back and watches his Dad, disheveled and barefoot, open the door of his room and bluster down the hallway. Madeline cries out for a nurse and Blake runs to find help.

Avoiding the elevators for obvious reasons, Norm sneaks into the empty stairwell and descends as quickly as he is able, and then breezes out of the Emergency Room exit unmolested by any authority.

Once clear of the facility, Norm stops and looks about him. There is a terrible unfamiliarity about his surroundings. He passes this off as effects of his delirium. He looks down at his bare feet and wishes he had grabbed his sandals from the room. They were right there in the closet! But the night is temperate, and the cool breeze is a salve to his fevered body. He's terribly thirsty, and he needs to move on.

He isn't sure where he's headed, but he has an idea it's over that hill.

As he approaches he looks around. It is, he reckons, about three in the morning and there is not a soul in sight, not a car on the road, and an ambience of gloom prevails. When he achieves the crest of the hill he notes what appears to be a downtown area beyond a dark bridge that seems to be bustling with light and energy. He perceives it as a happy refuge from the murky despondency all about him and he makes a beeline for that place.

After a few yards Norm hears a rustling behind him, and he stops and turns. He sees a man running toward him in the dark who eventually resolves into the person of... Father Owen?

"What the hell..." Norm whispers aloud. He doesn't like Owen. Thinks he's a pain-in-the-ass holy roller and first-class buttinski. At last the priest catches up to Norm, stops, reaches into his jacket pocket and whips out a bible, or a missal or whatever the hell you call them things priests use. Without even greeting Norm he launches into a practiced routine, which Norm hears as ridiculous nonsense.

"Domine Domine Domine blah blah blah Jesus and Mary blah blah holy God blessed this and that and sacred holy spirit blah blah..." and all the while making the sign of the cross with his right hand, book in his left.

And he goes on and on like this and Norm just stares at him with his jaw agape. After a few moments Norm turns his back on the reverend and walks away toward the bridge, but the plucky padre follows on his heels, droning ceaselessly.

"...yummy yummy Jesus bless the holy son of Mary Domine Domine yum yum, holy God and lord of all yummies bless us now and eternally blah blah blah forever Amen."

And as suddenly as he appeared, the feckless friar closes his little black book, turns and runs back down the road whence he came. Norm stares after him until the figure is absorbed into the dark.

"That was completely bizarre." Norm says aloud. But he is undeterred, turns and resumes his walk. The bridge is well in sight, and beyond that seems the promise of relief in the bright lights of the lively town square, the dark horrors of the night behind him at last.

With only a few yards to the bridge he hears another rustling behind him, and he turns, expecting the dreaded Father Owen about to make an encore appearance. Instead, the rustling resolves into a large, fit man dressed in running clothes jogging toward him. He stops and the two stand face-to-face. Norm recognizes the man as his boss at the paint store. His name is Mr. Berryman, but everybody calls him Boz.

Boz is out of breath. "Hey," he pants.

"Hi," Norm says. "What's going on?" he asks carefully.

Boz waves the question away. "Never mind that."

Norm always hated that about Boz the most—the stink of disrespect that always came out of his mouth even in the most harmless of conversations.

"Okaaaaaaayyyyy," Norm says. "What can I do for you?"

"Just stay put," he says, and Boz backs off a few paces. He inhales deeply, leaps high and snaps a swift kick right to Norm's breastbone, knocking him flat on his ass.

Norm can't even speak, barely breathe, as he looks up into the smirking face of his tormentor. Norm points at him, forcing his body to ask what his lungs won't let him.

Boz waves him off again with the same gesture. "Don't ask," he says, and he resumes his jog back down the road.

Norm lies in the middle of the road for a long space, incredibly weary and with a very sore chest. He figures he better get up and back on his way and he struggles to rise. He brushes himself off and, fervently hoping for no further visitations, trudges toward the bridge and to the hopeful place just beyond where he can escape the trials and tortures of what has become his recent existence.

It's an underpass, actually, the place he needs to traverse, of a railway bridge, age-pocked concrete festooned on the outside with mindless graffiti he can barely discern in the darkness. He looks through the bridge passage into the bright square of the town and sees all sorts of people milling about.

He knows he's doing the right thing. He's made it. At last. Another few yards and he's in the light.

"Hey you. Where the hell you think you're goin'?"

Blocking Norm's exit into the light is a trollish man, filthy-looking, dressed like bum. He's short, and he looks up at Norm belligerently.

"I'm talkin' to you, pal."

"I just want to get past the… the bridge here and see what's up-"

"*My* bridge."

"Pardon?"

"My bridge. *Mine.*"

"Well… what does that *mean?*"

"It means you gotta get past me."

The dankness and rank smell are making Norm's eyes water. "What do you… you want to fight? Is that it? Look, I'm sick. I need to-"

"Get the fighting idea out of your mind," the ogre says, and Norm is astonished to see that the hairy man is even taller than Norm is. When did that happen?

Norm's throat is so parched he can hardly speak. "Do you have any water?" he asks. "I gotta have some water."

"*My* water."

"Yes… will you *share* a bit with me?"

The troll looks disgusted but retreats into the blackness for a few seconds and returns with a wet washcloth.

Blake is disappointed. "I was hoping for, you know, a nice big gulp or two. Or eight."

"Well you can't. Just hold still." And the nasty thing, with amazing delicacy, dabs at Norm's shriveled lips and holds the washcloth steady for a few seconds while Norm greedily sucks at it. Then the ogre takes it away and tosses it aside.

It's not enough, but it helps. "So… you don't want me to pass? Do you want money? Because I-"

The troll laughs. "I don't care a rat's ass if you pass or not. Ain't up to me."

"Well, then why are…" and Norm looks over the ogre's shoulder and sees a small gaggle of people in the lit square beyond. He squints (forgot his glasses) and sees…

"Mom?"

Norm makes a move around the troll, but the troll grabs him by the back of his shirt and flings him away from the exit.

"But that's my Mom!" Norm cries. He sees his Dad standing next to her and someone else he can't make out.

Mom waves. "Hello, sweetheart!" she hollers.

Norm could just melt. "Hi Mom! Hi Dad!" he shouts. "I'm trying to get around this big oaf here and I'll give you a hug!"

"Hey!" the ogre looks hurt. Norm ignores him.

"No, honey," Mom cries. "Not now! Now's not the time!"

"Whaddaya *mean* now's not the time?"

"You need to go back to Maddy and Blake! They're worried!"

"But it's torture back there." Norm starts to cry. This has just been a *terrible* day.

"Pussy," the troll observes.

"Listen, hon!" Mom shouts. "We love you and miss you and you can come again when it's time, but you need to face your responsibilities at home! Understand? You're not ready for this!"

"Listen to your mother!" Dad adds in a loud gruff.

Norm at last sees the wisdom dawning in what they say and becomes resigned.

"Turn around now and piss off," the giant troll grunts.

Norm ignores the taunt, squints hard and finally discerns his uncle standing next to his Dad.

"Zeke?" he calls out. "Zeke is that you?"

Uncle Zeke waves back.

"Fuck you, Zeke!" Norm yells angrily. *"You piece of shit!"*

Zeke puts his head down and his Mom cries out, "Norman, now stop that this *instant!*"

"Do what your mother says, goddam it!' his Dad bellows.

Norm hated Zeke. *Everybody* hated Zeke. He was a perv and a leach. *So why are they so buddy-buddy over there?* he wonders. *Ah… hell with it.*

Norm waves at the trio. "Okay!" he cries. "I'm going back, I guess…"

"You'll see us again, honey!" Mom yells back.

"If you say so!"

Norm breathes a big sigh and gives the troll a sour look. "Thanks, it's been great," he says. "And I really *love* what you've done with the place."

"Fuck you. Get out." And he points. *"That* way."

Norm flips him the bird and starts the long trek back to the hospital.

He sort of trances out on the way, and before he knows it he's back at the Emergency Room doors, his slog completely free of unwanted visitations. He stumbles in and finds the stairway, trudges up, soaked in sweat stinging his eyes, he mops his face and enters the door to the third floor ICU. He staggers into 318 and there's Maddy and their son waiting for him like nothing's unusual. He's so tired he just wants to plop into sleep but stops dead when he sees himself on the bed.

"What the hell?"

"Hey sleepyhead," Maddy's voice is silky music. "You're awake."

Norm is so soaked in sweat that it looks like somebody turned the hose on him. He blinks open his eyes and smiles at his wife.

"Who was that in my bed?" he mumbles.

"What?" Maddy laughs. "Oh honey, you need to wake up. The fever is gone. You're going to be okay."

Norm snaps away from his fuzzy state at the touch of a hand on his. He looks up to the smiles of his son. He grabs Blake's hand and squeezes hard. "What happened?"

"You nearly left us, hon," Maddy says. "It was very close."

"Jesus, Maddy," Norm rasps. "Get me some goddam water before I die."

She holds out a full plastic cup which Norm drains forthwith. He notes the splendor of this sunny morning through the big windows.

"More."

"Let that settle, hon," Maddy says. "They said drink slow."

"Your heart was beating really fast and your temperature got to 106," Blake reports.

"And then your heart went into what he called flutter," Maddy explains, "and they had to shock you."

"Defibrillate," says Blake.

"Oh… it's still pretty sore…" Norm says. Madeline leans over and kisses the wet gown over his breastbone. She leaves her head there and Norm strokes her hair languidly.

"I hope you don't mind, Dad…"

Norm looks suspicious. "Mind what? What did you do?"

Maddy lifts her head and grins impishly at her boy.

"I asked Father Owen to give you Last Rites."

Norm begins laughing so hard he has to hold his chest to steady the discomfort.

"You were on the edge, Dad," he pleads. "I did what I thought needed to be done."

"That's okay, Blake. Always do what you think is right."

"I thought you'd be pissed at me."

"Surprise!" Norm says and they all laugh. The sense of intense relief brightens up the entire room. The entire world.

"So you can go home tomorrow, probably," Maddy says. "That way you can get back to work next week at the latest." She looks annoyed. "And that whatshisname Boz won't be too put out by all this."

Norm is quiet for a space, then he blurts, "Fuck Boz."

Blake laughs, but Maddy asks for clarification.

"I'm not going back there. We'll be okay. There's other jobs."

Maddy brightens at once and leans down to hug him. "I thought I'd never hear you say that. Good for you. Good for *us.*"

There is a rap on the doorjamb, and they behold Father Owen, popping by during his rounds. Owen knows he's on thin ice, and that Norm may well be displeased at his divine intervention, if indeed they even told him about it.

"Norman, I'm so glad you pulled through. We were with you through it all!" he says, pumping his fist.

Norm smiles at the priest. "You're alright, Owen."

The priest is relieved at Norm's pleasant reception. "It's Easter in a week," he reminds everyone. "See you at Mass?"

Norm's smile remains as he says, "Bye now, Owen."

Father Owen drops his head. "Hey. I gave it a shot. God bless you all." He waves and goes about his hallowed duties.

"More water," Norm orders, and Maddy complies. Drained in a gulp. "What I'd like is a beer."

"Maybe tomorrow," Maddy says. "Do you feel ready to go home?"

Norm sits up, swings his legs to the side of the bed and rests his arms around Maddy's shoulders. He looks at her deeply, and she at him.

"Maddy," he whispers, "I need to look at everything. Consider everything. I need to think. I need to go home."

And he kisses her.

80 03

496

Enemy of the People

Shine, Perishing Republic

While this America settles in the mould of its vulgarity,
    heavily thickening to empire,
And protest, only a bubble in the molten mass, pops
    and sighs out, and the mass hardens,

I sadly smiling remember that the flower fades to make fruit,
    the fruit rots to make earth.
Out of the mother; and through the spring exultances,
    ripeness and decadence; and home to the mother.

You making haste haste on decay: not blameworthy; life is good,
    be it stubbornly long or suddenly
A mortal splendor: meteors are not needed less than mountains:
    shine, perishing republic.

But for my children, I would have them keep their distance from
    the thickening center; corruption
Never has been compulsory, when the cities lie at the monster's
    feet there are left the mountains.

And boys, be in nothing so moderate as in love of man, a clever
    servant, insufferable master.
There is the trap that catches noblest spirits, that caught—they say—
    God, when he walked on earth.

—Robinson Jeffers, 1925
from *Roan Stallion, Tamar and Other Poems*

HIS ARREST

Michael Haas, shivering in his unlined trenchcoat, peered out through the pine branches at the long concrete dam raucously sheeting tons of water per blink into the roiling river below, churning up a cloudy mist that caught the 9 a.m. sunlight in a lovely way, a spectrum of colors in the vapor. He had no idea why he was there.

He turned from the sight and leaned against the railings, waiting for the man who left him the note at work, a man he did not know. Michael spied him on the asphalt path rising to meet him. He was a small man in a white... what was it? a white utility uniform of some kind. For a moment he felt a shot of anxiety. Michael had many enemies, but the message the man left was compelling enough to take the chance and meet face-to-face. Out here. In the middle of nowhere. Michael stepped forward to meet him.

The man offered his hand. He had to shout to be heard over the roaring of the dam waters. "MICHAEL HAAS?"

"THAT'S ME." They shook on it. "WHO ARE YOU?"

"CALL ME BOB."

"IS BOB YOUR NAME?"

"NO. WOULD YOU LIKE TO PICK A DIFFERENT ONE?" He said this with a disarming smile that, oddly, put Michael at ease.

"Well... WHAT CAN I DO FOR YOU BOB?"

"YOU'RE GOING TO BE ARRESTED. AROUND NOON IF MY GUESS IS CORRECT."

Now, you'd think Michael might ask why? But no; he knew why. What he wanted to know was-

"WHY ARE YOU TELLING ME THIS?"

"Let's just say I'm a fan."

"A WHAT?" he yelled.

"A FAN. OF YOUR WORK."

Bob nodded. "YOU SURE PICKED A NOISY PLACE TO MEET!"

"I PICKED A *SAFE* PLACE TO MEET."

They just stood in the noise for a moment. There just didn't seem to be much more to say.

'Bob' moved close to Michael and yelled into his ear. "GET YOUR AFFAIRS IN ORDER, MICHAEL. THERE'S NO WAY OUT." He looked at his watch. "YOU'VE GOT ABOUT THREE HOURS. MAYBE LESS. WE NEVER MET, UNDERSTAND? MY LIFE WON'T BE WORTH A COUNTERFIET DOLLAR BILL IF I'M CAUGHT HAVING ANYTHING TO DO WITH THIS. UNDERSTAND?"

Michael took the man's hand in both of his. "THANK YOU!" he shouted. "Thank you." The fellow nodded and slipped his hand away, turned and hurried back down the asphalt path.

Michael smiled at the thought of a counterfeit dollar. Those were the ones with George Washington's picture on the front—the very emblem of slavery, genocide, colonization, manifest destiny, and white supremacy.

When Michael got back to his car he wasted no time. He sent a text to his oldest grandchild, Nick, who was all of 16 and a junior in high school. He wrote,

Dear Nicky, I'm going to be arrested today and probably sent to prison. You probably can guess why. A kindly Samaritan risked his life to warn me, so I have this opportunity to write you. My big mouth and sloppy pen have finally got me in trouble. I'm not scared or ashamed, but I sure wish this wasn't happening. Please break this to the other kids, all four, from both families. Tell them the truth that best suits their ages, but don't lie to them. You mustn't lie to them. I have only one request - that you will try to visit me wherever they send me. Please. Just once is all I ask. Just once. It will mean the world to me. I'm old but I feel good and strong. Don't worry about me. You know how much I love you and the younger kids (they all look up to you, you know), and I know you love me too. God bless you. Love, Grampa

That was it. There was nothing else for him to do. Nothing he *dared* do. He wished most of all that he could contact Sly. He made a plan with Sly. Michael needed to get that plan in motion.

Michael would turn 70 this year. He yearned to touch his grandkids for one last time. He always put his hand on top of their heads when he saw them, or just when he passed them by. It was his way of blessing them. One time his granddaughter Anne asked him why he did this. He told her it gave them superpowers. She asked what these superpowers were, specifically, and Michael told her that if she knew they wouldn't work properly. She then asked, being the smartass nine year-old that she was, what was the good of it then? Michael said that the superpowers would come when she needed them most, and never ever to forget this important fact. She considered and was good with that, and the following weekend she explained the superpowers situation to the rest of the kids. Their reactions varied. He smiled remembering all this.

The five grandkids lived with their aunt, the sister of Michael's dead wife, who was not well and confined to bed for most of her day. It was Nick and his fifteen year-old sister Hannah who ran the house. The other children were ages thirteen, eleven, and nine—all healthy and often a real handful for the older pair.

Back to reality, and Michael was certain that 'Bob' was not the good Samaritan he appeared to be. A favorite tactic of the feds was to have a benevolent stranger tip you off to your imminent arrest, and then you were put under perfect surveillance for the few hours of grace that you imagined you had. It was a brilliant way to weed out 'co-conspirators,' discover 'treasonous' plans in the works, and isolate the panicky victim's friends who would likely require close scrutiny in the future.

He drove home. And waited. It was damn near 1 p.m. before they realized that the harmless text to his grandson was all they were going to get from him. They sent six armed agents in two cars.

HIS EXAMINATION

"All rise," announced the bailiff. "Court is in session. Honorable Judge Amos Ohlsson presiding."

All now seated, the Judge spoke. "We're here today to examine and make recommendation in the case of The People vs. Michael Haas.

The woman at the table facing Michael stood. "I'm Marcia Hillman, your honor, Examiner in this case." The Judge gave a courteous nod. "I understand we must decide between psychiatric or criminal proceedings going forward."

"Correct," the Judge said. "Proceed, Ms. Hillman."

She turned to face Michael. "We have designated nine different areas that we feel warrant investigation during your career as a nationally syndicated writer and radio host before you were righteously relieved of your duties. When we have finished our summary of your various crimes against the People, we believe that your incarceration, whether penal or psychiatric, will be the obvious remedy and just verdict for your misdeeds and mis-statements over the decades. We do not seek reprisal, we are concerned only with doing what is best for the People, and for yourself."

Michael smiled, and stared at his shoes.

"Do you understand why you're here and what I have just put forth to you?"

Michael looked up and scrutinized his interrogator. "Yes. I understand why you think I should be here, and I heard your little introduction. I understood it."

"Are you a Christian, Mr. Haas?

"What?" That was jarring. Why go there? "A Christian? I guess. I try to be. I'm bad at it."

"You defend Christianity in your writings and in your broadcasts."

"Mainly I defend them against scurrilous attacks. They're being martyred all over the world, by the dozens a day, and instead of coming to their defense we do nothing. We don't even offer them sanctuary anymore."

"Christians are dangerous."

"How so?"

"They represent the very pinnacle of superstition. The Fundamentalists pose a grave danger with their ideas that they want to impose on others."

"But you call anyone who even goes to church a fundamentalist."

"Again—they are the very pinnacle of superstition. They pose a grave danger with their ideas that they want to impose on others."

"You mean like you do?"

"I mean *superstition*, Mr. Haas. Superstition by which Christians have been at least as deadly to the world as your hated Muslims have been."

"I don't hate Muslims and I never said I did."

"Christians have killed millions under the banner of followers of Christ."

"These people were not followers of Christ."

"That's what they have claimed throughout history."

"If I call myself a Martian, does that make me a Martian?"

"Do you deny the slaughters of the Crusades? Those invasions?"

"They happened centuries ago. Christians are a threat to no one anymore. Actual followers of Christ *never* were. We are under a mandate to love one another; Islam's mandate is to kill the infidel. Surely even you must note the difference."

"The Christians are the biggest force against our progress as a nation that we have had to deal with."

"Good. I hope it gets worse for you. You can't win this."

She smiled. "We've already won. It's time to clean up." The prosecutor moseyed to her table, poured herself half a glass of water and drank it down, then sat and spoke while examining a sheaf of papers.

"Let's briefly consider your advocacy of the so-called Founding Fathers and the Old Constitution for more back-

502

ground on you before we formally begin. Your constant harping on these themes has caused much unnecessary turmoil. When the old Supreme Court system was dismantled recently you were among the most vociferous opponents of the People's Court. Don't you understand that we have based the new court very closely upon the old?"

Michael sat up in his chair and leaned forward. "Except for your 'living Constitution' nonsense. By picking and choosing and ignoring whole formative concepts, you've been able to interpret that document in whatever ways you see fit. Anything in order to justify your ends!"

"I'd advise you to stop right there, Mr. Haas," the Judge instructed. "You will henceforth answer the Examiner's questions succinctly and in a calm voice."

Michael sighed and closed his eyes. Sitting silently. He heard the shuffle of papers and murmurs of the observers.

"I will proceed without delay to Charge Number One: *Criminal Intolerance and Incitement to Violence on the Issue of Immigration.* Citations against you in print and during your broadcasts are so numerous that I will not take the Court's time to enumerate them. They are in the Record. I simply have two questions for you."

Michael opened his eyes and sat looking as neutral as he possibly could manage.

"First, what are your general views regarding immigration? And remember, the documentation against you is very bulky," she said, holding up a large binder. "I have nine of these binders, all full, for every charge against you. We will tolerate no lies or nonsense."

"Bulky isn't the same as accurate. But thanks for the warning," Michael said.

"Please answer the question. Shall I repeat it?"

"No. Please." And Michael paused to gather his thoughts. "When millions of people storm across your country's border, that's not immigration, that is an *invasion.* For years we were told that this was a humanitarian issue when it was actually just about getting voters for your party. Good plan. Worked pretty well."

This enraged the gallery and there was much hooting and derision against Michael's statement. The Judge uses the gavel to quiet things, making clear that he would clear the court if there was more of the same.

"Mr. Haas, that is exactly the kind of lie and distortion that has landed you where you sit right now. America welcomes all."

"Yes, but now that your power is absolute, you have all but closed the border and are moving toward the kind of restrictions that your opposition had begged you to implement when you, you know, actually *had* an opposition."

"You are wrong to conflate the two circumstances, so obviously that we will not bother to refute your nonsense. Now, about Islam…"

"Islam is incompatible with the Constitution. Or what the Constitution was about before you and your ilk got hold of it. Sharia Law is taking hold in whole counties in America. Sharia Law hurts women and homosexuals, and their holy book theologically mandates that they destroy the infidel." The crowd was getting agitated again. "What is so hard to understand-"

More agitation from the gallery until the gavel came down again and order is restored. This Judge seemed like he had a short fuse this morning.

"Mr. Haas," the Examiner said, "allowances must be made for cultural differences. Once again, your own testimony damns you and shows you for the racist, intolerant person you have become. And regarding Sharia Law? So far there is no problem."

"Yeah. That's what you say after you jump off a 60-story building. By the time you understand what's really happening it's too late. And what's all this about 'incitement to violence'? I never told anyone-"

"Really?" She pats Binder #1. "We have it all right here, Mr. Haas. Your listeners, your readership—many of these people have been arrested for violent crimes against the People after being exposed to your hate. You bear responsibility here."

"How can you prove this? I *never* incited anyone to violence. I mean... they all probably watched the same toothpaste commercial on TV, too. Why not blame that? You have just as much evidence there."

"Trying to reduce your crimes to the level of absurdity will avail you nothing, Mr. Haas, I assure you."

Michael sighed. He knows how this is going to go. He looks out the window, and wonders if he'll ever see the light of day again.

Examiner Hillman rises from her chair and walks around to the front of her table. "I will now proceed to Charge Number Two: *Verbal and Written Hate Crimes Against the LGBTQ Community.*" She picks up Binder #2 and holds it aloft. "We have many, many examples." She glares at Michael. "Well?"

"Well what? Was there a question in there somewhere?"

"How do you respond to the charge?"

"Well, first of all, I have nothing against homosexuals and have never said anything against them."

"Do you deny you have enraged the LGBTQ community with your-"

"I am against the idea that minors, children, should be exposed to drugs and surgery in a naïve and hurtful attempt to change their sex, and with the approval of parents and the partnership of physicians, who should both be jailed for child abuse. And one cannot change one's sex, anyway."

Another uproar from the crowd, another gavel bash and warning from the Judge, but the atmosphere was getting ominous.

"Mr. Hass, you-"

"I'm not finished. If you're an adult I don't care what you do with your body and couldn't care less what gender hallucination you want to embrace. You're a 60 year-old man and want to identify as a teenage Martian girl—well, god bless you and good luck to you, but I will not be compelled to share in or validate your hallucinations."

"I see," the Examiner said. "Since you're doing my job at least as well as I could, illustrating your hateful intolerance so perfectly, is there anything you would like to add on the subject?

"You're goddam right there is," Michael said. "If one is born a male, how can he say that he 'feels there is a woman inside him that wants to be free' or some such nonsense? How can a male know what a female 'feels'? No one even bothers to ask this question, they just accept a stupid statement like that as true. So he gets his genitals cut off, gets some plastic reconstruction, and starts taking hormones. I ask you—is that all there is to being a woman? Because if you think that's okay, then I have a hell of a lot higher idea of what a woman is than you do."

At this point the Judge had had enough, quelling the angry mob with difficulty, and finally clearing the courtroom of spectators. The Examiner sat, all smiles, waiting for the court to empty.

After the smoke cleared, all that remained was Michael, the Examiner, the Judge, the five Magistrates and the bailiff. When the Judge resumed the proceedings, Examiner Hillman stood and held up Binder #3.

"Charge Number Three: *Libel and Slander Against Regulations Regarding Obvious Hate Speech and Righteous Censorship.*"

Michael laughed. "Wow, now *that's* a beefy binder.'

The Examiner joined in the merriment and carefully displayed the stuffed file for all to wonder at.

"Yes. It is indeed a beefy bundle. So how do you respond to the charge?"

"The Bill of Rights we used to have-"

"We still have it, Mr. Haas."

"Well, this new one says that rights come from the State. That's incorrect."

506

"Oh, so you believe they're 'God-given' or some such superstitious nonsense?"

"I believe, most of us believed, that we have those rights simply by virtue of being human, you don't need to drag God into it. The State grants us *nothing*. The State is supposed to *defend* these rights for us, not pretend to dole them out."

"Do you have a point?"

"Yeah. The First Amendment was about protecting offensive speech. What other kind needs protection?"

"Mr. Hass, Hate Speech is not Free Speech."

"Of course it is. Why would you need a First Amendment if everyone just said and wrote inoffensive things? We need to know what haters think, and why they think that way, if nothing else. Censorship is a totalitarian evil. No one is smart enough, or impartial enough, to act as censor for a nation. Not even you."

The Judge had a spasm here. "Mr. Haas you will refrain from personal attacks."

Michael regarded the Judge, sighed, and nodded.

"You've dug such a nice deep hole for yourself on that subject, Mr. Hass," the Examiner said, picking up Binder #4. "Let's continue with your views on science."

"Or *your* idea of science, anyway."

"Charge Number Four: *The Propagation of Superstition and Outright Falsehood Against True Science*. Let's begin with your denial of Climate Change. How do you defend your writings and broadcasts? Remember: we have the evidence right here."

"Right. The binders." He thought for a space. "First of all, no one denies Climate Change. Everybody knows the climate changes. You just bundle all the people who don't believe humans cause it into the Climate Denier category to further your ends. Many object to the notion that humans cause climate change or can do anything about it. Hey—maybe they can and maybe they can't—I don't know, and I don't have a horse in that race, but it is simply not settled science. If it were, it would be obvious in that there would be no peer studies proving against the theory, but there are. Many. Climate Change as an issue is not about Science, it's about politics and control."

"Are you a scientist, Mr. Haas?"

"No."

"Well, thousands are, and 95% of them agree. And-"

"That's a ridiculous statistic."

"*And* I'm sure the court sees no point in providing a forum for more of your ignorance and lame excuses for hundreds of broadcasts and articles designed to pollute minds and endanger our Mother Earth."

"Then why haven't any of your 40-plus years of bogus predictions come to fruition?"

"Many have and many more are coming true as we speak. We will move on!"

Noting the Examiner's testy demeanor, the Judge moved for a half-hour recess. Michael, though free to move about, simply sat where he was, overwhelmed with depression and anger. Prone to dehydration, he shuffled to the drinking fountain and forced a few gulps, then returned to his seat, praying for a quick conclusion to all this.

Examiner Hillman returned from recess looking fresh as a daisy and all smiles. The bailiff called all to order, everyone sat down, and the trial resumed.

"Darwinism, Mr. Haas."

"What about it?"

"More of your science denial. You have written extensively against his teachings."

"Darwin cannot explain the origin of species. The fossil records he predicted we would find have never turned up and the mathematics of molecular biology, a science that didn't even *exist* in his time, disproves him. The top researchers know this now, but they can't convince you and yours to let go of your obsolete narrative because it's just too convenient."

"I thought you said you were not a scientist. So you're a mathematician?"

"No. But-"

"Darwin in his greatness has removed us from the superstitions of Creationists. Or do you think Adam and Eve popped into existence one day and-"

"It has nothing to do with Adam and Eve. I know the idea that you sprang from a monkey is dear to your heart but, once again, top scientists no longer hold this view. They postulate that a common ancestor is much more likely. But, again, none of this has filtered down. Darwin's intellectual daring will always be inspiring. The man will always be admired. But science has moved on, and you people will not let him go!"

"Once again, Mr. Haas, the record is clear. Darwin is obviously an insult to your religious superstitions. I believe that's enough on this subject."

Michael closed his eyes and took a deep breath. Will this never end? He already knew *how*. Now he just wanted to know when.

"Charge Number Five," the Examiner stood as she announced. *"Criminal Racism.* What do you have to say to this charge?"

"What, specifically, can you cite against me? What the hell can possibly be in that bulging binder of yours?"

"You obviously hold, as just one example, that African-Americans are inferior to whites. And that's just for starters"

"No, I do not. I said that, as a *group*, all races and nationalities have different characteristics, abilities and liabilities, that become evident upon analysis."

"THAT, Mr. Haas, is the very *definition* of Discrimination!"

"Discrimination is good! It's bigotry that's evil."

The Examiner laughed and sat back down. "Let me give you as much rope as you need, Mr. Haas. Please continue to explain how discrimination can ever be a good thing."

"We can leave race out of it. You need to find somebody for a couple hours of child-care so you can do some errands.

Your choices are the ladies down at the church or the folks at the crack-house. It's *discrimination* that allows you to make the sane choice here."

"Talk about races. That's where you most offend."

"Demographic studies are very clear that *groups* of people can be predicted to act certain ways, prefer certain things to others, share purchasing habits, believe certain things. The accuracy is often amazing. *That* is discrimination. It's simply the study of raw data and putting to use the observation that all groups are demonstrably not the same. That's benign. *Bigotry* is using this information to pre-judge an *individual.* That is a great evil and the foundation of most of the world's sickness."

"Please... go on. Give us an example."

"Okay. You want race. Blacks generally have more speed and agility than whites."

"Your use of the term 'blacks' is offensive."

"Tough. You hyphenating 'Americans' offends me. But you don't believe that that generalization I just made is obviously true? Okay. How 'bout this? We'll go visit a high school and each select a team for a game of basketball. I'll take five random black teens, and you can have, umm... three random white boys, an Hispanic and an Oriental kid. You have $100 to bet. Where is your money going to go? Be honest. If possible."

"You're digging yourself deeper."

"It's my shovel. Try this: In which case do you think there is more likelihood of a hate crime: when a black person walks alone through an all-white suburban neighborhood, or a white person walks alone through an inner city all-black neighborhood?"

"The answer is obvious."

"Not to you. I have been spat upon doing just that. It's much more likely to occur that the spit lands on the white guy in these instances. Where is the hate?"

"African-Americans cannot commit hate crimes. Theirs' is a natural reaction to centuries of oppression-"

"Oh, for Christ sake save it for the interns, lady."

The Judge reacted as though someone stuck him with a cattle-prod. "Mr. Haas! This examination will end with a contempt conviction with another comment like that!" He was red in the face. "Do you understand?"

"I understand, Judge."

The Examiner didn't miss a beat. "You've railed against African-American families."

"They don't have dads! The consequences are devastating! I have pointed out, which is not the same thing as 'railing against,' that education is a critical component in racial problems in America. Seventy-seven percent of black kids are born to single moms. This is a bad thing! The lowest single-mom rate belongs to Asians. The crime rate is vastly higher in blacks than in any group, and Asians have the lowest crime rate. Asians in America do the best academically, even surpassing whites. I suppose this is just a meaningless coincidence?"

"Mr. Haas, hate is hate."

Michael looked confused. "'Hate is hate'? *What the hell does that even mean?*"

"We are not surprised that this eludes you. We will move on." She fondles another binder, almost lovingly, and holds it aloft. "Charge Number Six: *Incitement to Violent Firearm Use Against the People.*"

"I never did any such thing."

"On the contrary. It might be what you're best known for."

"Your confiscation of firearms produced a bloodbath, and you still don't have a fraction of the guns in private hands."

She smiled a calm smile. "We're quite confident we have most of them, and the remainder-"

"No you're not, you just have to say that."

"And the hundreds of heroes who lost their lives disarming these domestic criminals will be forever remembered."

"They'll be rightly forgotten and even vilified as the useful idiots they were if sanity ever returns."

The Judge brought the gave down hard at this and gave Michael another stern warning. His last, the Judge promised.

"Statistics prove," Examiner Hillman continued, "beyond a reasonable doubt, that deadly weapons in the hands of Americans are far more of a threat to the People than nuclear weapons in the hands of Iran and North Korea."

"Wow…" Michael mused. "That's really nuts."

"We note your rudeness. It will go against you."

"Humans have a right to self-defense and to defend themselves against an out-of-control government. Those were the Founders' intentions."

"Your precious Second Amendment is gone forever, Mr. Haas. There is simply no more right to keep and bear murderous objects."

"Can we please move on. You're making me sick."

"You're making yourself sick because you cannot defend yourself with reason."

"Reason… odd that your mouth can actually sound that word."

The Examiner whirled to the Judge and motioned to belay his gavel and warning. "It's okay, your honor. Charge Number Seven: *Criminal Sexism.*"

"You forgot to hold the binder up."

"Why do you suppose we levy this particular charge, Mr. Haas?"

"Because I say that men and women are different?"

"They may usually *look* different, but this is superficial. You, for instance, would even deny them employment in certain areas."

"I would not deny any woman anything she's earned. But I know where you're going with this. In the fields of computer science, physics and engineering, all these classes and the jobs they lead to are populated overwhelmingly by males. Women are far more likely to work in caregiving jobs such as nursing, childcare, and elementary education. This is indicative of the nature of the sexes. Do you think we're forcing this on women?"

512

"The patriarchy of the past had conditioned women to have such desires, or to pretend to. We are taking care of that and the tide is turning to a more equitable playing field."

"No it isn't. Men and women are *different*. Their bodies symbolize the difference and it goes right to the core of a person. A woman has a void that she wants to be filled, and a man wants to do the filling."

"That's disgusting," the Examiner seethed.

The Judge brought down the hammer. "No more of that sort of thing, Haas."

Michael looked up at the Judge. "That's *Mister* Haas to you, your honor."

"No more of that sort of talk, *Mister* Haas. Actually, I'll end this with a contempt citation if the Examiner agrees, right now."

"Not necessary, your honor. We're almost done here, and I am not intimidated. Please just let him talk for the record. What about your statement that women want to be objectified? I suppose you will deny having put forth this infamous assertion?"

Michael chuckled. "No… no, you're correct. I did say that. I did it on a bet, but I stand by it."

"Oh, please do explain that one."

"Okay. I suggested to a round-table discussion on TV that women might appreciate being objectified. Of course, it was like I just said that toddlers should be forced to smoke a pack of Camels a day. It was chaos. So I bet them all $100 that I could give them a good example. A bit of fun. Well, you can't bet on TV, it turns out, so we had to make what we used to call a Gentleman's Bet. I suppose you can't call it that anymore, eh Marcia?"

"Refer to me as 'Examiner.' And get to the point. You're on thin ice."

"Okay. A woman has a rough morning and feels worn out and unattractive. She goes to the gym for a workout, and then to get her hair done. She walks out of the hair salon feeling a little better for her efforts and a handsome man passes her by, stops and turns and says, 'Ma'am I just gotta tell you, you're the prettiest woman I've seen all day long. You look great," nods, and continues on his way. Now, that man doesn't know her from Eve. He doesn't want anything from her, and she can tell he's sincere. Not like a friend who sees you got a haircut and says, 'Huh, looks great,' like, what are they supposed to say? So she knows he's not blowing smoke up her ass. I submit that that man has made that woman's day, *and he totally objectified her*. He knows nothing about her dreams and aspirations, her struggles or her beliefs. Not a thing. He treated her like an *object*. And she's loving it. I submit that there are situations in which women enjoy being objectified—it just depends on who's doing it and how they go about it."

A couple of the male Magistrates squirmed and chuckled at this, and the three women looked a little uncomfortable. Even the Examiner was at a loss for words, wondering how to best come back at this. Finally, she decided it would be prudent to simply feign disgust and move on.

"Charge Number Eight is *Slander and Libel Against a Woman's Right to an Abortion on Demand*. Explain yourself.

"I think it's murder and you have made it a sacrament."

"Your twisted philosophy aside, the People disagree with you, and in large numbers."

"Well, your polls and numbers are all lies, so how can we know this? There are many tens if not hundreds of millions of Americans who think it's murder. And if one agrees that a human life begins at conception, then one must agree that it's murder. There's no logical way around that conclusion. You're killing babies, sometimes as they're being born, and no one is being held accountable! People don't want that!"

"A woman has a right to choose."

"She can choose not to kill her baby. Maybe choose adoption. Maybe even choose not to have unprotected sex. Maybe even-"

"That's quite enough. You've already incriminated yourself a spectacular number of times on the stand so let's get this over with, shall we?

"Please. Yes."

"Charge Number Nine: *Slander and Libel Against the People's Socialism.* Our righteous moves to abolish the evils of capitalism once and for all have made tremendous strides, though admittedly, we have a long way to go. This, evidently, displeases you."

"Yes. It displeases me."

"Why's that?"

"Capitalism creates prosperity. Without it-"

"Businesses create *oppression*; it is *government* that creates prosperity."

"Are you gonna spew more phony stats at me? Please don't bother. Look at history. Can you not just look at history? I know that the Narrative commands you to ignore logic, evidence, and history—but can you just look, just for a moment, at history? Look at all the socialistic and communistic states. Argentina, Cuba, China. North Korea. Look at Pol Pot, and the old Soviet Union and what happened, what *had* to happen to it. Did you know that these governments and others like them killed 200 million of their own citizens in the 20th century alone and this doesn't even include war casualties? And before they went on their kill spree? They systematically disarmed their citizens. Sound familiar, Marcia?"

"It's you who are spouting the phony statistics, and the only reason socialism hasn't brought prosperity anytime in history is because the right people haven't been in charge."

"And naturally enough, that would be you."

"Well… I do my part, my small part for the People."

"And fascism is your religion."

"All right, Mr. Haas," the Judge had no more patience.

The Examiner petitioned her boss. "No, please, your honor. I'm okay. We need to get all this. Just please let this all play out."

515

Michael continued. "You view everything as political and that any action by the state is justified to achieve your goals. You take control, but not responsibility, for all aspects of people's lives, our health, our well-being, and you try to impose uniformity of thought and action, by force or by regulation and social pressure. Everything, including the economy and people's basic belief systems, must be aligned with your objectives. Any rival identity is part of the 'problem' and defined as the enemy. Your new America embodies all of these aspects. This is fascism."

"You are irrational and deluded."

"You're a monster, Marcia."

"Mister Haas!" cried the Judge.

"It would make me feel better if I could drum up a good rabid hate for you, but I can't. When you realize what you're doing, the terrible bidding of the sadistic jackasses you work for, this realization, whether you have it in this life or another, will break you. Harder than from any hate I could work up."

Marcia Hillman was pretending not to hear. "The People rest their case, your honor."

The Judge looked wrung out. "Sentencing will be in two weeks, March 25th at 9 a.m." And he slammed the gavel for the final time.

Michael smiled. "I'll try to make it, your honor."

"We're dismissed. Take him to holding."

"All rise," announced the bailiff. "Court is adjourned."

HIS INCARCERATION

It seemed to Michael that a criminal trial leading to prison, or a work camp was the no-brainer consequence of his examination, but he was wrong. Instead, it was decided that Michael Haas was too much a public figure with a large and still not easily managed following. So instead of tossing him in the slammer and throwing away the key, it was put forth to all, loudly and publicly, that Michael Haas was basically a good, if terribly misguided, man and simply required 'rehabilitation.' This demonstrated to all how Justice administered by the People was tempered by Mercy whenever it was possible (and strategically expedient).

Recovery Centers such as Bedford, Michael's new home, were new or recent, hi-tech and abundant, merrily sprinkled across the nation from sea to shining sea, and only the spiral razor-wire fencing and moats bounding the facility hinted at its true nature.

Soon after admission, Michael had a short round of ECT, or electroconvulsive therapy. Michael knew enough about the treatment to believe, correctly, that it had little to do with any perceived psychological issues Michael might be suspected of harboring. ECT is used for schizophrenia, acute mania, severe depression, bipolar disorder—all things which Michael had been happily spared in this lifetime, so he figured it was simply a punishment.

There were three treatments, with two days between sessions, and in the recovery between sessions two and last, Michael had an idea. He overheard discussion that confusion and memory loss, of the permanent variety, were risks of the treatment. He would embrace this strategy as part of his plan for his release.

After the third and final treatment, Michael presented a new persona to his handlers and to the other inhabitants of his little world. He became dull, monosyllabic and mostly chair-bound. He evinced interest in nothing at all and acted as though he was a man without a past. He ate his food, took his drugs, bathed, and took care of his hygiene to a degree that he maintained his independence and was not a bother to the staff. He knew this would be important.

He was tested, he was analyzed, he was interviewed, and his doctors hemmed and hawed over him for weeks before they concluded that Michael Hass as previously known had been transformed into pretty much an idiot. Oh well. These things happen!

And about those drugs of his. Other than the odd laxative and occasional sleep aid, there was really only one drug, a tiny yellow pill, that they insisted he take once a day. It really knocked him for a loop but there was no way to avoid taking it. Blood was tested every Friday for proper med levels and uncooperative patients would simply be given their drugs in an I.V. or by injection.

Michael took his drug six days a week and squirrelled the Saturday pill away for safekeeping. Part of his plan. His lab tests were within limits, and he consistently appeared so out of it that no one would ever suspect shenanigans from such a witless dullard. He also managed to conceal in his hidey-hole a reflex hammer, one of those little silver-handle jobs with the rubber triangular head that they bounce off your knee and such to test reflex responses. The doc left it on the nightstand and never even came back to look for it. It might come in handy. Might be part of the plan.

Of course, living such a life was immensely depressing and many times Michael was at his wit's end, contemplating the worst. It had been six months since his incarceration. What was hardest to bear was the fact that his grandson had not come to visit. Not a letter, not a call, although he was not sure that these would be permitted to him in any case.

But he lived in hope for it was all he had. He needed to protect his grandchildren, and it was for them that he had endured this numbing yet searing torture day after day, living in a drug fog and permitting himself not the smallest diversion, lest his true condition be made known. That would ruin his plan. That would destroy everything. That would extinguish hope.

Speaking of extinguishing, Michael would dearly have loved to extinguish the orderly who was assigned to him every weekday. He was rude, stupid and sadistic and his name was Hans. Big, fat, lazy, ugly Hans. He even ate Michael's food! Not the gruel and slop and swill that was his usual fare, but his Thursday dessert—a heavenly creampuff that for some inconceivable reason was magically envisioned and expertly accomplished. He only got to eat it the first week he was there. Then Hans decided it was his.

When dinner was brought to Michael on Thursday evening (he took his meals in his room), Hans was always there waiting. He would close the door after the porter left the room, then sidle up to the tray and snatch up Michael's creampuff, saying, "You don't want this, do you buddy?" and then proceed to stuff it in his big fat ugly face in two quick bites. What a pig! But Hans, too, had a part in Michael's plan.

So this was Michael Hass in his new life. But he felt he could not, even for the memory of his wife and the love of his grandchildren, last much longer.

Another month passed, and his hopes were answered. One of the social workers, Ms. Ellis, whom he saw everyday interacting with others though she had never spoken a word to Michael since his incarceration, came into his room on a Wednesday morning as if they were old pals. He was awake and dressed and sitting on the side of his bed.

"Good morning, Michael," she said. Nice big smile. A small, thin, youngish woman. Maybe Korean, he guessed.

Michael simply smiled in response.

Ms. Ellis pulled the little chair over and sat across from Michael.

"We've had a request from, well, actually several requests over the months from one of your grandchildren to visit you here. His name is Nicholas. Do you remember Nick?

Michael gave an idiot grin. "Nicky?" he said.

"Yes, Nicky," she said. "Well, we think there's no reason why that shouldn't happen. You've been with us long enough, you are a good patient, and as a reward, we thought letting Nick-"

"Nicky!"

"Yes… Nicky, we thought a visit would be a fine idea. Is there anything you would like to do with Nick, Nicky, when he comes tomorrow?"

"Walk in the tree path," Michael said slowly.

"Ah! The forest trails. How nice. We'll have to send Hans with you over there though. Is that okay?"

Michael nodded, still smiling like an imbecile.

"So, what do you think, tomorrow afternoon sometime?"

"After dinner."

"After dinner? That late? I don't know…"

"Walk after dinner. Makes me tired," he mumbled. "Good sleep then."

"Oh! Okay. Well… you're served here at 5:30 and I'll make sure Nicky comes at about six. How's that? Then you two and Hans can go around the forest trail together."

Big dumbass grin.

"Okay then!" Ms. Ellis stood. "Big day tomorrow!" And she took her leave.

Michael considered how incredibly lucky he was to have Nick come by on creampuff night!

Michael stood at his window, craning his neck for a better look at the forest trail area. Patients were allowed outside unsupervised but only in areas with close human or camera surveillance. There were no cameras on the forest trail, a stretch of woods a few hundred yards long, dense with birch and pines. It was early November, and it was not a popular place for a stroll. Fat-ass Hans would not be pleased at Michael's activity choice, which made the outing even more gratifying.

Michael was in the big chair in his room, waiting for his dinner tray. Timing was everything tonight and he was fretting. So many what-ifs. It could rain, for one thing—that would cancel the walk—and that looked like a possibility.

A knock on his open door and in came the food porter followed on her heels by the hoggish Hans, eyeing the creampuff on the tray. She set Michael up with her usual efficiency and started toward the door. Hans turned to follow, and Michael opened the palm of his hand, dropped four of his little yellow pills into the creampuff, pressing them inside the lovely pastry with his fingers, and licking his creamy fingers clean at the sound of the closing door. Yum! Hans turned and plodded back to the sitting Michael and his treasure, a line of drool at the corner of his lips in anticipation of his ecstasy.

"You don't need this, do you buddy?" Hans said as he reached over, snatched the creampuff, and in seconds it was in his maw and down his gullet. Two bites. Gross.

"I caa beeve yr mawgge me do uiss," Hans had mumbled through the stuffed hole in his face. He swallowed. "Did you hear me? I said I can't believe you're making me do this. You're a fucking moron and you wanna walk in this weather? I oughta smack you. You're lucky, you know. Some of you veggies get smacked around on this floor. Do this shit to me again and you'll see."

He wanted to go on explaining how lucky Michael was but there was a knock on the door that shut him right up. Hans opened the door to the apple of Michael's eye.

Michael stood and Nick rushed to embrace him. They both wept, and Michael was not pretending. They stayed in their embrace for a good half-minute. When they parted, Michael sat back down and Nick said, "Grampa, they told me what happened to you. I'm really sorry. I didn't know."

Michael looked down at the floor and nodded. "That's okay... that's okay..."

Hans, completely impervious to human sentiments, was growing impatient. "Maybe we should move it along, huh fellas? Looks like it might rain."

Nick turned his head to consider Hans, and Michael noted that Nick had instantly assessed what an ass Hans was, though it didn't take a genius. Nick, already sufficiently clad, helped Michael on with an overcoat from the closet while Hans went to fetch one for himself. When he had left the room, Michael whispered to his grandson.

"Listen, I'm all right. Things aren't as they appear. Play along. Understand?"

Nick stepped back as if slapped. "Oh my god. What's going on?"

Michael made the shoosh gesture with his index finger and Nick nodded okay. Hans blundered back into the room, bid them let's go, and the three of them headed slowly toward the elevator.

On the way down, Hans said to no one in particular, "Jesus, I'm tired."

After about ten minutes of strolling they were still short of the forest trail, with Michael setting what he hoped was not a suspiciously rapid pace for them all, as he typically treaded sluggishly wherever he went. Hans didn't look good. At one point Hans stopped walking. Michael and Nick turned to him and Nick asked if he was okay. They were still out in the open and if Hans were to collapse here they would be spotted. Hans just stood there for a moment and said, "I'm fine. Let's get this over with," and resumed the stroll.

They walked in silence for another minute, now finally at the trailhead. They entered the woods at a much slower pace than previously, until Hans stopped again, leaned against a birch tree, and slid down on his ass, out like a light.

Michael turned to his grandson. "I don't know how much time we have." He considered the snoring lump that was Hans. "I hope I didn't kill him."

"What?!"

"I drugged him." He turned back to Nick. "Listen, Nicky, I'm okay, I just have to pretend I'm all fucked up to get along here. I couldn't hold out much longer and I'm so glad to see you *I could explode!"*

At that they embraced again. Michael let the lad go and asked, "Did Sly contact you?"

"Oh my god. Sly? Yeah. A week or so after they put you in here I got a call from a guy called himself Sly."

"What'd he say?"

"He asked if I was ready."

"And you said?"

"I said what the hell are you talking about and he hung up. What should I have said?"

"Okay. That's okay. I couldn't tell you about Sly in my text to you, else they'd be gunning for him, and I couldn't get in touch with him for the same reason. But listen now."

"I'm listening."

"Long time ago, I suspected they'd come for me eventually. But I only really cared about one thing, and that's you and the other four kids."

"And?"

"Nicky, you gotta get out. And you gotta take the kids with you."

"Get out where?"

"Wherever Sly takes you. Probably the mountains."

"Mountains! What mountains? There's no mountains where we live! What the hell?"

"Calm down, Nicky. And listen to me. This blob next to me could wake up any second and we'd both be fucked."

"I'm listening. But geez…"

"Things are going to get worse. They might get better, but not before they get one hell of a lot worse. You're my grandchildren. Soon they'll be watching you. You'll never get out of their sight. You'll toe the line and become one of their commie robots or you'll pay a price you have no *idea* what price. The kids look up to you. This is the most important moment of your life. You need to save those kids, and yourself. They need you, Nicky. They need you like they needed their moms and dads before the war took them. You're their dad now. D'ya see?"

"Why will they watch us? Why will they bother us?"

"Because you're my grandchildren! You'll never escape their scrutiny. And also, because I'm going to kill fatboy there. And then I'm going to escape."

As if hearing someone call his name, Hans stirred and grunted, prompting Michael to hurry to conclude the lecture, but Nick spoke.

"But if you *don't* kill him and *don't* escape, then they won't bother us, right?"

"Not an option, Nicky. Life for all of you will be intolerable in the best case, and literally unlivable in the worst." He paused to let this sink in. "See, you need to follow the plan whether you want to or not. But I'd prefer you see the wisdom of it."

"No... you wouldn't do that to us."

"If I thought you were a very stupid lad with no regard for your responsibilities, I would agree with you. But I know you better. I know you won't let anything happen to them, and this is your only way out."

Michael let Nick consider all this for a space, looking askance at his granddad.

"Let's say I do this. Where are the mountains?" Nick asked.

"I don't know. And it's best I don't."

More reflection by Nick, but also more noisy stirrings by Hans.

"Time's up, Nicky."

He shot his grampa a most unaffectionate look. "Okay, let's say I agree to do it. What do I do?"

"Make a call when you get back. When it's answered say you want to order a pizza. He'll tell you you got the wrong number. Then you hang up and actually order a pizza. Got it? Don't forget to order a pizza. Doesn't matter where from. Then, the next day or two at most, Sly will show up. Be ready. No school for anyone. Do what he says and don't argue."

"What's the number?"

And Michael gave Nick the number to call and made him repeat it many times, Nick a little insulted that his grampa forgot about his brilliant memory. He also told Nick that each of the kids needs to be ready—pack one suitcase, backpack or other piece of luggage but no more than one each, something they could each carry, and not to share any of this information with his aunt or anyone else. This was crucial. If she divulged any of this, she would be carted away (at best) and the project's safety compromised.

"This will break her heart, Grampa," Nick said sadly, "for us to disappear. She's been good to us."

"She'd want this for you. She's old. She's near the end of her days. Besides, Sly will get word to her when the heat dies down a little. Trust him. And trust me," Michael hoped that was true.

Hans woke and tried to rise but couldn't and slumped back into oblivion. They waited for another five minutes. It was starting to get dark and they would become suspicious back at headquarters, so Michael told Nick to slap Hans around a little to stir him.

As Hans was coming to, Nick turned to his grandfather and said, "I might hate you for this. I haven't decided yet."

"I understand," Michael said sadly, "but please try to trust me here. You mean the world to me, Nicky."

They helped lumpy Hans to his feet.

"What the fuck happened to me?" he asked Nick.

"I don't know," Nick lied. "You just passed out for a while. I tried to wake you. Didn't know what to do so we just stood here waiting and hoping you'd wake up."

"Holy shit. We need to get back… my head… Jesus…"

Just then Hans's phone beeped, and a voice came through. "Mr. Gruber where are you?"

Hans got real big in the eyes and answered, "Just enjoying the last of our walk. On the way in now."

"Just checking."

Relief poured over the poor man as they started the walk back. Hans looked at Nick. "So I bet your granddad wasn't the best company, am I right or am I right?"

Nick laughed. "That's for damn sure. Not much of a conversationalist. Kind of annoying, actually." He glowered at his grampa as he spoke.

"Yeah, well I get the same five days a week! And never so much as a thank you."

"You're a saint!" the lad said. The building was in sight, and it started to rain.

There was only one way Michael would ever know if his plan had succeeded and that Sly was able to spirit away his grandkids. He knew that unless the authorities burst into Michael's room within the week to grill him on the whereabouts of those missing children, that all will have been lost.

If all stays quiet, that would mean Nicky would have decided to not proceed with the plan and hope his grampa was not stupid enough to endanger them with his own plan of murder and escape. That was too bitter to contemplate so, of course, his mind went there often.

If Sly had failed, as hard to imagine as that might be, Michael would be notified by the authorities that his grandchildren had become wards of the state. They would do this gloatingly, and all would be lost.

But Sly was amazing. He moved like a ghost. He was a legend, and many did not even believe he existed, that he was just a myth. But Michael had known him for years, they were tight, and he knew Sly was as real as it gets. It was Sly's vocation to spirit the willing and able away to a better place, hard living among a small but growing group of free-minded people, people willing to resist, and engage on every front when the time is ripe, and to be victorious. That was the dream, and sometimes the dream is enough.

Three days after Nick's visit, Michael was greeted by the ogre Hans while Michael was dressing for the day. Hans burst in, without knocking, and simply blurted, "Hey veggie, you're *fucked!*" and slammed the door shut.

Well, Michael already knew he was fucked, but *how* was he fucked? Goodly or badly? That, he suspected, would become clear in short order. Grateful for the heads-up, he went to his little hidey-hole in the molding and retrieved a wadded piece of tissue, also the almost forgotten reflex-hammer abandoned by the staff doctor many months ago. He clutched it, not by the six-inch stainless steel handle but by the orange triangular head—a molding of rubber secured by a thin band of steel. He held up his fist and briefly examined the wand of silver jutting from his fist between his middle and ring fingers. He nodded, satisfied, and stepped to the big chair, slipping the objects between the cushion and the arm and sat, waiting. His heart was pounding in his ears.

It was a full hour, the longest most tortured hour of his life, before Hans returned, this time as escort for the so-called 'Guardian' of the Bedford Institution (who everyone secretly referred to as 'warden'), a Mr. Grey. He was hoppin' mad. He glowered down at Michael like an avenging angel about to vent his righteous wrath.

"Mister Michael Haas?" he seethed loudly. Michael never knew it was possible to seethe loudly but there it was.

Michael kept it together enough to simply lift his head and smile idiotically.

"He's like a moron, sir," Hans inserted helpfully.

"Shut up," Grey said. "Where are your grandchildren?"

Michael split himself in two. On the inside he was so elated that he wanted to stand and cry out *Yes! Yes! It worked!,* but on the outside he frowned like a sad clown.

"Where are they, goddamn it!" Grey yelled in exasperation.

Michael started to cry and blubbered through his sobs, "Where are they? Are they all right?"

"You saw the oldest and then they all disappeared in a day. Are you really the moron you pretend to be? *Are you?"* Grey forced himself to regain his calm. "I'm going to get to the bottom of this. Today." He turned to Hans. "Get this person in a hospital gown and take him to an open seclusion room. Now."

Grey turned and bolted from the room. Hans followed and shut the door, turning to Michael but Michael was no longer in his chair. When Hans turned, Michael hammered Hans in the nose with an overhead closed fist and with all his might, and then he did it again, knocking Hans flat to the floor. Before Hans could react, blood sheeting from his broken nose, Michael was on top of him, straddling his fat belly, with his left hand over Hans's mouth and in his right hand, a six-inch silver spike spearing out from his fist. He positioned the spike to just below Hans's larynx and started to push in.

"How's this feel you bloated piece of shit?" he whispered to the terrified orderly.

He gathered himself for the final thrust, for the *coup de grace*.

And he stopped. And he looked away.

He sighed heavily and dismounted the petrified Hans, who stayed flat, gurgling with the blood from his broken nose flooding his throat, subdued and submissive, staring wide-eyed at his captor.

"I'm not like you," Michael said "Get up. And get out."

The orderly complied, slowly. He was indeed badly hurt. Hans stumbled to the door and through it. An alarm sounded.

HIS RELEASE

Michael quickly seized the wadded tissue from the cushion hideaway and unfurled it. There were sixteen little yellow pills in reserve. He gobbled it all, including the tissue, picked up his water cup and drank.

In an instant the room was filled with beefy orderlies and guards. They seized Michael mid-gulp, the plastic cup bouncing to the floor and dragged him away, down the corridor and to Isolation/Solitary No.3, opened the door, and brusquely deposited Michael onto the hard floor within. The door slammed and there he lay, staring in near-darkness at the concrete ceiling.

Michael Haas sensed the veil descending, bright and sparkling as he lay, and he laughed. He did right by his grandchildren, the only thing that mattered. They would live. They would have a life and they would steer their own course through it. He lazed, unmoving, no longer feeling his body and the veil fluttered and darkened.

After a short space the veil was murky, became opaque, and Michael's laughter turned to soft tears. Still, they were *happy* tears. No more tortures. No more pretending to be an imbecile. No more of the old life.

He sensed he was on his way out. He didn't know for sure where he was going but breathed out a last feeble giggle, knowing his final wishes—that wherever he was headed there was some measure of Peace. Or at least creampuffs as good as the ones here.

About Gerald Brennan

I was born on September 2, 1953, in Jessup, PA. At age two I moved to Dearborn, MI, where I lived with my family until my late teens. The eldest of six children, I went to Catholic school, and when my brain started working at about age 15, I left the Church, appalled by its many odd dogmas. It didn't help much that so many of our priests and nuns were mean-spirited and sadistic (in their defense, we were simply spectacularly 'negatively blessed' in that way). When we had philosophical questions, the answer was usually along the lines of "Shut up." It was in high school that I began to write down the music in my head.

Wandering in the desert for many years, I drank heavily, experimented with drugs, and studied music, science and philosophy. Though I never had any formal music education, living in Ann Arbor put many wonderful resources at my disposal, including many fine Steinway grands sprinkled merrily throughout the University of Michigan campus back in the day when there didn't need to be a lock on every door.

I became a good pianist in the following years, as well as composer. I had many musical adventures—breaking a Steinway grand playing Liszt at the University of Michigan music school, playing Liszt's American Steinway at the Smithsonian Museum in an impromptu recital that drew quite a wondrous crowd. I improvised madly (after all, this was Liszt's piano), and the crone that ran the joint nearly had a stroke as she screamed at me to STOP STOP!!! STOP!!! as I was summarily ejected from the premises. That was a real nice piano, incidentally. I may go on to fill a book with like tales, but not here.

I became a National Public Radio affiliate producer with WUOM, WVGR and WFUM out of the U-M. I produced hundreds of weekly programs in my decade there—including *The Musical Theatre, New Music, New Releases, From the Monophonic Era, Music of Our World, Excursions* and *Nocturne*. One of the highlights of my career as broadcaster included a carefully-engineered presentation of all nine symphonies of Beethoven, played *simultaneously*. In those days, it took two assistants, five turntables, four CD players, a few stopwatches and multiple attempts to get all that onto tape. The night it was premiered some listeners called the cops, who stormed the studios looking for Classical Music felons. There were many dozens of phone calls. Half the callers thought I was the coolest DJ ever; the other half wanted me dead, as soon as possible and as painfully as that could be accomplished. Now *that's* good radio.

In 1980 I organized the Ann Arbor-based Sinewave Studios for the development and propagation of new art music. I produced about 20 concerts and conducted the North American premier of Karlheinz Stockhausen's *Für kommende Zeiten* at the Detroit Institute of Art. I never asked Stockhausen's permission to do so and never paid him any royalties. I feel bad about that now that I am a creator who likes his own royalty money, but at the time it never occurred to me to pay him. Never even entered my head. You know when it *did* enter my head? *Years later when I was talking to him.* I considered, for the first time, as the words were coming out of my mouth, that I had never asked permission to do the premiere and never gave him a nickel. To his credit, he let it pass. This was contrary to his reputation and I have always been grateful to him for that.

My writing career started in 1984 when I wrote and self-published a booklet on starting a classical record collection. Borders Books agreed to carry it, and it finally made its way into the paws of a publisher. They asked me to expand it into a sure enough book and thus was born *Classical Records, Starting Your Collection*. After it was published, I took it to the Ann

Arbor News and asked them if they needed a music reviewer. Turned out they did, and so, all while I had the radio gig, I was reviewing the best acts in the world that came through town. It got old though, and when we radio producers all lost our jobs, I also quit reviewing. I found it to be spiritually corrosive to have to say negative things about other people's performances, even if they richly deserved it. That said, it did help feed me, my wife and my two kids.

Before all that I worked in record stores, including the famous Liberty Music. I also sold pianos, moved pianos, sold sheet music, managed U-M's record and sheet music store, and wrote for various national music journals.

In 1998, I was headhunted by a visionary fellow named Michael Erlewine, who decided that it would be a good idea to get hold of every album in the world and put every bit of information about it into a database. Eventually the idea included taking a photo of the album and doing sound samples. They started with a core of a few music geeks and began by going through their own collections. The company Erlewine founded was called All Media Guide (www.allmusic.com), which became the world's largest repository of product data and editorial information about music.

Erlewine asked me to assume the post of Director of Content of Classical Music at AMG, to create a department that would be devoted to Classical Music only. I jumped at it, and in four years my amazing staff and I, along with scores of excellent writers, amassed the data, created the classical website, and produced the giant reference book, *AMG Guide to Classical Music*, which I edited and saw published in 2005. My mission was accomplished; my staff was a well-oiled machine and easily the best and happiest of all AMG's departments. Then 'investor fatigue' set in among the shareholders and AMG was appointed a slick new president who knew little about what we did or why but was hired to sell the company at a good price to whomever. He disliked me and my open resistance to his schemes and I was fired. I had no hard feelings. I had completed my mission and it was time to go.

Now I write music and books, make recordings and give the rare recital.

Books include this one, also *Prince of Pines*, a dystopian male-adventure novel set in Michigan's Upper Peninsula; the recent *Jophiel*, a fantasy novel about the Classical Music world and an angel sent to Earth to help rejuvenate the dying Arts, *Song of Blood and Ashes*, a vampire tale set in contemporary Ireland and Ann Arbor, and *Classical Music & Recordings -- a Primer*, which is just what it says.

Musically, I've to-date got 80 songs published in three *SongBooks*, many chamber and orchestral pieces, piano works, a full-length Broadway-style musical called *Penelope*, choral works, and a large orchestral piece known as *Sinfonia Matrix*, which requires some 80-octillion years to be heard in its entirety. Therefore, performance versions are extracted depending upon available forces, duration required and occasion.

Available CDs include *Mythos* (piano pieces based upon Greek myth characters, recorded in recital and in-studio), *Five Fantasy Nocturnes* for piano, *Campfire—The Burning Psaltery* (a phantasmagorical piece for an innocent 12-string psaltery), *7 Solo Songs from Penelope*, and several CDs from the *SongBooks* recorded in studio and at home, by me and various performers.

Also available on CD is the electronically-based *Ambient Music Series*, which includes *Ambient Counterpoint, Grand Starbells, Monochrome Frescos, The Singing Moon,* and *Whisperings of Angels*.

Not-actually-available is the CD of *Beethoven's Nine Symphonies Played Simultaneously*. This is a digital recreation of the earlier radio project, this time featuring John Eliot Gardiner conducting all nine at once in a carefully tailored orgy of magnificent aural splendor. Like nothing you ever heard or will hear again. Why not available for sale? Because it is also the most magnificent copyright violation of all time—nine in the space of one. See, I don't fancy ending up in Classical Music Prison. I'm a good-lookin' old guy and there's some mean hombres in there, especially the violists.

All items detailed above are published by DreamStreet Press and available on Amazon or through DreamStreetPress.com.

Made in the USA
Middletown, DE
26 July 2023

35754560R00305